A Fatal Lie

A Fatal Lie

An Inspector Ian Rutledge Mystery

Charles Todd

HARPER LARGE PRINT

An Imprint of HarperCollinsPublishers

A FATAL LIE. Copyright © 2021 by Charles Todd. All rights reserved. Printed in the United States of America. No part of this book may be used or reproduced in any manner whatsoever without written permission except in the case of brief quotations embodied in critical articles and reviews. For information, address HarperCollins Publishers, 195 Broadway, New York, NY 10007.

HarperCollins books may be purchased for educational, business, or sales promotional use. For information, please e-mail the Special Markets Department at SPsales@harpercollins.com.

FIRST HARPER LARGE PRINT EDITION

ISBN: 978-0-06-306193-4

Library of Congress Cataloging-in-Publication Data is available upon request.

21 22 23 24 25   LSC   10 9 8 7 6 5 4 3 2 1

This book is especially for Angela Zeman. She was such a wonderful friend. A Rutledge fan. Multi-talented. An author. Attractive, fun, with a whole *résumé* of accomplishments. But most of all, she was a lovely *person*. And her loss has left a huge emptiness in the hearts of those who knew and loved her. Ours included. God bless.

***

And there are others to remember in a different way. Lady stole our hearts when she nearly gave her own life to save that of her little son. They went on to live a long happy life together. A gentle spirit, with a brave and loving heart, she was special.

Jingles was a shepherd whose early life taught him to be afraid, but nothing could take from him a loving heart. He found a forever home, loved to greet visitors and bark at strangers. If he accepted you and let you pet him, you knew you were honored.

Snickies, née Snickerdoodle, the freest of free spirits, fearless, a cat with wings, tiny as she was. She never grew *old*, even as she advanced in years, and to the end, she was that rarest of creatures, comfortable with herself. How she loved whipped cream!

And there is Max, big, loving, stubborn Max, who could bay like a hound, run away with enthusiasm, loved the out-of-doors and sleeping in the sun. He had such a rough start, but a loving home to the end made up for that.

Squilly, née Lily, Linda's first cat, had the most extraordinary green eyes, a wonderful disposition, and kept motherless kittens in her care until they found their way. And she lived with us for seventeen amazing years. A great talker, she was only our second cat who could say *Caroline*. Intrepid—we once found her on the roof—and loving, with a mind of her own, she had a firm grip on our hearts. She was—*Squill-will*.

We mustn't forget Thomasina (Tommy for short) who looked like her namesake in the famous book by that name. Only, Tommy was disabled and didn't know it. She jumped and walked and did everything else as if she had two straight front legs. A foundling, she was sweet, loving, and curious about everything. John loved her too. She left us before her time, this special marmalade cat, but gave us years of love before then.

Dear Boo rejected every other name offered to her. Found on the side of a road, injured but alive, she survived surgery small as she was, but one leg would never be right. That didn't bother her. Black from nose to tail, she was a wonderful cat, and she loved to be petted. You could hear her loud purr of joy across the room. She helped Charles work at the computer, keeping him company book after book, and wanted nothing more of life than to be loved in return. She, like Tommy, often inspected new covers, giving them her approval. Both left holes in our hearts, like so many rescues.

A Fatal Lie

1

The River Dee, Llangollen Valley
Early Spring 1921

On his sixth birthday, Roddy MacNabb was given a fishing pole by his pa, with promises to teach him how to use it. That was late July 1914, before the Bloody Hun started the war, and his pa had left the village with four of his friends and enlisted. He'd promised to be back before the end of the year, but the war had dragged on, and in 1915, his father had been killed at Bloody Passiondell, wherever that was.

The pole, long since put away, was in his granny's attics, and Roddy had only just found it last week, when he'd gone up there to fetch a box for her. He'd brought it down with him, but his mum had told him to take the Bloody Pole out to the shed and leave it there.

"There's to be no fishing," she'd told him. "Not while you're in school."

He'd watched his granny's mouth tighten at his mother's words. *She* didn't hold with cursing, but Mum had come from Liverpool, and he'd heard his Aunt May say that she'd been no better than she ought to be. Still, his father had somehow fallen in love with her and brought her home, and she'd stayed.

He didn't remember his real mum, she'd died when he was born. But his pa had told him this was his mum now, and he was to call her that. And so he had, because his pa was the best in the village, and he would have done anything to make him happy.

On Saturday, with no school and the schoolmaster ill with a chest, Roddy slipped away while his mum was having her usual late breakfast, took the fishing pole from the shed, and went off to the river.

The Dee here was within walking distance of the farm, and Roddy found himself thinking about his pa and fishing. He'd gone with his father a few times and still had a vague memory of what to do with the pole, once the hook was affixed to the line and a worm was put on it. He'd surreptitiously dug some worms out of the kitchen garden last night and put them into a tin. Most had crawled out, but there were still three left.

Whistling now, he could glimpse the river shining in the noon sun beyond the line of trees, and he told himself his father would be happy if he could see how tall his son had grown, and only twelve. And off to fish at last.

The sun was warm, but under the trees—their bare branches crossing over his head like the bones of wood holding up the church roof—the air was cooler. Or perhaps it was the water—he could hear it and smell it now. He came out onto the bank, stiff with the dried grasses of winter, and stood looking down at the drifting current. Too steep here to fish, he thought, and moved downstream a little, beyond the Telford Aqueduct soaring high above the valley. Everyone knew the Aqueduct, but unlike the Roman ones he'd read about in school, which were intended to carry drinking water, it bridged the wide gap between two cliffs, and made it possible for the narrowboats traveling along the canal up there to float right across from one side to the other. He'd heard the horses that pulled the narrowboats, the hollow sound their hooves made as they stepped out onto the path that ran beside the trough of water. It echoed, on a quiet day. He'd been afraid the first time he'd heard it, but his pa had told him about the horses, and once had even taken him up there to see the long boats and the ducks too. He barely remembered it now, that trip, but his father had bought him an ice and told him not to tell Mum.

Ahead was a lower spot on the bank, and Roddy moved quickly toward it, eager to try out the pole and catch his fish. He didn't notice what was in the water, not at first. He wasn't interested in the river, only the pole.

After two attempts he got the line on the pole, tied the hook to the end, then pushed the wriggling worm onto the hook. On his first try at casting, he caught the bush behind him, untangled the line finally, and tried again. This time he managed better, and the hook actually sailed out over the water and sank into the sunny depths.

Smiling, he wiggled the pole a little, felt it catch, and burst out laughing. He'd caught a fish, first thing! What would his pa think of that?

But when he tried to pull the line in, it wouldn't come, and as he pulled harder, he saw something move in the water, just below the surface. From where he stood, it appeared to be a rock or even a tangle of roots.

Whatever it was, it bobbed a little as he went on pulling, harder now, desperate to save his only hook, then it suddenly came free from whatever was holding it down.

And as it did, a face rose slowly out of the water. A face unlike any other he'd ever seen, white and torn and no longer human. Like something the water had taken and hadn't ever wanted to give back. The lump of whatever was attached to it rolled a little again, making the head move as well, and for an instant Roddy thought it was coming directly out of the water at him. He screamed as he dropped the pole and ran.

But no one on the narrowboat crossing high above his head heard him.

2

Chief Superintendent Markham was in a fine mood. He had been congratulated twice on the successful conclusion of a rather nasty murder inquiry in Norfolk—once by the Home Office, and again in an article in the *Times*.

Inspector Carlton had brought in the killer, covering himself with glory as well as the Yard, and he was currently basking in the Chief Superintendent's smile.

Inspector Rutledge, on the other hand, was still in his office, buried in paperwork. His last inquiry had stirred up a mare's nest, and Markham was apparently still smarting from that, because he'd seen to it for several weeks that Rutledge wasn't given a new assignment.

Rutledge had not complained—much to Markham's annoyance, according to Sergeant Gibson.

When the Chief Constable in a northern Welsh county asked the Yard to take charge of an inquiry into the death of a man found in the River Dee, Markham summoned Rutledge to his office, brusquely told him what was required of him, and said, "Sergeant Gibson will see that someone takes over the reports you were reviewing." He passed the file across the desk, nodded, and began to read another report already open on the green blotter. The air was chill with Markham's dislike.

Rutledge extricated himself from the office as smoothly as he could, collected what he needed from his own room, and informed Sergeant Gibson of the status of the reports on his desk.

Gibson grimaced. "Does this mean you're back in his lordship's good graces?"

"I doubt it. Northern Wales is rather like being sent to Coventry—out of sight and out of mind."

Gibson nodded. "There's that."

It was a Monday morning, overcast, cold. As he walked out of the Yard to his motorcar, Rutledge could smell the Thames, fetid with the receding tide. At his flat, he packed a valise, left a note for the daily, and then headed west through dreary outskirts and a succession of small towns before he reached open countryside.

By that time he was no longer able to ignore the voice coming from the rear seat.

It wasn't there, that voice. He knew it as clearly as he could see the ruts in the road unwinding ahead of the motorcar's bonnet. Corporal Hamish MacLeod was buried in the black mud of Flanders, and Rutledge had once stood by that grave and contemplated his own mortality.

It was the manner of Hamish's death that haunted him, and the guilt of that had turned into denial. By the end of the war he had brought Hamish home to England in the only way possible, *knowing* he was dead, but unable to free himself of the voice that had stayed with him in the trenches from the Battle of the Somme to the Armistice. It had followed him relentlessly, sometimes bitter, sometimes angry, and sometimes, for a mercy, even bearable. But always there. And with it, the memories of the war.

What he, Rutledge, feared above all was one day seeing the owner of the voice—and knowing beyond doubt that he had finally run mad. The only answer to that was the service revolver locked in the chest under his bed at the flat.

For it was he who had delivered the coup de grace that silenced Hamish forever. Military necessity. But even as Hamish had broken during the Somme, he himself had been on the ragged edge of shell shock. England had needed every man that July. No one walked back to the forward aid station and asked for relief from the horror. They withstood it as best they could, week after unbearable week, and hoped for death when the agony was too much.

Hamish was saying, "Ye ken, the Yard doubts ye. Else, they'd no' send ye to Wales for a drowning."

Rutledge didn't answer.

"Aye, ye can try to ignore the signs. But ye've seen them for yersel'."

Hamish was trying to goad him into a quarrel, but it was only a reflection of his own troubled mind.

Setting his teeth, he concentrated on the road ahead. There was nothing Hamish could say that he hadn't heard before, or thought, or dreamed of at night. Tried to ignore—but could never put completely out of his mind. It was there, had been since the trenches. A constant reminder of the war and what he'd done on that bloody nightmare of the Somme. Seemingly as real as if the living Hamish MacLeod traveled with him.

Rutledge could feel that presence growing stronger as he made his way into the Cotswolds. Waiting for him as it always did at the end of a long day. He had wanted to drive another twenty or so miles, but as he found himself in a village of butter-yellow stone reflecting the last of the evening light, he knew that it wasn't possible. There was a small, charming inn near the village center—as good a place as any to face the night. He ate his dinner in a dining room that was only half full. The food was good, the whisky with his tea even better, and he found himself relaxing for the first time in a very long while. Hoping it would last and he would sleep after all.

A woman across the room laughed. His back was to her, he couldn't see her face, but the laugh was rather like Kate's when she was truly amused. His whisky glass halfway to his lips, he paused, caught off guard.

But Kate was in London . . .

Setting his glass down, unfinished, he went up to the small room where Hamish was waiting in the shadows for him.

It was a long night. He'd been having nightmares more frequently of late, Hamish drawing him back into the war, filling him with guilt and despair and a longing for peace that always left him drained in the first light of dawn. As if in the blackness surrounding him the past came back more easily, slipping through the darkness in the room and in him until he couldn't hold it back any longer.

His last thought as the nightmare took its firm grip

on his mind was, *How could I ever do this to Kate? How could I ever let her see this part of me?*

Rutledge arrived at his destination, Cwmafon, on a Wednesday afternoon of soaking rain and lowering clouds that turned everything gray and dismal. Much like his own mood. In spite of a good sense of direction, as he'd driven deeper into northern Wales, he'd struggled with place-names he couldn't pronounce and others that weren't even on the English map he'd brought with him.

He finally found the country lane that followed the River Dee into the village he was after, saw the tiny police station next to a general store, and splashed through the puddles to the door.

The Constable behind the desk looked up as the door opened and a wet stranger stepped in.

"Good afternoon, sir. Constable Holcomb. How may I be of service?" He rose to meet the newcomer.

"Inspector Rutledge, Scotland Yard," he replied as he took off his hat and glanced down ruefully at the circle of rainwater expanding on the mat under his feet.

Holcomb smiled. "You made good time, sir. Never mind the rain. It's gone on for three days, but we are hoping for a bit of sun by tomorrow." There was a soft

Welsh lilt to his voice, but he was a fair man, broad-shouldered and stocky in build.

"That's good news."

Gesturing to the chair across from him, Holcomb sat down again. "Sorry to say, there's no good news about the body the boy found. We haven't identified him yet. Dr. Evans says he'd been in the river a few days, which hasn't helped. And from the look of him, we think he must have fallen from the Aqueduct. There was a lot of damage internally, consistent with such a fall. It's a long way."

He'd seen the Aqueduct. A towering array of arches with the top only a faint outline in the low clouds. "That puts his death around Thursday of last week."

"Yes, sir. I've made inquiries," the Constable went on. "But no one is missing from up there. No narrowboat owner or passenger, no visitor to the site. No stranger wandering about. You can walk across the Aqueduct, along the horse path. Easy to lose one's balance, looking down. If he fell at night, there might not have been anyone to see him start out—or go over."

"And no one missing down here?"

"Nor here," Holcomb agreed.

"Then we've not got much to be going on with."

The Constable sighed. "Sadly so, I'm afraid." Frowning, he added, "There was another case very like this one, three years ago. A body found on Mount Snowdon, spotted in a hollow by a sharp-eyed young woman on the cog railway to the summit. The little train hadn't run for several days—weather coming down—or likely he'd have been found earlier. A hiker, judging from his clothing, presumably caught in the storm. Took two months to prove it was a suicide. The Chief Constable has a long memory, sir. He'd like to see this inquiry concluded sooner rather than later."

Rutledge smiled grimly, thinking that the Chief Constable and Chief Superintendent Markham had much in common. He asked, "Any reason to believe our body was a suicide?"

"Not yet, sir. For one thing, he wasn't dressed for hiking. Nor did he appear to be down on his luck, as far as we can tell. But then you never know, do you, sir?" Holcomb rose. "A cuppa tea wouldn't go amiss just now, sir, given the day?"

"Thank you, Constable." Although the room was warm enough as it was, almost too warm.

Holcomb moved the kettle on a shelf above the small stove to its top, then poured in water from a jug sitting on the floor. As he busied himself with the cups and saucers, he added, "Roddy MacNabb is a good lad. The one who found the man in the river. Gave him a nasty shock, that did. He'd taken out a fishing pole, hoping to give it a try, and found a corpse instead. His gran sent for Dr. Evans, who had to give the lad something to calm him down a bit before they'd even got round to what he'd seen. Roddy was convinced the body was coming up out of the water after him. Which of course it never did. Dr. Evans discovered later that the hook from the pole had caught in the man's clothes, and as the lad pulled at what he thought was a fish, the body moved."

"How is the boy now?"

"Well enough. His gran wouldn't let him go to school. The other lads would have swarmed him, asking questions, which would bring it all back again." The kettle whistled and he set about making the tea. Bringing Rutledge a cup and then taking his own back to the desk, he sat down again. "There is one other thing. Roddy's stepmother. She's not from around here. MacNabb met her in Liverpool or some such before the war, brought her home, and married her. Against all advice. Still, he was a good man. Killed in the war. I wasn't all that surprised when Mrs. MacNabb wondered if the dead man might have something to do with her daughter-in-law."

Surprised, Rutledge said, "And does he, do you think?"

Holcomb frowned. "Begging your pardon, sir, but I

don't believe the dead man is her sort. There have been a few rumors over the years about Rosie MacNabb, none proved. She has a taste for trouble, you might say. Usually the sort that comes in trousers. But she's been careful never to push her mother-in-law far enough to send her packing. The feeling is that there was nothing much in Liverpool to draw her back. She'd as soon stay."

"Then why is this man not her sort?"

"He was short, sir. Just a bit over five feet." He considered the man across from him. "Rosie prefers them tall."

By the time they had finished their tea, the rain had stopped, but the clouds overhead were still heavy with moisture. Holcomb took Rutledge to the doctor's surgery, several houses down the road from the police station. Water stood everywhere, mirroring the gloomy sky. The house itself was not very large, but it was connected to a smaller cottage next door by an enclosed passage. The Constable led the way up the walk to the cottage. Knocking at the door, he waited. A woman came to answer the summons.

She was matronly, with a pretty face, dark hair, and a competent air about her.

"Afternoon, Mrs. Evans," Holcomb was saying.

"I've brought the Inspector from London to speak to the doctor."

"Of course." She smiled at Rutledge, then led them through a waiting room to the office beyond. Opening the door after a brief tap, she thrust her head in and said, "It's the Constable, my dear, with the man up from London."

"Send them in." The voice was gruff.

She opened the door wider, and the two men went inside. Dr. Evans was standing beside the mantelpiece, knocking the dottle from his pipe into the fire. He straightened, stuck the empty pipe into his pocket, and nodded to them.

He was older than his wife, graying, fifty perhaps, with spectacles that didn't hide the sharpness of eyes so dark they seemed to be black.

"Inspector Rutledge, Dr. Evans," Rutledge said, holding out his hand, and Evans shook it before settling them in front of his desk. Mrs. Evans had shut the door and gone away.

"Not much to tell you," he said, in the same gruff manner. "Dead, clearly fell from a high place. Given where he was found, that would most certainly be the Aqueduct. No water in his lungs to speak of, he didn't drown. But my guess is that he was in the Dee for two or three days."

"Was he alive when he fell? Or had he been killed and then dropped over the edge of the Aqueduct?"

"That's harder to judge. The river didn't do him any favors. Between that and his fall, any bruising or other signs of a struggle would be masked by the massive injuries he sustained almost immediately afterward. If he was alive, I suspect he saw his death coming. It's a long drop. Not a very pleasant thought." He shook his head. "Nasty business."

"Was there enough left of his face for a description?"

"I can only tell you that he had light brown hair, brown eyes, was barely five feet tall, and that three ribs had previously been cracked and healed with time. Age in his early thirties, I should think. You can see him, if you like. I doubt it will do you any good."

"Yes, I'd like to have a look. You are certain about where he fell from?"

"Given finding him in the water with those injuries, there was no other conclusion to draw. The only other possibility is having fallen from an aircraft. And Holcomb here can tell you there were none of those flying about in the week before he was discovered."

Rutledge glanced toward the Constable, saw the shake of his head, and turned back to Evans. "Anything about his clothing that might be helpful in finding out who he was?"

"Dark suit, not of the best quality but presentable enough. English made, I expect. There's a label in the shirt, but not, I think, from a known tailor. Holcomb here asked around, but no one seems to recognize the maker. The body was wearing no watch or ring, no watch chain. Of course, he might have had those, and they are either at the bottom of the Dee or in the pocket of whoever killed him—if, of course, this was murder. Not even a purse or loose coins in his pockets. One handkerchief, coarse linen, no initials. His boots were of good leather, reasonable wear and tear on the sole, and there was a hole in the right stocking, at the toe."

It was an oddly human finding.

"No overcoat, this time of year? Or hat?"

"No. He might well have left them somewhere. Or perhaps his killer took them."

Holcomb interjected, "We've searched for any belongings. All along the river where he might have come down. And a swath on either side of the banks. I've had local men out there looking. They know the Dee, they would have found a hat or coat. Or anything else."

"I must be sure. You're confident they were thorough?" Rutledge asked.

"We even went farther downstream in case some belongings drifted on, after the body lodged in the shallows."

Rutledge turned back to the doctor. "Murder? Or accident?"

"Impossible to say, medically. If he fell by accident, he'd have had some form of identification with him, surely. Still, if he didn't want to be identified, a suicide, he took care to see that he wasn't. If it was murder, his killer stripped him of anything useful to us. And that's what I reported to the Chief Constable. This death was probably not an accident." Dr. Evans rose. "Again I warn you, it isn't pleasant, what you're about to see. And he's been dead a week." He went to a cabinet, took out a small bottle of disinfectant, soaked three squares of gauze in it, and held out two of them. "You will be glad of this."

The back room, where the body was lying on a table, reeked of decayed flesh. Rutledge's mouth tightened as he recognized it and was for a moment back in the trenches, where the smell of rotting bodies had been omnipresent to the point of being commonplace. Unavoidable, and therefore best ignored. He held up the small square of gauze, as Holcomb and the doctor were doing. It wasn't a great deal of help.

The body was as Evans had said, badly damaged and in the river too long. It wouldn't have bloated, given the fall, sinking to the bottom of the river and moving with the current until it lodged in roots or against rocks.

Evans was right, also, that there was too little left of the face, reminding Rutledge of a leper he'd seen in France. He found himself thinking that the dead man's family wouldn't have recognized what was left. But the heavy bone at the nose, the squared line of the skeletal chin were indications of a strong face. On the other hand, brown hair and eyes were common enough in Wales and on the Welsh borders.

The man's clothing had been folded neatly on a smaller table against the wall, but it too smelled, as Rutledge touched the fabric of the man's suit and looked at the black boots. The handmade label stitched into the neckband of the shirt was faded, not new, but he could read the ornate script: *Banner.* Just beneath it was what appeared to be the tailor's mark, a needle with a loop of thread through the eye. He took out his notebook and made a rough sketch of the design.

The dead man had been dressed, he thought, to conduct business somewhere, not to take up work. Not a laborer, then. Turning away, he said, "Anything else that we can use?"

Evans gestured to the left arm. "There is one thing, but I doubt it will be helpful. On the forearm, just there. I can't make out what it might be."

Rutledge leaned closer for a better look. The skin

was broken, bits missing. But there *was* something. Holcomb came up to peer at it over his shoulder.

"It's not the same color as the skin around it. A tattoo, do you think?" Rutledge looked up at the doctor. "In the war, were you?"

Evans shook his head.

"It was a popular thing among the ranks. A sweetheart's name, one's regiment, a battle." Straightening up, Rutledge added, "I can't be sure, of course. But I think that's what we're seeing here. Do you have a magnifying glass?"

Evans nodded, opening a drawer against the wall. "Will this do?"

It was small, but Rutledge took it and held it over the dark patch. It magnified the rotting skin as much as it did the faded pattern. He handed the glass to Holcomb as he went on. "My guess is that our unknown body *was* in the war. And given how short he is, I'd say that could very well be the insignia of the Bantam Battalions."

Pressing the square of gauze hard against his nose, Holcomb peered at the discoloration. "I can't say I can make out a bantam rooster. Looks more like a"—he searched for the right comparison—"like a tree, don't you think? An oak, perhaps?"

Oaks were a popular tattoo, given their association with the Stuart King Charles II hiding in an oak tree during his escape from England and the clutches of Cromwell. Any number of pubs and inns had been named for that tree. There was even, Rutledge remembered, a Revenge-class battleship brought into service in November 1914 named *Royal Oak*.

Had the dead man served on her? It might prove to be the link between the body and the narrowboats. Had he once worked on them, before the war?

Ignoring the smell, Rutledge looked more closely at the faint pattern. Oak—or rooster?

The tree was generally shown in full leaf, and with a massive spread of roots below, the same width and depth as the tree was wide and tall.

The Bantam tattoo, as he remembered it, showed the rooster above with larger entwined *B*s below it.

But so much of the skin was missing, it was hard to determine any size here. He looked away, then returned to his inspection. There—at the bottom left. Was that the straight line of a *B*? There were no straight lines in roots . . .

Rutledge looked away once more, staring at the wall for an instant, then turned back to the arm before him. Leaves went up. A rooster's tail went down. He thought he could just pick out the faint blue line of half a feather.

The smell was getting to him, the trenches, the dead—

He moved back, trying to evade the odor of decaying death, but it seemed to be everywhere, distinctive, cloying, strong.

Taking a grip on the sudden flood of memories, he forced himself to think clearly.

There was nothing in what little was left of the design to indicate a tree. But there were a straight line and then a downward line with three short lines perpendicular to it. A possible *B*—a possible feather.

"I think not," Rutledge said, answering Holcomb. "But given the number of shorter men finally allowed to enlist in the Army by Kitchener, it doesn't narrow our search all that much. And short men were allowed to join the Navy, in due course."

"Well," said Holcomb, stepping back and handing the glass to Evans, "I'm fair flummoxed. It could be a tattoo right enough. I'll give you that. But I'm damned if I know what it might be showing."

Dr. Evans said, "The only thing in the Inspector's favor is the fact that the top appears to be larger on the right than on the left. A rooster has a small head to the left, large body in the center, and larger tail to the right. Still, that could be a problem with the torn skin and not the design."

"There's little else to be going forward with. I'll look into the Bantams to see if the body can be identified through the regiments."

Holcomb shot him a look of relief as Rutledge started for the door. Evans followed, with Holcomb at his heels, coughing sharply.

The air in the passage seemed fresh and sweet by comparison as the doctor shut the door firmly behind them. Back in the office, Evans didn't sit down.

"I've given you all I can. I don't recognize this man, and nor does Holcomb, and we know most of the men in the village and on the surrounding farms. Besides that, so far we have no missing person query. I don't think our body is actually ours. You'd be better off inquiring among the narrowboats that cross on the Aqueduct."

Beyond the door to the waiting room, Rutledge could hear voices, and so could the doctor. Patients waiting.

Hamish spoke suddenly, jarring Rutledge.

"He's no' a man wi' imagination, yon doctor."

Holcomb glanced at Rutledge, who said briskly, covering his reaction, "Thank you, Dr. Evans. If I have more questions, I'll be in touch."

"Can't think what they might be, but you'll be welcome to come again."

And then they were passing through the curious

stares in the crowded waiting room and out onto the street.

Holcomb looked back at the closed door of the surgery, then said, "Well, he's right, I expect. It's our body because the poor sod landed here. But not our inquiry, do you think? Sir?"

A man no one wanted. The thought passed through Rutledge's mind. Inconveniently dead on their patch.

Or was he?

Time would tell.

"At the moment, he's still ours." They started in the direction of the station. "Who should I speak to at the Aqueduct?"

"I've not spent much time up there. Once after a thief who'd strayed our way. He'd been robbing the boats over that winter. Went with my brother another time when he was looking for work." He shrugged. "We don't have that much in common with the narrowboat folks."

"Where is your brother now? Did he find work there?"

"No, no experience handling the craft. But it was worth a try, he kept telling me he wasn't cut out for farming. Until of course he met a lass who was a farmer's daughter." He cleared his throat. "Lost him in the war, died of gangrene during the Somme Offensive."

It had been hot that July, the dying and the dead everywhere, and no time to save half of them. It would have been easy to die as gangrene set in, taking the leg and then the man.

Shutting out the past with an effort, Rutledge nodded. "I'm sorry."

Holcomb shrugged. "Nice memorial brass in the chapel so he'll be remembered. But I'd rather have had him home, leg or no leg."

They finished the short walk in silence.

"You'll want to speak to the lad who found the body," Holcomb said when they reached the police station.

"Yes." He glanced at his watch. "This should be as good a time as any."

"He can't add much to what the doctor told you, but he's a good lad, and still shaken by what happened."

Rutledge crossed to the motorcar. "You'll show me the way?"

"Happy to, sir." He turned the crank for Rutledge and then got in beside him.

"Straight through the village, and the first left. After that, it's not far."

The farmhouse sat back in a windbreak of mature trees that must have been planted at the time it was built. Gray stone, a slate roof, and an urn of early pansies by the door. It could have been any one of the farms Rutledge had passed, driving into Wales.

A woman came to the door as they stepped out of the motorcar. She was tall, with graying hair that still had a hint of dark red in it, and an attractive face that was lined with worry at the moment.

Holcomb said in a low voice, "Her husband's great-grandfather came from Scotland to work on the Aqueduct. MacNabb. Met a Welsh lass and married her. When the work was done on the Aqueduct, he stayed."

Rutledge was taking off his hat. "Mrs. MacNabb? My name is Rutledge. I've been sent by Scotland Yard to look into the death of the man your grandson found by the river."

She nodded to Holcomb, then said quietly to Rutledge, "We were expecting you to call. My grandson has nightmares now. I hope you'll be gentle with him." And she opened the door wider, to allow them to step in.

The parlor was lit by windows on two sides, today letting in only the gray light, but Rutledge could picture it on a sunny day, the yellow-and-lavender wallpaper reflecting it in every corner.

Over the mantel in pride of place was a painting of a man in Highland kit, standing by a loch where trees climbed the surrounding hills.

She saw Rutledge's glance and smiled slightly. "My husband's great-grandfather's father, and mine. I'm a cousin as well as a wife. It was sent to him after his father's death. I sometimes think its purpose was to make my great-grandfather homesick. But they hadn't seen eye to eye in life, and there was nothing for Robbie back there." Abruptly changing the subject, she said, "May I offer you tea?"

"Thank you, no," Rutledge said, smiling and taking one of the overstuffed chairs she indicated. "I think it best if we keep our visit short."

She nodded. "I won't be a moment." And then she was back with the gangling boy of eleven or twelve who had gone fishing and found a dead man.

His face was rather pale, and a sprinkle of freckles stood out across his nose. He said politely in a low voice, "How do you do?"

Holcomb leaned forward, but Rutledge was there before he could speak. "Hallo. Roddy, is it? My name is Rutledge, I've come from London to find out what I can about the man you discovered. It would help me search for answers if you could tell me a little about what happened to you."

It wasn't what the boy had expected. He said, "I can't tell you much. I hardly looked at him."

"I've seen him," Rutledge said, nodding. "It was

very unpleasant. But I was wondering. Was he floating when you got to the riverbank? Or caught in the shallows somehow?"

"I don't know," Roddy replied. "I didn't see him at first. Not until my hook caught in his coat, and—and I pulled. I didn't know it—I had no idea what it was. Until he rolled over."

"It must have been a dreadful shock," Rutledge agreed. "That particular place in the river. Downstream from the Aqueduct, do you think?"

"About half a mile," the boy said, nodding. "It wasn't overhead. But I could hear sounds from up there."

"Anything or anyone in the vicinity of where you were fishing, along the river just there?"

"I don't think so." He glanced uneasily at his grandmother. "I wasn't—I shouldn't have been out there, fishing. But I found the pole, you see, and I wanted to try it. I thought it best to stay out of sight."

There had been a search of both banks, upstream and downstream, but nothing had been found, and now there was no indication that others had come searching for the dead body before Roddy's discovery.

Rutledge nodded. "I'd have done the same. Good fishing in the Dee, do you think?"

"I don't know. I hadn't tried before."

"Why did you choose that particular spot?"

"It was flatter just there, I could get to the water more easily."

"And no one had been there before you? No footprints or other signs of anyone about?"

"No. I wasn't really looking—but I'd have—I'd have moved on if I'd seen other people." He lifted a shoulder, not looking at his grandmother. "I should have been helping. It was a Saturday."

Somewhere in the house a door slammed, making the boy jump and glance anxiously at his grandmother. Before she could say anything, they heard brisk footsteps, and the door to the parlor swung open. A younger woman stepped in. Mrs. MacNabb introduced her daughter-in-law without any inflection in her voice or change in her expression, but her gray eyes were as hard as flint.

Even dressed as a farmer's widow, it was clear what sort of woman Roddy's stepmother had been. It was there in her face and the way she moved forward, her gaze on Rutledge, prepared to be the center of attention.

Roddy had moved back toward his grandmother, eyes down, looking at no one and nothing.

But before she could ask to be introduced, Rutledge rose, smiled pleasantly, and said, "Mrs. MacNabb, I believe? We were just leaving. A few questions for

Roddy, in the course of my inquiries. He's a good lad. You must be quite proud of him."

Holcomb was on his feet as well, following Rutledge toward the door.

Rutledge let him pass, looked at the elder Mrs. MacNabb, and said, "Thank you. We won't trouble you again." And to Roddy, he added, "You were a brave lad."

The boy mumbled something. The grandmother followed them to the door, and shut it after them.

Rutledge strode to the motorcar. Holcomb was already turning the crank.

"I wasn't going to give her a chance to interfere," he said grimly.

"If I'd found a body out here, along the river or the road, I'd not have been surprised to see it was her. I don't know how the grandmother puts up with her. Did you learn anything from the boy?"

"Only that no one was still searching the river for the body. We can't be sure of that, of course, they could have come and gone long before Roddy went fishing."

"Falling from that height, there wouldn't be any question the man was dead."

"I don't think a murderer would have cared either way," Rutledge replied. "But if no one else came looking for him, it could mean he had no friends up there wondering where he'd got to. Therefore he was very likely a stranger."

But before driving back into town, Rutledge asked Holcomb to show him where the body had been drifting when Roddy MacNabb's hook brought it to light.

The sun was just struggling to break through when they reached the spot.

The ground was trampled and muddy still where the men had worked to bring the corpse in and others had come to stare. The little clearing was no longer a tempting place to stop and try for a fish. Holcomb looked around it and shook his head. "It was bad luck the dead man got caught on something here. For a killer, that is. If it'd stayed midstream, now, it might have floated well away."

"That was very likely what a killer hoped for." As Rutledge turned to go, he looked up at the graceful dark red brick aqueduct, towering far above his head, the very top section gray cast iron. He realized that the top of the structure must be where the waterway and the horse path were carried across. Eighteen slender pillars rose from the valley floor in arches that ran from right to left, bridging the gap from side to side. A span of near 1,000 feet, if he was any judge, and a good 120 feet high. Yet the waterway itself was invisible from here. In fact, at first glance one could almost believe the Romans had built it.

"Elegant piece of work, isn't it?"

"That it is." Holcomb shaded his eyes as a shout echoed from above, and another voice answered it.

"What if our man's killer waited to make his move until he was certain his victim would go into the river? Where the body had a good chance of being carried away downstream, possibly never found?" Rutledge asked thoughtfully. "If he did, it speaks of premeditation, not an argument that got out of hand. It's a place to start."

"A different world up there," the Constable agreed darkly. "Not one I know."

3

Early the next morning, Rutledge left the village and made his way along back roads toward the top of the Aqueduct. The rain had gone, as Constable Holcomb had foretold, leaving a bright day with a bit of a breeze.

When he reached the head of the northern cliff, he felt an even greater appreciation for the stunning piece of engineering that Telford had created in 1805. It was still an amazing construction. His godfather, the architect, had always claimed that Thomas Telford was a man before his time, and Rutledge had no difficulty in believing that here.

A community of sorts had grown up where the engineers and workmen had put up their temporary lodgings in the 1800s, but now the waterway belonged to the narrowboat men. Leaving his motorcar under some trees where the main canal coming down from the north broadened into a basin, Rutledge walked past a scattering of cottages, and then where the basin narrowed again, he found shops that catered to them as well as to craft passing through.

There was an odd sense of isolation here. He'd come through Trefor, just to the north, where there was some industry, and even a railway station, although it had been closed until the next train was due. Here it felt as if life were suspended until the next narrowboats passed along the canal and over the Aqueduct. It was almost unnaturally quiet, no children running about, no wives gossiping along the path, no dogs barking as he went by. Holcomb had been right. It was a different world.

Rutledge walked into one of the smaller shops, and was surprised to find it too all but empty.

Nodding to the man behind the display of goods, restocking a handful of tins, he asked for a cup of tea.

"Any table you like," the man replied, and Rutledge chose one by the front window, looking out on the waterway as it narrowed toward the crossing. Then he turned for a better view of the way he'd come in.

As he'd left his motorcar he'd noticed the single narrowboat, long, high in the water, and barely six feet

wide, tied up in the basin. It was a sleek black with pol-
ished brass fittings. In the sunlight dappling the dark
water, it had looked freshly painted. He could observe
it now. He hadn't wanted to appear unduly interested
in it or attract attention to himself until he'd got a better
feeling for this place.

The man came over with his tea and set the cup
down. Noticing the direction of Rutledge's gaze, he
said, "My cousin's boat."

"Indeed? Does he live on it?" he asked casually.

"No, his cottage is just over there." He gestured to
a stand of trees on the far side of the basin. But his
tone of voice indicated an affront, as if Rutledge had
insulted his cousin.

"I don't know much about narrowboats," Rutledge
said affably, as if he hadn't noticed. "I thought families
usually lived on board."

"Those that do are no better than gypsies," the man
retorted.

"Are they? I hadn't known." He poured milk into
his cup, then added, "How long are the boats?"

"Seventy-two feet, most of them. If they're to nav-
igate some of the canals and many of the locks, they
can't be any longer. Even so, they must fit sideways
into some of the older locks."

Rutledge turned toward the Aqueduct. "It's damned

narrow, out there," he said. "Are all the aqueducts like that?"

"I expect they are. One boat at a time, going or coming. And just enough room beside the boat for the horse pulling the rope and the man walking him."

"What do they carry, most of the time?"

"Whatever's called for. Aggregate. Slate. Goods. Quarry stone. Brick. Even people, sometimes. During the war, now, there were nearly five hundred boats using this canal. Did my dad's heart good to see them, he said. He was a narrowboat man. I never was. My mother's father kept the shop, and I took over from him."

"Do many visitors come to watch the boats cross over?"

"Sometimes in the summer, there will be a dozen or so about. Wanting a float across, some of them. As if these were pleasure boats."

"This time of year?"

"You're the first this week." He studied Rutledge. "What brings you here?"

"I was expecting to meet a friend."

There was a wariness now in the man's manner. "Not this side of the crossing. I've heard of no strangers about."

But Rutledge hadn't told him whether the friend was local or an outsider.

"You might remember him if you had seen him. Short, just over five feet tall. Good shoulders. Light brown hair, a strong nose." It was the best description he could offer.

The shopkeeper shook his head. "He never came in here." There was a firmness now in the denial. Cutting off further questions.

Was that really so? Or only a part of the truth? If the victim hadn't come in—had he been somewhere outside? On one of the boats that had come through?

Reserving judgment, Rutledge said, "Are you sure of that? I was held up in Shrewsbury for several days. I'd not like to think I'd missed him." He stirred his tea, staring out now at the black narrowboat. The problem was, he himself was in the dark about the victim's movements. Shrugging slightly, he added, "Is there an inn, this side of the Aqueduct? Somewhere he might have stayed? Or left a message?"

The shopkeeper was frowning now. "Never been a call for one. The men coming through on the narrowboats sleep aboard."

"What about the far side?"

"The far side?" The shopkeeper stared at him, as if he'd asked about the far side of the moon.

"I don't relish the long drive around. How do I cross the Aqueduct to the southern end?"

"By the towpath."

"Any chance of taking one of the narrowboats across? I don't fancy walking. Heights trouble me."

"You'll have to speak to one of the owners. They don't as a rule care for passengers. Not when there's goods aboard. Sometimes if they're empty." He glanced at Rutledge's cup. "Finished, are you?"

Rutledge rose and followed him to the counter, where he paid for the tea. But at the door he paused. "I'm curious. Why do you say the narrowboats with families living aboard are no better than gypsies? Are they a thieving lot? Should I be wary of them?"

"They're ignorant. Illiterate. No schooling for themselves, nor for the little ones. Families crowded into cabins hardly big enough for the man at the tiller. Sleeping there, cooking there. Born there as often as not, and dying there too. Poor and dirty—you can smell the boats as they pass."

Rutledge thought he was exaggerating. "But not thieving, no police records, surely."

The man replied sourly, "Who knows? They've no roots, they come and go as they please, traveling up and down the canals year after year."

"Do many come through here?"

"More since the railroads came. Hard times, then. Some couldn't pay for a boat and a house on shore. But that's less space for cargo, isn't it, and without a full load, they earn less. Gypsies."

The railroads had come through decades ago. But old prejudices died hard. With a nod, Rutledge stepped out into the sunshine and walked on to where the black boat was moored.

It was handsome, if a little funereal. There was a painted rose by the well of the tiller, and lacy curtains at all the windows. Two had flower pots in them as well. It was hard to say whether this particular boat carried goods or passengers, but it appeared to ride high in the water, a sign that it was empty now. He walked the length, looking at the well in the bow. The man at the tiller would have to stand to see down the length of the craft and over the slightly raised prow.

The tow rope lay coiled neatly on the boards. It appeared to be dry, as if it hadn't been used in several days. He turned, wondering where the horse was stabled when not in service, and saw one or two outbuildings beyond the cottages.

Ducks came running as he moved on around the basin, then lost interest as he ignored them and looked around at the cottages scattered about. For the most part they were modest and kept trim. He wondered where the children here went to school. In his brief survey, he hadn't noticed a building large enough to be a school.

He turned and retraced his steps toward the Aqueduct. Closer to it, he realized that the trough of water and the towpath beside it could be no more than twelve feet wide. While the water, shimmering now in the sunlight, seemed suspended in air, the towpath on the eastern side appeared to be dangerously narrow. The closer he got to the edge, the longer the Aqueduct seemed to stretch before him. And then he was looking down at the green Llangollen Valley, fields and trees and the line of the river over a hundred feet below. In the distance upriver he could just pick out the roofs of Roddy's village.

" 'Ware." Hamish's keen hearing had picked up the approach of someone behind him, and Rutledge stepped away from the drop, turning to see who had followed him. He'd half expected it to be the shopkeeper, but it was a younger man, in his late thirties. He walked with a limp, but stopped at once as Rutledge turned. And stood there not six paces away.

"Careful," he said in the rhythmic accent of the Welsh. "You'd not wish to fall all that way."

"No."

"First time here?" the man asked.

"Yes, it is."

"Impressive sight."

Rutledge asked, "Live here, do you?"

"On the far side. Yes."

"I thought you might be the owner of that handsome black narrowboat."

The man grinned cheekily. "Me? Not likely." And without another word, he set out across the towpath, walking jauntily, as if the height didn't worry him. Rutledge watched him cross and then disappear on the southern end.

Making certain there was no one else coming up behind him—and no one about to cross from the other side—Rutledge himself stepped out onto the towpath. It was barely more than five and a half feet wide, with little or no protection against falling, he thought, keeping his gaze on the far end and walking steadily. Soon he was a quarter of the way across, and he couldn't stop himself from glancing down at the fields and trees and the dark line of the river below.

But that was dizzying, not the best of ideas, and he quickly brought his gaze back from the sheer drop and fixed it on his goal. The tow horses, he thought, must wear blinders to keep them firmly on the path. Or did they, like he himself, still sense that drop so close to them?

He cast another quick look down, regretting it almost at once.

How easy it would be to turn quickly and shove someone off the path!

Had the man screamed as he fell? Or had it been too sudden, the shock keeping him from crying out until it was almost too late?

The wonder was, he hadn't taken his killer with him . . .

Rutledge's mouth was dry as he reached the far end, and Hamish was hammering at him in the back of his mind. Trying to ignore the deep Scots voice, he continued into the village. It was more or less a mirror of the one he'd left. There was the line of the narrow waterway that carried on a short distance over solid ground before widening into a basin, and beyond the basin, the southern canal disappeared among a stand of trees. If there was an inn, he couldn't see it. And then the sound of hooves caught his attention. Looking up, toward the basin, he realized there were several narrowboats approaching from the south, just coming into view. They were in line, and he counted four of them, the horses plodding steadily, heads down, in his direction. The horses pricked up their ears as the basin came into view, and he thought they must know the routine, a brief stop before the crossing. One of the men leading them called out, and a woman appeared at the door of a cottage on the far side of it.

He began to walk toward the boats. There was an older man with a thin gray beard squatting close by the towpath, a long hemp rope spread out by him. He appeared to be inspecting it inch by inch.

When he was near enough to the man, Rutledge called pleasantly, as if he were only a chance visitor, "Hallo. Remarkable place, this. Live here, do you?"

"Aye." The response was cautious. And he didn't look up after the first swift glance Rutledge's way, his attention on the rope.

"I couldn't help but wonder. What's it like here in a storm? Or in winter? Surely the horses can't make that crossing if it's icy? Or cold enough for the water to start to freeze?"

The man stared up at him now. "Some days it's shut down. Aye."

"I just walked across myself. I don't fancy walking back," he said with a rueful smile. "Too damned narrow for my taste. Even in such good weather. Do you suppose one of those boats will let me step on board?"

The man said, curiosity and something else in his gaze, "English, are you?"

"Yes. I've never been here before." He launched into the story he'd told the shopkeeper, about the friend he was meeting. "Have you seen him about, by any chance? I don't want to miss him, after coming all this way."

The man shook his head. "Doubt he's been over here."

"Are you sure? I'd like to find him."

"If he was on one of the passing boats, I'd not have noticed him."

"Why? Would he have been inside, not sitting in the bow?"

"Not inside, if she carried cargo."

"Surely you must know most of the men at the tiller. And those leading the horses. They must come and go through here often enough."

The man dropped his gaze to the rope again, moving it slowly but steadily through his fingers. "Not always. Mostly I know the narrowboats."

It was a close community of men who made their living on or from the waterway. Rutledge could see that they weren't likely to give a stranger any more information than was necessary. Nor did he think they would be likely to help an English policeman, if he'd shown his identification instead.

But he said, as he looked back toward the crossing, "That's a dangerous place. Ever have accidents there?"

The man lifted his head again, his dark eyes giving nothing away as he regarded Rutledge. "The horses and the lads know their business."

"I'm sure they do. But one misstep, one foot tangled

in the tow rope, one instant of losing one's concentration—I can see it happening."

"But then you aren't a boatman," he retorted and went back to his rope, closing the conversation.

Rutledge walked on, watching the horses pulling the narrowboats toward him. They walked steadily, at a pace, the tow rope not always taut where each boat's momentum eased the effort to pull it. The boatmen, standing in the stern, watching the bow down the spine of their boats, sometimes shouted to each other or to someone they saw on shore. But for the most part they concentrated on their craft as they pulled into the basin and half a dozen people came out to greet them.

There were three men and a boy of perhaps fifteen leading the horses, moving close by their bridles, and Rutledge saw that the horses did indeed wear blinders.

As the boats eased to a stop, the tow ropes slacking off and dipping into the water, the horses were led forward and allowed to drink.

He walked toward them, and when he reached the elder of the three men, he said, "Thirsty work, I take it."

The man looked up. "Man and beast."

"Worked the narrowboats long, have you?"

"I have."

"What about the man at the tiller?"

"My son. We take turns."

The lead boat was a dark green, with yellow trim. There were curtains at the windows, and he could see that the other two boats had them as well. There would be no way to know what the boat was carrying. Or who was aboard. Rutledge noticed two flower pots on a low shelf in the bow of the boat where a boy led the horse. A sign that a family lived aboard? And then a curtain in the boat bringing up the rear twitched, and a child's face appeared in the window for an instant, then disappeared.

"Do you think he'd allow me to travel back across the Aqueduct with him? I left my motorcar over there."

"You can ask."

Rutledge walked on and did, offering a pound note as he asked his favor.

The younger man took it, glanced to see that his father wasn't watching, and pocketed it quickly. "In the bow. Don't stand. I need to see."

But it was nearly a quarter of an hour before they moved out of the basin and toward the Aqueduct.

The boat came close enough that Rutledge could step on board, then moved into the stream toward the crossing as the horse took up the strain, the older man talking quietly to the animal. And the boat glided silently toward the waterway.

The horse was out in front, stepping onto the path, and the boat moved with it, the man at the tiller guiding it smoothly into place, still the first boat in line.

Neither the horse nor the man leading it seemed to notice the drop so perilously close as the boat seemed to fill the waterway and move quietly along, the sound of hooves the only distraction. Rutledge rose slightly to look down into the valley from the safety of the bow. The view was quite impressive. But he couldn't pick out the spot where Roddy had found the body.

Sitting again, he watched the horse putting its feet down with the assurance that the path was there, and the man moving beside it, glancing back along the line of the boat toward the tiller a time or two, then studying Rutledge when he thought he wasn't being seen.

They reached the far side, glided on into the basin there, and Rutledge was put ashore. He thanked the man at the tiller with a wave, and walked on to where he'd left his motorcar.

If the dead man had come here, no one was about to admit to seeing him. The police had already been here to ask questions, and a stranger coming after them wasn't very likely to be taken into anyone's confidence.

As Rutledge bent to turn the crank, Hamish said, "Ye ken, if he came at night, who was to see?"

"I'd not care to cross on that towpath in the dark."

"Aye, it would depend on how much he wanted to reach the far side."

But what was he looking for that couldn't wait until the morning? And how had he got here in the first place? The police hadn't found a motorcar. Train service was sporadic. Had he walked? From where?

Remembering the child's face at the window, Rutledge realized that a dozen men, alive or dead, might be behind those pretty lace curtains. Who would know—or guess? And if one was tossed over the bow on the opposite side of the narrowboat from the towpath, it wouldn't disturb the horse making its careful way across.

How easy was it to leave the horse to find its own way? Or to leave the tiller untended?

But the channel of water over the Aqueduct was barely wider than the boat. There was no place for it to go, once it started across. Lash the tiller, and it would stay on course. The boat's length would assure that.

It would be nearly impossible to track every narrowboat that had crossed the Aqueduct in the past ten days, much less interview their owners. Not until the police were in possession of sufficient information to make an interview worthwhile.

Rutledge got behind the wheel of the motorcar, then

sat there for a moment or two, thinking. Finally he turned his back on the Aqueduct, his mind made up.

The Bantam Battalions had had their beginning in Birkenhead, on the Cheshire coast, early in the war. The average height of men in England was five feet six inches. The Army had set as its regulation height anyone above five feet four, then dropped that to five three. But men shorter than that had clamored to join as well, and General Kitchener had listened, allowing the Bantam Battalions to recruit men between five feet and five three. The initial advertisements had brought in not dozens but hundreds of shorter men eager to serve their country. One had reportedly offered to fight any six men of regulation height, to prove his mettle. The first battalion's officers were of regulation height, and that had been true throughout the war, until the Bantams had been assimilated into other regiments toward the end. More than a few had gone into the new tanks, where space was cramped even for them.

Rutledge had known one of the Bantam officers in France. Word was, Alasdair Dale had retired to Chester at war's end, to return to his former occupation, that of solicitor.

It had also been rumored that Alasdair was planning to write a history of the Bantams. To set the record straight. Whether he'd got round to it or not, he'd had the best working knowledge of the Battalions of anyone Rutledge could think of. If the gossip was right, he'd written most of the wills of the first recruits. Wills had been required by the Army, and most men took that philosophically, but a few had seen it as stepping on their graves. Rutledge had had his own drawn up in the months after his parents' death, making provision for his younger sister, Frances. But the Army had insisted on a more current one, as several years had passed.

The city of Chester was not that far from the Telford Aqueduct, only a few hours' drive. Once a Roman garrison, it had preserved the walls the legions had built, rebuilding and restoring them well into the Middle Ages. Behind them, Charles I had tried to hold the city during the Civil War. And they were still standing, the city's pride. Set on the same River Dee where the body had been found, only closer to the sea, Chester had a long history of trade and industry, but its real glory was the tall, elegant black-and-white Tudor houses that graced street after street.

Driving into the city through one of the gates, Rutledge glanced at some of the houses. In the late afternoon sun, the glazing reflected the light, and the white plaster with its dark hatchwork of beams seemed to have defied the centuries.

He wasn't certain just where Alasdair's chambers were, but he finally found them not far from the Cathedral. Set into the dark green door, the heavy brass knocker was shaped like a gloved fist, but there was lacy fringe to the cuff. Rutledge remembered as he lifted it that a gloved fist was on the family's coat of arms.

A clerk answered the summons, leading Rutledge through the narrow entry into a room that spoke quietly of old money. He gave his name, and the clerk disappeared through a door, returning shortly. "Mr. Dale will see you, sir. This way, if you please."

Down a passage lined with paintings of waterbirds, Alasdair was waiting by the door to his office. He was nearly as tall as Rutledge, only a few years older, with sandy hair and blue eyes. As Rutledge started toward him, he said, "Well, I never thought you'd make it to Chester, but here you are. Don't tell me there's a murder in the city that I haven't been told of?"

They shook hands as Rutledge replied, "Not here, but not that far away. I need your expertise."

"The law? Or do I know the victim—or the murderer?"

They moved into the paneled room, and Alasdair was gesturing toward one of the leather chairs across from his desk.

"Actually, I need to know something about the Bantams."

"Do you indeed?" Interested, Dale leaned back in his chair. "What's this in aid of?"

Rutledge described the dead man he'd seen in Wales.

"You do know, that description could fit half a regiment? As for the tattoo, I daresay there must be half as many men again who got such a one. If not when they enlisted, at least before they shipped out. Have you considered your man might be in the Navy, not the Bantams?"

"You're depressingly unhelpful. Did you ever write that history?"

Dale grinned. "Good God, man, we're talking about the stories of thirty-odd thousand soldiers! But I've got a box room full of notes. I found collecting information was much more my thing than sitting down and collating it. My friends tell me to hire someone to write the book. But somehow I don't think it would be the same." The grin faded. "I knew those men. They were damned good soldiers. They deserve a history far better than anything I might write."

"You're too close to it. Five years from now you might see it differently."

"I hope that's true. But I shan't hold my breath." He picked up a pen from the blotter, toyed with it for a moment, then set it down again. "I've had trouble fitting back into my old life. It didn't help that I lost my wife in the middle of the war. I can't settle, somehow. Even my work doesn't satisfy me the way it did in 1914. Don't misunderstand me. God knows I don't miss the war. I do miss the comradeship. We counted on one another, it was a brotherhood born of necessity. Nothing like anything I'd known at university before the war. And I haven't found it since." He cleared his throat. "Too many of us died. They haunt me. The friends who didn't make it."

He couldn't meet Rutledge's gaze, looking instead at a painting of a swan landing on a lake fringed with reeds and grasses. It hung on the wall to his left.

Rutledge said carefully, "I think they haunt most of us. None of us expected to survive. What we did had nothing to do with who deserved to live. It was a lottery, and some of us won. God alone knows why."

Dale took a deep breath, as if to steady himself. Then he said in a different tone of voice, "Back to this dead man of yours. Any good reason to think he was Welsh? Other than the fact he was found there?"

"Not so far. The only other bit of evidence is that his shirt came from a tailor. There's a handmade label in the collar. The shirt is a fairly decent grade of cloth, but the label indicates a smaller, possibly local firm.

Anything strike you about the name Banner?" Taking out his notebook, he passed it to Dale, open to the page where he'd drawn the design.

"Someone has ambitions, looking to come up in the world. I don't recognize it—not an establishment I'm likely to know. But I'd advise you to speak to a few tailors here in Chester. One of them might be familiar with it."

"Yes, I was considering that. Meanwhile—how popular was that Bantam tattoo?"

"At a guess? Thousands of men got it. A matter of pride. You are welcome to go through my notes. But you already know that the first two battalions were local men, then the idea spread, and we had men as far away as Nottingham. Fairly soon, other towns all over England were following in our footsteps, raising companies. Still, if this man was killed in Wales, he could well be from Cheshire. Or any of the neighboring counties. Less likely to be from Glasgow, say, or Suffolk. That's still a fair number of men to track down."

"What about the narrowboats? Do they have a reputation for trouble? If I were a boatman and looking for a place to rid myself of a body, the Aqueduct would be my first choice."

"I'd say they're no more likely to be killers than

any other occupation. On the other hand, there's one thing in your favor, Ian—there's never been an overall English canal system. They've always been local enterprises. Bits and pieces, wherever it was possible to link rivers with waterways and make it easier to carry loads of goods, instead of hauling them overland. If this man's killer is a narrowboat man, then it's likely that he met his victim close to that particular canal. Which brings us back to the possibility that your body is Welsh. Or your killer may be. As a rule, boatmen put down roots where they worked."

Which fit all too well with the reception he'd encountered at the Aqueduct. Rutledge grimaced. "You make it sound hopeless."

"I'm being realistic. Now, if you could give me a name, I could probably find your man in my notes. Any time between now and Whitsunday, if you nagged me."

"Meanwhile, a murderer goes free."

Dale shrugged. "I know. I do have photographs of various companies of Bantams. It was a popular thing to take one, and after the war I found many of the photographers and begged copies. I'll gladly let you search through them."

"His face was too badly damaged. I could make a guess at the shape of the nose and the chin, but that's about it."

"When you have more, come back. I'll do what I can to give you a name."

Leaving his motorcar where it was, Rutledge sought out the city's tailor shops. The more upscale clerks shook their heads and denied any knowledge of anyone by the name of Banner. But on a back street not far from Ye Old Boot pub, he was more successful.

The older man who came to help him looked at the sketch Rutledge had made and frowned. "I don't know if Banner is still in business," he said. "He came here as an assistant in 1904, and learned the trade. Some years later, when there was an opening in a shop closer to home, he took it. I was sorry to lose him, to tell the truth. But his parents were getting on, and he was worried about them. I might still have his direction." He looked around the shop as if expecting it to materialize out of the air, then went to a small room in the back where he kept his files.

As he opened a drawer stuffed full of letters and began to sort through them, Rutledge groaned inwardly, thinking it would take most of the day to find anything.

But haphazard as the man's system might appear to anyone else, he quickly found the packet of letters he was looking for, took them out, and began to thumb through them. Near the end, he pulled one out.

"Yes, here it is. Banner. He took over when the owner retired and added his name to the sign. Llangollen." He looked up. "That's in Wales. Do you know it?"

Rutledge had in fact passed through it. And it sat on the River Dee not far from the village where Roddy had caught the body with his fishhook. "Yes."

He showed Rutledge the letterhead. It read *BANNER* and beneath it was the direction: *113 High Street.*

Rutledge thanked him for his help and promised to give Banner the man's regards, then left the shop.

He drove back the way he'd come, through flat farm country that spread out before him, fallow fields already plowed and waiting to be sown. After crossing the border into Wales, the land began to roll more as Rutledge neared Llangollen.

It was a prosperous but hilly town, and after he'd found a place to leave his motorcar, he walked uphill toward the center. He found 113 with no difficulty, and looked at the window on the street. There was a tasteful display of shirts and ties, an array of shoes, and several bolts of cloth. Stepping through the door, he saw that Banner must have prospered, because one side of the shop held haberdashery goods, while the other was clearly for tailoring.

A young assistant came out to greet him, and Rutledge asked to speak to the owner. He was led to an office no larger than the one in Chester, filled to the ceiling with files and bits of cloth in every color and of every quality.

Banner was seated at the desk in the center of the room but made to rise as his assistant spoke to him.

He was fair, with a ruddy complexion and light blue eyes. As he rose, Rutledge realized that he had a club foot. He came forward, limping but smiling, and asked, "Good afternoon. How may I help you, sir?"

Rutledge glanced toward the assistant, and Banner said quietly, "I think you might have a look at that new bolt of tweed. I'm not sure it's up to our standards."

The assistant left, and Banner turned expectantly toward Rutledge.

He held out his identification and explained what had brought him to the shop.

Banner frowned. "I've many clients who ask for custom-made shirts."

Rutledge described the dead man and the shirt that he'd been wearing. "And it had a label in the collar with your name on it. At a guess, the shirt was made in the last year or so. There was very little wear."

"Yes, that's very likely my work. But I'm afraid it doesn't help me find a name for you. We've served a fair number of Bantams, you see. That description could fit half of them."

He opened his notebook and showed Banner the sketch he'd made. "A needle. Have you always used that? Or is it recent?"

His eyebrows rising, Banner said, "I use no mark. Just my name." He rubbed his chin thoughtfully. "But I did put that symbol in the label of a shirt. Once. It was during the war, the man's wife wished to have new shirts and a suit of clothes made up for her husband as a surprise when he came home from France. She told me he'd broadened out in the Army, and she had his new measurements. She wanted him to know everything was bespoke." He smiled deprecatingly at the memory. "She was rather pretty, reminded me of my late wife. I saw no harm in giving her a mark."

"Then you must know who she is," Rutledge persisted.

"Indeed." He opened another drawer, sorted through some papers there, and brought out a folded sheet. "I was hoping to do more business with her." He opened it, glanced at it, then passed the sheet to Rutledge.

"And did you?" he asked as he read the name written there in elegant copperplate script. *Mrs. Ruth Milford. The Mill. Crowley. Shropshire.* The date of purchase was there as well. Looking up at Banner, he said, "That's rather a long way to come for a tailor. How did she discover you?"

"Sadly, no." Banner shrugged. "I never saw her again. I believe she told me she was in Llangollen visiting a friend. I expect that's how she found me."

"Do you know her name, this friend?"

"I never met him."

"Him?"

"I saw him once, he was waiting outside to carry her purchases. He was an officer. That's all I recall."

"He wasn't her husband?"

"Not if the measurements she provided me were those of her husband. *He* was quite short. This man was a good ten inches or so taller."

4

Walking back to his motorcar, Rutledge considered what Banner had told him. Who was the other man? A relative? If he was willing to wait outside the tailor's shop, he could be a friend. Or a lover. And what had brought Ruth Milford to Llangollen, if she lived in Shropshire? The village where the dead man had been found was only a handful of miles away from Llangollen, just a little farther down the River Dee . . . Was *he* her husband? Finally wearing a shirt she had ordered for him years earlier?

What was the connection with Wales? It had to be more than coincidence.

He consulted his watch. If he left straightaway for Shropshire, he could be out of the worst of the Welsh hills by dusk, then find somewhere to stay the night.

Taking a map from the pocket in the driver's door, he spread it out across the bonnet and looked at the roads.

The village where Mrs. Milford lived was, in a way, familiar ground, for the Long Mynd and the Stiperstones were fairly close by. He'd never been there, but he knew where they were and what they were. The Long Mynd was a great gash between two ridges, popular with hikers, and the Stiperstones were a strange jagged rock formation jutting from the ground and said to be haunted by the Devil.

Satisfied that he knew his way, he folded the map again and put it back in the pocket.

It took him ten minutes to find a shop where he could order sandwiches and fill his Thermos with tea, then he set out.

The flat countryside had vanished, and the roads seemed to have been designed to thwart any driver intent on making good time. They twisted and turned with the land, were interrupted by crossroads without fingerposts, and twice he made the wrong choice and had to turn back. He was still north of Oswestry when at last he found an inn for the night.

Late the next morning he was held up short of Shrewsbury by a puncture in a tire. A hole in the roadway, masked by rainwater, was deeper than it appeared. The miracle, he told himself after swearing at the delay, was that it hadn't happened in the desolate hills in Wales. But by the time he'd found a garage and the mechanic had found a replacement for his tire, he'd lost most of the day.

And so it was well after dusk when he reached the outskirts of Crowley. It was, he realized, hardly more than a hamlet. Lamps were already lit in the windows of several farmhouses along the road, and then it turned slightly, and he found himself among a dozen or more small houses. They were more the size of cottages, in fact, only a handful boasting an upper story. There were no names on any of them, and instead of being clustered around a village church or green, these were strung out on the road. In fact, there *was* no church, nor a green. And although he drove through twice, carefully searching, there wasn't a cottage called The Mill. What's more, in this failing light, he couldn't see a pond or a stream that would support a waterwheel.

Some thirty yards from the last cottage and set on a slight rise was a pub. He could just make out the unlit sign—The Pit and The Pony. And that was all that Crowley could boast.

Hamish said, "Ye ken, she lied to yon tailor."

"Still, that shirt was given to the dead man at some point in time. Which tells me it reached her when Banner posted it to her. The question is, where does she live if not Crowley?"

There was a tiny general store, closed for the night, but he stopped to peer through its windows. He couldn't see a post office inside, the surest source of information about anyone in a village.

Reversing for a second time, he drove up to the pub. Although he could see that there was a lamp burning in a window, he was nearly sure that it too was closed.

There was a yard to one side of the pub, empty save for a single bicycle, which was propped against the wall.

He left his motorcar beside it, and removing his hat, he walked over to the side door, reaching for the knob, expecting to find it locked. To his surprise, the door opened under his hand. He stepped inside.

At once he could see why the name was appropriate. There were photographs everywhere of miners, their gear, and the mine heads. Many of these appeared to have been taken over a period of years, because some of the photographs were beginning to fade a little.

Like the yard, the pub was empty, except for a young woman sweeping a small drift of dust into a pan.

She straightened up, looking quickly toward the new arrival as if she had been expecting someone. He could have sworn there was hope in her pretty face, but it faded almost at once, leaving it drawn. He wondered if she had been ill.

"We're closed this evening," she told him. "My barman is unwell."

"I'm sorry to hear that. I was hoping for a room for the night, and perhaps my dinner," Rutledge said pleasantly. "But I'm actually looking for the house of a Mrs. Milford. Ruth Milford. Do you happen to know where I could find her? I believe she lives in a place called The Mill."

Her expression was wary now. "And who is looking for her?"

"My name is Rutledge. I'm from London."

"London?" Wariness became fear. "You just missed her, love. She left for Shrewsbury this morning."

He didn't need Hamish, stirring in the back of his mind, to tell him that very likely Mrs. Milford had never left the village, that she was standing before him now.

He set his hat down on the nearest table. "As it happens, I've come to ask for information about her husband. Perhaps you know him, and can help me?"

Frowning, she put the broom aside very carefully.

"What sort of information are you after? I don't know him very well."

There were only two lamps lit, one by the front window that he'd noticed coming up the rise, and the other on the bar. She looked him up and down, then stepped to one side, so that her face was partly in the shadow of a post that was part of the framework of the bar, setting it off from the tables.

"His full name, for a start."

"Samuel Arthur Francis Milford."

"Can you describe him for me? I've never met him."

"Brown hair. Brown eyes."

"A tall man?"

"Short."

"In the Bantams, was he?"

She put up a hand to stop him. "Why would you come all the way from *London* to ask such questions?" She spoke the word with ridicule, as if she hadn't believed him. "Who are you, and why are you really here?"

"Actually," he said gently, "I'm with Scotland Yard. In London. And it's my duty to ask these questions because there has been an accident—" He broke off as she paled and reached out for the post, as if for support.

"What do you mean, an accident? To Sam? Is he all right? *Tell me.* What has happened?"

"Mrs. Milford? Perhaps you should sit down."

"*Tell me*," she repeated roughly, no longer denying her name. But she turned and sat down in the nearest chair, as though needing time to brace herself.

"I was called to a village near Llangollen, in Wales. On the River Dee." He came forward and took the chair across from her. "There had been a death, Mrs. Milford, and it is possible that the man whose body was found could be your husband."

She shook her head, hope reviving. "You must have the wrong man. He can't be my husband. Sam has never been to Llangollen," she told him flatly. "Now I must ask you to leave. As I said, we're closed."

He took out his notebook. "During the war, did you order a shirt from a tailor in Llangollen, and ask him to sew a label into the collar, with this design?" He showed her the drawing he'd made. "The tailor told me he'd only used such a label once."

But she couldn't answer him. As she looked at the design, a flood of emotions chased each other across her face. Shock—denial—realization—and finally acceptance.

And she broke down then, drawing her apron up to her face to hide her tears.

There wasn't a friend or family member here to help

her through the worst of the shock. To give her a little privacy, Rutledge rose and went through the open door behind the bar into the small kitchen.

The cooker was banked but hot enough still to make tea, and he quickly found what he needed. Even as he worked, he could hear her weeping, anguished sobs. He had always hated having to break such news to the families of victims. There was never anything to say that could offer comfort. And that was a helpless feeling.

She had recognized the design on the shirt, and must have remembered too that she had been with another man at the time. Who was he? A relative? A friend? A lover? And was he still in Llangollen, close by where Sam was found?

Hamish said, "Was she telling the truth? That she didna' know he was in Wales?"

I think she was. He'd almost answered Hamish aloud, and cursed himself for the lapse.

Giving the pot time to steep, Rutledge went back to the grieving woman and simply sat there across from her, offering whatever solace his presence might give her, alone as she was. But it didn't appear to help. He returned to the kitchen, found a serving tray, and brought two cups of tea back to the table, hers very sweet to help with the shock, and set them down. Pushing hers forward, he resumed his seat.

"Mrs. Milford—" he began.

She shook her head, dropping the apron and not caring now if he saw her ravaged face. "Is it true? That this man might be Sam? Couldn't you be wrong? I can't think why he would be in Wales, of all places. He's never been there." She was pleading with him, never taking her gaze from his face.

"I'm afraid it must be true. He was just a little over five feet tall, wearing the shirt I described to you, and there was a tattoo on his left forearm. It appeared to be the insignia of the Bantams."

She closed her eyes. "I can't go on," she said in a strained voice. "I can't endure any more."

Rutledge took that to mean she recognized the description.

"I'm sorry to be the bearer of such news," he went on gently. "But I must ask, there's no one else. Do you have any idea what your husband's business was in Wales? Why he went there?"

Ruth Milford stared at him. "I've lost everything now," she said finally. "There's nothing left, I can't go on. It's my fault—it's all my fault. And I can't *bear* it."

He wondered if she had even heard his questions. "Drink a little tea. It will help," he told her, pushing her cup closer to her. "Is there someone in the village I can bring to you? A woman relative? A friend?"

She obediently reached for the cup. Her hands were shaking, and she had to use both to steady the cup and lift it to her mouth. Ignoring the question, she asked tentatively, "Was he—was he alone when he died?"

He took that to mean whether anyone had been there with him, but before he could answer the door opened and a man came through, calling, "Ruthie? I just heard about Will—" He broke off, frowning, as he saw the two people at the table, drinking tea. But he couldn't at first see Ruth's face, for she had leaned back into the shadows again. "Sorry. I didn't know the pub was open. I'd heard it was closed, that's why I came over. Is Will feeling any better then?"

She cleared her throat. "I haven't spoken to him since the morning," she replied huskily, and then added, her voice breaking, "Donald. It's *Sam*."

Rutledge had risen as Donald moved quickly across the room, dropping into the chair Rutledge had just vacated. He reached for Ruth's hand as she set the cup down, and held it tightly.

"What's happened? Tell me, I'll take you to him."

"He's dead," she replied, her voice empty of feeling. "Sam is dead."

Donald looked from her to Rutledge. "Is that true? I don't understand. Who are you?"

"My name is Rutledge. Scotland Yard. I was called to Wales to investigate when a body was discovered in the River Dee."

"*Sam's* body?" he repeated blankly. "In *Wales*? When? Are you sure?"

"He was found on Saturday last. We have good reason to believe it must be Milford. Do you recall a tattoo on his left arm, the insignia of the Bantam Battalions?"

"Yes, of course I do. Surely there's more than a tattoo to go on? There must be thousands of Bantams in Shropshire—even in Wales, for that matter. The first battalion raised was in Cheshire."

"There is other evidence," Rutledge said, not wanting to mention the shirt and the tailor in Llangollen to him. "That's what led me to Mrs. Milford. Can you tell me what took Mr. Milford to Wales?"

"I didn't know he'd gone there." He glanced at Mrs. Milford, then turned back to Rutledge. "I thought he was in Shrewsbury."

Mrs. Milford began to weep again. "He was. It was about Tildy. It's always about Tildy."

Rutledge asked, "Do you know, does she have a photograph of Milford? It would help to have it." It would not help identify the body, but it might be useful in tracking Milford's movements.

"Ruthie?"

"At the house. In my bedroom."

"Is there anyone—a woman—who might come and sit with her?" Rutledge asked in a low voice.

"My wife, Nan. She and Ruthie are cousins. I'll fetch her, and that photograph." Rising, he hesitated. "It's a shock—I can't bring myself to believe—what *happened*?"

Rutledge moved away from where Ruth was still sitting, and Donald followed him. "That's one of the reasons why I'm here. If Milford was meeting someone in Wales, perhaps that person could help us find out more."

"Yes, I see. But what *happened*?" he persisted.

"He was found in the Dee, near a small village," Rutledge told him. "He'd had a fall."

"A fall? From where?"

"It appears he fell from a height."

Donald frowned. "I know there are mountains in Wales—I can't think why Sam was climbing one."

"Have you been there?" Rutledge asked with interest.

"No." He gestured toward the bar. "I help out in

here whenever Sam is away. Seeing to supplies, paying creditors. We've had a few travelers from Wales."

"Anyone in particular? Anyone who might have known Milford, or who had some reason to contact him here?"

Donald shrugged. "I doubt it. That's to say they're only stopping for the night, and are gone the next day. I never heard of Sam speaking privately with any of them." He glanced toward Ruth Milford again. "I'd better go."

Rutledge turned to see that she had put her head down on the table, cradled by her arms. Even from here he could tell that she was shivering.

"Go on."

He crossed to the table, took off his heavy coat, and wrapped it around Mrs. Milford's shoulders. She didn't lift her head but seemed to huddle into the warmth from his body as well as the thick wool. He moved her teacup, hardly touched.

Waiting for Donald, and leaving Mrs. Milford to her grieving, he had a moment to look around the pub. It was L-shaped, the longer leg of the L filled with tables and the bar. The shorter leg was more spacious, with a second hearth, the dartboard, and fewer tables. The bar had been prosperous once, but it was beginning to show a shabbiness that couldn't, he thought, be completely the fault of the war. Where were the miners or their descendants, from the framed photographs everywhere? There were mine lamps and other paraphernalia mounted high on the walls. Someone had kept these dusted, he noticed.

But there was no one to ask.

The door opened again, and a woman rushed in. She had the same auburn hair and brown eyes as her cousin, and they were much alike. Rutledge would have thought they were sisters, if he hadn't known otherwise.

She hurried to Ruth, kneeling beside her chair, her arms around her. "Oh, my dear. Donald told me. Is it true?"

"That's what *he* said, Nan," Ruth replied wanly, nodding in Rutledge's direction. "It must be so." The tears began again. "What am I to *do*?"

Nancy turned on Rutledge. "How could you break it to her like this? Last *Saturday*?" she demanded. "This news could have waited an hour longer! Why didn't you come to me first? Nancy Blake, Ruth's cousin. Everyone knows us. Anyone could have directed you to us."

He said, "I came to the inn looking for the Milford house. She began asking questions, refusing to tell me anything until I answered them." He realized that sounded as if he thought she might be protecting Mrs. Milford. "As you might have done."

Nan shot a quick glance toward the door, as if looking for her husband. Rutledge couldn't quite read it.

Ruth touched her cousin's shoulder. "Don't blame the Inspector, Nan. It's my fault. He told me he'd come from London—I thought he was a solicitor—I was afraid to tell him anything, with Sam away. I hoped to put him off." She put her hands over her eyes again, and her voice was only a thread. "Everything is my fault. It has been from the start. Tildy—" She couldn't go on.

"Nonsense," Nan replied briskly, turning back to her and taking her hands again. "It was never your fault. Never. What happened to Tildy was not something any of us could prevent. And Sam grieved for her as much as you did. As all of us did."

"And now Sam's dead. We'll never know why . . ." Her voice trailed off.

Rutledge watched the two women. This wasn't the first time that Ruth Milford had blamed herself for what happened. Had they quarreled? he wondered. And her husband had left her? There was the other man, outside the tailor shop in Llangollen. Had Milford somehow discovered his existence, and gone to Wales to confront him?

Just then the side door opened again, and Donald came in, holding a silver frame. He looked across at the two women, then handed the frame to Rutledge. "Here." And without waiting to see what the man from London made of it, he moved on toward his wife and her cousin as Nan coaxed her to drink a little more of the tea.

Rutledge turned the frame over. Samuel Milford had a good face. The chin was square, and the prominent nose was well shaped. An attractive man, broad-shouldered, straight-backed, staring into the camera with confidence, smiling a little. The uniform he was wearing was indeed that of the Bantams. His rank was Corporal.

Rutledge remembered the battered features lying on Dr. Evans's table. Hardly recognizable now.

Hamish said, catching him off guard, "He's no' the sort ye'd expect to find himself murdered."

Rutledge was thinking much the same thing. He looked at the photograph again, wishing he'd had it with him when he'd spoken to the man in the shop or the narrowboat men, rather than a vague description. It had been too easy for them to deny having seen the victim.

Hamish disagreed. "If his death had to do with the narrowboats, no' even a photograph would ha' helped identify yon body. They keep themselves to themselves."

And it was very likely true. He'd felt the resistance toward outsiders while he was there.

Donald came back across the room. "I need to know—what's to be done about bringing him home? She'll want him buried here, not in Wales. I dread to think what it will cost, but I'll find the money. God knows, I've done what I can to keep the pub going."

"I'll put you in touch with a Dr. Evans. He will help you make the necessary arrangements. There will be certain—formalities, of course." He wasn't ready to discuss an inquest with Blake, and so he gestured to the mining theme. "Was there a mine near here? Is that why there're so many photographs about?"

"There was. A lead mine. Well, two of them. The smaller one has been closed for years. They'd shut down the larger operation too, then opened it up during the war. There's talk it could be closed permanently in the next year or so. Bad for business here, of course. The uncertainty." He glanced toward the frames on the wall. "Ruthie's father put those up. I expect he could put a name to every face. During the war there were German prisoners working The Bog. They weren't allowed up here, and business fell off sharp with the lads away fighting. Come to that, we've not had all that much custom since. Not the way it once was when Ruthie's father was alive."

Rutledge made certain the women were occupied, and then said, "I need to examine Milford's wardrobe. Although Mrs. Milford confirmed that the clothes the dead man was wearing were indeed the ones she'd given him, I want to be very sure that her memory is accurate. This might be the best time to go to the house."

Blake hesitated. "I must ask Ruthie. It's her house, after all."

"We don't need to distress her more than we have already. My motorcar is outside, as you've seen."

Blake reluctantly agreed, and the two men went out the side door.

The house was one of the handful of two-story dwellings. Even so, it was small. They went in through the kitchen door, Blake saying as they stepped inside, "We've never had call to lock our doors. This way."

They went up the narrow main staircase. There were four very small rooms above, and Blake said as they passed the first door, "That was Ruthie's mother's room. She and Sam slept in this one." He opened the door and stepped aside.

There was room for only a bed, two chairs, a tall chest, a smaller one with a mirror above it, and a night-stand. There was no armoire, just a curtain in one corner that set off the space where clothes hung on pegs. Rutledge looked through them, then said, "I see no shirts here."

"In the chest, then?"

Rutledge crossed the room to pull out drawers one at a time. In the third he found Sam Milford's shirts. He lifted them out, took them to the bed, and carefully went through them.

None of them had the Banner mark in their collars.

Satisfied, and feeling claustrophobic in the small space, Rutledge nodded to Blake. "Thank you. But it was necessary to be sure."

"I don't see why those shirts were so important," Blake said as they went back down the stairs and out to the motorcar. "They look just like all the rest he's ever worn. Sam liked nice shirts, and it wasn't vanity." He searched for the right word. "He took pride in his appearance. And Ruth knew how to starch them." There was almost a touch of envy. "Nan never could quite get it right."

But Banner's mark wasn't visible when Milford was wearing the Llangollen shirt. Blake had probably never seen it.

"It's a matter of thoroughness. I'm sure Mrs. Milford would be relieved to discover we'd made a mistake." But he knew now that he hadn't been wrong.

They returned to the pub in silence. The wind had picked up, and overhead the stars were brilliant in the cold night sky. Rutledge had watched them spin across the horizon countless nights in the trenches, waiting for the next attack or still on edge from the last one. He looked back at the road as they went up the rise.

"Why was the Milford house called The Mill?" he asked.

"The Mill? There's no mill in Crowley. Who told you that?"

Rutledge let it go. Mrs. Milford might not have wished to give Banner the address of the pub or even a cottage. Perhaps *The Mill* sounded more like the home of a woman placing a large order.

They had just walked through the side door when they met Ruth and Nan coming toward them.

"I'm taking her home," Nan said. "My house," she amended. "She needs to be in bed with a hot water bottle and a little whisky to help her sleep."

"Yes, that's for the best," Rutledge agreed. "I will need to talk to her in the morning, when she's a little stronger."

Donald regarded him. "Here. Were you thinking of staying the night in the inn?"

"I believe there are rooms," Rutledge replied as Hamish said quietly, " 'Ware." For there was something menacing now about Nan's husband.

"Best to move on," he said. "You've done what you came for. You can give me that doctor's name and where he's to be found. Nan and I'll see to Ruthie. There've been rats in the bedrooms. They're closed for the rat catcher to come. That's what sickened Will. The rats. There's a good inn two villages on. The train comes in there."

"Donald—" Ruth began, but he ignored her.

"I'm sorry to disappoint you," Rutledge replied. "But this isn't finished. I'll take my chances with the rats." There had been colonies of them in the trenches.

Ruth Milford said, wearily, "Donald doesn't want it to be Sam. Any more than I do. But it must be—he was wearing my shirt. The one I had made up for him when he came home."

"You can't be sure—" Blake said sharply.

"I can. I ordered it from a tailor. As a surprise. And no, it was my own money, it didn't come from the pub." To Rutledge she added, "Nan and Donald want to sell up and move away from here. Sam and I wanted to stay, I was hoping to buy them out, but they can't leave me now, not to run the pub on my own. Not if Sam is dead." Something changed suddenly in her face, and she went on with rising alarm, "Was—was Sam alone when he died? Was anyone with him?" It was the second time she'd asked. Was it the lover in Llangollen she was worrying about?

"We don't know. I'm sorry."

She shook her head, his coat slipping from her shoulders. "What do you mean, you don't know? Surely—"

"Ruthie—" Nan cut across her words.

"So far, we haven't found anyone who witnessed his fall. And until we do, we can't be sure whether he was alone at the time or not."

Her face drained of what little color it had had. "I'll want to know. You must tell me, as soon as you know."

"I promise," he told her and retrieved his coat.

And Nan led her to the door.

Rutledge watched her go. "Is it far? I can drive them," he said to Blake.

"No."

"Then show me my room."

Blake opened his mouth to argue again, thought better of it, and turned toward the far side of the bar, where a door opened onto a staircase.

They went up together, and Rutledge took the larger of the two rooms he was shown. Blake was about to leave him, but he asked, "I didn't want to press Mrs. Milford. But she said something earlier that I didn't understand. That it was about someone. Tildy?"

Blake shook his head. "Best you ask Nan tomorrow." And he was off down the stairs before Rutledge could reply.

There were no rats in the night. But Hamish was waiting in the dark when Rutledge had retrieved his valise from the motorcar, undressed, and turned out the single lamp on the table by his bed.

He was dressed and sitting in the bar working on his notes when Nan Blake came in with a tray with his breakfast on it.

"Good morning," he greeted her, rising. "That's very thoughtful of you. How is your cousin this morning?"

"She's still sleeping. There were some powders left over when her mother was ill. I gave her one. It was the only way she could rest." She began to lay out his food on the next table, away from his notebook and pen.

"I'm glad you're here. I need to ask a few questions that might upset her. For one," he went on before she could object, "I was told that everyone thought Milford was in Shrewsbury. How did he go there and when?"

"There are trains to Shrewsbury, two villages over. Donald took him in the dogcart."

"Was he wearing a heavy outer coat? A hat?"

She glared at him. "Of course he was."

"And he was carrying a valise?"

"Brown calf."

But none of these things had been found—neither hat, coat, nor valise.

"When did he leave?"

"Monday last."

That was almost two weeks ago, now. Time enough to reach the Telford Aqueduct.

"And you are quite certain he went to Shrewsbury?"

"Of course he did," Nan snapped. "Sam wasn't a liar. If he told us he was going to Shrewsbury, then he did."

"He had business there?"

She answered him defensively. "There have been—issues—with our vendors. Well, credit issues, if you must know. He was hoping to persuade them that in the spring, custom here will pick up. There are attractions here—the Long Mynd, the Stiperstones, the ruins of the lead mine, and its village. There have been stories that the mine is haunted. And there's the Devil's Chair on the Stiperstones. People already come to Long Mynd. It's not that far away."

"Was he meeting anyone in particular in Shrewsbury?"

"No. Only with the bank and the brewery people. The shops we buy from. To be fair, Donald does it too, he's been such a brick, and he's even gone away to find work to help us when money was short. But there's something about Sam that reassures people." Her voice caught. "Reassured them. He could persuade them that the pub could go on for a long time." And then, rounding on him, she made it plain why she had brought his breakfast. And it clearly wasn't out of kindness.

Standing before him, arms akimbo, she went on in a flat tone of voice. "You might tell Ruthie that Sam Milford fell down a Welsh mountain, where he had no reason to be in the first place. But I don't believe a word of that. I want the truth, or Scotland Yard or not, I'm sending Donald for the Constable."

And so he told her. About the Telford Aqueduct, about the boy finding the body, about the condition of the dead man. He told her about the shirt and about the tattoo and what he could read in the ravaged face. But not about the officer with Ruth.

"Once I saw the photograph, I could accept the very real possibility that the man in Dr. Evans's surgery is Samuel Milford. I didn't lie to your cousin. I told her the truth. Just not all of it. She was barely able to take in his death. I expected to give her the rest of the account today."

Nan sat ungracefully into the nearest chair, pale enough that he thought for a moment that she was going to faint or be quite sick.

"Dear God," she said finally, bringing herself to look at him for the first time since he'd given her the details. All he'd withheld was Banner's account of the tall officer who had waited outside the tailor shop while Ruth Milford ordered a suit of clothes for her husband. That, he thought, was something he would ask Ruth Milford about when they were alone.

He said nothing, letting her absorb the shock. Then she whispered, almost to herself, "He's been dead a week? How did we not *know*? Not feel something was wrong?" She took a deep, unsteady breath, trying to rally, turning on him again. "If you tell my cousin how badly Sam was injured—how he must have died— you'll answer to *me*. There will be no open coffin by the time we can bury him. She can think of him in there as she knew him when he left here on Monday last. He'll want to be buried in his uniform. It's in a chest under his bed. I'll find it and press it properly. You can take it back with you to this Dr. Evans, and see that the undertakers have it."

"I will agree to that, if you'll tell me why Mrs. Milford felt that she was to blame for her husband's death. Had they quarreled? Did she feel that she had driven him to leave by something she'd done?"

"To blame? No, of course not, she did nothing of the sort." She was indignant now, and yet as she continued, he had the feeling that she was choosing her words carefully. "She's had a very—unhappy life. Not in her marriage, mind you. Sam made her very happy. But she feels that her own troubles have spilled over on her family. That Sam must have died because she *did* love him so much. That we've all been through all manner of hardships because she wants to keep the pub in the family. Donald wants better opportunities—you can't blame him, he didn't grow up in Crowley. He doesn't have the same feeling about it. But now Sam is gone—" She shrugged, unable to finish the sentence. "We'll grow old and die here, like her mum and dad. But that's because the lead mine is closing. It isn't because of Ruthie."

"Do you know anyone who might wish Sam Milford harm? Who might wish to see him dead?"

Her gaze focused on his face, a frown forming between her brown eyes. "What are you asking me?"

"We found his body, but we didn't find his hat or his winter coat or his valise. The question is, where are they? Why did he go to Wales, if he had told you he was only going as far as Shrewsbury? What happened in Shrewsbury? Why did he leave there?"

"I don't understand."

"I'm here in Crowley not only to be sure of his identification, but to begin the search for answers surrounding his death. It's very likely, given the circumstances, that Milford was murdered."

5

Nan Blake had been shocked by the suggestion that Sam Milford had been a victim of murder. She told him roundly that Sam wasn't a troublemaker, he wasn't the sort of man to stir up people or cause problems. "Donald is the opposite, he doesn't think, he brings trouble down on himself. That's why Sam went to Shrewsbury instead."

"Did you expect him to be gone this long?"

"Sometimes—it's hard when you must beg for help. For faith in the pub when there's so little hope left. The longer he was away, the more we worried that this time he wouldn't find the money we need. We thought—we thought no one was willing to listen, and he was still trying. It would be like Sam, not to give up. Not to come back with nothing." She found her handkerchief and blew her nose. "He couldn't have been murdered. He came through the war, for God's sake, with only a few cracked ribs to show for it. He didn't know anyone in Wales. I don't understand why he was even there."

"Where would he stay, when he went to Shrewsbury?"

She named a small, inexpensive hotel near the Abbey. "It's all he could afford. We could afford," she amended.

"How long did he expect to be in Shrewsbury?"

"As long as necessary, he said. I've told you, sometimes it takes time, persuading people to listen when they only want what's owed them. I went once, just before Sam and Donald were demobbed. And I got nowhere, because no one was willing to give money to a woman. 'This isn't London, you know,'" she ended, mimicking a banker or the owner of a firm. "We were so grateful when Donald came home, and then Sam followed him six weeks later. It was a miracle, having both of them come safely home. Now this."

"I gather neither Blake nor Milford is from Crowley."

"Donald is from Ludlow. Sam grew up in Chester. He came to Shropshire to look at a bit of property his parents had left him. Ruth was in Shrewsbury to take care of some business for her father. This was in 1912. Both of them had to sit and wait for over an hour in the solicitor's office until he'd finished speaking to another client. They talked, and after the solicitor had seen the other man out and was apologizing for the delay, Sam asked him to introduce them. Then he turned to Ruth and asked if she'd have tea with him afterward. It was a good match."

Nan went away soon after, leaving him to finish his now-cold breakfast in peace, telling Rutledge that she must talk to her husband. "I've never known anyone who was murdered. I don't quite know how to think about Sam being *killed*."

He spent the rest of the morning walking through Crowley, speaking to the other residents, moving from house to house, keeping his questions simple.

Word hadn't spread yet that Sam Milford was dead, much less murdered. The Blakes apparently hadn't told anyone else, and Ruth Milford was still in a drugged sleep.

As he was about to begin with the nearest cottage, Hamish said, "It's possible it was of a purpose, gie'ing her yon drugs."

"We'll know the answer to that soon enough. Either she wakes by noon, of her own accord, or you are right, the Blakes have a reason to keep her where I can't question her."

A family by the name of Baker lived in the first cottage he visited, an older man and his wife in the next, and a widow in the third. He could see how difficult life must be for these people, whom progress had left behind. Most didn't have the money to move on, like the Blakes, while others clung to the only world they knew, waiting for a miracle.

They had known that Milford had gone to Shrewsbury—they had seen him leave with Blake in the dogcart—and they were shrewd enough to guess why such a trip was necessary. As for the length of time Milford had been gone, they had put it down to difficulties he'd encountered, for as Mr. Baker had bitterly informed Rutledge, "If the mines hadn't begun to run out of lead, none of this would have happened. The bankers and the brewers, they'd be at the door to welcome you and ask how much you needed. Now it's just the opposite, they don't want to talk to you. But Sam was never one to give up, was he?"

They professed surprise that something had happened to him. It was clear that they liked the man, and everyone had asked how Ruthie was holding up under the news of his death.

Rutledge answered their questions but quickly realized that no one in Crowley held a grudge against Milford. If anything, his return from the war had offered hope. He had been in a way a natural leader, in a hamlet where no one knew how to take the lead.

"You never noticed how short he was, once you got used to it," another man told Rutledge. "There was something about him, a strength. You knew you could trust him."

And a woman had said, "He was shorter than Ruthie, you know. But he was more of a man than her cousin's husband, wasn't he? He was the best thing that could have happened to her, Sam was. I don't know how she will go on without him."

Which made it all the more a mystery why Sam Milford had been in Wales instead of pleading his case in Shrewsbury. As far as anyone knew, he had neither family nor connections over the border.

By the time he'd reached the last cottage but one, Rutledge had already realized that his next course of action was to trace Milford's movements in Shrewsbury. And then a Mrs. Esterly, a widow, came to the door, peered up at him over her spectacles, and said, "I've watched you making your way here. And I'm curious to know why. Do come in, young man. The parlor is just there."

It was as feminine as a lady's boudoir. Lace-edged curtains, delicate china figurines on every flat surface, fringed shawls in pastel colors spread over every piece of furniture.

As soon as Rutledge had introduced himself, Mrs. Esterly gave him no opportunity to say more, leaping in with her own eager questions.

"Will is my nephew. I've heard about poor Sam. *Such* a tragedy. Tell me, will Ruth stay in Crowley, now, do you think? Keep The Pit and The Pony open?"

"I don't think she's in any frame of mind to think about the future," he answered.

"Well, even if she tries, she's bound to lose it. I don't see how she can manage on her own. The poor dear. Life hasn't been kind to her. And Nan will surely persuade her to give up the struggle. Ruth will miss The Pit and The Pony. And what will the rest of us do?"

He made some polite answer, but Mrs. Esterly went on asking questions, not always giving him an opportunity to respond. Lonely and alone, she was making the most of her audience, even offering him tea to keep him there a little longer when she feared he was about to leave.

Refusing the offer as courteously as he could, he was looking for an opening to thank her for helping in his inquiries when a name popped up in her rambling monologue that caught his attention.

"Of course, she hasn't been the same since that business about Tildy," Mrs. Esterly was saying, changing directions. "*Such* a tragedy. I've never understood the whole story. But I've heard from Mrs. Warren that Ruth blames herself. Although I can't see how. It wasn't her doing, was it?"

Mrs. Warren lived in the sixth house with her brother. She hadn't mentioned Tildy.

But Ruth Milford had last night. Several times . . .

And Blake had told Rutledge to speak to Nan. But there had been no opportunity at breakfast.

"Who is Tildy?" he asked, interrupting the flow of words more sharply than he'd intended.

"Her little daughter, of course." As if he should know without asking. "Matilda. She was named after Ruth's mother. Such a pretty little thing. Sam adored her, you could see that in the way he carried on about her. The apple of his eye, he said more than once. But that was Sam Milford for you, *such* a good father."

Rutledge searched his memory. There had been no signs of a child in the Milford house . . .

"And what became of Tildy?"

"Didn't Ruth tell you? But then she'd have been too upset about Sam dying like that, off in the wilds of Wales, where there was no one of his own with him as he drew his last breath? I can understand that—I expect I'll be alone when my time comes. I've tried to accept that, but it's hard."

Ruth had also asked if Sam had been alone at the end—

"Was Tildy with him?" Rutledge asked. Then what had become of her? Why hadn't they found a child wandering about without a parent?

It was a disturbing prospect.

"No. Oh, goodness, no. Didn't anyone tell you? She lost Tildy almost a year ago. *Such* a tragedy that was. And the way it happened. I'm sure I don't know how Ruth kept her sanity after that."

A dead child, then.

"She blamed herself?" That might well explain why she believed she was at fault in her husband's death as well.

"Oh, yes. Sam was distraught over Tildy, but he was trying to keep Ruth from killing herself in her anguish."

"Literally killing herself?" he asked, frowning.

"I wouldn't have been surprised. No, not at all. But she couldn't eat nor sleep, nor find any peace. Like a wild soul, she was. I never saw anything like it. Donald and Nan, upset as *they* were, had to manage the pub without her or Sam. He sat by her, night after night, comforting her as best he could. I heard he feared she'd lose her reason. Do you have children, Inspector? No? Then you won't know how they suffered. But I saw it, and I can tell you, it was pitiful. But then Tildy was so young. Only two and a half. How can anyone not grieve over such a dear little girl?"

He extricated himself from Mrs. Esterly's house with some difficulty, spoke to the family in the last house in the village, then walked back to the pub.

Hamish was saying, "A wasted morning. Ye havena' learned anything that would shed light on the dead man's reasons for traveling to Wales."

"I've learned enough about his character to wonder why he was pushed off the Aqueduct. Was there a side to Sam Milford that no one in Crowley saw?"

But there was no answer to that.

The pub was open when he got there, as the tall thin man by the name of Will had recovered sufficiently to take charge while Ruth and the Blakes grieved.

He looked up as Rutledge walked in. "The man from London?" he asked, as if there were dozens of strangers wandering about.

"Rutledge," he answered, nodding.

"The cooker's up. A cup of tea and maybe a sandwich?"

"Yes. Thank you." He took off his coat, tossed it over the back of a chair, then sat down at the bar. "You were under the weather last night?"

"I get these thundering headaches sometimes. Even opening my eyes to the light makes me worse. I just lie in a dark room until the pain has passed." He shrugged. "I haven't had one since late February. Ruthie understands." Bringing a cloth out from under the bar, he wiped at an invisible spot. "I can't believe Sam is gone."

"I'm told he went to Shrewsbury. About pub supplies."

"Aye, the brewery was threatening to cut us off. What's a pub without drink? I ask you!" He put the cloth away.

Commiserating, Rutledge smiled. "Not a happy place. But then I'm told that your custom has fallen off?"

"You've seen Crowley. How much can so few people drink? All the young ones have gone off to war and not come back. I was wounded outside Ypres—there's a bit of brass in my back still. It causes terrible spasms. Doctor says it might be the reason for my headaches. Pressure on the spine." He shook his head. "I'm one of the lucky ones, they tell me. I survived. But it's hard to forget the war when one wrong move sets me off."

"Live here, do you?" He'd stopped at every house, but he hadn't seen Will. Only his aunt.

"My dad owns a farm outside Crowley. What I make

here helps out my family there. When the mine was operating, neither my dad nor the pub could keep up, the demand was so great. All those miners? A hungry and thirsty lot." With a nod, he went into the kitchen to fill Rutledge's order.

He limped heavily. And Rutledge thought there was more than a bit of brass from a shell in his back. Very likely there had been a machine gunner's bullet in his knee as well.

Following Will as far as the kitchen doorway, Rutledge asked, "Was there any other reason why Sam might have gone to Shrewsbury?"

"Not that I know of. He never mentioned any to me. But then I don't understand why he was in Wales when he died. Are you sure the dead man is Sam?"

"Certain enough to ask questions."

"I thought—Nan said you'd come to break the news."

"A policeman always has questions. We aren't sure ourselves what took him to Wales."

Will grunted. "Knowing Sam, he was likely to be helping someone."

"All the way to Wales?"

"All the same, I'll wager that's what's happened."

"Have you seen Mrs. Milford this morning?"

"She was in a while ago. To return the cellar keys. That's when she told me. I was that shocked."

"Then I'll speak to her myself. Is she still staying with the Blakes?"

"I expect so."

But when Rutledge got there, he discovered that Ruth had gone home. It was only next door. He walked across and knocked.

She came to open the door herself, pale and unsteady still, but more in command. "I'd hoped you'd gone," she said, stepping aside to allow him to enter.

The front room was comfortable, but showed the lack of resources to keep it up. The carpet was worn in places, and the furnishings were of a style popular in King Edward's day.

"I'll be leaving shortly. For Shrewsbury. I'm taking your husband's photograph with me, but I'll return it as soon as possible."

"I wish you wouldn't take it." She didn't ask him to sit. "Nan told me—you believe Sam didn't fall by accident. You believe he was murdered." He could see the hurt in her eyes as she took a deep breath. "You've got it all wrong, you know. That isn't Sam in Wales. When you look at him again, you'll see that. It's the only reason I am willing to let his photograph out of my sight."

He didn't argue with her. Instead he promised, "I'll see that nothing happens to it."

"Why would anyone harm Sam? It makes no sense," she went on, brushing a tendril of her dark red hair back into place. "I can't get the thought of it out of my mind."

Rutledge asked, "Do you know anyone in Llangollen, Mrs. Milford? Friends or family that your husband might have visited—perhaps to ask for help to keep the pub afloat?"

She flushed. "No. I don't have any family in Wales."

"Perhaps your husband has relatives there—or friends from the Bantams."

"He wouldn't leave Shrewsbury without telling me his plans. Don't you see, you've upset our lives for nothing. Sam will be home today or tomorrow."

But even as she said it, he could see that she only half believed any of it. It was a way of putting off the inevitable, putting off facing having to accept her husband's death for a few more days.

"Mr. Banner—the tailor where you had clothes made up for your husband—saw you with another man. An officer, who waited for you outside the shop. And you told the tailor you were in the town to visit with friends."

"He's mistaken," she said harshly. "How could he be sure of such a trivial thing as that? After all these years? He must have had dozens of people in and out of his shop since then."

"Then why *were* you there?"

"I took a brief holiday. It was after my mother's last illness. I was tired, upset, I needed to get away. Even for a few days. I went to school in Shrewsbury, I know people there, and I didn't want to be reminded of my loss."

"There are many towns closer than Llangollen. Why *there*?" he persisted.

"I told you, it was an escape," she retorted, angry now. "Just an escape."

He let it go, knowing she felt cornered and wasn't likely to tell him more.

"I'll need to speak to your family solicitor. Can you give me his direction?"

"He's in Shrewsbury. Hastings and Hastings. Anyone can tell you how to find his chambers. Now, if you don't mind, I need to be left alone."

Shrewsbury was not that far away, less than twenty miles to the north of Crowley, and he made good time despite the state of the roads. The town had been built in a loop of the River Severn, making it almost an island. Walls were added to its defenses, and a castle guarded the only way in by land, but the great Norman abbey had been built outside that protected perimeter. Rutledge passed it on his way across the English Bridge.

He spent the first hour and a half canvassing the breweries there. Although it was Saturday, there was always someone in the office willing to speak to him. But none of them had seen Sam Milford in several weeks.

"Nigh on a month now," one brewer told Rutledge. "Unlike him not to stop in when he's here."

At his last call—at the Old Salop Brewery, in Chester Street—Andrew Clark, the manager, was just leaving when Rutledge found the office. He was told that Milford had stopped by early one morning almost a fortnight ago, but on other business, nothing to do with the pub. Clark added, "He'd hoped to speak to my sister. She's a patron of the local orphanage, and she was away last week, collecting a child from a farm east of here. Father dead, mother unable to carry on. Sad business. But Dora is up to it. She adores children, but has none of her own. Husband died on the Somme. Matthew Radley, that was. Fine man. Fine."

"I'm sorry."

Clark shrugged. "It's my hope that she'll find someone and marry again. But she won't even consider it."

"In her own time, perhaps?"

"Yes, I expect so. But you'd think—" He broke off, shaking his head.

"Why was Milford interested in speaking to her?"

"He lost a child, you know. It's been good for him, taking an interest in the little ones. And it's been good for Dora too, I expect." He shuffled some papers on his desk. "But back to what brought you here, Mr. Rutledge. You might go to Crowley. Sam is sure to be home by now."

Rutledge thanked him and left without telling him that Milford was dead. It served no purpose, Clark would learn of it soon enough, but he didn't want the news running ahead of him before he'd finished his search.

He was halfway to the hotel where Milford usually stayed when he remembered.

Ruth Milford had said, *It was about Tildy. It's always about Tildy.*

In spite of what Clark had told him—Dora, after all, was his sister—had Sam Milford had an affair with her? Drawn together by their love of children and their sense of loss? He for a child, she for her husband? Grief could create a strong bond that might change into love.

And that put a different perspective on Ruth Milford's relationship with her husband. Still, he had died in Wales, a long way from Crowley.

Hamish said, "Aye—but there's the officer who was wi' her in Llangollen, and that's no' verra far from yon Aqueduct."

"True enough." He answered aloud, and then cursed himself. But would a man she hadn't seen in several years kill for her? It was hard to believe, although in Rutledge's experience at the Yard, stranger things had happened. Or had Ruth killed to be with *him*?

"Aye," Hamish said, picking up on the thought, "so far, yon officer and yon tailor are the only connection between Llangollen and Crowley."

How would the officer have recognized Milford? His size alone was not enough. Unless he knew when to expect Milford—and where he might be staying. But turn it around the other way. Milford had gone in search of the officer, and met his match, killed in self-defense . . .

Until he knew more about both men, he had to stay with the possibility that something from Milford's past had caught up with him. After all, he hadn't lived in Crowley most of his life. What, in fact, was in his past?

Rutledge found the hotel, rather forlorn on its shabby corner but with a fine view of the dark red stone towers of the once-great Abbey, now only a shadow of itself.

The young man at Reception smiled, thinking Rutledge had come to ask for a room.

Instead he showed his identification and said as he put it away again, "I'm looking for one Samuel Milford, from Crowley. I believe he has been staying here?"

Alarmed, the man said, "Here? Has he done something wrong?"

Rutledge smiled. "We hope he can help us with our inquiries."

The man pulled the guest book from a drawer, nearly dropped it, and opened it at the place where a black ribbon marked the latest entries.

"He arrived on the Monday of the week before last, arranged for an early lunch on Tuesday—then he left straightaway, even though he'd booked his room for three days."

"Did he meet anyone here at the hotel? Or has anyone called to speak with him?"

"I don't believe so, but I'm on duty only during the day. Still, he was a quiet guest, no trouble at all, and he's stayed with us before."

"The lunch on Tuesday. Did he dine alone?"

"Yes. He booked a table for one. He was expecting a letter, I believe, and it arrived by messenger shortly after he came down from his room."

"Who sent the letter, do you know?"

"I'm sorry—the messenger insisted on taking it to the dining room and handing it to Mr. Milford personally."

"What do you remember about the messenger?" When the clerk hesitated, Rutledge added, "It could be important."

"Only that I'd never seen her before."

"Her?"

"Yes. She came in, asked for Mr. Milford, went into the dining room, was there no more than a minute, and then she left. She was wearing dark clothing, very plain, and a cap rather than a hat. I was told she arrived by bicycle."

"Can you describe her? Would you recognize her again?"

He shook his head ruefully. "I couldn't even tell you what color her hair was. It was hidden beneath the cap."

Dora Radley? he wondered. But it could have been anyone.

"Did she sound like someone from Shropshire?" The accent was noticeable.

"She asked for Mr. Milford by name. Just that. I couldn't judge where she came from." But he had been curious about her, had remembered her.

"Tall? Short?"

"More middle height, I think. Slim."

"And Milford left immediately after his lunch?"

"Yes. I said goodbye, wished him a safe journey home, and he went out the door."

"Did he have a motorcar?"

"I believe he came to Shrewsbury by train. A cabbie brought him to the door."

"And he left the same way?"

The clerk shook his head. "I'm sorry, I was busy with Mrs. Dunham. She wanted to book her dinner for seven rather than eight. I didn't see how he left. But there are cabbies over by the Abbey. He could have found one there."

"Did he have a valise? An overcoat and hat?"

"Well, yes, of course. The weather had taken a turn, and it was quite cold here week before last. Felt more like winter than spring. And I took up his valise myself. He was late for a meeting, he said."

"What was Mr. Milford's state of mind after the letter arrived? Did it appear to upset him?"

"If it had, I didn't notice. Rather, he seemed very much himself."

After a few more questions, Rutledge thanked the clerk and left.

In his motorcar once more, he considered his next step. He needed to know if Milford had a will and what the disposal of his property might be.

The chambers of Hastings and Hastings was on a short street just beyond the center of Shrewsbury.

But it was closed, and when he called in at the police station afterward, he was told that the Inspector in charge, a man by the name of Carson, had gone for the day.

There was nothing he could do about it.

Resigned to losing the rest of the day and the next as well, he considered what to do.

It would behoove him to find a hotel.

In the end, he went back to the one where Milford had stayed, and asked for the man's room. It was vacant, and he took it.

Hamish, derisive, asked, "Do ye expect his ghost to speak to ye there?"

Rutledge, facing a frustrating day of inactivity, said only as he unlocked the room door, "For answers, I'd speak to the Devil."

At exactly nine o'clock on Monday morning, Rutledge presented himself at the elegant door of Hastings and Hastings.

It was small as chambers went, with an elderly clerk who greeted Rutledge formally and asked his business.

"I'm looking for the solicitor who represents the

Milford family in Crowley." He took out his identification and offered it to the man.

"I see." He looked up. "Shall I inform Mr. Hastings that this is a police matter?"

"Yes. Official business."

The man nodded and walked to a door to his right. Five minutes later he was back, and he escorted Rutledge down a dimly lit passage. There were five doors along it, two on each side closed.

The clerk tapped lightly on the last one, at the end, and then opened it.

"Mr. Hastings," the clerk said formally, and then closed the door after Rutledge stepped inside.

Hastings was standing behind his desk, a stooped, gray-haired man wearing a rimless pince-nez. He looked tired. "Good afternoon, Mr. Rutledge." He gestured to the chair in front of his desk, then resumed his seat as Rutledge sat down. "I understand you are with Scotland Yard. How may I help you?"

"I've come about the affairs of Samuel Milford, late of Crowley. One of your clients, I'm told. He was found dead along the banks of the River Dee, near Llangollen. Wales. Evidence leads us to believe he fell or was pushed from the Telford Aqueduct. It would be helpful to know how his will stands."

Hastings had frowned at the news, shaking his head.

"I am sorry to hear it. Mr. Milford was a good man. I can't quite understand. Why do you believe he could have been pushed to his death? And why should he have been murdered?"

"I don't have those answers. Not yet," Rutledge replied. "That's one of the reasons I've come here. Do you know of anyone with whom he might have quarreled? Were there debts, for instance, or legal matters pending, any trouble at all that might shed light on what happened in Wales?"

"He had no vices that I'm aware of. He liked a good wine, but he was no tippler, and he had no enemies that I'm aware of. He wasn't one for gaming, or women. In fact, my impression is that he was very much in love with his wife. He was even-tempered, and steady. Did you know that he was a Sergeant in the Bantams?"

He had been a Corporal in the photograph.

"Yes, I did."

And then Hastings added somberly, "He didn't care to talk about France. I didn't like to pry, but I wanted to know—" He took a deep breath. "I lost my son and my nephews in the war. It would help to know how they died."

"Did you receive a letter from your son's commanding officer?"

He winced. "There were three, and very much

the same. My son's and my sister's sons'. A fine soldier, liked by his men, he didn't suffer, and we must be proud of him, for he gave his life for his King and Country. That isn't terribly reassuring, is it?"

Rutledge had written hundreds of letters very much like these—every officer felt it was a duty and responsibility to write to the families of the dead, reassuring them as much as he could, even when the man had died screaming in agony. The truth was often too distressing for grieving parents or wives. And so trite words were often the kindest.

He said, choosing his own words with care, understanding all too well how such letters were written, "Most casualties died at once. Others lived to be taken back for care. But the doctors could only do so much, and it was not unusual to lose severely wounded men. The Sisters were quite good, and very kind. They sat with the man throughout his ordeal, and wrote letters where they could—he might dictate them if he was conscious. Much of the time he would be given something for the pain, but he could ask the Sisters to take down any messages. Even if he couldn't write."

He told himself it was not a lie, only a generalization. But as he spoke, something changed in Hastings's face. A tightness there smoothed a little.

"Thank you," he said quietly, with old-fashioned

courtesy. "Clearly you were there. And I am grateful for your understanding." He cleared his throat and ruffled the pages before him. After a moment he went on. "As to Mr. Milford. His affairs were in order, although The Pit and The Pony had been a drain on his finances. He had inherited money, not a fortune of course, but more than sufficient under ordinary circumstances."

"How does his will stand?"

Hastings rose, searched for the proper box, then fished out and scanned the several pages. Coming back to his desk, he said, "As you would expect. His Last Will and Testament drawn up at the time he enlisted in the Bantams was straightforward. His estate went to his wife, Ruth Hensley Milford, with a small bequest for the woman who had attended his father in his last illness. That was replaced by one he drew up on his return from France. The woman in the earlier will had since died, and that clause was removed. His estate went to his wife, as it had done before. And he included their child, Matilda Patricia Milford, with a trust fund to see her to the age of twenty-five, to be used for her upbringing, her education, and her wedding, if she chose to marry. In the event the child Matilda died before reaching the age of twenty-five, funds set aside for her in accordance with his will reverted to her mother, Ruth Milford."

Which, Rutledge realized, might give Ruth Milford

a very good reason to rid herself of her child. Was she that desperate to save the pub? It behooved him now to look into just how Tildy had died. He was about to speak, when Hastings held up a hand, moving to another document in his hand.

"The final will was drawn up a year ago."

"A third will?"

"Indeed. It left the bulk of Milford's estate to his wife, as before. There was a small bequest for one Will Esterly, who helped Mrs. Milford keep the pub open after he was invalided out late in 1915. And there was a separate fund to be used after Mr. Milford's death to continue his search for his daughter. Any monies left in that fund after she was found were to revert to the trust."

Rutledge said, "To search for his daughter?" The Milfords had met in Reception in these very chambers. Something about property . . . "Was he married before he met Mrs. Milford?"

Hastings looked up from the papers in front of him. "No." He examined Rutledge's face. "Surely you were told? Matilda Patricia Milford went missing. Nearly a year ago. The family has been searching for her ever since."

Rutledge stared at Hastings, rapidly revising all he'd been told.

Mrs. Esterly had referred to Tildy as *lost*. A euphemism for death. The solicitor had used the word himself just now, referring to his son and his nephews killed in France. And children died young from any number of illnesses—typhoid, measles, diphtheria—as well as inherited diseases. It was a tragedy many families had to endure. Rutledge had also taken it that way, recognizing that Ruth Milford found it difficult to deal with her husband's murder and might find it even harder to speak of Tildy as dead.

"I didn't know," he said finally. "What happened?"

6

Hastings leaned back in his chair. "It was a disturbing business. The police came to interview me about the family. Mrs. Milford had taken the child for an outing in her pram. It was quite chilly that day, and she had put a shawl over the pram's opening to protect Matilda from the wind. A neighbor, Mrs. Esterly, saw her and called to her as Mrs. Milford was about to turn and go back the way she'd come. It seems there was a jar of honey on a shelf and the older woman was unable to reach it. Mrs. Milford looked in on Matilda, saw that she was asleep. She went into the house, brought down the jar, and left. Shortly afterward, she reached her own house, and there was a small parcel on the front step. She picked that up and took it inside, out of the way of the pram, then came back to bring that in as well. She hung up her coat and hat, then turned to lift away the shawl. The pram was empty. Matilda wasn't in there. It was thought at first that she had awakened and climbed out, wandering off on her own. A child of that age, not yet three, couldn't have got far. There was a thorough search, to no avail. Sadly, the child was never found."

Lost, indeed.

"Good God." He understood now why Mrs. Milford had said over and over again that she was to blame. For Tildy, and for her husband. Had he been searching for their missing child, and somehow learned that she might be in Wales? That was a more likely reason for going there than looking for the officer. "What did the police have to say?"

"Very little. The child might as well have vanished. And I was told there's no Constable in Crowley. Not since 1910, when the incumbent died. I understand Crowley is hardly more than a hamlet, and he was never replaced. But the police had to be sent for, and it was dark when the Constable from a neighboring village arrived. Everyone continued searching, but it was really at first light that the search began in earnest. Not just in the village, but as far as the Stiperstones and The Bog, the main lead mine. There are people still working there. Little Bog, the smaller abandoned lead mine, was combed but yielded nothing. Mr. Milford was out of his mind with worry. He even went into the mine shafts, as deep as he dared go—farther than the police were willing to look—but there was never any hint of what had become of Matilda. Then or in the weeks that followed. I needn't tell you how this affected everyone."

He could imagine the search. Door to door, even the general store and the pub itself, then ever widening to look any place that a child might have been taken and then abandoned. Alive—or dead.

"No one sent for the Yard?"

"It was not thought necessary. The police questioned Ruth Milford over and over again. She had spent ten minutes in the shop before stopping at Mrs. Esterly's house, in both instances leaving the pram just outside the door. But you understand, in neither instance had anyone else actually seen the child. Only the pram with the shawl over the opening. For nearly a fortnight the police suspected that Ruth Milford had done something with the little girl, then taken the empty pram out for all to see and assume that Matilda was in there. It was the only reasonable explanation. Crowley is not a busy city or at a crossroads. No one had noticed any strangers about that day."

"Was she arrested?"

"She was questioned until she broke down and a doctor had to be summoned. He ruled that she was in no state for further questioning."

"You seem to know the details. Were you called in as the family solicitor?"

"I was. And I must tell you, I feared for Ruth Milford's sanity."

"Was there no ransom request? You indicated that Sam Milford had money."

"The police considered that as well. No ransom demand was ever made, you see. The police did wish to question Milford's half sister, because a Mrs. Nancy Blake had reported hard feelings between brother and sister at one time. Some trouble at the wedding, as I recall. But it came to nothing."

"Half sister?" No one in Crowley had mentioned her.

"Yes. Milford's father was married twice, with a daughter from the first union and a son from the second. The daughter—her name is Susan Elizabeth—was unstable, and had been in and out of care. She had threatened her brother several times, once publicly at their father's funeral, and she had come to the house shortly before their father died and attacked his caregiver. The woman who was to receive the bequest in the first will. But the police couldn't find Susan, although there was a countywide search, a missing person's report, an offer of a reward for any news."

"The parcel that Mrs. Milford had set in the house to make way for the pram? Had it been posted? What was inside?"

"That was rather odd, you know. There was only Mrs. Milford's word that it had been waiting on the step. Inside was a single baby shoe. Quite old, the leather shriveled and cracking. The police were prepared to believe that Ruth had put it there herself, to give her a third opportunity to leave the pram outside for all to see. Before she'd made her discovery. The closest post offices had no record of a parcel being delivered to Crowley that week."

"And no charges were ever made, no inquest held?"

"No to both. No—er—body has been found. And Mr. Milford refused to let the police charge his wife. He was prepared to say that he had done away with the little girl himself."

"Where was he at the time this happened?"

"On his way home from Shrewsbury. He arrived an hour after the child was discovered missing."

Hastings drew a sheet of paper toward him, and in elegant script wrote down a name. "This is the Inspector here in Shrewsbury who was put in charge of the inquiry, after the nearest village Constable realized he needed further assistance. Fenton was on the brink of retirement—he'd stayed on for the duration of the war, and his replacement arrived three months after the events of that June. He took his retirement then, citing his age and health. But you'll find him at this address." He passed the sheet to Rutledge. "I've told you what I recall of the matter, but he can tell you what, if anything, the police discovered and didn't reveal. They sometimes do that, hold back until they find the offender. Well. You are a policeman, you'll know that."

Rutledge thanked him, but wasn't ready to conclude the interview. He said, "Milford's father. Were you his solicitor as well?"

"Yes, there was property in Shropshire that belonged to him, and I handled his will and the sale of his house after his death."

"What provisions did he make for his daughter from the first marriage?"

"He left money to have her privately cared for. He blamed his first wife for Susan's state of mind. She killed herself—the first Mrs. Milford—and the child found her hanging in the kitchen, when she came home from school for her midday meal. It scarred her, according to her father, and there was no turning back the clock.

But he refused to have her admitted to an asylum, because he didn't feel it would help her. Instead he looked after her until he died." He rearranged a letter opener lying beside the blotter. The handle was in the shape of the Eiffel Tower. Noticing Rutledge's interest, he held it up. It was heavy brass and very beautifully made. "A gift from my son after a brief leave in Paris. He knew I'd followed the building of the tower with some interest. I'd wanted to be an engineer, but my father had insisted I join the family's firm. But that's neither here nor there. Apparently the first Mrs. Milford was unstable as well. Perhaps the daughter had inherited that. And the sight of her mother hanging brought on what might not have made an appearance, in a happier home."

"What reason was given for her suicide?"

"I was told she never really recovered her health after childbirth."

Preparing to take his leave, Rutledge said, "I'll speak to—" He referred to the sheet. "To Inspector Fenton. Meanwhile, I can be reached through the Yard, if you remember anything else that might help. You don't have any way of contacting Susan Milford?"

"Sadly none. And the police never found her. Mr. Milford—her brother, not her father—always feared she'd follow in her mother's footsteps and take her own life. That her disappearance was indicative of that."

Hastings saw him out. Rutledge returned to the motorcar and sat in it for several minutes before getting out again to turn the crank.

Hamish said, "It was no' what ye expected, coming here."

"Not at all." He closed his eyes and went on silently. *They should have told me about Matilda. I wonder why they were satisfied to let me believe she was dead. Even though they're still searching for her. Dear God, this explains Milford's friendship with Dora. The brewery manager's sister. She's been working with orphaned children. Did Milford hope that whoever had taken Tildy might dispose of her as an orphan, rather than kill her? A body would lead to the police, a reopening of the case, a hunt for her murderer, while one more orphan in need of care wouldn't raise any questions or suspicion at all. But did that mean he believed his wife had got rid of her own daughter? Was that why he didn't take her into his confidence about Dora—or Wales? What did he know that we don't?*

Hamish replied thoughtfully, "Aye, but see it anither way. If yon widow had an eye for Milford, it would ha' been easy for her to dispose of the lass and put blame on the mother."

I'm not certain Milford knew Mrs. Radley before Tildy's disappearance. But it was worth looking into.

Rutledge found Inspector Fenton's house easily enough, following the directions given him by the solicitor. It was a semidetached, in a street of similar dwellings. Well kept, with stone vases on the steps and a small garden, still dormant, in the circle of the drive.

He left his motorcar on the street, and as he went up the short walk, he saw that several of the first-floor windows were inset with stained glass in various patterns in the style of the Pre-Raphaelites.

When he knocked, there was no response.

He knocked again, and then a man opened the door the merest crack. He was of middle height, portly, and hadn't shaved in days. His clothes were stained, appearing to have been slept in.

"And you want?" he asked, his voice a little slurred. But Rutledge could smell the whisky on his breath and in his sweat.

"Inspector Rutledge, Scotland Yard. I'm in charge of an inquiry into a death in Wales." He'd kept his voice

neutral. "It may have some connection with the disappearance of Tildy Milford."

Fenton's eyes suddenly focused on Rutledge's face.
"I don't understand."

"We don't know why her father was in Wales. It's
possible that he was searching for her, and his search
led him there. His death is being treated as suspicious."

Fenton shook his head, as if to clear it. "Sam Milford?"

"Yes."

"Come back tomorrow, when I can think straight."
And he shut the door before Rutledge could stop him.

He knocked again, but no one came. Finally he went
back to his motorcar, and found the police station where
Fenton had been assigned.

He asked for Inspector Carson, showing his identification to the new man on the desk.

The Constable said, "Sir. Is this a courtesy call or
Yard business?"

"Yard business." Something in his voice told the
young Constable that the London policeman was not to
be put off.

He led the way down a short passage to a door on
the right.

"Sir? Inspector Rutledge to see you. From the Yard."

Carson had been sitting at his desk in his shirtsleeves, reviewing a file. He looked up, saw Rutledge in the doorway, and stood, reaching for his coat.

Rutledge put his age down to his early thirties, and the scar that ran from his neck into his hair looked very much like a shrapnel wound. "Come in. Trying to catch up on station files. Sit down, do."

Rutledge took one of the chairs in front of the cluttered desk as Carson resumed his own seat, set aside the open file, and asked, "How can we assist Scotland Yard?"

Rutledge repeated what he'd told Inspector Fenton. "I wonder if you can help me with the background?"

Carson shook his head ruefully. "I didn't arrive on the scene until that August. I was demobbed in the spring, and spent several weeks in hospital. Still have my left leg, but its mate wouldn't recognize it in broad daylight. Still, it's healing. More scars than flesh, sad to say, although I can walk now. So far I haven't been required to chase down a felon."

Rutledge laughed with him. "What matters is that you survived the war."

"Damned near didn't. Ran afoul of a Hun machine-gun nest as they retreated north. Lost seven men before I could get a grenade in amongst them. Then I lost consciousness and woke up in a base hospital near the coast. Apparently they got me there by train. It was all that saved my leg. But you aren't here to discuss my medical history. Inspector Fenton dealt with that inquiry. Everyone in the station was unsettled by the disappearance. She was such a lovely little girl, by all accounts, bright red hair and green eyes. Cheerful, smiling, the sort of child anyone stopped to admire. The entire village turned out to search, and we brought in men from every corner of the county, everyone who could be spared."

"Why do you think she was taken?"

"Well, that's a good question, isn't it? Fenton considered the mother, who had the best opportunity to dispose of her. He also wondered if someone passing through, dining or staying at the inn, might have seen her. The problem was, the mother had no motive. She seemed to dote on the child. And so did Milford. He wasn't the father, you know. But he took the child to his heart, according to Fenton, and treated her as his own flesh and blood."

"What do you mean, Milford wasn't Tildy's father?"

"She was a little over a year old when he came home from France. Ruth Milford claimed she met Milford in London and the child was conceived then. But Fenton couldn't find any record of her husband having been given leave early in 1917. According to the file, Fenton suspected she'd had an affair. Of course, it could have been something else, something worse."

"Rape?"

"Fenton sent requests out all over Shropshire, Cheshire—as far away as Gloucestershire, and there is no record of an incident involving Ruth."

"Did Fenton search under her maiden name?"

Carson shook his head. "No luck there either. One theory was, she was jealous of her husband's love for a child that wasn't his and got rid of her. Or alternatively, Milford himself only pretended to care for Matilda, planning to be rid of her as soon as *he* could. Neither motive could be proved."

Rutledge said, "The family told me nothing about this. Nor did their neighbors."

"The neighbors don't know. It's a well-kept family secret. But they loved the little girl. And they went through hell, Rutledge. The entire village. The loss, the finger-pointing, the mystery that left everyone guessing. I expect it wasn't something they wished to relive."

"This changes the inquiry. It's no longer just about Milford's death. Was he in Llangollen to find out what happened there to his wife? Or was he looking for his child? Or both?"

"Mrs. Milford had no connection with the town, as far as we know."

But she had. And kept it to herself.

Then how had Milford found out? The shirt? But Banner would surely have told him if Milford had been there earlier, asking questions . . .

Carson was saying, "It nearly killed Fenton. This business. He'd lost a son to cancer at Matilda's age. He wanted to find her alive. And when he failed, he started to drink heavily. Fortunately, he was old enough to retire. We let him take his pension and leave." He sighed. "A great many people spent a great deal of time searching, and we turned up nothing. I reviewed the reports when I took over, and I couldn't fault a single thing that Fenton did to find her."

"Do you think she's alive?"

"God, I don't know. How was she taken, with no one seeing it happen? Who wanted her and for what? Lost children can suffer any number of fates. You know that, and so do I. Someone could have taken her to use or to sell. Or perhaps to replace a child lost. I'm told some women are so disturbed by a child dying that they will do anything to stop the pain. Speak to Fenton. He's lived with this inquiry longer than I have."

Rutledge thanked him and left.

He'd seen Fenton. The man was still drinking.

And Rutledge had his doubts about the reliability of Fenton's memory, if this had been going on for nearly a year.

Still, it would be worthwhile to call on him tomorrow, to see what he remembered about the inquiry. There was always something that was never put into the reports. He himself had been guilty of that, keeping secrets that didn't need to be exposed, protecting the innocent who had already suffered enough, leaving no word of doubt that might linger and be used to cause trouble later for the dead. He had stayed with the evidence, cold hard proof where there was no question of guilt. There were any number of reasons to use discretion.

At ten the next morning, Rutledge knocked at the door of the Fenton house, without much hope of finding the man sober enough to speak to him, regardless of what he'd said about the morrow.

There was a long wait, going far toward supporting his reservations.

But then the door opened, and Fenton looked out at him.

"I'm not as sober as I'd hoped to be," he said. "But you'll have to make do with that."

He'd bathed and shaved, his clothing was neat and

tidy. But his face reflected the effort he'd made. He was pale, with dark circles under his eyes, and his left hand shook as it gripped the edge of the door.

"I'll take my chances," Rutledge replied.

Moving back, Fenton allowed him to step into the foyer, then took him to a room in the rear of the house that had once been his study. It reeked of cigarette smoke and stale alcohol and food.

"This is where I live," Fenton was saying. "My wife refuses to allow me in any other part of the house. I'm not against that decision. I'm neither good company nor a good husband. She's out at the moment. Some church meeting or other." There was something behind the words, a flatness and despair. As though he had lost his faith.

He moved a pile of newspapers from a chair and gestured to Rutledge to sit down. "I'd offer you tea. But I'm not allowed in the kitchen."

Rutledge glanced at the newspapers spilled onto the floor. They were nearly a year old.

"What's your interest in the Milford case? I don't remember if you told me yesterday. My memory isn't at its best."

Rutledge said, "Sam Milford appears to have been murdered in Wales. I was dispatched by Scotland Yard to look into the death, and it's very likely that his fall from the Telford Aqueduct was not an accident. There were no witnesses, and the body had no identification. I am told that his family believed he was in Shrewsbury this past week, on business related to financial problems at The Pit and The Pony pub."

"Sam is dead?" Fenton stared blankly at Rutledge. "Good God." He'd moved to the only other chair in the middle of the chaos, this time setting a tray of food on the floor—a half-eaten breakfast. "I couldn't swallow it," he added apologetically. "And the maid hasn't come yet to collect it." Frowning in concentration, he said, "You said no identification. How did you trace Sam?"

"He was wearing a shirt that his wife had bought for him to have when the war was finally over. It had a label that I was able to trace to a tailor. He was a careful shop owner, and kept records of clients who might wish to do more business with him. That's how I found Ruth Milford in Crowley."

"That was good work," Fenton said approvingly.

"While I was informing Mrs. Milford of her husband's likely murder, I was told by everyone that the Milfords had lost a daughter. I took that to mean that she had died in childhood. It wasn't until I was speaking to Mr. Hastings, the family's solicitor, that I learned the truth—that Tildy had gone missing. And no one knows what became of her. I spoke to Inspector Carson, your successor, and he told me about the efforts you'd made to find the child. That too was good work."

Fenton looked away. "Hardly. We never found her." There was something in his voice that indicated the pain of his failure.

"You had a personal connection to the case?" He already knew the answer. But it was important to him to understand what had driven Fenton to try so hard, and then destroy his own life by drinking himself to death.

Fenton sighed. "I thought I'd put it behind me. Years ago. I had to, I had a wife and another child to support. I lost my son to cancer. We had the best doctors, we did everything that was humanly possible to save him. We prayed for him until we were hoarse. And we never left his bedside until it was over. It was the worst week of my life. I am not sure why the disappearance of little Tildy brought that back to me so vividly, but it did." He got up and went to his desk, shuffling through papers in one of the drawers.

"I had a copy made. Mrs. Blake had shown me the film negative. This is Tildy Milford." He brought the photograph to Rutledge and stood there while he looked at it.

She was sitting on a table, a white cloth with embroidered flowers—lilacs? He couldn't be sure—covering it. She was wearing a pastel dress. He could tell because it wasn't as white as the cloth. It too had a pattern of flowers, these around the throat and hem.

He'd expected an extraordinarily pretty child. But Tildy had a sweet face, a smile that was charming, and eyes that were alight with happiness. Her hair was curly, not quite blond, not quite dark. He'd been told it was a bright red. There was a ribbon in it, apparently the same shade as the dress.

"It was her birthday. She'd had cake and gifts, and she'd enjoyed all the attention. This according to Nancy Blake. I've never seen Tildy, you understand. Just this photograph. But I have one of my son, a very similar pose, just after his second birthday. There was something—that same expression in the eyes, that joy, that sweetness—it took my breath away. When I came home, I took out the photograph of Jonathan, to make certain I hadn't imagined that expression. I hadn't. And all the pain I'd fought my way through came rushing back. Twenty-seven years after he'd died. I swore I'd find Tildy. That I'd bring her home safely. And in spite of everything I could think to do, I failed."

A silence followed. Rutledge said nothing. *I'm sorry* seemed trite.

Fenton struggled to cope with his own emotional confession, then said in a very different voice, "You must understand. I let none of these feelings in any way affect my judgments or decisions. I kept a clear head. But driving me day and night was that memory."

It was the policeman speaking now, not the grieving father.

"You questioned Ruth Milford relentlessly. Why?"

"She was shocked and terrified by what had happened. But there was something—I felt she hadn't been completely honest about something. I never could put my finger on what it was. I even considered the possibility that the child had died, and because she knew how much Sam loved the little girl, she had tried to conceal it. Disposing of the body so that the finality of death was never acknowledged, although by the end of the inquiry and the inquest, some of us believed Tildy must have been dead."

"Why?"

"I don't need to tell you what can happen to children. None of it good. And there were no sightings, nothing at all. Red-haired children with green eyes aren't that common. That might be why she was taken. She was unusual. And she caught the eye of someone."

"Did you check everyone who had come to the pub?"

"We couldn't possibly have traced all of them. But yes, everyone who had stayed the night there and could have seen her. Her parents were proud of her, they didn't keep her at home with a nanny while they were working at The Pit and The Pony, they let her play in a little pen they set up by the hearth. And that might have been her undoing. But no one we managed to trace had any reason to harm her. All of them had alibis and no motive we could establish."

"Still, they might have told someone. Without realizing what they might have set in motion by doing so."

"And how do you trace those people? It's impossible."

"What about the villagers?"

"That went nowhere. Half of them didn't have real alibis. One was ironing in her kitchen, another working at his father's farm in full view of his mother. Another was having a quiet nap after his lunch. Again, we couldn't find a motive. Nothing that would make a neighbor harm the child. We considered covetousness, revenge for some slight, even viciousness and unnatural desire."

Rutledge himself had interviewed the villagers in

his attempt to learn more about Sam Milford, and he had come to the same conclusions about them. There was nothing to alarm him, just as nothing had alarmed Fenton.

"There were no strangers in Crowley that day?"

"If there was, no one saw him. Or her." He took a deep breath. "We even searched for Milford's sister. Half sister. But no one had seen her since shortly after her father's death. And this was before the war, mind you. Still. I kept an open mind."

"Who was the child's father?"

"We never got to the bottom of that. According to Mrs. Blake, Mrs. Milford met her husband in London early in 1917, and the child was conceived then. The neighbors told us the same story. But that's not likely. Milford was never sent to London on any mission. The odd thing was, Milford clearly considered the child to be his, and in spite of the fact that he was distraught, he defended his wife fiercely when we suspected her."

This agreed with what Rutledge had heard from Inspector Carson.

"How did she manage to persuade her husband to accept such a story, when he must have known it was not possible?"

"She was quite clever. From what I've been able to piece together, she consulted a doctor in London when she realized she might be pregnant. I have tried to trace this man, but it's likely that she gave him a false name. He must have confirmed her fears, because when she returned to Crowley, she told everyone that she had traveled to London because she had got word that Sergeant Milford would be there over the weekend, something to do with secret orders. They spent several days together, according to her account. No one appeared to question this. A month later, when the pregnancy was announced, the entire village was happy for her. She then told everyone that the doctor she was seeing in Shrewsbury had ordered her to take care, or she'd suffer a miscarriage. And so when the baby was born a fortnight early, no one suspected that it was a full-term child. Mrs. Blake assured us that Ruth had told the good news to her husband in a letter, and he had been overjoyed. Of course, she could have done no such thing. And yet my impression of Ruth Milford has always been that she doesn't lie as a rule. So the fact that she was able to carry off this lie has worried me. It means she could have successfully lied about other matters."

"And yet when her husband came home and discovered he had a daughter, he accepted her. Supported her, even."

"I don't believe she could have admitted to an affair.

Which leaves us with an assault. She would have had to tell him about the assault and the pregnancy early on. Everyone must have been eager to write to him and congratulate him on the prospect of becoming a father, and she couldn't risk him spurning her. I was told she came to Shrewsbury alone, to meet his train and welcome him home from France. That was probably why, to see if he was still supportive of her. She took Tildy with her, I believe, and Sam never doubted Ruth. To me or anyone else I spoke to."

"Do you think that this assault actually took place?" he asked, remembering the officer outside Banner's shop in Llangollen.

"It could have happened while Ruth was in Oswestry. Attending a funeral. The timing is right. All I know is, she never spoke to the police there, or anyone at the railway stations she passed through. Nor to a priest. But according to Mrs. Blake, Ruth was distressed when she came home, and that would most certainly support the fact that something untoward had happened."

"Whose funeral was it? Do you know?"

"A classmate from the school she'd attended for a year or two. We did speak to the family of that friend. Ruth was there, and appeared to be herself the entire weekend. The family had found her to be a rock—

their words, mind you—which didn't agree with what Mrs. Blake was saying about her distress when she came home. When we questioned Ruth about her state of mind then, she told us the services for her friend had reminded her of her mother's recent death."

"It could have happened after the funeral. On her way back to Crowley. Was she traveling alone?"

"She was, that's true. But, of course, there was no way to prove or disprove that it happened then. Except that she wasn't free to leave Crowley whenever she pleased. Not with the pub to see to. When we questioned Will Esterly, he told us that he'd taken over for her three times in the new year while she went to Shrewsbury, settling her mother's estate. He seemed surprised that it had taken so long, given such a small estate, but he knew it was difficult for her. Then the journey to London, either to visit a doctor or visit with Sam, take your pick. Finally there was the one to attend the funeral. Once she learned she was pregnant, he said, she was fearful about traveling."

"Was one of those journeys to Shrewsbury in March 1917?" When Ruth was in Llangollen ordering clothing from Banner? Had she lied to everyone about where she actually was, using her mother's legal affairs as her excuse?

"I believe it was. Carson has my files about the case, or I could look."

"Any evidence that Mrs. Milford had been unfaithful to her husband during the war? Then or at any other time while he was away?"

"None that we could discover. And I don't see how she could. She'd have to ask Will or Mrs. Blake to take over, and she couldn't very well tell them why. And it would be impossible to invite a lover to the pub, the whole of Crowley would start to gossip."

"If it was an assault, could her attacker have been in the Army? Home on leave? Possibly even recovering from wounds? That would explain why she didn't pursue the assault, knowing he was traveling also and well away by the time she reached Crowley—out of her reach."

"No idea. It was dark, I expect, or there would have been possible witnesses. And she could claim she never saw him clearly."

"Returning to Tildy. Was there anyone in Crowley that you had second thoughts about? Someone who might have taken a fancy to her? Or someone who saw her every day, and would have been trusted by the child? Will, who helped in the pub, for instance."

Fenton took his time answering.

"Will Esterly? No. I did wonder several times about Mrs. Blake's husband. Donald."

"Did you?" Rutledge was surprised.

"The thing is, he had no motive for harming her. Or none that I could find. He threw himself into the search like a man demented. Hardly slept, in fact."

"Would the loss of Tildy persuade her parents to give up the pub? It's what the Blakes have wanted for some time."

Fenton considered the possibility. "If that was his intent, it didn't have the effect he was looking for. Ruth and Sam were even more intent on keeping the pub open. If only because if whoever had taken the child had second thoughts, they would be there to receive their daughter. After all, a child that young couldn't possibly identify her kidnappers. It would be safe enough to leave her where she could be found quickly."

"And Sam was apparently still searching. Only I don't think he told his wife what he was doing."

"Didn't want to get her hopes up. I'd probably do the same, myself, in his shoes."

"What did you leave out of your final report?"

Fenton looked away.

"There's often something."

"No. I never did any such thing."

Rutledge had a feeling he was lying.

But nothing he could say convinced Fenton to be honest with him.

His last question, as Fenton was looking drained of emotion and thought, was about the shoe that Ruth Milford had found in the hand-delivered parcel left on her house steps.

Fenton said, "I always wondered why that shoe wasn't left *before* the child's disappearance. It would have been far more effective as a threat. But then the sender might well have found it much harder to take the child. The family would have been on guard."

7

Rutledge left soon after, half convinced that Fenton would turn to the bottle again as soon as his visitor was out the door.

Hamish said, "Was it a' about his son? Yon policeman's concern for Tildy?"

"That's a very good question. He was about to retire. Many men find it hard to give up the authority of a policeman for a quiet life where no one jumps to his orders."

Still, even that failed to explain Fenton's drinking. What had driven him to the bottle, to forget?

Unsatisfied, he went back to the police station.

The Constable on duty said, "He's interviewing a suspect, sir. I don't know if he wishes to be interrupted."

"I have a question to put to him. I'll wait if need be."

But it was a good half hour before Carson could see him.

Carson said, "So you met with Fenton. I'm surprised you got him to answer his door. Much less talk to you coherently."

"He spent an agonizing night sobering up sufficiently to remember Tildy. Why?"

"I've told you. He lost a child very close in age to Tildy. Cancer."

"Yes, and he used the same excuse not half an hour ago. I've no doubt his dead son made another child's loss feel more personal. But it goes deeper, I think. I'd hoped you could tell me."

"Good luck in finding your answer to that. I don't know Fenton well enough even to make a guess."

It was clear that Carson had no further interest in the matter. His attention was already straying to the open file next to the blotter on his desk. Rutledge thanked him and left.

Turning the crank, he went back over what the hotel clerk had told him about the letter that Milford had been waiting for. He'd left the hotel immediately afterward. But where had he gone? Not back to Crowley. He'd told no one his plans, which indicated he hadn't expected to be gone long enough for anyone to begin to wonder where he was. And yet somehow Milford had arrived in the vicinity of Llangollen.

Was it merely a coincidence that Milford had been killed not far from where his wife had ordered a suit of clothes for him while an officer waited for her outside Banner's tailor shop? Or had he somehow learned about this man—who might have been Tildy's father? How had Sam Milford made the leap from Shrewsbury to Llangollen?

And that brought Rutledge round to Dora, Andrew Clark's sister. Was she the woman who had brought Milford the letter? If so, what did she know about it?

He didn't know how to find her. He'd have to speak to her brother first. And tell him that Milford was dead.

He found a foreman at the brewery, and used his Yard authority to obtain Clark's direction.

Clark was no happier to see him this morning than Carson had been. And protective of his sister, he was reluctant to give Rutledge any personal information about her, once he had been told that Milford was dead, and in suspicious circumstances.

"She's got nothing to do with this business. Leave her out of it. She's had enough tragedy in her life."

"I can find out what I need to know from the police," he said finally. "And I don't believe she would care for that."

More than a little angry, Clark said, "If you upset her over Milford's death, you'll answer to me. London policeman or not."

"I have no intention of upsetting her. I need information about her work with orphans. Milford was interested in that as well. I need to know where it might have taken him, and why."

"He'd lost a child. For all I know he was considering adoption."

"Still."

Clark left Rutledge standing at the door, came back a moment later with something written on a slip of paper, and handed it to him. "Now I'd appreciate it if you left."

Clark's reaction told him far more than the man himself would ever have revealed. Dora Radley had feelings for Sam Milford, just as he, Rutledge, had expected from the start. But were they returned?

And additional proof, if that was needed, lay in the address he'd been given: Maple Street. No one at number 18 knew Dora Radley. When he tried a neighbor, to confirm what he'd just been told, the householder suggested he try Elm or Oak, instead.

"There's sometimes confusion over which species of tree," he said with a wry smile.

Rutledge went to Elm first, and stopped before number 18. It was a modest bungalow in a quiet street of similar dwellings. He went up the short walk, tapped on the door, and after a moment a pretty woman with fair hair and hazel eyes answered. She was wearing a very becoming dress of deep brown with cinnamon trim. Redness around her nose and eyes indicated she had been crying. She said politely, "How may I help you?"

"Mrs. Radley? My name is Rutledge," he replied. "I'm from Scotland Yard. I'm looking into a matter that you may be familiar with. I'd like to speak to you about Samuel Milford, and his daughter, Tildy."

"Oh. I—I was just going out—"

"It won't take long."

"My brother just told me. Sam—Mr. Milford is dead. Is—is that true?"

So that was why Clark had sent him on a wild goose chase to Maple. To give his sister the news himself.

"I'm afraid so."

"I don't understand. What happened? He said—an accident?"

Damn Clark, Rutledge said to himself. And to Mrs. Radley, "I am sorry to be the bearer of bad news.

But there's a possibility that Milford's death was not an accident. That he was killed. I've been asked to investigate."

"Kil—" She stared at him, trying to make sense of what he'd said. Shaking her head, she began to deny it. "Not Sam. No, I can't believe that. You—you must have it wrong."

Her reaction was much like Ruth Milford's. He found that only reinforced his view that Dora Radley had been in love with Milford—or thought she was.

"I'm sorry," he said again, more gently this time. "I'm afraid it's true. I had hoped you'd be willing to help with our inquiries."

After another brief hesitation, she said, "Oh. I don't know how. But—yes. Please. Come in."

The parlor was a pleasant room, a pale green with white trim and darker greens in the drapes and the upholstery. He took the chair she indicated, declined her offer of tea, and was about to give her a moment to compose herself, when she said, "Tell me, please. What happened to Sam—to him?"

"He fell. We have reason to believe he was pushed." He didn't give her any more details than that. He didn't think it was necessary.

"Dear God," she said softly, then clearing her

throat, she added, "I'd only just seen him, you know. He always looked me up when he was in Shrewsbury. I work with children being placed in orphanages. It was never likely that Tildy would be one of them, but it gave him hope, you see. Some of the children have had very difficult childhoods. Mistreated, abandoned, no warmth or love in their short lives. Others are given up because their mother can no longer care for them. She's ill, dead, drinks heavily—there are myriad reasons, of course. Not the sort of place for Tildy to be found, but he was desperate, and hope is sometimes all one has."

"How did you meet him?"

"He was there one day, at the brewery, and we were introduced. My brother mentioned my work, because I'd just stopped by after a rather difficult morning, and he knew I was upset. Sam began to ask questions about the orphaned children."

"What sort of questions?"

"How we found parents for them, when the children were waifs and we didn't know where they had come from. How much children resembled their mothers, and whether we could establish who a parent was by looking for that resemblance. What traits were passed on. Like being left-handed or tall or having green eyes or bad teeth. I thought he was just being polite, putting me at ease by asking about my work. It wasn't until later, when I was told that Tildy had disappeared, that I realized what he was asking was how much she might have changed in the months since he had last seen her, and whether he would still recognize her. It was rather sad. He loved her, you see."

But *was* that why he was asking?

Dora, unaware of Rutledge's doubts, was still speaking. "And then he asked me to look out for Tildy. How could I say no? However impossible it might be for her to be brought in, what if she were? What if the person who'd taken her had regrets or something, and didn't know of a way to be rid of the problem? We've had children left on the doorstep. Too young to tell us who they are, where their parents are, or how to find them."

There were tears welling in her eyes as she went on to describe some of the children she cared for. "It's heartbreaking work. But someone kind can make such a difference in their lives."

"Did Sam have any theories about what had become of Tildy?"

"He always spoke of her in the present. As if he felt she was still alive. I found that quite touching. And for his sake, and of course his wife's," she added quickly,

"I prayed that he was right. But mostly we are overwhelmed by widows from the war. Sometimes they simply can't cope any longer, and want their child to have a better life. I can't tell you that it's any better. But many of them believe it will be. Hard for the child to understand that. All he or she knows is abandonment and loss."

Was that what Tildy had felt? She would have missed her mother and father. He was beginning to understand, on a very different level, what Fenton might have tried to tell him.

And then he broached the issue that had really brought him here.

"Why did Milford leave Shrewsbury without telling anyone, and set out for Wales? I've learned that someone brought a letter to him at his hotel, and immediately afterward he left the city. A woman. Was that you? The next sighting is in Llangollen, where he was killed."

She flushed in embarrassment. "I don't know anything about a letter—I've never—I *would* never go to his hotel."

He believed her. The embarrassment was too deep to be feigned. She might care for Sam Milford, Rutledge realized, but she would not chase him. Which meant there must be another woman in Shrewsbury who was privy to his secrets, one who hadn't been found yet.

"Did he ever mention his sister to you?"

"I never knew he had a sister. But then we were talking about the recent past most of the time. Mine or his. I expect it never came up."

"Then it's very unlikely that you would know if he had enemies, someone he disliked, or perhaps someone who disliked him?"

"In the war, I think, there was something that happened. He said once that he'd done things that haunted him, but he'd got one decision right, even if he'd paid a dear price for it."

"Did he tell you what that decision was?" God knew, he himself had done things that haunted him. He couldn't stand in judgment of Sam Milford.

"He wouldn't tell me. He hadn't even told his wife." She looked away. "Soon after that, he asked me about Oswestry."

"What was his interest in Oswestry?" It was an English market town almost on the Welsh border. The town where Ruth Milford had gone to a funeral, and Fenton had wondered if that was where she'd been assaulted. It was also on the road to Llangollen . . . "Was it connected to what he might have done in the war?"

"I-I'm not really sure. He was looking to find someone he could trust there. Someone he could speak to. And, of course, my first thought was that he was asking if there was someone like me in the town, someone who looked after orphans. He laughed and said it had to do with the pub. But that couldn't be true, could it? They'd never deliver as far away as Crowley. Still, I did give him the name of a dairy farmer just outside of the town, a man related to a friend. And the next few times he came to Shrewsbury, he'd spend only a day or two here on pub affairs, then go to Oswestry."

Sam Milford *was* searching for Tildy's father . . .

Did he believe he'd had something to do with the child's disappearance?

Rutledge found a garage and topped up his petrol, then set out for Oswestry, some twenty miles or so northwest of Shrewsbury. But the dairy farm was just north of the town, and he had a little trouble finding it.

The owner, one Ted Brewster, was washing down the milking shed. A herd of black-and-white cows waited at the yard gate, ready to come in. A few were lowing, but most of them were quietly standing there.

Rutledge had seen him as he drove down the farm lane and passed between the main barn and the milking shed. The farmer had looked up, begun to stow away the hose pipe he'd been using, and was standing by the entrance to the shed as Rutledge drew up and stepped out of the motorcar.

Underfoot the yard was muddy and unspeakable. He had had the foresight to put his Wellingtons in the well of the passenger's seat and quickly changed his boots before walking over to meet Brewster.

He gave his name, used Dora's as his reference, and added, "I believe you know a man I'm looking for. Sam Milford."

The farmer's Shropshire accent was so thick Rutledge had trouble at first understanding him.

"I know him. Why are you looking for him?"

"I was just in Shrewsbury, and I was told I'd missed him, he'd gone on to Oswestry. I knew him in the war."

"You don't look much like a Bantam," Brewster said, surveying Rutledge's height.

He laughed. "I was in another regiment, but our paths crossed. A good man, Sam. I was coming north, he'd always told me that he would welcome a visit. I stopped in Crowley, as well. If I don't find him soon, I'm afraid I'll miss him altogether. I thought perhaps he stayed with you whenever he was in town?"

"Farm's too far out. Sent him to my sister. She has a spare room to let."

"Is he staying there?" Rutledge tried to put excitement and enthusiasm into his voice. "We can dine together tonight, and I can get on my way tomorrow."

"He's not there. Spent one night with Betty, so she says, and then was off."

"Damn," Rutledge said. "To Chester, I hope? That's where I'm heading."

"Didn't tell me. You'll have to ask Betts."

Holding on to his patience, Rutledge said, "And where will I find her?"

"Betty Turnbull." He gave Rutledge her direction, but had to repeat it for him.

"Thank you. I appreciate your help."

"Didn't help. Wasn't here."

Rutledge splashed through the mud back to the motorcar while Brewster walked down to open the gate. The milk cows came through in orderly fashion, as if they knew their usual place in the shed. Reversing carefully, he turned back toward the town.

He found Betty in a rowhouse, midway down the long street, and opened the gate into the little walled garden. Tapping at the door, he waited, and finally a woman answered. Her hair was darker, but otherwise she looked very much like her brother. "Mrs. Turnbull?"

"Who's wanting to know?"

"I was at your brother's farm just now," he told her, and at once she glanced down at his feet and saw the muddy Wellingtons he was wearing. As if doubting his word. "Ted tells me that Sam Milford often stayed with you when he was in Oswestry."

"He does. Rents the room at the back. But he's not here now. Left two weeks ago. You'll find him back at home, like as not."

"I missed him there as well. Do you know where he might have gone? Chester? Wales?"

"Doubt he's going there. He's been looking for someone in Oswestry. No name, no description to speak of. Red hair, he said. And a cleft chin. Needle in the hay, if you ask me."

Rutledge tried to recall the photograph of Tildy. *Did* she have a cleft chin? It wasn't pronounced in the photograph, but she was very small, and those who knew her well might see it, even if the camera failed to capture it.

Hamish said, "Or ye ken, Mrs. Milford made it up to satisfy her husband, when he asked what she remembered about the man who attacked her."

Ignoring the voice, Rutledge asked, "Did he tell you why he wished to find this person?" Had Milford been searching for Tildy—or her father? Or both?

"He was collecting a debt. He said."

An interesting way of putting it, Rutledge thought, given the circumstances.

"If he was looking for someone here, why did he leave Oswestry?"

Hamish commented, jolting him, "Yon narrowboats wi' their curtains at a' the windows. A hundred orphans could be hidden inside, and no one the wiser."

She lifted a shoulder, a slight shrug, distancing herself from Milford's decisions. "You must ask him when you find him. I needed the money, and so when he was staying here, I'd help him search. Two pairs of eyes were better than one, he said. Besides, I lived here, and nobody took any notice of me walking about day or night. I could have seen someone he'd missed."

"And did you?"

She shook her head. "That bright a color isn't usual. Most have darker red hair."

Auburn, like Ruth and her cousin. But then a child's hair could darken. A schoolmate of his had been quite fair when he was seven, and then his hair began to darken until it was brown by the time he was twenty.

"Were you looking for a man—or a child?"

"It didn't matter, he said. A long-lost cousin he was trying to find. Something to do with the family, he said. I didn't care to pry. He paid me well. I was willing to help him."

"I wonder—Milford had borrowed a book from me—a small collection of poetry, *Wings of Fire*. It was signed by the author, and has sentimental value to me. I was going to ask him for it. As I'm here—do you know if it's in his room?"

"I don't go in there. He's paid for that room to the end of the month." Her mouth tightened.

She didn't know him. He could see that she was not about to jeopardize what Milford was paying her by allowing a stranger to poke about. Whatever excuse he might offer. And he thought that as long as she believed Milford was alive, she wouldn't touch his belongings herself.

At the same time, he was not ready to tell her that Milford was dead. Not until he had learned as much as he could about the man's movements in Oswestry and what had led him north to Llangollen.

Tomorrow would do.

He thanked her, and left.

Rutledge had never been sent to Oswestry by the Yard, and the town had few visible treasures to offer visitors, beyond a rich history. But if he remembered correctly, this was the home of Wilfred Owen. Only a year or so younger than Rutledge, Owen had been killed toward the end of the war. But Rutledge had read some of Owen's verse, as well as O.A. Manning's, and had admired both.

He spent what was left of the light walking through the town, finding an excuse to loiter here or there, searching for anyone with bright red hair. Looking into shop windows, standing on the motte and appearing to stare at what little was left of the ancient castle, strolling along Bailey Head market, even watching three women walking into St. Oswald's on Church Street. But it was a cold afternoon, and most men were wearing hats or caps, while the few women about had on hats or covered their heads with a silk scarf against the chill.

He hadn't expected it to be easy to pick out hair color. Still, he noticed three people with red hair. The first was a boy of about seven, lagging behind his parents as they strolled down a quiet street. But the child's eyes were brown, not green, even though his lopsided wool cap had revealed a forelock of bright red gold, and his face was a sea of gold freckles as he passed Rutledge and gave him a shy grin.

On Curlew Street, he encountered a woman just leaving a friend's house, pausing on the steps for a last word. A curling tendril of hair had escaped her very becoming hat, and he could see that it was red. He stopped to ask for directions, as an excuse to approach her. But her eyes were hazel, not green.

The thin man just crossing another street wasn't wearing a hat, his thick red hair blowing in the wind as he hurried on. He had a slight limp, but carried himself like a soldier. Rutledge easily caught up with him, only to realize on closer inspection that his coloring was darker, and he possessed a receding chin that had neither dimple nor cleft. It wasn't possible to determine the color of his eyes, but he was too slight a figure to have taken on Sam Milford on the trestle over the River Dee and come out the winner, even with the advantage of a few more inches in height.

Rutledge was beginning to understand just how difficult Milford's search had been.

Hamish said, "It's late, the streets are nearly empty. Tomorrow if the day is fair, ye'll have better luck."

But Rutledge wasn't as certain. How many times had Milford been to Oswestry—and he'd had no luck? He'd moved on, finally, into Wales, and the Aqueduct. That was barely another twenty-some miles farther north. But what had led him there? What had he learned in Oswestry that had taken him to the boats? Betty Turnbull didn't appear to know—or was keeping to herself anything she might have learned, helping Milford.

"It's no' sich a great distance," Hamish reminded him. "A narrowboat man could have family here, a brother—a cousin. And had come down for a visit. It's no' impossible."

It didn't matter what Milford had discovered, he'd apparently abandoned Oswestry as a destination. And that had led to his death. The question now was, had someone followed him north, or had Milford's unexpected appearance there suddenly presented a very real danger to someone with secrets?

"Ye've come full circle," Hamish told him.

Rutledge spent Tuesday night in Oswestry. Traveling to the Aqueduct last week, at the start of the inquiry, he'd taken the main roads to the Dee. Now he preferred to follow Sam Milford, and look for any traces there might be of him along the way. That was best done in daylight.

Still, after dinner at the inn where he'd found a room, he was restless and walked for two hours, finding himself at one point in front of Betty Turnbull's rowhouse. It was late, there was only one light on, and that at a first-floor window. As he watched, it went out, and the house was pitched into darkness.

She hadn't known that Milford had gone north, instead of turning back toward Shrewsbury and then home. Or at least she denied knowing about the change in his plans. Which was it?

Milford had paid her for her help in searching the town, and for a room at the rear of her house . . .

What did he leave in that room that might be useful?

Rutledge was just considering that when Hamish said softly, "'Ware." As he'd so often done in the trenches on night watches, when his sharp hearing had caught a sound before Rutledge had picked it up.

Rutledge wheeled to find a burly man coming toward him.

"Evening," he said, but Hamish had warned him, that sixth sense, and so he was prepared when the man spoke brusquely.

"Lingering about in the dark, mate?" There was a strong odor of beer on his breath.

"No. Deciding that it was too late to call on Mrs. Turnbull. I'll have to return in the morning."

"You're up to trouble, more likely," the man replied, the brusqueness changing to belligerence. "I've been watching, mate. From my window over there. You've stood here a full ten minutes or more. Waiting for the old woman's light to go out, before you go in?"

"If I'd wanted to go in, I'd have gone around the back," he said reasonably. "Easier in that way."

"I've half a mind to haul you up to Constable, and let him decide."

"I wouldn't if I were you. You'll regret it."

Something had changed in Rutledge's voice, and the man was still sober enough to catch it. But he said, "It's my street, mate."

Rutledge didn't respond.

Uneasy suddenly, the man seemed to be debating what to do next. It was impossible for Rutledge to see his face clearly, but the confusion was there in the way his weight shifted.

Rutledge finally spoke. "If you see Mrs. Turnbull in the morning, tell her Inspector Rutledge will be calling on her at nine. Good evening."

He walked on, his shoulders tensed against attack, but the man stayed where he was.

True to his word, Rutledge was at the door of the rowhouse at nine sharp the next morning. He'd already left his room at the inn, and he expected to be on the road north within an hour. But there was unfinished business with Mrs. Turnbull.

As he knocked he wondered whether the neighbor he'd encountered last night was still on guard. But he didn't turn to look in that direction while he waited for Betty Turnbull to answer.

When she didn't, he used his fist, loud enough this time to be heard in the back of the house, in the event she was in the kitchen.

No response.

Glancing up, he saw that the curtains were still drawn in the bedroom where he'd seen the light go out last evening. Had she left early, to do her marketing?

Trying the latch, he found the door still locked.

He moved back toward the road, where his motorcar was waiting, for a better view of the bedroom window. And as he did, he looked up to see a door across the road open, and the burly, unshaven resident coming to stand in the opening.

Calling to him, Rutledge asked, "Does Mrs. Turnbull usually sleep this late?"

"Her's an early riser," he answered. "Meets the milk van coming up the road."

He turned back. There was something about that closed curtain. Drawn tight, no shred of light coming through a crack. He could feel his unease increasing.

"Fetch the Constable," he called to the man. "Straightaway."

The man said something over his shoulder to someone unseen in the house behind him and came striding across to where Rutledge had his hand on the gate into the tiny walled garden that led up to the door.

"What's happening?" He stared at Rutledge, frowning. "You were here last night."

"I was. And Mrs. Turnbull isn't answering. Find that Constable, *now*. I'm going round to the back."

"Not out of my sight, you aren't. Constable can wait."

Rutledge took out his identification, and the man squinted for a better look. But he stood his ground. "If you're going round back, I'm coming as well."

"Then show me the way."

There was a narrow access passage between two of the houses just down the way, and the two men walked swiftly toward it, went through the dimly lit, littered area, and came out on a scruffy alley where the back gardens of the next street over stopped only four or five feet from those belonging to Betty Turnbull's street. They quickly identified the house they were after, and the neighbor didn't hesitate. He forced the wooden door in the garden wall and dashed inside, avoiding the clutter, the chicken coop, the small shed, and a line for hanging out the wash.

He was about to crash through the kitchen door as well, when Rutledge stopped him. He reached out, touched the door latch, and it swung inward.

The man looked at him, about to step over the threshold.

"No. A matter for the police." And Rutledge moved ahead of him, working slowly through the small ground-floor rooms, then starting up the stairs. The neighbor followed at his heels, refusing an order to stay in the kitchen.

The first bedroom door they came to was shut, and Rutledge opened it. The mattress was rolled up, sheets covering the furniture. Unused.

They opened the other, and behind Rutledge, the other man drew in a harsh breath. "Oh, my God."

She was lying in bed, her hands composed, quiet, seemingly at rest. Except for the large feather pillow that covered her face and head. The room was tidy, as if her killer had removed any sign of a struggle. But for the pillow, still in place, she might have been sleeping.

The neighbor rounded on Rutledge. "I should have taken you to Constable last night. This would never have happened—I should have known what I'd seen—"

"Be quiet," Rutledge cut him short impatiently. "What's your name, man?"

"Waggoner. Bruce Waggoner—"

Rutledge said, "Go and find the Constable. Or I'll leave you here to guard the body and go myself."

The man took a last look at Betty Turnbull's body lying there. "Yes. All right, then."

"And this is an order. Don't spread the news on

your way, do you hear me? No one but the Constable is to be told."

But Waggoner was already hurrying away. Rutledge heard his boots clattering down the steps. He was out the front door, banging it shut behind him. Rutledge winced.

He stayed where he was. The tidiness of the murder was unexpected. Most killers left the body as it lay, any overturned furniture where it had fallen. Someone had taken time to look around him—or her—and removed all traces that anyone else had been there. Except for that pillow still across the face.

In spite of the curtains, the morning sun was bright in the room, casting pale squares of light across the floor. Warming the room, giving it life.

The fittings were cheap, the bed brass, the curtains white with purple tulips splashed across the broad hem in a clumsy but pretty enough pattern. The bedspread was lavender with a scalloped edge in white, not always even, and the covered chair in the corner was the same shade as the tulips. He'd noticed a sewing machine in the vacant room, and he wondered if she had made the curtains, spread, and slipcover herself, to create what she saw as a charming bedroom.

Then, leaving her there, he quickly went to the third door at the top of the stairs, and found what must have been the room taken by Sam Milford. No one would have thought to look for him here, in this run-down street.

It too was tidy, the bed made, the top of the tall chest empty of personal belongings like purse, watch, or cuffs. No shaving gear on the table by the bed, nothing in the wardrobe but a single shirt that looked as if it might have fit a larger man.

"He didna' truly live here," Hamish commented.

"No. It was simply a place to spend the night. Then why did she have to die?"

"Ye ken, a woman might think of tidying the room after killing her. No' a man."

And the set of the mind behind that tidying worried Rutledge. Steady, organized . . .

In many ways, the same kind of thinking that had gone into Milford's death. Just the right distance above the River Dee to make certain the body would fall into the water. And the coolness of the mind that risked the possibility that a flailing man about to plummet to his death might take his killer with him as he was pushed off the horse trace.

But what drove it, that mind?

Too soon to make a guess at that, he told himself, and set about a swift but methodical search of the room.

If anything had been there, Sam Milford—or Mrs. Turnbull's killer—had taken it.

He remembered that the bedroom light had remained on, while he stood on the road and looked up at it. Was the killer searching even then? Or finishing his neat arrangement of the room?

He felt a wave of regret. He had seen the light—he should have knocked. Even if Mrs. Turnbull was already dead, at least it might have shaken her killer into making a mistake.

He heard the street door open and close, and stepped out to the head of the stairs. Waggoner was following a uniformed Constable up them, a thin man with a long thin face and bony nose.

He didn't speak until he was on a level with Rutledge, looking up at the man from London from beneath the brim of his helmet. "Sir," he said. "Constable Drew. You're Scotland Yard?"

Rutledge took out his identification and held it up. "Yes. I'm in Oswestry on other business, and called on Mrs. Turnbull yesterday. She was alive and well then, and not under duress of any kind. I'd say she was killed around ten last night. At any rate, after she'd retired to bed. In there."

He gestured toward the bedroom, and Constable

Drew stepped in there. "There's no doubt she's dead," he commented, "but why didn't he take away the pillow to be sure?"

"Perhaps he did, and then decided to put it back in place. Not on the floor. Nothing appears to be disturbed, but I have a feeling the room was thoroughly searched."

Drew had stepped to the side of the bed, lifting the pillow and looking down into the dead face. "Why was that, sir?" He gently put the pillow back where he'd found it.

"Because the room is neat. Not even the bedspread is disturbed. She might have hung up her clothing, but her comb and brush are too perfectly placed. The chair is in the same position it always was, in the small dents in the carpet it had made through years of someone sitting there. Look at her bedroom slippers. Side by side just under the bed. The lamp is just where it must have been. And yet a struggle must have taken place. I met her, I can't picture her dying quietly."

Constable Drew followed Rutledge's pointing finger around the room, taking in what the other man had noticed. And what he himself had not. He shot a quick glance toward Rutledge, then went back to the exhibits before him.

"What was he looking for, sir? If he was searching?"

"That I don't know. There isn't much here that would entice anyone bent on theft, and the rest of the house is tidy as well. But there on the mantelpiece are several cheap plates with pretty pictures on them. To someone desperate for money, they might possibly bring in a little. What's more—see there—she's still wearing her wedding ring. If I'm not mistaken, that's gold. It would bring in much more."

"Mr. Waggoner tells me she was a widow, sir. He and his wife have known her for a number of years. Said she was quiet, a good neighbor. And that she'd recently taken in an occasional lodger. In fact he believes there was a man staying here in the past week or so. Could he have done this?"

"That man, sadly for my own inquiry, is already dead. He was killed a fortnight ago. His room is just there."

The Constable went to see, and came back to the bedroom. "Didn't leave much behind."

"No. He had personal business in Oswestry, and I think he was concerned about spending more than he could afford, while here. And Mrs. Turnbull was happy to have the money." *No Oswestry hotel bills to explain to Ruth or her cousin and husband,* he added to himself.

"If *he* wasn't the killer, sir, could he have been the

cause? Someone came here looking for him, and she was in the way?"

"Possibly, unless of course her killer already knew that the lodger was dead. Or it could have been someone else altogether, also looking for the lodger."

Waggoner, hanging back during the discussion between the two policemen, said, "I don't care what you think—he couldn't have come to kill Betty. It has to be the lodger, one way or another. I've told you, we've known her for years, and there was nothing in her life that would have led to *this*."

"I'll have to report this to the station," Constable Drew said, turning to Rutledge. "Unless you wish to lead the inquiry, sir?"

"No. Treat it as a local matter for the moment. Until we have more to be going on with."

Drew left then. Waggoner, lingering near the stairs, said, "I can't believe this has happened. Yes, there have been fights on the road, mostly young layabouts who have no work and no one to manage them. My neighbor two houses down is nasty when he's got a skinful. Still, it's a quiet enough place on the whole."

"Did you ever meet her lodger?"

"No. Saw him a time or two. Little man. Carried himself well, kept himself to himself."

"How did he get around?"

"Walked. Like the rest of us. I have a bicycle, but I don't like leaving it in town and having it pinched."

"Where do you work?"

"Me? Stevedore before I met my wife. Carpenter now. She'd come to Liverpool to visit her granny, and I lived next door."

Liverpool. That was where Roddy's mother had come from.

Waggoner wiped his hand across his mouth. "Must we stand here where we can see her? It's obscene, her lying there with the pillow on her head."

An Inspector Preston came back with Constable Drew, a doctor, and two other Constables who were already knocking on neighboring doors.

Rutledge repeated what he'd told Drew, and let them get on with it. From the doorway of the bedroom, he heard the doctor confirm that Mrs. Turnbull was deceased, and that the time of death was the previous evening. "Nine? Ten?"

Waggoner volunteered that she had a brother living nearby, saving Rutledge from having to explain how he'd found the farm.

When the formalities were finished, Rutledge said to Preston, "I have other business in Llangollen. But I'd like a copy of your report sent to Sergeant Gibson at the Yard. In the event what happened here has any bearing on the death I'm investigating in Wales."

The two men walked out together, and out of hearing of the men busy in the room upstairs, Rutledge gave a brief outline of his search for Milford's killer. He carefully omitted details that he was not ready to share. Tildy's parentage for one.

Preston didn't speak until he was finished, then asked Rutledge, "Why should this missing child be on my patch? If she was abducted by someone who had seen her in the pub, she might be anywhere. Wales. Ireland. Scotland."

Rutledge was watching two small boys who were examining his motorcar with awe, touching the body, peering into the driver's side to look at the dials. Beyond them in the road, a cluster of neighbors, drawn by the arrival of the police, silently stared at the two men.

"That's what we don't know. If Milford found anything here—even believed he might have done—he kept it to himself. For one thing, he wouldn't have wanted to raise his wife's hopes. For another, he might not have known where to place his trust. He paid Mrs. Turnbull for a room. Someone might offer to pay her more to betray him. She was a convenience, in a sense, not a co-conspirator."

"There's that," Preston agreed. "All right, then. I'm needed upstairs. Keep me informed as well."

"I shall."

He watched Preston stride back inside and shut the door, then walked on to the motorcar.

Why had Betty Turnbull had to die?

If Sam Milford had indeed kept everything close to his chest, then his secrets had died with him. She should have been safe enough.

Had her killer taken anything? Or was he afraid of something *she* knew, or may have guessed?

He stood by the motorcar, staring up at the house. He'd watched that light in the bedroom window go out. The killer was very likely still there, seeing to the room. And afterward, searching Milford's.

Hamish said, "Ye ken, her death might ha' no connection wi' yon lodger. She could ha' been killed for ither reasons entirely."

And that was quite true. He had to keep that in mind. It was one of the reasons he hadn't wanted to take over the inquiry. Preston appeared to be a good man. Let him ferret out Mrs. Turnbull's secrets, and see what he uncovered.

Still, the niggling feeling that he'd overlooked something wouldn't go away.

He stood there, head down, staring at the withered grass beneath his feet. In his memory he examined both rooms again.

Betty Turnbull had made curtains and a chair cover and a coverlet for the bed. They weren't worn, they were fairly new. Where had she come by the money to buy the fabric? Was it the rent she had been paid?

And suddenly he knew what he'd missed. Very likely what he was looking for was in neither her room nor Milford's.

He went back to the house, took the stairs two at a time, and before Preston had even realized he was there, stepped quietly out of sight.

8

The spare room offered nothing in the way of a hiding place, except in the rolled-up mattress on the bed, and someone, Preston most likely, had already flattened it, and the drawers from the chest against the far wall had already been examined—one of them hadn't been completely closed again, a space of about half an inch showing someone had pulled it out after he himself had looked into this room.

Preston too was searching . . .

Not a man to underestimate, he warned himself as he crossed the room and lifted the pretty cover, shaped like a tea caddy, over the head of the sewing machine. It was the same dark purple cloth as the chair in her bedroom.

And there it was.

A small square of paper. Hardly noticeable among the packets of needles and pins, scissors, bobbins, and thimbles there.

He pocketed it, his back to the door, and then replaced the cover.

As he turned, Preston stepped into the room.

"You're back," he said, stating the obvious in a querying tone of voice.

"I hadn't searched the sewing machine. It was the only place I hadn't looked," he said truthfully. "It's a woman's, and a man might not have thought to look there as a hiding place. I hadn't. You?"

Preston said wryly, "No. I didn't. Any luck?"

Rutledge smiled and lifted the cover a second time. "Thimble, needle packet, a cotton reel—"

"Any other clever ideas?"

"Sadly no. But I'd noticed that she'd taken pride in her handiwork." He shrugged, a slight lift of a shoulder. "Worth a try."

"Next time, ask me to try instead. I'd appreciate it."

"Point taken," Rutledge answered, and as Preston left the doorway, he nodded to the Constable, then took his time going down the stairs and out to the motorcar. And all the way, he could feel Preston's eyes boring into his back from the bedroom window. Still wondering.

He made a point of turning the crank and driving away. The growing crowd opened their ranks to let him through, but in his mirror he saw that Preston had sent a Constable down to guard the now closed door.

He was well outside Oswestry before he pulled to the side of the road, took the small square of paper from his pocket, and unfolded it.

Inside were two postal stamps.

Under them, in small, neat handwriting, was a name, *Alyssa*, and after that, *Bed*. The rest of *Bed* had been scratched out, as if the writer was uncertain of the spelling or even of the remainder of the word. Bedford? Bedbury? Bedcock? Beddes? Beddings? Beddoes? Beddesford? Beddingham? Bedwin?

It was impossible to guess.

He held the paper upside down, then looked carefully at the reverse. But nothing leaped out at him.

Hamish said, "It could be the name of a woman she was sewing for."

True enough. And if so, it would have been left just where he'd found it, with the sewing machine.

No use to the killer, no use to him.

But he folded it again and put it safely in his notebook, before turning back to the road and carrying on toward Llangollen.

He took the road that went around the Aqueduct, to the railway station in Trefor. It had been closed the last time he was here. It had been near enough to the noon hour for the stationmaster to go home to his lunch.

He came down from the flyover and into the station yard. The platform was long and narrow, with a covering, and across the dual tracks, houses backed up nearly to the track fencing.

The stationmaster was there, this late in the afternoon. He was graying and had lost an eye, but he looked up when Rutledge stepped into the tiny waiting room. "Afternoon, sir," he said in a gruff voice.

"Afternoon," Rutledge replied affably. "I'm looking for a friend." He'd brought in the photograph without its frame. "He and I were supposed to meet at the Aqueduct. He was going one way, I another, and it was a good chance for us to spend a little time together. Haven't seen him since the war, you know. Good man in a fight. Glad to have him at my back."

Rutledge placed the photograph flat on the countertop. "His wife is worried about him. As am I. But there's no trace of him after he left Oswestry. Did he by chance come up by train?" He gave the date, gambling that he was right. "A Thursday."

"There wasn't a passenger that day, but there was the day before. The Wednesday. A short man got down. That's a Bantam uniform he's wearing in the photograph, I see. Could have been him. Nice enough, as I remember."

"Did he have a valise with him?"

"I expect he did. Most do, if they're going to the quarry works. Or the firebrick works at Ruabon. We don't run that many trains south. Unless the Family is coming up, of course." He said the word as if Rutledge should know them.

"Family?"

"Aye, there's a big house here. Handsome brick. Trefor House, it's called, but the Family seldom comes, not since the war."

"Who are they?"

A little affronted, the stationmaster said, "The Grants, of course. Bought the house in bad condition in the old Queen's time, and restored it and the grounds. The heir was killed at Passchendaele. Sad, that. He was a fine young man."

"Who is the heir now?"

"I don't know. Perhaps there isn't one. Rumor says they might put the house up for sale again. Pity, if they do. But there you are, the lad's gone, isn't he? Like so many others." He shook his head. "Flower of England, the newspapers called all those young men."

Rutledge brought the stationmaster's attention back to the photograph.

"My friend," he said, touching the edge.

"If that was your friend, aye. He went out and stood by the entrance for ten minutes or so, then came in again and asked if the branch line was running that day to the Aqueduct. But it wasn't. He then asked how far it might be to walk. I told him roughly an hour and a half. He nodded, and set out."

"And you are sure it was this man you saw?"

"I wouldn't swear to it under oath, you understand, but if you want my opinion, it was him." He regarded Rutledge for a moment. "Was it you he was expecting to meet him here?"

"I was to meet him at the Aqueduct, but he could have hoped I'd drive up here for him, once I discovered there was no train that day. Are you sure of the date?"

"Aye, that Wednesday. And you missed him?"

Rutledge said wryly, "I don't understand how I could have done. If you saw him setting out, he should have reached the Aqueduct a little before me. But then I don't know what it was that brought him to the Aqueduct in the first place. It was just convenient for me as well to meet him there. That's why I suggested it."

"He never came back here. I was on duty that night— even though there was no train coming through."

"There were no other passengers that day? Getting down—or waiting to take the train?" he asked, taking up the photograph. "Just my friend?"

"It was a quiet afternoon. Often is, this time of year." He scratched his chin. "As I recall, your friend did have a return ticket. He asked when the train left on the Thursday."

"Any visitors in the town who might have come by motorcar?"

"There was someone going up to the house earlier. My wife thought it might be regarding the sale. Likely an estate agent."

"You never saw him? No? Could your wife describe him to me?"

"I doubt she saw more than his shoulders and his hat in the motorcar. It wasn't close by, at all."

"I see," Rutledge answered. And he did. Milford wouldn't be coming back to Trefor for the return to Oswestry. Instead, he'd fallen to his death.

After leaving the station, he drove up to the Hall. It was indeed a handsome house, brick faced with white

stone. More or less an H in style and Georgian in design. Turning, he looked out. The view over the valley
was stunning.

There was no one about to ask questions regarding
an estate agent. But the house had an emptiness about
it that spoke of standing vacant for some time.

Although he walked around the house, the sense
of emptiness increased. No one on the sunny terrace,
drapes pulled to in all the rooms on the ground floor,
not even a family dog to bark at strangers straying too
close. But as he started back to the motorcar, a man in
work clothes, a pick and a spade in his hands, stepped
out of a shed. He saw Rutledge and called to him.

"Help you, sir?" His accent was Welsh.

"Good afternoon. I was told the house had a visitor
a fortnight ago. A Wednesday that would be." He gave
the date. "I'd very much like to speak to him, if he's
still here. I understand the house might be put up for
sale."

"He was only here for a quarter of an hour, at most.
Came to pick up some papers, he said. Fetched them
and left. I was working in the drive just then."

"A regular visitor?"

"Not to say regular. The Family isn't at home. But
if they need anything, they send for him to see to it. He
has a key."

"Do you know his name?"

"No, he'd never give it to the likes of me." He gave Rutledge a cheeky grin. "Nor did you."

Rutledge returned the grin. "The name is Gibson," he said, thanked the man, and walked back to his motorcar.

He made his way back to the station and the road that carried on to the Aqueduct, covering the distance that Sam Milford had walked in no time at all behind the wheel of the powerful motorcar. But as he drove, he tried to picture the man trudging along the road, perhaps looking over his shoulder in the hope of a lift from the person he was expecting to meet, or failing that, a farm cart going his way.

What had Betty Turnbull said? *A needle in the hay.*

And yet, in spite of everything, he had not only identified Sam Milford, but he'd also traced him to Crowley, then followed his movements from there all the way to the place where he'd been killed. It had taken nearly a week.

But he still didn't know why Milford had come all this way. Except for the narrowboats, there was nothing at the Aqueduct.

Milford could well have told Betty whatever he'd thought she'd accept, spinning her a tale that she believed, while keeping his real search to himself. Just as he himself had spun a tale for the stationmaster, and then put off the gardener at the Hall with a name that wouldn't mean anything to people in this part of Wales. No sense in putting the wind up if someone gossiped.

Hamish said, "Aye. But what if she'd questioned someone without telling him, and stumbled on something she shouldna' ha' discovered?"

Rutledge only had her word that they were looking for anyone with bright red hair . . .

If she did, did she tell Milford? Or use it in some other fashion that saw her murdered? Blackmail?

"It was the money she wanted. No' the information. She would take it fra' both parties."

In the silence of the motorcar, he found himself agreeing with Hamish.

Hamish said, "And what of the child?"

"Let's hope she's alive," Rutledge said grimly. "There must have been two matters on Milford's mind, in all this. Find the child, if she was still living, and once she was found—or her death acknowledged— find the person who had done this. He must have come here for one or the other reason."

Hamish said, "Ye ken, if this was no' for the child at a', if it had only to do with the man, the lass would ha' still been the lure. To bring him to a place where he could be killed."

"In which case," Rutledge said, "she's dead. No longer needed."

"Aye," Hamish replied morosely. "A killer wandering about wi' a wee lass in hand, crying for her mither, is likely to attract unwanted attention. He would ha' tired of her soon enough."

Rutledge reached the northern end of the Aqueduct and almost at once noticed the subdued atmosphere, very different from the first time he'd been there. A number of narrowboats anchored in the basin, a dark green, two less funereal black ones, a pair of reds, and a bright yellow and green. They seemed to be empty of cargo, floating high in the water today.

He left the motorcar out of sight in the trees and started past the houses, toward the shops. Clusters of people, men and women, stood closer to the crossing, in the waning sunlight near the shops, talking quietly, sometimes looking over their shoulders. Some of them stared at Rutledge as he walked by, but no one spoke or asked his business, or even met his glance.

His initial intention was to stay clear of the little shop where he'd ordered tea before, and instead try to find the old man he'd met across the Aqueduct on that first visit. He looked in the shop window to see how crowded it was, then changed his mind when he realized it was as empty today as it had been then. He went inside, shutting the door behind him.

The shopkeeper looked up, frowning.

"Good day," he said, as if he'd never seen the man in his doorway before. But Rutledge had caught the flicker of recognition before it was quelled.

The shop was empty, and Rutledge said, "No custom today?"

"The police have just left. Not even an hour ago. Everyone is on edge."

"What's happened?" He hadn't passed them on his way here. Had they turned off toward Llangollen instead of proceeding to Trefor?

At first he didn't think the man was going to answer him. Then, fiddling with the displays on either side of the register, he said finally, "There's been trouble."

"Serious trouble, if the police were called," Rutledge said easily. "I saw the narrowboats in the basin. Fighting among the men, was it?"

The shopkeeper regarded him sourly. Then he gave a little shrug. "Joseph Burton was found dead yesterday morning. Floating in the north basin." He gestured toward the door and his right. "This one."

"And who is Burton when he's at home?"

"Brother of one of the narrowboat owners." The shopkeeper glanced out at the crowd. Some were already beginning to wander away, back to their houses.

Rutledge waited.

"Walked the horse mostly. He was suspected of theft twice over. And last year, his brother threw him out. Joseph disappeared for a bit—some said he'd been taken on by the firebrick company in Trefor, then they let him go for troublemaking. Whatever the truth of it was, he was back after Boxing Day, hanging about, picking up work where he could find it." Then, as if he realized he'd said too much, he looked hard at Rutledge. "What'll you have? Besides gossip."

"Tea," he said, and then added, "a sandwich, if you have one."

"Egg?"

"That will do."

The shopkeeper set about the order, slicing bread and taking the egg salad from a heavy crock and spreading it thickly between two slices of bread. It looked dry.

"How did this man die? Was he drunk and fell into the water? What did the police have to say?" Rutledge walked over to the door, and keeping his voice merely curious, fought down his impatience.

"I was told there wasn't any marks on him, when

they pulled him out. They reckoned he'd been drunk and fell in. That was last night. Today the police came back and searched all the narrowboats, then took away Steve Fuller. I told you, Joseph worked for his brother back in the day."

"Have they indeed?" Rutledge answered, surprised. He walked over to the table where he'd sat on his first visit. "Which narrowboat is Fuller's, do you know?"

The shopkeeper brought over the sandwich and a cup of tea, setting them down without fanfare. "Yon yellow-and-green one."

He could just see it from where he was sitting.

"And what does rumor say about Fuller?"

"That he's not guilty, of course. Steve has a temper on him, right enough. And uses his fists sometimes before he uses his head. But he's no killer."

Hamish was saying quietly, "Could the woman have been wrong about Bed—?"

The two names weren't close. *Bed* versus *Bur.*

But he asked anyway. "Does Burton have a family?"

"Aye, he does. A wife. She left him some years ago."

"What is her name?"

"Here, what do you want to know for?"

"Passing the time."

"It's Hester."

Rutledge turned his attention back to the shopkeeper. Some people were beginning to make their way toward the shop. "Anyone here or across the Aqueduct by the name of Bedford? Or was it Beddoes? I didn't hear the last name clearly."

"There's none of either name here."

"I was here a week ago. Looking for a man I was to meet. He never came. Was Burton here then?"

"Likely he was. Why?"

Rutledge got up, took the photograph from his pocket, and walked to the counter. "I was searching for this man."

"Don't know him."

"You must have served him something. He walked here from the train, an hour and a half on the road. He'd have been tired and thirsty. And he'd have been looking for someone. You told me before that you hadn't seen him. But I think you did. Someone pushed him off the Aqueduct that same day—or evening. And I'll have the police back here again, if I'm not told the truth." There was steel in his voice, this time, and the shopkeeper glanced quickly at his face.

"What is this man to you?" He poked a thick finger at the photograph.

"He arrived on a Wednesday afternoon. The station-master in Trefor remembered him. There was no train to the Aqueduct that day, and so this man walked here.

On Saturday morning he was found dead, his body in the River Dee just below the Aqueduct. According to the doctor who examined him, he'd fallen from a great height. That pointed to the Aqueduct. The horse walk. It happened a fortnight ago. And no one up here admits to having seen him, spoken to him, watched him walk out across the Aqueduct."

"Here, I don't want any trouble—"

"You knew he'd died. The account of finding him in the river would have reached here. You were aware of it when I came here the first time asking questions. And you lied to me then. The police will want to know why. They will be asking if he fell—or was pushed. I have every reason to believe he was killed, that he didn't fall by accident. It's your choice. Talk to me—or explain yourself to them."

"I want no trouble—" he repeated.

"I am in a position to make a great deal of trouble for you. Ask the police to search this shop and your house for evidence—take you in for questioning. Speak to everyone who was here when that man fell—keep the narrowboats here indefinitely until the police are satisfied that they have their man. For this killing, and Joseph Burton's."

"You can't do that."

"I'm afraid I can. If you don't believe me, watch."

There was a heavy silence.

Rutledge said nothing, his gaze firmly on the shop-keeper as the man silently argued with himself. In the end, the threat won.

"All right. I'll admit to seeing him. The man in that photograph was here. He came in late on that Wednesday afternoon, ordered an ale, then asked if he could leave his valise behind the counter while he looked for someone. He wouldn't tell me who it was. Just that he wanted to speak to him about a personal matter. He finished his ale and went out, then came back again just as I was closing up at seven. It was already dark. I asked if he'd found whoever it was he was searching for. He told me he hadn't, that the man was expected in the next hour or so, on one of the narrowboats coming up from the south. Then he asked if there was a place where he could spend the night, since it would be too late to walk back to Trefor. I told him there wasn't, but that he could sleep on the bench back there." He turned slightly to point to a bench in the rear of the shop near the displays of boat gear. "He took his valise with him, and he left. I never saw him again."

"And that didn't worry you? You didn't wonder what had become of him?"

"When I opened the shop door Thursday morning, there was no sign of him, nothing to show that he'd slept here. I'd left a blanket on the counter—it was still there. I thought he'd found the man he was after and gone with him on the narrowboat."

"Why didn't you tell me that when I came here, asking questions?"

"That was almost a week later. You said *you* were to meet him and had missed him. But *he* was looking for someone on a narrowboat. I wasn't sure what to believe, and I didn't want any part of it."

Rutledge took a chance. "No. You lied to me, because Joseph Burton was the man my friend was hoping to meet. And you knew Burton's reputation for being a troublemaker."

"I've said—he never told me—I swear he didn't."

"But you saw them together, didn't you? As you were closing up here, and going home."

"Yes, all right. They were standing out there in the dark, talking. The two of them. Near where the Aqueduct begins. I saw money change hands. I didn't like the look of it. I was glad he hadn't come back to sleep in the shop. I didn't want to be involved."

"Change hands how?"

"That man in the photograph gave Burton money."

"When did you see Burton next?"

"Not until two or three days later. He walked in, ordered breakfast, cheeky as ever."

"And you said nothing to him about the man who had come here to talk to him? Or about someone asking questions?"

"Why should I? I told you, it was none of my affair."

"Was Burton here when I came before?"

There was a long silence. Then the shopkeeper said, "He came up behind you, when you walked down to the edge of the Aqueduct. Then went over past you. Jaunty man, dark hair."

Rutledge remembered him. He'd crossed as if accustomed to the height and the narrowness of the horse walk, as if he'd done it hundreds of times. For his brother's narrowboat. If it was Joseph Burton who had pushed Sam Milford from the Aqueduct, he'd known how to do it without falling with him.

What had Sam Milford come here to ask Joseph Burton? Had he paid him for information he believed the man possessed? And then had he been lured to his death, thinking he was with a man he could trust to help him?

Or perhaps the more pressing question was, who had sent Sam Milford here, to contact a man who had already been paid to kill him?

Was that how it had happened?

Rutledge put the photograph of Sam Milford away. "I'll speak to the police."

"Here! You said—"

"I don't think it was Steve Fuller who killed Burton. I'll tell them that. But first I want a statement from you. Now. Putting down everything you've told me."

There was an argument—the shopkeeper clearly had no wish to find himself part of a police inquiry. Rutledge wondered if he'd ever been guilty of taking smuggled goods from the narrowboat owners. But he let that go.

An hour later, the laboriously written statement folded and safely tucked into his notebook, Rutledge thanked the man and left.

He did stop at the police station in Trefor, and with the permission of Inspector Walsh, an older man with a heavy Welsh accent, he interviewed Steven Fuller.

Very little of substance came from that, except for one interesting exchange.

Fuller, slim, with thinning hair and a stoop, said, "I was never close to Joseph. He was my half brother, and we had little enough in common. Except for Mum, of course. But he was never what he might have been. Always looking for an easier way. Like his pa. I gave him work, and he stole from one of the other narrowboats. I could never prove it, but it was my reputation or his, and I let him go. Mum was all right with that, but my stepfather blamed me, not him. I avoided Joseph after that." He took a deep breath. "I'm sorry he's dead. But truth be told, I don't have to worry about him pushing me off the Aqueduct some dark night, when I don't see him coming."

Rutledge asked, "*Do* you believe he'd kill you?"

"I always had a feeling he might. I can't say why." He shook his head. "It was just a way about him. It was always there. To see what he could get away with."

"Did he come into money lately? More than he ought to have?"

"I don't know. He was always trying to borrow from Mum. But his pockets were empty when he was pulled from the basin. A shilling, a sixpence, and a ha'penny. It was all he had to his name."

"Where did he sleep? Did anyone look there?"

"The police did. It's little more than a shed, out beyond the wood. I was with the police when they searched." He grimaced. "Dreadful way to live. But any money he had slipped through his fingers like water."

"Nothing out of place?" Rutledge persisted. "Perhaps a valise you didn't recognize?"

Steve Fuller shook his head. "Just an odd bit of white cloth over Joseph's pillow. No idea where that came from. Half a circle, just lying there."

Afterward, Walsh showed Rutledge the scrap.

He fingered it, looking at the half-moon. A white scallop. And he'd swear that it would have matched the scalloped hem of Betty Turnbull's handmade coverlet.

"I'd like to keep this, if I could," he told Walsh.

The Inspector said, "It doesn't match anything in the shambles he called home. Still. To do this properly, you'll give me a receipt."

Rutledge dashed off one on the pad lying on Walsh's desk. "I don't think he killed his brother," he said as he handed the sheet to the man in front of him.

"I doubt he did it myself. Still, he told me he was always half-afraid his brother would do for him. And that's motive too. To have it over and done with, and Burton the one dead. Doctor found bruising on the back of his neck, where his head had been held underwater. Even if Fuller had tried to kill Burton, I don't see him finishing it, once the victim began to struggle. But that's for the inquest to decide."

"Any strangers about? Someone unaccounted for?"

Walsh shook his head. "No strangers about that I've been able to discover. There was a woman here the night before Burton was killed. Or so one of the women living close by the basin claimed. Glimpsed her in a window on one of the narrowboats, she said. But the boatmen swear there was only cargo aboard, headed south."

"Any truth to that?"

Walsh said, "Who knows? I wondered if she was trying to protect Steve Fuller, muddying the waters, so to speak. Mary Jones is a cousin on Fuller's mother's side." He frowned. "People come and go all the time, there at the Aqueduct. Mostly on the narrowboats, but on foot as well. And it's damned dark up there at night. Nobody saw anything when Burton was killed. That could be true—or not. Still, no one has come forward."

"At the inquest, will you ask that Fuller be bound over for trial?"

"There's not much choice in the matter, is there?"

Rutledge went back to the Aqueduct, and with the help of the very reluctant shopkeeper, he found Mary Jones.

She was more respectable than he'd thought, from Walsh's description. She was tall and slender, on the edge of pretty, with dark hair and a look in her dark gray eyes that he'd seen many times before, the speculative look of a woman who sees any man as a chance to better herself. But she held herself well, and faced him squarely, once he'd identified himself as a policeman.

When he asked about the woman she claimed to have glimpsed, she lifted her chin. "I'm no liar," she told him flatly. "I saw her face at that window. She lifted the lace curtain, like, and looked out. But there were people about, and she was gone in a flash. That's what I saw. Like it or leave it."

"Which boat?"

"That I can't tell you. I wasn't paying attention until I saw her face. One of the black ones, maybe."

"Did you see this woman again?"

"No."

"Did anyone see your cousin kill his half brother?"

"Steve was afraid of Joseph. But I can't see him trying to kill him. He's not got the nerve."

"Do you think Joseph ever killed anyone?"

She considered her answer for a moment. "If he ever did, he'd make certain not to be caught."

Thanking her, Rutledge spent another hour finding the owners of the narrowboats. But to a man they swore they hadn't brought a woman with them on board.

Rutledge had a feeling that the man in one of the red boats was lying, boldly facing his wife down as she listened to the question. "Whoever said she was on my boat," he declared, "is either drunk or malicious."

"It was another woman who saw her," Rutledge informed him. "Why would she lie?"

"Stirring up trouble, at a guess." He grinned down

at his wife. "She'd have my head—or worse—if she caught me bringing another woman here."

"You're chasing a wraith," Hamish told him as Rutledge walked away. "If she was here at all, she's no' here now. D'ye truly think she's the murderer?"

He had no answer to that.

In the end, he drove back to Oswestry in the dark, and in his hotel room looked again at the small white half circle he'd brought with him.

Before going to bed, he went back to the Turnbull house in the night, and with his torch shielded, matched the small bit of cloth to the coverlet.

Except for the edges, which would have been sewn under with tiny, almost invisible stitches to hold it in place, like all the others in the pretty little pattern, the half circle was a perfect fit. Type of cloth, quality and thickness, shade. It was all there.

Looking around, Rutledge found a scrap box in the front room, next to what must have been Betty Turnbull's favorite chair. It was wood, well used, and had her initials carved into the dark top. When he knelt beside it and opened it, he found half a dozen more such bits of cloth inside. And purple and lavender as well as other colors.

He hadn't seen it earlier—he'd left the downstairs

to the local police. But the killer, searching for something, had discovered it, and on a whim, taken at least one bit from it. And then, on another whim—or on purpose—he or she had left it on a dead man's pillow up at the Aqueduct.

Rutledge emptied the box, then returned the contents as tidy as they had been when he'd lifted the top.

The killer, he thought, knew he was being hunted.

Betty would surely have told him about the policeman from London . . .

And now he, Rutledge, was being played with.

9

Rutledge was tired, late as it was, but he sat at the small table in his room that served as a desk and added what he'd learned at the Aqueduct to his notebook. Staring at what he'd written, he was all too aware of what he was facing now.

Milford's killer had dealt with the two people he had been forced to use to bring the former Bantam to him. He'd left them alive as long as no one found or questioned them.

Once Rutledge had spoken to Betty Turnbull, her fate had been sealed, and Burton's as well. They had to die, because they had somehow communicated with the killer. And knew enough about him—or her—to be a danger.

He took out the scrap of cloth again and moved it

about in his fingers, thinking how much easier police-work would be if bits of evidence could speak.

What could this one tell him? He lifted it and smelled it. No scent on it. Just the dry odor of clean cloth. Nothing that might have been Macassar oil or French perfume to point to a man or a woman. No cigarette smoke lingering in the tiny pattern of squares that had been produced by a weaving machine as the cotton was made into a running bolt of cloth.

Nothing at all, in fact.

He put it away again, left his notebook on the table beside his fountain pen, and undressed for bed.

Tomorrow was another day—but he had no new leads to follow.

Only what a canny woman had hidden in her precious sewing machine.

The morning dawned gray, heavy clouds rolling in from the west, sweeping over the Welsh mountains and sliding down into Oswestry and other border towns.

These Marches, the towns that kept guard on the border between England and Wales, had seen a great deal of fighting over the centuries. The Welsh had been hard to tame, and Welshmen like Llewellyn and Glendower had kept the English on their toes.

He remembered tales he'd been told once in South Wales, how the Welsh had watched their English invaders build an impregnable ring of castles to contain their warring neighbor. And when a castle was finished, the Welshmen had swarmed down out of the mountains and taken it over, turning the tables on their invaders.

He was thinking about that at breakfast when Inspector Preston came to the door of the dining room, hesitated a moment, and then crossed to his table.

"Good morning," he said briskly, helping himself to a chair. "Rumor whispered that you were back in Oswestry."

"So I am," Rutledge said, and waited.

"What are you after?"

"Information, mostly. Any news to pass on about the late Mrs. Turnbull?"

Preston stretched his legs and sighed. "To be honest? No. Nothing. As one of my Constables told me this morning, it was as if she had tidily killed herself, leaving nothing to disturb my inquiry. Even replacing that pillow over her face, once it was done, to prevent my men from being unsettled when they came into her room."

"Your Constable might well be right," Rutledge agreed.

"And you, in your wanderings. What did you find out?"

"I went to Trefor. And the Aqueduct. It appears that the person who might well have pushed Sam Milford over the edge of the horse walk was himself found dead just before I got there. Apparent drowning, until the doctor found bruising on the back of the victim's neck, where he'd been held down. No proof, you understand, that Burton *was* the killer. Still, he was one of the last people seen with Milford, and he's a known troublemaker, always in need of money. If offered enough, he could well have turned to murder. Inspector Walsh had taken the dead man's half brother into custody. But I can almost promise you he had nothing to do with it. A motive, yes—he admitted to that. It's my view that Joseph Burton was killed by the same person who smothered Betty Turnbull in her bed. It's likely that both victims could have identified him— or at least pointed us in the right direction, if we'd known what to ask them."

"And so you've left me and this Inspector Walsh a body each, and nowhere to turn for answers. Not very kind of you, is it?"

"I'd like very much to have those answers for my own inquiry."

Preston studied him. "You're an odd bird."

"How so?" He finished his tea and pushed the cup away.

"There's something you haven't told me. About this business."

"What makes you think that?" Rutledge parried.

"I don't know. There was Mrs. Turnbull lying on her bed, and you went haring off to Wales, pursuing Milford while you had a warmer body to hand. What took you there?"

"The way Milford died."

"And what was he doing there?"

"Ah, now that's the mystery, my friend. I don't know. I wish I did." He looked around the room, but there was no one close enough to overhear. "A year ago, the Milfords lost a child."

"That's a sad business." Preston nodded. "Turned his mind, did it?"

"It's still possible she's not dead," Rutledge replied. "You assumed she was, as I had done. But no, she was taken by a stranger. As far as we know. Neither she nor her body has been found. I'm convinced that Milford was searching for her. Or her captor. Both, I should think. He talked to people, and either he was led to the Aqueduct on purpose, to put him where he could more easily be killed—or he discovered something that took him there."

"You're saying that he might never have traced his daughter after all. That he was killed to stop him from getting too close with his search."

"Sadly, that could be the case." He rubbed his eyes. He hadn't slept well the previous night.

"Poor sod." Preston moved the place settings about in front of him. "You think the child is dead. That she served her purpose, and was dispatched."

"Or she's out there somewhere, and if Milford can't find her, I must. Either way, dead or alive. Because if I find her, it's possible I will also find her father's killer."

But Sam Milford hadn't been her father . . .

Preston rose. "I don't envy you. But I have nothing to give you. Not a shred of evidence that would lead me to my victim's killer."

"There's the old hill fort on the edge of the city. Any recent bodies found out there that might have a bearing on what I'm doing?" It was an outside chance. He'd had his fill of prehistoric ruins on the Marlborough plain in Wiltshire, he didn't relish searching another one. Still, he couldn't ignore it.

Preston shook his head. "Nothing that couldn't be fixed with a warning. Popular in summer with lads stealing cigarettes and giving them a try."

He was about to turn away.

Rutledge stopped him. "By the way. Do you know anyone called Alyssa?"

"Alyssa? That's an old name, I think? Something my grandmother might have been called instead of Alice. You might ask a Rector or sexton about that. Or search the churchyards yourself." His gaze sharpened speculatively at Rutledge. "Is that the child's name?"

"She was—is—called Matilda. No, Alyssa is a name I recently came across. I don't know that it has any significance at all."

"I've spoken to Mrs. Turnbull's family, hoping to find something I could use. Not an Alyssa among them. But our agreement stands, I think. We share what we find. However tentative it might be."

"Yes." But Rutledge said nothing about the scallop in his notebook as Preston nodded curtly and walked away.

He was climbing the stairs to his room when something Preston had said stopped him halfway.

Search the old churchyards . . .

It had been more a taunt than a suggestion. But it was worth considering. If nothing else, one of the old stones might yield a surname. And the gravestones wouldn't hurry back to Preston bearing tales of what the London man was searching for . . .

He took the remaining steps two at a time and fetched his coat, hat, and gloves from his room.

Rutledge began with St. Oswald's. A handsome church surrounded by its churchyard, down a street of shops and houses. While the grass under his feet was wet, the day had brightened and warmed considerably, toying with spring. As he quartered the ground, trying to read the headstones and the table tomb inscriptions, many of them dark with age and lichen invasions, he began to think he was wasting his time. There were nearly as many Welsh names here, he realized, as English, a reflection of the town's troubled past—invaded and conquered, borders shifting with each newcomer, half destroyed by war and fire and finally, Cromwell's depredations. Oswestry seemed to have lost its sense of self and was still trying to make the best of it. So unlike Shrewsbury, with its great Abbey and castle, or Ludlow, with its half-timbered houses settled below the castle's ridge.

In some of the grave rectangles, daffodil tips were beginning to push up through the wet earth. Tiny, green, and fragile. He walked carefully, making a point not to step on any of them.

He'd nearly given up when he saw a smaller headstone half-hidden behind two large table tombs to a Davies, *père et fils*.

Too small to matter, he told himself, but he squatted on the damp ground, careful of the edges of his coat, and looked at what was written there. But it was nearly undecipherable. He took off his gloves and with his fingernail, scraped at the shallow letters until some semblance of shape began to appear.

BELOVED

He kept working.

WIFE AND MOTHER

DEPARTED THIS LIFE 2 APRIL, 1861

He had to pull a handful of grass away to see what followed.

And there it was.

ALYSSA BED—

The rest of the name—just as on the square of paper he'd found in Betty Turnbull's sewing machine—was impossible to read.

He felt a sense of elation, standing up, his cramped legs complaining, and dusting his hands before pulling his gloves over his cold fingers once more.

But what did this grave mean? What had it to do with the murder of three people, and the disappearance of Tildy Milford?

Hamish didn't speak. And he himself was at a loss.

He squatted once more, giving the sunken headstone and grave all his attention. And then, finally, he saw it, a darker line that wasn't grass or earth.

Taking a deep breath, he pulled off his gloves again, but he had to dig his nails in to bring any force to bear on whatever it was. And then, up it popped, as if he'd stumbled on the right way to wriggle it out.

It was a packet made of oiled cloth.

He opened it to find a slim leather case of the kind that would fit in a man's pocket, in which he might carry four cigars for later use. Brown, supple, of good quality leather properly dressed.

Why would anyone leave a relatively new cigar case in the grave of a woman dead for sixty years?

He lifted the top, but the leather case was empty.

Was this how Betty Turnbull and whoever was hunting Sam Milford communicated? He could leave money in here—or instructions. She could leave answers and information. It was safe enough, surely.

Whoever had put the case here had had to improvise. There had been no time to set up a better system. One could buy such a case and the oiled cloth anywhere.

Rising to his feet again, he could see that he was now visible from the street beyond the churchyard wall.

Had Betty stood in a shop window across the way, her curiosity getting the better of her, and watched to see who came to Alyssa's grave?

Was that why she had to die?

But how had this person contacted her in the beginning? A sheet of paper slipped under the door in the middle of the night? Aware that she had just taken in a lodger and therefore might be interested in other ways to make money? It was not a very efficient method, but then finding a trustworthy collaborator was never easy, and there would still be uncertainty, suspicion. It was the nature of conspiracy.

He was still holding the cigar case. Turning it over, he looked for initials. But there were none. Whoever had left this hidden wouldn't have been so careless as to have left a case with a crest or initials or a firm's symbol embossed on it.

Looking down at it, he frowned.

Was this the first personal clue to the identity of a killer? The brand of cigar he sometimes smoked? The case he carried them in? Or a woman's father might have smoked . . .

It was not a cheap brand. Edwardian. Grenadiers, he thought, judging the case.

Still frowning, he sniffed the interior. He'd been

right. Good tobacco scent still lingered in the leather. Cuban, possibly. He had friends who smoked them.

Slipping the top back down over the bottom to close the case, he put it in his coat pocket, then set about tidying up the narrow crack where it had been hidden. When he was satisfied that no one strolling by to keep an eye on the grave would notice anything missing, he walked away, going around the church to the intersecting street. Then he continued briskly to the hotel from there.

But where to go from Oswestry?

Hamish had the answer. "Back to the lass in Shrewsbury. Dora."

Passing a tobacconist on his way back to his motorcar, he stepped inside.

It was like many in London and elsewhere: dark woods, wares spread out in an array of containers so that a man might browse before choosing. Small as it was, there were three racks of pipes, one of them holding elegant Meerschaum from Turkey, delicate carved faces and designs that caught the eye. There were humidors for sale, instruments for cutting, and an array of cases.

The air was heady with the scent of tobacco and a hint of something else, a different world far away.

The owner stepped out from behind a curtain leading to the rear of the shop, smiled at Rutledge, and asked how he could assist him. Then noticing his particular interest in the cases, he moved toward them as well.

"We happen to have an excellent selection at the moment," the owner was saying.

But Rutledge took out the one he'd found in the churchyard. "What can you tell me about this?"

"The case? Yes. Excellent leather, calf of course, and quite a nice color. We have some similar to that, as well as more exotic leathers."

"Can you tell where it was made? Who might have sold it?"

He was still fingering the leather. "While it's a fine maker, of course, it's widely available." Handing it back to Rutledge, he added, "This one is plain, but we offer a service if the buyer wishes to have the case initialed or a crest put on. During the war it was popular for young officers to have their regimental badge on the case. I've had them ordered by parents as well, to be gifted to the young man."

But no one had done that here.

Rutledge thanked him, and left.

Rutledge went out of his way to make a stop at the dairy farm. But Ted Brewster, he was told by a woman whose eyes were red from crying, was seeing to funeral arrangements for his sister.

He didn't leave a message. Thanking her, he went back across the muddy yard, listening to the lowing of a single cow that had wandered up to the milking gate, her dark brown eyes fixed on the shed on the far side.

It was late when he reached Shrewsbury, the town's lights a beacon as he came in from Oswestry, crossing over the Welsh Bridge after long stretches of dark and twisty roads. Before finding a room, he swung through the now-familiar streets to where Dora Radley lived.

The house was dark, no lamps showing. But he had waited outside as Betty Turnbull had been murdered and her house ransacked. He would not risk this again.

Leaving the motorcar a little way down the tree-lined street, he walked back to the house and knocked at the door.

No one came to answer the summons.

He tried twice more.

And finally, a lamp bloomed in what appeared to be the stair hall. The lovely colored glass came to life, and he could hear someone turning the latch.

The door opened a crack. "Alex? Is anything wrong?" And then she saw the black shape on her doorstep and said sharply, "Oh—!" She hurriedly began to shut the door.

Rutledge said quickly, "Mrs. Radley, it's Ian Rutledge. I need to speak to you, please. It's rather urgent."

"Rutledge—? Yes, yes. Will tomorrow do? I've had a difficult day, and I was hoping for a quiet evening."

"I am so sorry to be calling at this hour," he said, keeping his voice polite, apologetic. "I've just arrived from Oswestry, you see. And I think it best if we talk now. Tonight. It's rather urgent." He'd used the same words before, but he repeated them now.

She opened the door a little, and he could see her features, and how her eyes shone in the light reflected from the lamp to the door and back to her face. He realized she must have been crying.

"Have you found Matilda? Is that it?" She tried to imbue her voice with a measure of enthusiasm, but it rang false.

"No. Sadly."

Falling silent, Dora looked down. He realized that while she was fully dressed, as far as he could tell, her slim feet were bare beneath the dark blue leather slippers.

Resignation in her voice and face, she said, "Give me ten minutes, please." And this time she shut the door before he could respond.

He stayed where he was, on the step by the door, waiting with what patience he could muster. Five minutes passed, then another five, and he began to wonder if she had succeeded in putting him off until morning.

Rutledge was on the point of knocking again when the door opened almost under his hand.

Her hair was dressed properly, and there were stockings and shoes on her feet.

She led him into the parlor, turning up a lamp as she did, then sat down across from the chair she'd offered him.

With the curtains drawn against the night, the fire dying back in the grate, and only one lamp lit, there was an oddly intimate feeling to the room. But he thought she was trying to hide the ravages of tears, unaware of how the scene might appear to him.

"I will tell you that I had to cope with a very difficult death today," she began firmly. "And if your reasons for being here are not as urgent as you say, I will leave you to show yourself out."

Earlier, she had helped him for Sam Milford's sake. But she owed Rutledge nothing more now, and he wasn't completely certain she was even in danger. Still. He dared not risk walking away without a warning.

He chose his words carefully. "I have news as well,

and equally difficult to pass on. But for your own safety, I must."

"But you said that Matilda hasn't been found?"

"If you recall, I asked you for a contact in Oswestry. I didn't want to go to the police, I didn't want the local people to begin searching on their own, and possibly at cross purposes."

"Yes, yes, I told you to try the Brewster farm." She was impatient.

"As I did. It was too far from the town to be useful to me, but Brewster in turn passed me to his sister Betty. I must ask you, did you send Milford to Brewster?"

"Of course. I don't know anyone else in that town. And I knew him through someone at the orphanage— another worker there. It was all I could do for either of you."

"Milford found an ally in Betty Turnbull. Brewster's sister, the one who lives in the town. Evidently she helped him search for Tildy or her captors. And Milford paid her for that. As he should have done. Unfortunately, either he was seen in the town, or someone was watching his movements from the start. But that person began paying Betty as well, to report whatever it was Milford was doing, what success he had, even where he might search next. I can't prove it, but I believe that whoever it was used Betty Turnbull to guide Milford north to what was to be his death at the Aqueduct."

She had listened, but she hadn't really understood what he was telling her. Still wrapped in her grief for the death earlier in the day, she said, "That sounds rather far-fetched. Guesswork, leading yourself to the answers you need."

"Is it so far-fetched?" He kept his gaze on her face. "Betty Turnbull was killed while I was in Oswestry. Someone came into her house, smothered her in her bed, and searched everywhere for something. Whether he found it or not, I don't know. Still, there was nothing in the house to help the police with their inquiries." He wasn't ready to tell her what he'd discovered.

Horror had spread across her face as she listened, erasing the grief and stress as he watched.

"Dear God. Are you—are you trying to tell me that I had a part in that poor woman's death? Because I sent you and Sam Milford to her brother?"

He hadn't meant that at all. He looked down, realized that he was still holding his hat in his hand. He set it on the table at his elbow, buying himself a little time.

"No—in no way are you responsible for what happened. It's just that I'm worried. I have no real reason to believe that Mrs. Turnbull's killer knows about you.

But I was there in Oswestry when she was killed, and it has put me on my guard. I want you to be on yours as well. It will do no harm, you know."

She stared at him, still horrified. "I hardly know anything about you. You come here at this hour of night, talking about murder and killers, telling me that I could be in some danger—how am I to judge whether any of this is true or not? I tried to help you, for Sam— for Mr. Milford's—sake. Because I believed he might have wanted me to. And instead, you *threaten* me—"

"It isn't a threat, it's a warning. I'm Scotland Yard, Mrs. Radley. You have only to speak to Inspector Carson, if you aren't convinced of that."

Shaking her head, she said, "I don't know what to think or to believe." Biting her lip, she looked down at her hands. Beginning to cry in spite of her determination not to, she added, "I've had enough of death today. One of our little girls died. She'd never been strong, but we thought—we hoped—" Struggling to regain her control, she rose and hurried out of the room.

He sat there, waiting. Not wanting to leave her in this state, not sure where to find her brother at this hour.

Ten minutes later she came back. A little more composed. And a faint hint of whisky or brandy on her breath as she spoke.

"I'd hoped you'd left. Very well. You have warned me, Inspector. I don't quite know what to do with that information. But I thank you. Now please have the courtesy to go."

Rutledge said, "I have to know. Has anyone else asked you about Sam Milford?"

"I don't know. A woman at the center where I help with the children. I'd brought him there a time or two. She asked if I thought he might be interested in adopting a child. Oh, and there was a man in the tea shop where Mr. Milford and I stopped one day. I went in there again, on my own, and he was there as well. He asked if the gentleman I'd been with was once with the Bantams. He thought perhaps he knew him. But when I gave him a name, he frowned, shook his head, and said something like, 'Oh, I'm glad I didn't speak. I'd taken him for an old school chum.'"

"On that earlier visit, did Milford see this man?"

"I don't—well, he must have done, of course."

"And he didn't appear to recognize the other man?"

"If he did, he never indicated that he had."

"Can you describe him, please?"

She seemed flustered by the question. "I—I think he was quite ordinary. Dark, I believe? Pleasant. Perhaps in his middle thirties? Medium height, as I recall. I don't know that I would recognize him on the street, if I should see him again." Her eyes grew wide. "*Should* I need to recognize him? Are you saying I ought to be wary of him?"

"I don't know. But yes, to be safe, it would do no harm to avoid him."

"Oh, dear God. I shan't feel *safe* anywhere now. I've done nothing to deserve this, surely?"

And yet she had unwittingly sent Milford to Brewster. It was at least possible that he'd been followed. All the way to Mrs. Turnbull's house.

Hamish startled him, commenting, "What else has she done, unaware?"

That was the crux of the matter. Rutledge didn't know. He couldn't protect her from a threat he wasn't aware of.

Trying to help her as best he could, he said, "The police can offer you protection."

"Oh, yes, and have my neighbors wondering what I might have done, to attract the notice of the police?" She tried to make him understand. "I'm a young war widow, Inspector. I have to be circumspect. At church on Sundays, working with the children, at social gatherings, I have to know my place. I mustn't speak to another woman's husband in certain ways. I must be sure not to shake hands too firmly or with any warmth. I mustn't look too closely at a man, or seem too interested in him. I must not seem too forward or vivacious or laugh too much at something he says. It's quite difficult. And here I've entertained a visitor late at night. You've been here before. There will be questions about that, but I shall have to tell people that you were a cousin, traveling to London or Chester, bringing me family news. I don't like to lie. But I shall have to. The police will only make matters worse."

He was taken aback, the unexpected attack leaving him momentarily speechless.

Then he said, rising, "I'm sorry. It was my intention to do what my experience dictated. To let you know that you must be on your guard. I've done that. I'll leave quietly. If you need to speak to me, I'll come to your brother's house or office. It will be for the best."

"Thank you."

He retrieved his hat, walked to the door, and stepped out into the night. Standing well away from the step, he said, "Good night," and turning, walked briskly down to the street without looking back. The door was already closed behind him. He kept going until he'd come to his motorcar.

Later, in his spartan room at the hotel, he stood by the window looking down at the street.

Hamish said, "D'ye believe her?"

"Yes."

"And yon man in the tea shop?"

"Milford didn't take note of him. But if he didn't know the kidnapper, he could have been sitting five feet from the man without realizing who he was." Turning from the window, he began to pace, thinking.

"What's behind this whole affair? A child's abduction. Three murders. If the point was to destroy Sam Milford, the killer is finished. His intention carried out. If he was unaware that the child wasn't Milford's, then she was merely a pawn. To make him suffer, then let him die."

"Why no' let him live on, wi' the knowledge that yon lass was oot there somewhere, and he couldna' save her or change what was happening to her for the rest of her life?"

Was she loved? Was she cared for? Was she suffering too? That would haunt any father.

But Sam Milford was made of sterner stuff. He was actively looking for that child or whoever had taken her. And so he posed a threat that had to be dealt with.

What had he done, to be taunted in such a way? What sadistic pleasure had been taken from this tragedy?

Hamish said, "There's the dead man's sister. She didna' have any love for her brother."

Rutledge stopped in midstride.

There had been talk of an unknown woman in one of the narrowboats, just before Joseph Burton was drowned.

The bit of scalloped cloth on the dead man's pillow.

All this time, he'd been looking for a man. For Tildy's natural father. For her kidnapper.

What if from the start, Milford hadn't confided in his wife about his search because he feared that Tildy had been taken by his own sister . . .

Rutledge had no idea what she looked like, or where to find her. Or even if she was still alive. Hastings hadn't been very sure of that himself, and he was her solicitor.

The question was, could Milford's sister smother a woman in her bed? Drown a man in the narrowboat basin? Could she kill her own brother?

He couldn't answer that until he found her.

He had to start all over again, change everything he'd thought he'd known about this entire inquiry.

If only to rule her out.

There was no going forward until he did.

10

The best source of information for the last known whereabouts of Susan Milford was the family solicitor, Hastings. If her brother had known how to find her, if they had stayed in touch, that connection had died with him.

Hastings was in this morning. He was, in fact, just saying farewell to a client, a well-dressed woman wearing a fur stole and an expensive hat, as Rutledge was coming into the chambers. Without a flicker of recognition, Hastings continued his conversation with the woman as they crossed the room.

"It will be in hand, Mrs. Lacey-Smith, and I shall have the papers ready to send to you by Monday week, never fear."

She was in her forties, smiling back at him with the

assurance that she was in good hands. "Thank you, Edwin. You always know what's best." And then with a polite nod to the man standing to one side, opening the door for her to step in the street, she was gone.

Hastings's gaze was still on the door for a moment longer, then he turned briskly to Rutledge, saying, "A visit from Scotland Yard never bodes well. Come back, if you please."

Leading the way down the passage to his room, he was silent, but once he had shut the door, he added, "From your expression, I must assume there is no news of Tildy. Or if there is, it is not good."

"Nothing to report."

"Well, then, tell me what's on your mind."

And Rutledge did, giving him an abbreviated account of events both in Oswestry and at the Aqueduct. At the end of it, he touched briefly on his concern for Mrs. Radley.

"I don't know the motive of this killer. And therefore I don't know what he—or she—feels is threatening. Mrs. Radley needed to be informed."

"I know of her. I'm told she has thrown herself wholeheartedly into Good Works. I'm not convinced that that is best for her. But that's beside the point. Have you come to ask me to keep an eye on Mrs. Radley? Her solicitor is a friend, he'll work with me."

"No, I've come about another matter. It's time to find Susan Milford."

"I must tell you what I believe there as well. She is troubled. She's been a thorn in her brother's side from the start, and I have no idea just what she might be capable of, in her need to make his life as wretched as her own. That said, I strongly doubt that such a list would include kidnapping or murder."

"Nevertheless. As a policeman, I must rule her out."

Hastings toyed with the letter opener beside the blotter. "I have told you that I lost touch with her. In spite of all I could do." He paused, then went on. "I can't even be sure that she's still alive."

"It's what I do. Find people."

Hastings rose, went to the cabinet against the interior wall, and opened it. Reaching for what he wanted, he carried the box back to his desk, and there he took out a sheaf of papers.

"The tragedy of Susan Milford," he said, laying these out on the blotter. Sifting quickly through the various sheets, some of them clipped together, others only single, he began, "She was in care in Ludlow. For two years. One day she walked away from there, and although the police *searched*"—he glanced pointedly at Rutledge—"they did not for some time *find* her." He turned over another sheet. "She was discovered a year later in Betws y Coed, in Wales. That would be late summer 1917. She was brought up before the magistrate there for an unhealthy interest in the child of a neighbor."

"Unhealthy?"

"The mother believed she had designs on the child. She hovered over it, questioned her care of it, told her that she was not fit to be the mother of one so bright. But Susan told the magistrate that the mother was neglectful and uninterested in the child's well-being. As it happened, the child's maternal grandmother confessed to the magistrate that she herself had had words with her daughter over just that issue. And the case was dismissed, after the magistrate placed the child in the grandmother's charge. Shortly after that, Susan left the village. That was three and a half years ago."

"And you don't know if she is still in Wales or has gone elsewhere?"

"I have made inquiries. Her brother was in France, it was my duty to keep an eye on her. But as I've told you, these led nowhere."

"How much does she know about her brother's life?"

"Since the war? I have no idea. When he was married, she refused to be in the wedding party, and if she was in the church, no one saw her there. She came to the reception, but before she could do whatever mischief she'd intended, she was quietly taken home. She was inebriated. Or so everyone believed. I was never convinced of that, I thought it was to be her excuse afterward for her misbehavior."

"And you have no information beyond Betws y Coed?"

Hastings glanced at the papers again. "We were never sure, you see. She very likely changed her name, possibly even her appearance. There was a woman in Aberystwyth who moved on before we could make a determination. Some time later, a woman was doing clerical work for a slate mine. We couldn't be sure why she was doing such menial work, whether this meant she had run through her inheritance or simply liked what she was doing. But she too slipped away before we could be certain."

Hastings played with the letter opener for a moment. Rutledge was beginning to realize that this was a habit, a tactic, while he considered how much or how little to reveal.

"Please understand. Susan can be quite charming—she can make people like her, trust her, protect her, even, by alerting her to the fact that someone has been coming around, asking questions about her. Then they deny ever having seen her, in the misguided belief that they are helping her elude her pursuers. We couldn't prove it, of course, but we thought it was very likely that this was the case, every time we got close. God knows what tales she spins of persecution, but this is no raving lunatic, wild-eyed and wild of hair, mind you. You could pass her on the street, and take her for a young woman of good family quietly going about her own affairs."

"How *does* she live?"

"Her money was in trust until she was twenty-five. She gained full control of it two days later. Emptied her accounts, save for nominal sums that allowed them to remain open. How much or little is left of that trust only she knows."

Hamish said, "Ye ken, yon sister is devious enough to plan a murder."

Rutledge tried to ignore him, but Hamish was right. She had to be found.

"The very last time you had certain word of her was in Betws y Coed?"

"Yes. Nothing since then. Just—silence."

"Then why do you believe she might be dead?"

There was the play with the letter opener again. Then Hastings opened a desk drawer, drew out several letters, chose one of them, and put the rest back where he'd found them.

"This was after the trouble with the young woman and her baby."

He handed over an envelope. It was addressed to the solicitor and had been posted in Betws y Coed. That date matched the date on the folded sheet inside.

There was no greeting or signature. Just the dark scrawl of angry words.

Why anyone would think I could harm a child, when I was once the child harmed, I can't imagine. I am tired. My bones ache with it. There's the river here, but it's not deep enough. I'll have to find another way. Better to end it now than go on suffering. Tell Sam I didn't hate him. I just hated that they didn't love me as much as they loved him. I wasn't so different, was I? I wasn't ugly or misshapen or short or fat or even evil. I just wasn't what they'd wanted. Try living with that. It makes one bitter, it sours life after a while. So why go on with it? If I'd had any sense, I'd have done it long ago, while they were all still alive. Maybe the dead child would have been given a little affection, a candle in the church on my birthday or a thought for me at Christmas. Wouldn't Susan have loved the tree? Look, the first snow—Susan loved sledding, didn't she? Oh, how she loved wading in the sea! I might have been someone then. Now I'm just dead, and might as well finish that and make it true. Nobody wanted me alive. I'll see nobody finds my body. I'd rather the crows have it than my family. I'm not going to lie quiet in the family plot. I promise you that.

For the first time, Susan Milford seemed real to Rutledge. The black splash of ink on the page was rife with anger and pain and something more, a loneliness so deep it couldn't be measured.

He read it a second time, then passed the envelope back to Hastings, who put it carefully away. Not looking at Rutledge. How much was dramatizing her situation, and how much was sincere? He wasn't able to judge.

"You should have shown me that in the beginning."

"I'd hoped it would never be necessary. I never showed it to Milford. It seemed somehow too—personal."

"Do you think that that's how she truly felt?"

"Yes. Oh, yes. Only I never knew how to put it into words. She did."

Rutledge left soon after.

Betws y Coed was some sixty or seventy miles from Shrewsbury, he thought. Possibly farther, given the condition of the roads, and the fact that none of them save Watling Street—built by the Romans—ran straight. But before he could leave Shrewsbury, there was one more matter to attend to.

He found the hotel in the center of town that had a telephone—he recalled it from another inquiry—and put through a call to Scotland Yard.

Sergeant Gibson was closeted with the Chief Superintendent, and Rutledge was forced to wait for nearly three-quarters of an hour before the telephone in the little alcove began to ring.

He answered it quickly, and was glad to hear the gruff voice at the other end give his name.

"Sergeant. I need information. Are there any Yard inquiries in north Wales regarding a woman being taken up for anything to do with the abduction of a young child?"

He gave the particulars he knew, well aware that these were scant and of little use to Gibson, who seemed to manage a wide correspondence with half of England and had more facts at his fingertips than any dozen other men at the Yard. Behind Gibson's back, some of the men called it witchcraft, and were only half joking. It did appear to be uncanny at times, the way the Sergeant could recall a pertinent fact or a whispered hint or even a Constable in a far-flung village who had the right answer.

"I'll have to give it some thought, sir," Gibson replied,

sounding as if it might take him half the night to scour his memory.

But Rutledge knew better than to push. He took a deep breath, hoping Gibson couldn't hear that down the line, and said, "It would be very helpful. And I'd like to know if anyone in Wales—in the mountains or along the coastline—has come across a female body in the last three and a half years."

He could almost read the silence. *You're wanting too much, you're not the only Inspector clamoring for information, you know.*

Finally Gibson said with resignation, "I'll do my best, sir."

"And if you please, Sergeant. Could you leave a message with the Chief Superintendent? The dead man in the River Dee near the village of Llangollen has been identified. He may not have been alone when he was pushed from the Aqueduct into the river below. I'm having to trace a missing child now, to be certain she wasn't with him. I'll report again as soon as I have further information."

Interest picked up in the Sergeant's voice. "Ah. The woman. Sir."

"Possibly. Yes. That's why I must track her down as soon as I can."

"Nasty business when children are involved."

"Yes." It wasn't all quite true, not the way he'd told it to Gibson. But the point was to find the information as soon as possible. "Thank you. I'll be at this telephone. The Prince Rupert Hotel, Shrewsbury."

And so he spent a day wandering Shrewsbury, exploring what was left of the great Abbey ruins that had once dominated the little town, along with the castle. It was truncated now, but still intriguing. He walked there for the better part of two hours, listening to his footsteps echoing on the stone, no one about. If the monks who once lived here had left any trace other than the worn seats in the choir and the worn treads on the stone steps, he couldn't find it. Their voices raised in song and prayer had vanished with the Reformation.

If he was searching for a measure of peace, he didn't find it either.

He came back to the telephone twice in the course of the afternoon, and then around five o'clock he was just stepping into the alcove passage when the telephone began to ring.

It was Gibson.

"Strange that you should ask, sir." And he began to read from a Welsh police report.

Gibson had found the Betws y Coed case that went before the local magistrate, in much the same detail as Rutledge had been given by the solicitor, Hastings. There had been no case against Susan Milford, after all, and the charge was dismissed without prejudice.

Rutledge listened carefully to the report, but he heard nothing that was new or useful.

As Gibson finished, he asked, "And that was all you've found so far?"

"All there is to report. Sir. It was an unusual request. And there's this, mind you, some matters aren't passed on to London. They are dealt with locally, and if that's successful, it's not reported."

There was nothing to be gained—and much to lose—by annoying Sergeant Gibson for not finding the answers he was seeking. And for all he knew, Gibson was right, they hadn't been reported.

"Yes, I take your point. Sorry, Gibson, it's just that I was looking for something more, and that's not your fault." He tried to lighten his voice, hoping that would travel down the wires to London. "And bones, Gibson. Have you found any bones for me?"

"It took most of the day to find the report, sir. The bones will have to wait."

But Rutledge couldn't wait another day in Shrewsbury. He wanted to reach Wales and hear for himself what Susan Milford had or had not done.

"I'll put through a call when I find another telephone. That will have to do."

"Suit yourself, sir."

And Gibson rang off.

It was late on that night when he drove into Betws y
Coed, a village lying in the Conwy River valley. He
managed to find a room in a small hotel on the main
street. Well before the railways came, the village had
become a major coaching stop for the Irish Mail, traveling between London and the port at Holyhead, where
ferries made the crossing. And soon it had begun to
cater to summer visitors as well. Walkers, mostly, the
sleepy clerk confided in him, come to see the Falls and
take in the fresh air from the surrounding forest.

Rutledge rose early for breakfast. It was more than
a fortnight now since the death of Sam Milford. And
he was no closer to the man's killer. As soon as he'd
finished his meal, he walked across the green and the
railway tracks to find the magistrate.

He was in and willing to talk about the case against
Susan Milford. "I remember it because it was unnecessary, you see. There were better avenues for protecting
the child without frightening the mother. The police,
the church. The grandmother, even."

"Would she have taken the child away from the mother? Physically removing her?" Rutledge asked.

"I have no idea—it never came to that, of course. I sorted it out as best I could, given the flaring tempers, and from what I learned afterward, the child was better off with the grandmother in the first place. Felt rather like King Solomon, you know."

"And Miss Milford?"

"Perfectly polite, of course, but there was something about the way she saw the matter. Black and white. Far too personally. Too intense, too set on having her way."

"Did you see her again after the case was dismissed?"

"She was here and there in the village, I couldn't very well have missed her. Always at a distance, of course. She never approached me." He frowned. "And then she wasn't here, and I noticed that too."

"Did gossip whisper any information about where she might have gone?"

"I didn't hear it if there was. My wife would have mentioned it, I think."

"When was this?"

"Oh, I don't know. Does it matter? I can consult my records, if you wish."

"Possibly. Yes, it might well matter."

Rising, the magistrate ran his finger along a line of

boxes on the shelf against the wall. The finger stopped, and he took down the box it was pointing to. He brought it back to the desk, began to search the contents, frowning as he worked.

"Yes, here it is, I should think. Right. This was fourth September, 1917. Yes. It unexpectedly turned rather cold. The initial complaint was that the child was inadequately dressed to be out in the weather, and the two women—mother of the child and Miss Milford—had words outside a yarn shop on the main street. The next day the mother brought the child out in a sunbonnet and shawl. Flaunting her authority as parent. Miss Milford told her she was a fool and too stupid to be anyone's mother."

He looked up. "Shall I go on? Yes? It escalated from there, another encounter nearly coming to blows on the green. Near the end of the month, a Constable was sent for, the child's mother claiming that Miss Milford told her that the child would be better cared for by the town cat, and that she would personally see to it that the cat was given a chance to prove her words. The mother took this hyperbole as a threat, and began screaming. Very likely having seen the Constable nearby, because he was there at once and took Miss Milford into custody for endangering the life of the child in the pram."

He began to fold the papers and return them neatly to their proper place.

Although Susan Milford hadn't touched the child in question, had this confrontation stayed with her and eventually led her to take Tildy away from her mother? That, Rutledge thought, was a stretch, but then if Susan was disturbed, she might believe that Tildy would not be loved and cared for. That she was in need of rescue from a father who couldn't accept her as his own. But Sam *had* accepted the child.

Assuming, of course, that Susan was alive at the end of the war, when her brother came home to discover he was a father.

"Did you feel in any way that Miss Milford was a threat to herself?"

The magistrate considered him. "Are you asking me if I believed the young woman was suicidal? It never crossed my mind. She appeared to be satisfied by the resolution of the case." He pursed his lips in thought. "But now that you bring it up. That intensity of hers . . . If the verdict had gone against her, if she had failed to save that child from its mother, if she believed that something might well happen to it because the mother was careless, perhaps she might conclude that suicide was a more dramatic way of making her point. But that's hindsight, isn't it?"

Rutledge was still mulling that over as he left the little courthouse shortly afterward. Was it worry about the child that had precipitated that despairing letter to Hastings? And then when the child was given to its grandmother, suicide was neither necessary nor useful to get her way.

"It could have had verra' little to do with the child," Hamish pointed out. "Yon letter could have had different roots."

And no more than coincidental with the worry over the child.

Bones or no bones, he'd have to keep looking.

And then he had his very first bit of luck.

Someone was calling to him, and he turned to see the magistrate hurrying after him, waving something.

Rutledge walked back down the street to meet him.

"I'm glad I caught you up. My wife reminded me. Well, I expect she's just as happy to get this out of the house." He shoved a slim book into Rutledge's hand. "Susan Milford's. She'd been reading it while she was waiting for the case to be heard. I expect she forgot it when the verdict was handed down. It sat there on the table in the public room until someone thought to look inside and saw her name. She could well have moved on by then."

Rutledge turned it over. It was a small, cheaply

printed little book of Welsh legends. He found the name scrawled inside in the same heavy ink as the letter.

"Thank you. If I find her, I'll return it."

"I never asked. Why are you looking for her?"

"She's been missing for some time. Her family is anxious."

"Not terribly anxious. If they haven't begun searching for her until now."

Rutledge smiled.

"Well. I wish you luck." And he was gone, trotting back toward the courthouse.

He tossed the little book into his valise when he reached his room, and then stood at the long windows, looking down on the street. It was a pleasant little village, but he wasn't seeing the view. He had come here, verified everything that Hastings had told him. Where to, now?

Just where had Susan Milford gone from here?

There's the river here, but it's not deep enough. I'll have to find another way.

Wales wasn't large, but there were tiny villages everywhere, any one of them a potential hiding place.

"No' too small," Hamish suggested. "Too small, and they ask too many questions."

"Take away half of them, and it's still a mare's nest."

He turned back to the room, went to his valise, and took out the slim book on legends and myths.

It was a Victorian collection of Welsh stories, very likely inspired by Tennyson's *Idylls of the King*. Rutledge tried to recall when they came out. His father had possessed a lovely leather volume with the twelve poems relating the story of King Arthur, his rise and his fall. He had read to his son and daughter from it, his voice alive with the feel of the story and the glory of the words, and they had loved listening to him.

And the *Idylls* had revived interest in the old stories and legends of Wales.

Rutledge went back to the title page. The little volume was printed in 1875. That was about right, he thought.

Leafing through the pages, he found a series of tales, all of them heroic in nature as men fought the dark forces arrayed against them. Kings helping kings, faithful retainers saving the day, servants acting for beleaguered masters.

One of the dark forces was a scream.

Intrigued, he kept skimming through the tales. And he found one that was marked with a blot of ink. The same thick black ink that Susan Milford favored for her correspondence.

It was another story of courage and service and

battles with evil. There was a note from the editors at the bottom of the first page, informing the reader that this story was not as old as some of the other legends and myths, but was included for completeness.

And it was about a woman who took her cowardly brother's place in a bloody battle, drugging him so that he would sleep through it, then stealing away with his armor and his horse. She destroyed the enemy but was killed in the battle, and everyone believed that it was the brother who had died. The army's grief was overwhelming, the victory tarnished by the death of such a great warrior. The brother, coming on the scene as the army wept for him, realized what his sister had done. Ashamed, he slipped away and let the army bury her in his place, a monument she deserved and he didn't.

Rutledge, finishing the convoluted tale, closed the book.

Helpful in understanding Susan, perhaps, but not much use in finding her . . .

Hamish said, "The lass was buried. There would be a tomb."

Wales was full of mystical places. There was even a tomb somewhere to a gallant dog.

He found a bookshop on the main street, a tiny place owned by a man who might have been a troglodyte in his dark cubby beneath the stairs. But he knew his books, and he found what Rutledge was after. A 1901 guidebook of Great Britain, designed in the style of the far better-known work of Karl Baedeker. It was not in the best condition, clearly well used, but it was intact.

He went back to his hotel, stopping only for sandwiches and a refill of tea for his Thermos.

And he scoured the fine print on the thin pages for what he wanted. The grave of Gwian the Brave.

It was nearly seven thirty in the evening before he found it.

A village in the mountains where three rivers came together. There was a cairn in a field just beyond, in the shadow of a ridge.

He stared at the name—then went back to the guidebook. He recalled seeing a glossary in the back, explaining the meaning of some Welsh terms.

Bedd, he discovered, meant "grave of." Then Beddgwian must mean the grave of Gwian.

Rubbing his tired eyes, he sat there for several minutes, then rose and closed the curtains at the windows.

What was the connection between this place and Susan Milford?

Had she read the story of Gwian, and felt an attraction to the heroine? Or something else, a friend, a sanctuary, the distance from Betws y Coed, or even mere curiosity about the legend? The only way to find out was to go there. And hope for another clue, even if she had moved on. His inclination was to go down to his motorcar and set out straightaway. His good sense warned him that it was far too late to drive those twisting mountain roads tonight.

He'd made the right decision.

There were places where the road was nothing more than a track that nearly lost itself several times. He was heading in the direction of Mount Snowdon, the high peak in northern Wales that was famous for its cog railway to the summit. But here he was in forest, steep drops on first this side and then that, while rivers far below were in spate with the winter runoff. A time or two, he wasn't certain there was room for the motorcar to pass through, and then the road would open out just enough to make the next turning. Once he stopped to check the map, taking out his military compass to be sure he hadn't missed his way somewhere.

Looking down as he folded his map, he noticed the carpet of bluebells just beyond his tires, already up and waiting for warmer weather to bloom.

By fits and starts he finally made his way to Beddgwian.

It was hardly a village, he thought, so much as a place where the road, rushing down the hill to cross the river over a pretty little stone bridge, suddenly realized that it had come up against the steep face of a cliff. And with no other choice to make, it split, one turning to the left, one to the right.

Houses straggled down the hill on the left, and then the right, but most of them clustered around the bridge and beneath the shelter of the cliff face. People passing by stared at the big dark red motorcar, then at him, as if he'd suddenly fallen from the sky into their small world.

The stares, he noticed, were reserved, but not unfriendly.

Finding a place to reverse, he went back up to the hotel perched on a plot of land overlooking a wooded hillside that fell away sharply to the river below.

He'd been surprised to see it there, but it was a welcome sight too.

Pulling into the bare patch of ground across the road from the steps, he got out and went in.

The hotel was older than it appeared on the outside. He stepped into a narrow hall that widened into Reception, but there was no one at the desk. Noticing the bell, he rang it, and after a moment someone came out from the kitchen, a young woman wiping her hands on her apron.

"Can I help you, sir?" she asked in the rhythmic

speech of the Welsh. Then she added apologetically, "I'm afraid we're closed. It's off-season."

"Is it, indeed?" he said pleasantly, smiling for her. "I was hoping for a room, if that's possible?"

"I dunno, sir. I'll have to ask Mrs. Thomas." With a bob that might have been a hint of a curtsy, she disappeared through a door to one side of the desk.

Five minutes later she was back. "Mrs. Thomas says, one room won't make that much work. Number seven, second floor. Unless you'd prefer a room in the back, sir? The road can be noisy."

He hadn't passed another vehicle since two o'clock in the afternoon. "I'll take my chances with the traffic."

She smiled. "If you'll sign the register, please, sir?"

He did, putting down *Rutledge. London.*

She had watched him write, and as *London* flowed from his pen, she said, "That's ever so far. How did you find us?"

"Luck, I think." He gestured around him. "I hadn't expected to find such a place as this in such a small village."

"Oh, we aren't the only hotel, sir. There's one across the bridge and to your right."

"Who generally stays here?"

"Walkers, sir. There's fishing as well. Trout and salmon. And people stop here on their way to Mount

Snowdon. There's a copper mine not far away. The directors sometimes choose the hotel for meetings."

He thanked her and went up to his room, looking down at the road and his motorcar across the way. Just then there was a roaring noise and someone came down the hill at great speed on a motorcycle, quickly disappearing from view as it rounded the slight curve before the road went straight to the bridge.

So much for traffic keeping him awake.

He walked down to the village proper, where the road divided. Houses, shops, a small general store on this side of the little bridge, and a shop that sold souvenirs just across the road. To his surprise, it was open.

He went over there, and found that it specialized in paintings of the area—mostly mountain, woodland, and river views—and in woolen goods, which the owner, a young woman, claimed were entirely handmade. Looking at them, he thought she might be right. Concentrating on the paintings hanging on the wall of the smaller back room, he said casually, "These are quite good."

The young woman flushed pink at the praise. "They sell rather well," she replied, but he thought she was the artist.

He said, "I don't see any views of the famous grave."

She looked at him as if she didn't know what he was

talking about, then smothered a laugh. "It's a fiction, sir. I've lived here all my life and never seen the grave. My father told me once that he'd come across a cairn in a field. But he wasn't all that certain it was a grave."

If the story was old, twelfth century or earlier, there might not be a grave as such, he reminded himself. Cairns, or piles of heavy stone, were often erected over the bodies of warriors, and those who came to pay tribute would add a stone to the pile, increasing its size and thus its importance.

"That's too bad. I'd come to see if it was true, that Gwian was buried here."

She looked at him, a twinkle in her eye. "I don't think I ever met anyone who actually came to see the grave."

Rutledge laughed. "Is there a Constable in the village?" he asked then.

She was still amused. "Ah, and what would you do with a policeman, arrest whoever made up that legend?"

"It's the name of the village," he pointed out.

"And so it is."

Someone came through the outer door, setting a little bell jingling, and with a nod, she went to see who it was.

Rutledge looked at the paintings again. The cliff

face in sunlight, leaves floating in a pool where the river deepened, several views of the little stone bridge and the hotel. But no cairn.

He'd hoped not to have to reveal he was Scotland Yard, but speaking to the Constable now seemed unavoidable if he was to ask questions about Susan Milford.

Moving into the main room, he caught the young woman and the man who had just come in standing with their heads together, laughing. He thought she had told the man about the strange Englishman hunting for the Gwian cairn.

They turned guiltily, looking at him.

The fair-haired man was not much older than Rutledge, a bad scar across his nose and one cheek. It looked like a shrapnel wound, and when the man moved away from the young woman, it was awkwardly done, as if one leg troubled him.

"I'm so sorry," she said, the color rising in her face again. "Is there anything else I could help you with, sir?"

"Thank you, no," he said and, with a nod, went past them to the door.

He stood in the tiny scrap of yard at the edge of the road, and looked toward the bridge, hoping to pick out just where the police station might be.

The door opened and closed behind him, and the

man said, "Sorry. We aren't usually that rude toward visitors. But locally that legend is not given much credence."

Rutledge turned. "I happened across a book of myths and legends while I was at Betws y Coed."

The man said, "Betws? I grew up there. Shepherd's the name. Geoff Shepherd."

"Ian Rutledge."

Shepherd gestured across the bridge. "The pub is just over there. Opening time, I think. Join me for a drink?"

Rutledge nodded and the two men walked on toward the bridge, then crossed the road where it widened a little to form the junction. High above their heads, the rounded dome of the cliff top caught the last rays of the sun.

He'd been right about the wound, he thought, as Shepherd limped heavily beside him.

"What brings you here, besides literary curiosity?"

Rutledge laughed. "I'm on my way to Snowdon," he said. "This was just a diversion."

"Good food at the hotel," Shepherd said. "Be sure to dine there tonight."

They found a table in a corner of the pub, and Rutledge bought the first half. Bringing their glasses over, he sat down and said, "Tell me about the village."

"Nothing to tell, really. Oh—yes—there's a true story you might enjoy. One of Victoria's sons came to visit Beddgwian. It was an unexpected honor, but the village was up to it. They did what they could, bringing out flags and bunting, someone even found an ornate arch and a length of carpet to welcome him into the hotel. There was a lot of jostling as everyone tried to see the prince arrive. I don't know precisely what they were expecting, but they missed him entirely. He was only a boy, and just walked quietly past everyone and into the hotel without any pomp or circumstance while they were watching for a great personage."

Rutledge smiled. "Disappointment indeed. What brought you from Betws?"

Shepherd said, "I'm what passes as the local doctor. They had a need."

"Are you, indeed?"

"It's a remarkably healthy village. An occasional farm accident. Not much call for my services. That suits me."

Rutledge could hear the undertones in his voice. "In the war, were you?"

"Surgeon. I'd be happy if I never saw another scalpel."

He understood. The doctors at the Front had worked on torn bodies until they were ready to drop from exhaustion, then worked around the clock again, one man after another laid on their tables and no respite from the broken bodies and blood and hopelessness.

"You?"

Rutledge nodded, and gave his regiment.

"God. The Somme. I was there." A shadow passed across his face.

They drank in silence.

Then Shepherd said, "Why are you really here?"

11

Rutledge let the words hang in the air between them. Then he said, "I don't know what you mean."

"Yes, you do. You came from Betws y Coed. Who sent you?"

"No one sent me."

"That silly business about the grave. You could have thought of a better excuse. Or just come and knocked at my door. We're civilized here. We don't bite."

"Sorry. You've got it wrong."

"Have I? I'm not a fool. I've only to look at you to know you come from London. Who sent you? Lambert or Cunningham?"

"Gibson," Rutledge replied after a moment.

"I don't know him. Is he a partner?"

"He's a policeman."

Shepherd's blue eyes widened. "For God's sake, what are they going to do? Arrest me?"

"Depends on what they think you've done."

"I didn't know that disappointing one's father was a crime."

Rutledge said nothing.

Shepherd swore under his breath, long and with feeling. "You can turn around and drive back to London, and tell them to go to hell."

Rutledge reached into his pocket, took out his identification, and placed it on the table between them.

The other man stared at it.

"I'm here for reasons of my own," Rutledge said quietly. "And I'd like to keep it that way."

Shepherd gave a bark of a laugh, but there was no humor in it. "Damn it, are you telling me the truth?"

"Unless you've murdered three people in the past fortnight or so, I've got no more interest in you than I do in that cairn." He kept his tone light.

"Well, I'll be damned." He drank his ale, and then shook his head. "My turn to say I'm sorry. My father has never given up on the notion that what I want to do with my life is work in London hospitals side by side with him. Lambert and Cunningham are his solicitors. They are indefatigable in their efforts to find me, wherever I go. As if I can be worn down by their pleas and their promises and their persistence."

"Oddly enough, my father was a solicitor. He wanted me to join the firm as well."

"But you escaped."

"I think in the end, he was pleased for me." He didn't add that his father had died soon after he'd made his choice of career, and he had never known what he'd really felt about it.

Shepherd lifted his glass in a mock toast. Then setting it down again, he said, "You can't seriously believe there's a murderer hiding out in Beddgwian."

"Given the difficulty in getting in and out of here, I'm beginning to have my doubts." He changed tactics. "I'm also searching for a missing child."

The man across from him went still. "What do you mean, a missing child?"

"Just that. A child who was taken from her family a year ago."

Shepherd drained his glass. "This isn't the place to talk after all. You'd better come with me. I think I've made a terrible mistake."

Again they walked in silence, taking the right fork of the road to a cottage that was just out of sight of the stone bridge.

"My surgery," Shepherd said wryly, leading the way up the short path to the door. Inside he took Rutledge into the little back room that he used to confer with patients. It was cold, no fire lit against the still-early spring chill in the air at these heights. But one was laid on the hearth, and Shepherd busied himself lighting it.

When it was burning to his satisfaction, he sat down not at his desk but in the chair across from Rutledge.

"There's a woman here in town—well, *was*, actually. I haven't seen her in some time. She lives in that small house that sits back in the trees just beyond the hotel. You probably haven't noticed it. The house was to let, and she took it about three years ago. Arrived almost in the dark of night, you might say. One day the house was empty, the next it was occupied. She kept to herself. I wasn't here then, still in France. Then one day the house was closed again, and she was gone. One of the local women thought she might have been recovering from an illness. She ordered from the shops, had it delivered, but she was sometimes seen walking in the early morning or late in the evening."

Rutledge waited.

"Last summer she was back again. I saw her a time or two, and that's when I was told about her. I kept an eye open, in the event she needed help, but she never consulted me. I told myself she might have been recovering from tuberculosis, and the mountain air was good for her."

When he paused again, Rutledge said, "Go on."

"We have heavy mists sometimes. Thick white cloying mists. They come down in the night, and sometimes don't lift until midday. It was about ten o'clock on such a morning when I was summoned to the police station. Constable Jones is a good man, but this was beyond his ability to cope. I arrived at the station to find him dealing with a frantic woman. She was barefoot, cuts on her face and arms. She had come flying into the station, screaming for him to find her child. That the child was missing, and she couldn't find her in that mist. I realized as soon as I saw her who she was, the woman from the little house."

He got up to stir the fire. Standing at the hearth, his back to Rutledge, he said, "She kept repeating her story. That she'd awakened this morning, started down to prepare breakfast, only to find the front door standing wide. She couldn't see the path, much less the road beyond. Closing the door, she went on to her kitchen, and when the porridge was ready, she went to call her small daughter. But the child never answered her, and when she went up to her room, it was empty. The bedclothes were dragged off the bed, but no sign of the child. She began to search the house, then remembered the open door. Terrified that the child had got up in the night, gone out into the mists, and lost her way, she ran out to the road, calling for her. There was no response. She ran down the slope toward the river, searched along the water, and then climbed up again to the road. A van coming down the hill narrowly missed her—someone at the hotel recalled hearing brakes and shouting. But the woman ran on, arriving at the station, banging on the door, begging Jones to hurry."

"And did you search for this child?"

"My first thought was to calm her down—until then we'd heard only a garbled version of the story, piecing it together as best we could. I tried to make her swallow something, but she kept pushing the glass away, telling me she had to keep looking, pleading with us to send out search parties. The child was still in her nightclothes, no coat, and the woman had no idea how long she'd been outside. I told Jones to summon all the men he could, that we needed to search." He shook his head. "There was no child, Rutledge. When Jones went to the house, he found it just as she'd said. But there was no sign of a child. No clothes, no dolls, nothing to indicate there had ever been one there in that house."

Caught off guard, Rutledge said, "You mean she was alone in that house all along?"

"Apparently."

"What happened?"

"Jones got his wife in there—into the station—and she gave the woman a cup of tea that I'd put something in. It was the only thing we could do. She slept for nearly ten hours. By that time, we'd conducted a search, but we'd found nothing. When she woke up, she began to scream for the child again. And I had no choice, I had to give her something. Two days later, she was finally calm enough to be questioned. I think she was afraid we'd give her more sedatives if she didn't cooperate. That's when she told us that she had lost a child, and was still suffering from the shock of it. That she would wake up and find herself back in that moment, and have to relive it."

When Rutledge said nothing, the doctor looked away.

"The thing is, she'd never had a child. It was all a delusion. Start to finish. I tried to find out if there were friends—relatives—someone who could look after her. Failing that, I tried to find a place that would take her in and help her. Before I could do more, she went away.

Just packed up what she wanted and walked away from here. We haven't seen her since."

"What was her name?"

"Ruth Middleton, or so she said. War widow. But I don't think any of it was true. Several things in her possession had initials on them. We discovered them when we searched the house. A leather handbag, handkerchiefs in her drawer. A pin in the jewelry case. Even her valise. *SEM*. When I tried to ask her about that, she told me I had no right to search her things, and got quite angry. But she told the Constable that the items were hers, that the initials stood for Serena Ruth Edmonds Middleton, but she didn't care for Serena and had always used Ruth. We couldn't prove or disprove that. My mother never liked her first name, she never used it. I could hardly fault Mrs. Middleton." He paused. "Whether she was actually married or not, I thought it best to leave that alone."

SEM could also stand for Susan Elizabeth Milford . . .

"And the child's name?"

"Gwennie. Gwendolyn."

"Has anyone lived there since then?"

"No. And local people tend to avoid it."

"Is it possible to go into the house without attracting unwelcome attention? I'd like to have a look."

"There's nothing to find. It was furnished with what was left by the previous tenants."

"Still."

They left the pub to walk back up the long hill. The sun had gone behind the dome of the cliff, casting dark shadows here and there, although overhead the sky was still blue. As they came in sight of the hotel, Rutledge noticed the smaller house in the trees.

Shepherd led the way to the door, opened it, and they stepped inside. It was dim in the entry, and cold. Any life or laughter that had been in the house had left.

Rutledge stood there, listening to the nature of the silence. But it told him very little. "Is the door always unlocked?"

"I don't think any of us lock our doors here."

"All right. Let's begin."

And with Shepherd trailing him, Rutledge went through the house room by room, searching carefully and thoroughly.

Someone had removed the burned porridge from the cooker, but the smell lingered. That was the only indication that anyone had ever lived here.

He went up the steps, his boots echoing on the treads, and into the two bedrooms at the top of the stairs.

In the smaller of the two, the mattress was unrolled, the sheets on it were clean, and they were covered by a dark green blanket, one edge of it still trailing across the floor, just as the woman had described it to the police. But the little chest was empty, the table under the window bare, and there was nothing in the alcove where clothes could be hung on pegs.

Moving on to the other bedroom, he could see the back of the hotel from the windows, and what appeared to be a kitchen garden just beyond. Again he searched, and again he came away with nothing, until the bottom drawer of the chest caught a little and he had to work at it to bring it all the way out.

It was empty. But as he lifted it clear, something slid without a sound to the floor.

"Wait," Shepherd said, pointing.

Rutledge put the drawer back into place and picked up what lay there.

It was a slim bit of ribbon, silk, he thought, and it was a soft pale green. Just the color to thread through a small child's reddish-gold hair and tie in a bow at the top of her head.

Looking at it more closely, he thought he saw a single hair caught in the silk, but it slipped through his fingers onto the floor, and he couldn't find it again.

"Wishful thinking," Hamish taunted as Rutledge tried to ignore the voice.

"What is it?" Shepherd asked sharply.

Rutledge shook his head. "A bit of trim," he answered, holding out the ribbon.

They left soon after, and on the steps as Shepherd was about to walk down toward the village, Rutledge asked, "That was no accidental encounter in the shop, was it?"

Shepherd looked at him, then said, "All right. No. I saw you walking down the hill in your London clothes. I couldn't ignore that. The shop owner is a friend, I can stop in. It seemed—simpler—to take a closer look."

With that he nodded and went briskly down to the road, the limp pronounced even as he tried to make it less so.

Rutledge watched him halfway down the hill. Then he walked across to the hotel entrance.

At first light next morning, Rutledge set out on his own, a walking stick borrowed from the ornate stand in the hotel's lounge. He'd replaced his boots with his Wellingtons, wore a heavy jumper under a coat, and carried his torch from the motorcar.

It was very dark under the trees, but quiet enough

that he thought he could just hear the stream running at the bottom of the sloping hill. He went down the road, crossed the bridge, and turned left, soon finding himself in relatively flat meadows as the valley spread out. Overhead the sun was just brushing the sky with light, while below it was barely dawn.

And then the light began to overspread the meadows, and he could see every tree and bush and stone sharply outlined.

It took him some time to find what he was after. He'd nearly missed it.

In an open space, he discovered what first appeared to be rubble, a scattering of stones where they were not a natural feature.

And he thought this could be all that was left of a warrior's grave.

Someone had pulled down what might well have been a cairn in the distant past. Tossing the stones this way and that. Violently, smaller stones landing some good few feet away, as if thrown with angry abandon.

How recent was this destruction? And who had done it?

Hamish said, "Ye canna' know if it was yon sister."

True enough, he thought, grimly looking at what was left.

But he'd wager his pay for the next year that he'd

guessed right. Idle hands hadn't done this out of curiosity or a sense of mischief. This was destruction on a personal and malevolent scale.

Turning away, finally, he set himself to consider Susan Milford's current state of mind, and where she might be now. And how real that missing child might be.

On the long walk back to the village and then up the hill to the hotel, he saw no one. Only a quarreling flock of crows, chasing each other through the trees, then climbing to the rounded top of the cliff and disappearing from his view.

He was working out a timetable as he crossed the bridge.

She *could* have taken Tildy. And she could have had her brother killed to stop him from searching for the child. Then finished what she'd begun by smothering Mrs. Turnbull in her bed and drowning Joseph Burton. There were spaces of time where she might have traveled anywhere.

The woman's face that had been seen in the narrowboat window . . .

Was that Susan Milford? Or had the narrowboat owner taken a woman along with whatever cargo he'd been carrying, then got her out of sight fast, before anyone could even prove she'd been there? They were human, the boatmen. It had probably happened hundreds of times over the years. Those pretty lace curtains could conceal a multitude of people or things.

By the time he'd reached the hotel he'd nearly decided that his best course of action was to drive back to the Aqueduct and make absolutely certain who the woman was. If he had to take every man there into custody until he found his answer.

He was on his way upstairs when he stopped at the first landing.

The hotel and the house. Next door.

Swinging around, he went back down the stairs and into the bar.

The young woman who had been on the Reception desk when he arrived was putting clean glasses in the racks, frowning in concentration as she handled the more fragile wineglasses.

Taking a seat at the bar, he waited until all of the glasses were in their proper places. Then he said ruefully, "I went out walking this morning. And missed my breakfast. Is it possible to have something in here?"

A little flustered by his smile, she said, "Well then, what is it that you'd like?"

"Eggs, bacon. Toast. Tea."

"Let me ask in the kitchen."

When she returned, she was pink, and he thought she'd had to be rather more persuasive than she'd anticipated. "Yes, it's all right. Would you like a table?" She glanced toward the dining room, with its windows looking out at the road and the trees that ran down to the river.

"No need for any fuss. This will be fine." Talking to her was the only reason he'd ordered breakfast.

She seemed pleased. "You live in London? What's it like, London?"

"Busy. Crowded. Exciting sometimes."

"Have you ever seen the King?"

"I have." But that was when he'd been in France, and the King had stopped in one of the base hospitals to cheer the wounded.

"And the Queen? Her pearls are so beautiful."

"I'm told she enjoys wearing them."

"It must be wonderful to go to plays and the opera. I've never been more than ten miles from where I was born."

A man poked his head around the door and handed her a tray with Rutledge's breakfast on it. As she set the silverware and plates out in front of him, he used the opening she had given him.

"You must know everyone in the village, then." He

smiled again. "Was the house next door once part of the hotel?"

He'd picked the right person to question.

Her face closed slightly, the forthrightness of the Welsh vanishing. "It was built for one of the hotel's owners. Ages ago. Then a new owner didn't care for it, and it was sold off." She gestured toward Reception. "There's a story about the hotel, framed and in the entrance. You might want to read it, if you're interested."

"Did the hotel ever send meals across to the woman who had taken the house a year or so ago?" He deliberately set his question in the past.

"Sometimes." She turned and found a cloth, cleaning the top of the bar with it. Ill at ease.

"Sad story, that. I heard someone talking about it in the village. Something about a child missing. Was it ever found?"

"As to that," she began, "I couldn't say."

"Surely there was a search. It isn't still missing? Or is it dead?"

Her gaze flew back to his face. "I never saw a child when I took her dinner across. They *asked* me, and I had to tell them the truth. But there was always enough for two on the trays."

"I don't understand," he said quietly, in an effort to encourage her.

Clearly uncomfortable, she said, "I didn't know what to believe. But I'd spoken to her, she was quite nice. And then she ran into the village that morning, screaming for help—everyone heard her. Why would she make up such a story, if it weren't true? Why would she claim that there was a child missing, if there wasn't?"

"Did she stop looking? When everyone else did?"

"I don't know—no—I'd see her walking at all hours. Once Dr. Shepherd stopped sedating her. They were trying to find a hospital—asylum—a safe place. I told her, I warned her. And then she was gone. In the middle of the night. I was afraid then that I'd done a wrong thing." She looked thoroughly wretched. She must be all of sixteen, seventeen. Hardly more than a child herself.

"Just—vanished?" Shepherd hadn't told him that.

The young woman flushed a dark red, glancing over her shoulder. "I don't know. She gave me a letter. She asked me to put it in with the hotel post, so that no one would know."

"When was this?" Neither Shepherd nor the Constable had mentioned a letter.

"Only four or five days before she went away." She frowned, thinking.

Which meant she could have killed her brother. But why?

"Do you remember the name on the letter? Or the address?"

"I think it might have been to her solicitor. Handler? Hampton? Something like that."

Damn the man! He hadn't mentioned that letter! Why was Hastings playing a double game?

Had he sent someone for her—known from the start that she was in Beddgwian and never said a word? Knew where she was *now*—and talked about suicide instead?

"But where would she go, if this house was her home?" He kept his voice gentle, mildly interested, yet concerned.

"She told me she had to be sure. 'I have to know.' She said it twice. Then she told me 'I was a stolen child, I know what happens to them.' I asked her *who* had taken her, but she wouldn't tell me. She just begged me not to tell anyone the things we'd talked about. And I didn't. Still, it's weighed on my conscience." She bit her lower lip. "My mother says she was mad, that she ought to be shut away. But she didn't sound mad to me. Just afraid."

He remembered the book of myths and legends. Stolen children seemed to figure prominently in such tales. Had she borrowed from that, to appeal to this young woman's sympathy? Or had the stories fed her own delusions?

"Much would depend on where she went from here. Whether she had a safe place to go."

"I asked her that. I was fearful for her. But she said she could always go back to one friend who had stood by her."

"But she didn't tell you who that might be?"

"I don't think she trusted me with that. I'd not have told. It would—" She broke off as someone called to her from Reception. "Oh! I promised—" And she hurried away, leaving him to finish his breakfast alone.

He took the bit of green ribbon from his pocket, smoothing it out on the wooden bar. Then put it safely away again.

What to make of that?

And where to go from here? Back to Hastings in Shrewsbury?

"He'll no' tell the truth."

Rutledge agreed. It would be a waste of time.

He left some coins on the bar for the young woman, and went to his room. Taking out his notebook, he went back through his notes. What had Hastings told him on that first visit?

And there it was. It was suspected that Susan Milford, who had money in her own name, had, for reasons known only to her, worked at a slate quarry. But Hastings's people hadn't been able to verify that because when someone went to the quarry, the workers there had lied. They swore that no one of Susan's description had ever been there. Apparently protecting her.

Would she go there again? Test that same loyalty once more?

The young woman at the hotel had been protective, even though her mother had believed their neighbor belonged in care.

It was worth a try.

Slate was to the north what coal had been to the south of the country.

Rutledge spent the rest of that day driving from one quarry to another. They were massive operations, heavy beds of slate stretching right through the earth, and there were deep caverns underground where it had been removed around the miners until only slender pillars held the roof high above their heads. It came in colors, the Welsh slate, from almost black it was so dark to blue and red and even gray. Some of the men who'd worked at the face had dug the deep tunnels under German lines in France, and crammed them with gunpowder. He'd worked with them, laying the fuses that set them off. They were a breed apart, like the coal miners of the south.

He knew how to talk to them.

And late in the afternoon he came to what he was seeking, the place where Susan Milford had worked and made friends.

He discovered that in a roundabout way, leaving his motorcar on the main road and walking in.

Halfway to the buildings at the mine itself, he found a short, thickset man of about twenty-three breaking up some of the heavy blue slate into thinner slabs.

He kept working as Rutledge approached, and when the stranger stopped just feet from where he was bending over, looking for the right place to split a slab, he snapped, "Chips fly. You'd best be on your way to the top."

"By any chance, do you know a Tom Morgan, who was on the Somme '16?"

"No Morgans here." He split the slab perfectly.

"Pity. He and I set a fuse together. He was a good man. I'd hoped he'd made it."

The workman turned to stare at him. "I helped dig another tunnel." And he gave the coordinates. "Something went wrong. It didn't go on time. And a good thing. We broke through, and it would have got us."

Rutledge didn't think the man was short enough to have been a Bantam. Five feet five? At least that.

He was turning back to the slabs. "They'll be coming for this lot in an hour. I can't stop. Or I'll lose *this* pay." He gave Rutledge a curt explanation. It was, it seemed, his punishment for not making it to the foreman's hut in time to earn a day's pay. Instead they'd set him to fill a smaller order, and he was still angry about it.

"Give me five minutes of your time, and I'll pay you what they'd have paid you for a full day on the job."

The man squinted at him in the sunlight. "Why would you do that?"

"I've got my reasons. I work for a solicitor in Shrewsbury. He's lost one of his clients. He'd like to know she's safe. That's all. He's too old to make the journey himself. For my sins, he sent me. I don't know her. Just a name. Susan."

"My sister knows her. Wild Susan, she calls her."

"Sounds like Mr. Hastings's client."

"She's not here now. But they're airing the bedding. In the event she comes."

"Where will she be staying?"

"With my sister. She took over as manager when my father was crippled in a fall." He nodded back down the road that Rutledge had climbed. "There's a house in the village."

Rutledge said, "I'll thank you not to mention my visit or Mr. Hastings. He's got her best interests in this matter. He'll leave her where she is as long as she's safe. Learned his lesson last time she was here." It was a risk telling the younger man this much. Susan could slip away again, if she heard. She would know—whether Hastings had assistants or not.

He'd just handed the man a folded note when over their heads a gruff voice called, "Here? What's this? What does *he* want?" he added to the younger man.

"Stopped for directions." He was already splitting another slab, his back to Rutledge.

"Where are you heading?" he shouted at Rutledge.

"Snowdon."

"You're off your road." And he proceeded to shout directions. There was menace in his voice, and he shifted the tool in his hand to back up the warning. But Rutledge already had what he wanted. The last thing he needed was to have either man tell Susan Milford about his visit.

Rutledge, looking up at the man where he straddled a long ridge, said neutrally, "Thank you." And he was already on his way back down the road rising between huge piles of broken slate.

He didn't turn to see. But he knew the newcomer was watching him every step of the way.

When he thought Rutledge was out of earshot, he called to the younger man. "What did he want?"

"He said. Directions."

Rutledge made a point not to slow as he carried on as if driving to Snowdon, in the event other eyes were curious about his presence here. But he thought he could just see a house where the bedding had been stuffed out the open window to air. Waiting for Susan Milford to arrive?

12

It was a long drive back to Shropshire and thence to Crowley.

Twice he was nearly bogged down in the thick mud of back roads as the fair weather broke and rain followed him most of the way, overtaking him in sweeping sheets. He had hoped to cross over into England but finally had to call it a night still miles from the border. Unable to sleep for the rain beating down on the motorcar roof just over his head, he was on the road again by four. The rain had slowed to a patter, and he made better time.

It was well before dawn when Rutledge found a way around Oswestry, where an alert Constable might notice his motorcar passing through the dark and empty streets and report that to Inspector Preston.

Passing through Shrewsbury, he encountered fog by the river, and he pressed on, although he had intended to look in on Dora Radley.

Crowley was no more than ten minutes away when he noticed someone walking along the edge of the road in the distance. Before he'd caught up with whoever it was, the figure on foot had turned down the road that led to the smaller of the two lead mines, the one that had been closed for some years.

Rutledge frowned. There was something about the way the figure moved that made him slow down as he approached the same turning. A shorter stride, the way the shoulders were carried.

Although the walker was wearing trousers, he was nearly sure it was a woman. Not a man.

Where had she come from—and where was she going this early on a quiet morning? This was a desolate stretch of road. He hadn't seen another vehicle since Church Stretton. And the turning led nowhere but to a deserted village.

He pulled to the verge just out of sight of the turning, so that if she looked back she wouldn't readily see his motorcar. He didn't wish to frighten her. But she had had no knapsack with her, and in spite of the trousers, she hadn't looked to be the usual walker, and it was the wrong season for walking.

After several minutes he got out.

The cold rain from Wales was hardly more than a damp, drifting mist now, but unpleasant still, enough to keep most people indoors by the fire unless they had pressing business outside.

Leaving the motorcar where it was, Rutledge took his torch from the boot and changed into his Wellingtons. Then he started down the overgrown lane in a ground-covering jog. He caught sight of her twice, still heading toward the mine. She never looked back. If he'd had any doubt before, he was certain now it was a woman.

He had a rough idea of what lay ahead. He could already see the pointing finger of the chimney marking the pithead, and before very long he could pick out the stone mine buildings and then cottage roofs.

It never ceased to amaze him that nature could take over so quickly. Many feet had over two centuries trod any grass into beaten earth, but vines and briars and saplings had already begun to take over the man-made structures with their broken, empty windows and fallen walls, and all the equipment worth salvaging from the pithead had long since been sold or carried off. Bats had taken up residence in the tunnel and shafts, and crows fought for whatever they could find. He could hear them now, fussing at the unexpected visitor.

The Romans had mined lead, and later it had roofed medieval castles and churches and great houses. It came into its own with gunpowder and lead for bullets. But here at Little Bog, the lead had finally vanished after fits and starts. And the miners had moved on to The Bog and Snailbeach, if they could find work there.

He stood in the shadow of the building where gunpowder had been stored and watched the crows lifting off and challenging the woman as she moved on. And then the crows settled.

Where was she? And had she seen him?

The crows hadn't.

The front of the powder barn was open, part of it falling into ruin where the main door had been. He slipped inside, to wait.

And stopped short.

The dry end of the powder barn, protected still by a mostly intact roof and three very solid walls, had become a campsite.

There was bedding on a straw pallet against the rear wall of the rectangular building, and in front of that, a stone circle that contained ashes of a fire. Someone had lived here, cooked here. *Was* living here and cooking here.

He took out his torch and began a sweep with the light, noting the bundle that might be cooking gear, and nearby was a wooden box that might well hold a larder. There was no latrine, but in the woods where the crows had been fussing might well be facilities. And the village must have had a well, although in the opening near him, there was a pail collecting rainwater, and he could hear the drip-drip from a broken beam overhead as it fell from that height into the bucket. In the dampness he could just detect a faint trace of the black powder that had once been stored here for blasting.

The question was, had it all been taken away?

He had only stepped into the opening, and he looked down. His boots had left a wet imprint. Backing carefully away, he saw other prints, smaller ones.

He'd been right about the woman.

But who was she and why was she living like this, when there were rooms in The Pit and The Pony?

He didn't like it. Flicking off his torch, he carefully made his way from the powder barn toward the nearest cottage and from there moved to a point where he could watch the powder barn from a distance.

But she never came.

There were any number of buildings here, including a small chapel or church, the mine operator's house, a hall for the men to gather, a tiny general store. All in a state of disrepair. When had this particular mine failed? He remembered something about 1884, but wasn't sure of the date. Thirty-some years of slowly disintegrating.

A mouse scuttled past his feet, scurrying for shelter down a hole by the wall.

What had brought the woman here *now*, living alone in a place surely haunted by whatever lived off the land—foxes and stoats and badgers?

Two hours passed without sighting her, and the crows were quiet, he could just see them in one of the trees at the edge of the clearing.

Very carefully, with skills learned on the battlefield, he extricated himself, breaking off any possibility of contact.

But when he got back to his own motorcar, he quartered the surrounding mile. And there, well hidden by a tree that had come down in some long-ago storm, was a 1914 Sunbeam motorcycle complete with sidecar, shielded by khaki canvas that looked as if it had come from the Army—half a tent? On top of that were laid handfuls of winter grass and vines and other easily come-by bits that helped conceal it from a casual passerby.

Hamish startled him. "Ye ken, ye could tek away a wee child in yon sidecar. And who would see?"

"Possibly. We can't be sure."

"A motorcycle doesna' have to stay on the roads. It can go cross-country, weil oot o' sight."

Rutledge wanted to believe him. But there was no *proof.*

"Susan Milford was in Wales. She may still be there, preparing to arrive at the quarry any day now."

"*Expected* to arrive, aye," Hamish argued. "And a' eyes are there, waiting for her. The question is, what does she want sae near to Crowley?"

Rutledge took a deep breath, then started back toward his own motorcar.

Hamish said derisively, "Who else could she be? Ye can tak' her in for questioning. But ye willna' do it."

"There's nothing for her here. Her brother is dead. The child is still unaccounted for. It doesn't make sense that she would come to Shropshire."

"Unless she's come for a reason. Ruth is still alive. And you've come back. There was no place for ye to go but here. No' after the quarry."

Rutledge said nothing.

"Ye know more than you ought. About Milford, about yon Turnbull woman, about Joseph Burton," Hamish persisted.

"I don't think shooting policemen is on her docket."

"Oh, aye?"

Rutledge turned the crank, then got into the motorcar, driving down the main road toward Crowley.

"Tonight," he said to Hamish. "We'll see what we find tonight."

The flare of hope in Ruth Milford's face as he walked through the pub's door was like a lash. He'd brought her news of her husband's death—and couldn't find her child.

"I'm sorry," Rutledge said quickly. "I have no news for you. Good or bad."

Fighting back tears, she said, "I tried not to hope."

She came around from behind the bar and said, "There's food left from lunch. I was just going to have a sandwich."

She brought plates for two, and sat down opposite him. "Is Sam coming home soon?"

"I haven't been to the river. I've been searching for his sister."

"What does she have to do with anything?" she asked in surprise.

"It's what the police do," he said. "Search for any possible connection with the family. Or anyone who can add anything to one's store of information. Looking for a pattern to emerge."

"Well, I can tell you that Sam wasn't certain she was still alive."

"Why?"

"He hadn't heard from her during the war. Not even a postcard. Nor had I. Not that I'd expected to, mind you. And there was nothing when he came home, not even a note to tell him she was glad he survived the war. I didn't meet her until our wedding—for Sam's sake I tried to be polite, but I didn't particularly care for her. Nor she me, for that matter. I could tell."

"I'm told she's mad as a hatter." He waited for her reply.

Frowning, Ruth said, "I wouldn't call her mad. She's twisted in some way that I don't understand. And I never felt that she wanted Sam to be happy, to get on with his life. Still, he felt responsible for her after their father died. I couldn't understand why, given how she behaved toward him. But Sam wasn't one to walk away. That was one of the things I loved about him."

"Would she try to hurt you or your husband?"

"How do you mean?"

"For instance, would she—let's take the pub. Would she try to burn it down, so that you couldn't live here any longer? Or knowing how much you loved Tildy, would she wish to take her away? Leaving you to grieve and suffer?"

Ruth stared at him in alarm. "Surely—you can't be serious?"

Rutledge said, "I'm sorry, I must ask. It's—routine."

"I don't even want to think about—that's *horrible*."

"The solicitor. Hastings. Would he protect her?"

"I'm sure he worries about her. He's rather Victorian in some ways, isn't he? Polite and kind and always happy to help. I wouldn't be surprised if she made his life wretched too, just because she could."

He nearly choked on his sandwich at her description of the man. Then he remembered the woman in the fur stole that Hastings had escorted to the door, the epitome of courtesy.

He said, "He's your solicitor now. You might wish to find a younger man, more in step with the present." It wasn't his place to give her advice, but nor could he tell her that Hastings was Machiavellian. Even if she would believe him.

He pushed his plate away, and brought up the subject that he'd avoided before. They were alone in the pub, there was no one to overhear.

"Mrs. Milford. It's painful, I'm sure, but I must ask you about Tildy's real father."

Color flared in her face, and she started to rise, but he said, "No, you must listen to me. What do you know about this man? His name? Where he lives? I have to pursue the possibility that he discovered you had a daughter, and he decided to come for her."

"He never knew—I never told him. Why should I? After—after what had happened." She was speaking rapidly now, trying to evade talking about the past.

"You could have rid yourself of the child, and no one the wiser."

"Why? It wasn't Tildy's fault, was it? I love—loved—her as much as I would have done if she had been Sam's and mine. More, because she was the innocent victim here."

"But she wasn't Sam's. She had a father."

"No! By law she *is* Sam's child. He never repudiated her!" She was angry now.

"Because he was the man he was. And he loved her as much as you did. That's to his credit. But let's consider the other issue here. That somehow the man who attacked you discovered Tildy's existence, and decided he must have her. He took you by force. What was to stop him from taking Tildy from you by force as well? Surely you must have considered that possibility? When she went missing?" He used the word deliberately, not the euphemism *lost*.

"I tell you, he never knew she existed! I saw to that. I made *certain* that Tildy wasn't ever to know. I did everything in my power to protect her—" She broke off, afraid that in her fury she was about to say too much. Taking a deep breath, she added in a shaking voice, "I did what had to be done."

And for a split second, as she said that, he found himself wondering if somehow she had made absolutely and finally certain of Tildy's safety by doing away with the man who had fathered her.

He couldn't quite see her as a murderer. But women with children to protect could find resources within themselves to do what had to be done. Even if it included murder.

"Aye, but yon husband didna' believe he was deid," Hamish said.

He caught himself in time, and didn't answer. Ruth was looking away, her eyes on the windows, seeing something he couldn't read.

After a moment she said forlornly, "Why *my* child? Why Tildy? How could anyone be so very cruel?"

And that, Rutledge thought, whether she liked it or not, brought them back to Sam Milford's sister.

He used the excuse that he wanted to review the actual kidnapping again, and in the afternoon, questioned Ruth, her cousin, and her cousin's husband. They couldn't add anything new, they had been over this with the police at the time, and with Rutledge twice.

When they had finished, he brought out his note-book and took the bit of ribbon from it, holding it up for the three of them to see.

Ruth cried out as if she'd been stabbed in the heart.

Donald got to his feet, swearing at Rutledge, his face twisted in anguish.

Ruth reached for the ribbon. "She was wearing it. It was in her hair the day she was taken. Where did you find it? You *must* tell me, I have to know—in God's name—"

"Can you be perfectly sure of that? It could be a similar ribbon—"

But Nan and Donald supported her, Nan saying over and over, "That's Tildy's, it was one of Ruth's favorite bows for her hair. I'd recognize it anywhere."

"I found it in an empty house in Wales."

They stared at him, their questions tumbling over each other in their anxiety.

But he said only, "The woman's name was Ruth Middleton. Does that mean anything to you?"

It didn't. He hadn't expected it to.

Ruth was in tears now. "Does this mean she's alive? Please—"

But whether Gwennie—Tildy—or a child that didn't exist—had lived in that house, or not, he didn't know. And so he couldn't answer them.

Afterward, when Nan had taken Ruth home, Donald told Rutledge what he thought of him. "I hope you got what you wanted with that display of cruelty. But for my money you ought to be taken off this inquiry and someone else put in charge. It was mean, vicious, unnecessary. Ruth was beginning to heal. Then you gave her hope, and now it will all have to be done again. The weeping, the nights pacing the floor, the grieving. You ought to be ashamed of that."

"I had to know," he said quietly. "Who else would recognize that bit of ribbon but Tildy's family?"

"Who is this Middleton woman? What's she to Ruth or Sam or Tildy?"

"I don't know. Not yet."

"How did she come to have that ribbon?"

"I wish I knew. It was the only thing in an empty house that didn't appear to belong there. According to the police in the village, she lived alone there."

Donald began to pace. "Was she the kidnapper?"

"If she was, according to the police, there was no child with her."

"Then what did she do with Tildy?"

"I don't know."

"It was your business to know. Why didn't you *make* her tell you?"

"She had gone away. They weren't expecting her to come back."

Donald swore. Then, rounding on Rutledge again, he said, "You're leaving in the morning. And I don't want to see you cross Ruth's threshold again until you can bring her daughter to her."

"It's what I've been trying to do," Rutledge said grimly. "But so far, I have only a bit of ribbon. That doesn't bode well for the truth."

He was alone in the pub after nine that evening.

Will had served him his dinner, telling him stiffly that Ruth wouldn't be available to see him off in the morning. And no one else had come in. Rutledge wasn't sure whether that was by design or happenstance.

He waited until the last lights had gone out in the village, and then quietly set out in his motorcar to where he'd left it when he'd first seen the figure walking toward Little Bog.

The motorcycle was still hidden, just as it had been earlier. As far as he could tell in the dark, without using his torch, it hadn't been moved.

Walking on, he listened to the night sounds. The rain had stopped in late afternoon, but the sky was still overcast, cutting down on the ambient light. But the road had been well used in its day and, despite the encroaching weeds, was still a pale ribbon unspooling before him as he approached the ruins.

He came in a roundabout way. The village had been built on a semicircular plan, with the works in the center and the stand of trees beyond that, closing the circle. Moving silently, he found the corner of a house from which he could just see into the black interior of the powder barn.

A light flickered there, and as his eyes adjusted, he could see that it was from a flame—a fire on the hearth.

There was no shadow moving back and forth across the orange flickers.

She was not in there. He could feel it.

More alert than ever, he stood watch.

But the dancing flames held him, taking him back to the war and the precious warmth of the candle in his dugout, where he kept his company records and his diary and wrote letters to the relatives of the dead.

He could feel himself drifting back there, to the sound of Hamish's voice just outside the cloth that hid his light from German snipers.

Rutledge struggled against the draw of the past, of the war. He could hear the shells now, ranging first, finding their target soon enough. And the scramble to get out of their path, to pick up the wounded and carry them to safety. Such as it was.

He was being sucked into the darkness of his mind, and he fought now, his teeth clenched, his hold on the unlit torch all but a death grip.

He hadn't expected this—he hadn't been *prepared*. And yet the nightmare rolled on.

He wouldn't scream. *He wouldn't—!*

Hamish said softly, " *'Ware!*"

And somehow he heard the word and clung to it, rising up from the depths and shadows and feeling the rough stone edge of the cottage biting into his shoulder as he leaned hard into it.

He'd heard nothing. But Hamish had.

A footstep? He couldn't remember.

Something.

He began to realize then. The fire on the little stone hearth was a decoy. It was there to draw whoever had come.

Refusing to believe that she could have seen him— or that one betraying footprint—in the afternoon, he waited until moonrise.

But she never came to the powder barn. And when he moved closer as the fire began to burn down, shadows changing in the uneven light, he knew she'd been clever.

Where *had* she set her night camp? In the trees? The boarded entrance to a shaft? In what was left of the main building, where the manager must have had an office?

The ruins were full of choices. If he searched, she would see him long before he saw her. And disappear again.

While he had no choice but to retreat.

Why had she come here? What had drawn her to the place where that child had been taken? Where her brother and his wife had lived?

The questions rang through his head all the way back to the motorcar.

Had she been here before and knew it was a sanctuary of sorts? Or was there something she had come for, was waiting for?

According to the man in the slate quarry, Susan Milford was expected there.

But he remembered hearing a motorcycle racing down the hill outside his hotel room window. Had that been her, on her way to the quarry, and the man had lied to him?

Then who was here?

A red fox vixen trotted across his path, nose up, sniffing the night air.

A thought flashed through his mind as he watched

her disappear. If Susan Milford had a familiar, as witches were said to do, it would be a fox . . .

Hamish said as Rutledge bent to turn the motorcar's crank, "Ye ken, if it *is* her, it could be trouble for its ain sake."

Hamish could very well be right.

He didn't sleep well, after he got himself quietly back into the inn. It was just after three in the morning when he heard a noise downstairs. His first thought was that Will had come to start the bread and leave it to rise. There was no bakery in Crowley.

But he got up, left his boots where they were, and opened his door as quietly as he could. There was only darkness and silence from the head of the stairs. He made his way there and started down. As he did, he heard the quiet click of the door that led to the yard.

Someone had gone out. He sniffed the air. No scent of yeast and dough. Moving quietly still, he brought back a mental picture of where the tables and chairs had been in the evening and avoided them in the darkness as his eyes began to adjust.

There was no one in the yard as he reached the door and peered out. He thought he saw a shape by the barn, but it was too vague to be sure.

He waited, but didn't see any further movement.

Nan or Donald could have come back for something. But at this hour?

Short of lighting all the lamps, there was no way to tell if anything was missing or had been taken.

After a time, he went back to bed, and finally fell into an uneasy sleep.

He was finishing his breakfast in the morning when Ruth came in through the main door. She hesitated as she saw him sitting there, then gathered her courage and strode briskly toward the kitchen. She gave him a cold nod in passing, but didn't speak.

She came back with a tray and began to set several tables with silverware and cups. Halfway through, she stopped, and he heard her say, "That's odd."

He looked up, saw that she was staring at the line of frames around the wall, those her father had put up of the miners in his day.

One of them was missing, an empty space. It was at the end of the row that ran over the doorway and into the corner, where the line turned and came toward the main wall.

Rising, he walked over to where she was standing.

"What is it?" he asked.

She turned on him, accusing. "Did you take that photograph down?"

"No. Why should I take it?"

"Well, it's missing."

"What was the photograph of?"

He expected her to say that it was one of the miners or possibly the machinery that they were working.

"It was when Sam enlisted. He'd come back to the pub, and everyone was eager to buy him a drink, slapping him on the back, wishing him well. He'd wanted to join up, but he was too short. They wouldn't have him. And then the call came for the Bantams, and he was off to Chester on the next train, eager to do his bit. I was against it, but he told me he couldn't serve men in a bar when he could fight for his country. That he had to go and show them that he was as good a soldier as any man. And I let him go." Her voice caught on the last word, as if she still felt a deep regret for all that had happened between the time she had sent him off to war and the day he'd come home again, finally.

"Who would take such a thing?" she asked. "*When? You* were the only one here for dinner last night." And then, sadly, "I gave you my best photograph of him. Why did you need that one too?"

"I give you my word. I don't have it. I'd looked at these, yes, but I hadn't noticed that particular one. Or if I had, I didn't know what it signified."

But he didn't think she believed him.

Had he been right after all? That Susan Milford

had come back to Crowley? But for a photograph? It didn't make any sense. How had she even known it was there? She must have seen his motorcar in the yard, must have known someone was staying in the pub. And yet she had slipped in and taken it as quietly as a thief in the night. *Was* she making trouble for Ruth, as Hamish had said? If so, she'd succeeded. He was about to tell Ruth what he'd heard in the night, then stopped himself in time.

She already felt violated, believing that someone had come in and taken something else from her. He didn't need to confirm her worst fears.

He left soon afterward and this time drove all the way into the old ruins, up to the front of the powder barn, and blew his horn.

But when he got out and went inside to look, it was swept clean. There was no sign that anyone had been there. Only the lingering smell of woodsmoke from the little fire. Even the stones had been taken out and thrown somewhere, so that the woman's presence was wiped clean.

When he was certain that she was no longer anywhere in the ruins, he went back to where the motorcycle had been hidden.

It too was gone.

She'd got what she came for.

But why was that particular photograph important? How had she known it would hurt Ruth to lose it?

Rutledge couldn't believe that the Susan Milford that he'd been hunting was sentimental enough to want a photograph of her late brother.

But then, odder things had happened.

He got back into the motorcar, finally, and was on his way to Shrewsbury when a herd of cattle blocked his way. The farmer, touching his cap at Rutledge, moved them on, but while he was waiting for the last cow to meander across the road, he could have sworn he heard a motorcycle in the distance, traveling in the same direction.

He sped up as soon as his road was clear. But he never caught up with it.

13

He came into Shrewsbury by the Abbey once more, and then threaded his way to Church Street and the Prince Rupert.

Watching the Wednesday-morning traffic around him, he was about to turn into the yard when he saw what looked like the end of a Sunbeam motorcycle already there. Swerving back into the road, he went around the corner, out of sight, and left his motorcar there.

Walking back, he stepped into the hotel and found a porter carrying a valise up to a room. He took the man aside and asked, "That motorcycle in the yard. Do you know who it belongs to? I think it might be a friend's."

"The Sunbeam, sir? That belongs to Mr. Milford."

"Sam Milford?"

"Yes, sir. He's kept rooms here for years. Since the war, to my certain knowledge. He comes and goes, a busy man. A quiet guest."

"Small world, isn't it?" he said affably, and gave the man something for his trouble. When the porter was out of sight, Rutledge left.

Sam Milford had always stayed at a small, inexpensive, and unpretentious hotel in a very different part of town. The Pit and The Pony couldn't afford any better accommodations—or so Rutledge had been told. He wondered now if Milford's other reason was to avoid his sister. But then how had he known where his sister was staying?

Rutledge kept walking until he'd reached the street where Hastings and Hastings had chambers. Finding a shallow doorway several houses away, he waited.

An hour passed, and he moved on to another vantage point, patient and watchful.

It was nearly two o'clock when his vigil was finally rewarded.

A slim figure in a man's black-and-khaki riding dress walked down the street, felt hat pulled low over his features. But he didn't stop at the solicitor's door.

Instead he went past, and turned down a service alley between two other buildings. An hour later he came back the same way and walked on.

A tall boy? A short man? Or a woman in a man's clothes?

Rutledge set out to follow at a distance.

But Shrewsbury was a town of what the locals called shuts. Passages running between and under buildings, where it was impossible to keep his quarry in sight. And in the third shut, he lost her. Whether she had ducked into a shop on the far side or found another way out, he didn't know.

It was tempting to book his dinner in the Prince Rupert dining room to see who came to sit at Sam Milford's table. He had never seen a photograph of Susan, he had only Hastings's description to guide him. And that was not reliable.

But Rutledge himself was not ready to be seen. As long as she didn't know he was there, he was free to track her.

What role had Susan Milford played here? Was she a murderer? Had she been responsible for taking Tildy? If so, what had she done with the child? Was she haunted by that, and suffering delusions in Beddgwian?

Hastings had the answers—he must have them. But he would surely lie. Speaking to him would only serve to put the solicitor and Susan Milford on their guard.

He went back to the Prince Rupert, its handsome Tudor facade bright in the afternoon sun, and found a tea shop down the way where he could sit at a table that offered him a view of the hotel's entrance. But she didn't come back there. Or if she did, he never saw her.

Then, just as the owner of the tea shop informed him that it was closing for the day, he glimpsed the Sunbeam pulling out of the hotel yard and turning his way.

He hastily paid for his tea and hurried up the street to where he'd left his own vehicle.

Where had she gone from the hotel? South to Crowley and Little Bog? Or across the river and on to Wales? But she had the photograph now . . .

He cursed the crank, then was behind the wheel, heading as fast as he dared through the town's busy streets toward the Welsh Bridge and the road west. He crossed over it and was into the outskirts of Shrewsbury without sighting the Sunbeam.

Hamish said tersely, "Ye guessed wrong."

"We'll have to see," he retorted, and kept his eyes on the road ahead.

It wasn't until he was well on his way to Oswestry with nothing but instinct leading him that in the distance he caught sight of the Sunbeam again, just rounding a bend in the road.

She was heading back to Wales.

Cold air had followed the rain, sweeping in and dropping drifts of late snow in the mountains. Shaded roads were slippery with ice, almost invisible until a driver was nearly on it.

Even here the motorcycle was running fast. Sometimes he found tracks in the pristine white snowfall, and at other times he could hear a faint echo across a valley. His motorcar ran almost silently, but its passage also betrayed him from time to time, as the road narrowed and the speeding tires, gripping the wet surface, made slushing sounds.

She had stopped for petrol—as he himself had had to do—and had found a small hotel beyond the Swallow Falls outside Betws y Coed for the night. He had nearly missed that, catching up to her unawares, and spent a cold night in the motorcar, back in the village, to let her get ahead once more.

If she knew she was being followed, she appeared not to care. But he rather thought the Sunbeam's own noise masked his.

By late afternoon on the second day, they were close to the quarry, and he hung well back. If she was as clever as he thought, she'd find a place along the last stretch of road and lie in wait for anyone who was behind her. It was a Thursday—another week had passed since Milford had fallen to his death.

And Rutledge was no closer to finding his killer . . .

Nibbling at the back of his mind was Chief Inspector Markham's silence. By this time in most inquiries, he was asking for a report, urging Rutledge to find answers, arguing that the simplest solutions were often the right solutions. It was how Markham saw duty.

Doubling back on himself, he left his motorcar below the quarry as before, this time hidden behind a deserted cottage, inside a barn with a roof that had half fallen in. There was barely enough room for the Rolls to pass. Then he walked back to the quarry.

Instead of approaching the quarry office by way of the road, he began to look for access over the vast spread of rubble slate.

It was slippery work, but he was dressed for it, and his gloved hands took the brunt of sharp corners and edges. Working his way as if he were climbing a cliff face, he chose his path as carefully as he could.

The first hurdle was the hardest, he thought, as he came out on a lorry road that led far into the quarry site. Below him, barely ten feet away, dizzying depths opened up, and he realized just how deep the quarry was—deeper than the Aqueduct was tall. Looking up, he could see right across the gaping space, to abandoned caverns open to the elements, where the miners had had to leave one face and open up another over the years. It was rather, he thought, what the surface of the moon looked like, barren and inhospitable. Then he noticed men working on the far side of the gap, loading a lorry. They were tiny.

He was standing on a rough track, one side ending in more deserted caverns and the other, the left, appearing to head back toward the pithead. He walked without haste, hoping not to attract attention. He found a place where he could lie atop a heap of rubble and use his field glasses, but it was unstable and he almost came to grief trying to climb down again. Forty yards on there was another pile that appeared to be more stable, and he moved on to that.

From there he could just see a line of buildings in the distance.

The glasses brought them into sharp focus, and he began to observe the people moving about the cleared area in front of them.

There must be, he thought, one shift presently down in the pit. And various working parties on the surface appeared to deal with the vast amount of rubble that could still be salvaged. Others were loading slate in pallets onto a lorry.

A woman came out of one of the shops, bringing something to a dog lying in a patch of watery sun, and he turned toward her.

She was not as tall as the average height of a man—five feet six. Possibly five feet two or three? He judged her in relation to the lorry and the other figures in the yard. Dark hair curled out from the edges of a silk kerchief, and she wore a heavy coat, cut like a man's, and buttoned to the throat. Trousers instead of a skirt, as if that made getting around easier. Her stride was easy, long. But he didn't recognize it.

She turned to say something over her shoulder, and then another woman came out, and the dog went to her, wagging its tail in welcome.

The second woman bent to fondle his ears, all the while speaking to the first woman.

She was taller, five feet five? And slim, wearing trousers crammed into high boots, a blue scarf at her neck. Fair hair was done up in a knot at the back of her head, and a dark green coat was draped over her shoulders, as if she'd only stepped out for a brief word to the dog. When she walked on to speak to the lorry driver hailing her, he recognized that stride. Susan Milford or not, this was the woman from the Crowley road and from Shrewsbury.

She was just turning back toward the building when Rutledge heard a grinding of gears and a rumble.

While he'd been staring through the glasses, intent on what was happening below, one of the lorries from deep inside the quarry had started back toward the main buildings, and it was nearly on him.

He scrambled down from his perch, nearly lost his footing, and swore as his ankle took the brunt of his misstep. He was only just able to get down behind a large slab of blue slate as the lorry came up the slight rise just behind him. The heavy tires passed within inches of the slab, crunching into broken bits of slate that formed the road and spewing them out behind. He could just see the driver, eyes straight ahead, taking his time. There was a several-hundred-foot drop almost at his elbow as the road narrowed.

And then he was past the pinch point, and moving a little faster.

Exhaling with relief, Rutledge let him move well out of sight before he himself stirred.

With his glasses, he managed to follow the truck's approach to the main building. The second woman had gone back inside, leaving her companion to deal with it.

Scanning the open yard, he searched it from one end to the other, then swung the glasses back again, nearer the buildings this time, set out of the path of the huge lorries with their heavy loads.

And there it was, the motorcycle. Or the front wheel, to be exact, barely visible from his vantage point, but he recognized it at once. A Sunbeam.

It was warm on the slates, even the pale sun adding a little to that warmth, out of the wind that was eddying little dust clouds in the wake of the lorry.

The woman didn't appear again until the lorry had been checked and sent on its way, down the long drive to the main road, out of his range of sight. Then she stepped out with two cups in her hand, passing one to her friend. They appeared to be on good terms, talking quietly. This then was very likely the woman Susan Milford had trusted.

He thought she was very likely one of the people he'd intended to speak to, when he'd come here earlier. Before he'd been warned off.

He waited again, watchful.

And then he heard a voice shouting roughly somewhere behind his position. Turning quickly, he dislodged some loose scree and nearly lost his field glasses. Gripping them, he looked down past the toes of his boots and saw a man coming fast up the slope below him.

He'd been seen, and there was nothing for it but to let events take their course. He wasn't sure-footed enough up here to risk a fall or a broken ankle. And he knew he couldn't outrun the man, who moved with the grace of a mountain goat, at home up here on the heights of the quarry.

Getting himself down to the road, he stood there as the red-faced man came pounding up and slid to a stop.

"Who the—bloody hell—are you?" he was demanding, bending forward in a menacing stance.

Rutledge said, "Scotland Yard." And as he did, he realized that the man had a pry bar in one large fist, gripping it like a weapon. "Put that down," he ordered then. "Here's my identification."

He reached carefully into a pocket, pulling it out and holding it up in front of the angry man. A foreman? Or just another worker here? He couldn't be sure.

But the man wasn't interested. Still holding the pry bar ready to strike, he said, "Who let you in here? What are you after?"

"I'm a policeman," Rutledge repeated, his own voice hard and cold.

"We'll see what Theresa has to say." He lifted the bar threateningly, and added, "Go on. You were so eager to spy, let's give you a closer look."

Rutledge realized that the man clearly wasn't protecting the quarry, as he'd first thought, but the women he'd been watching.

Without a word, he turned and started along the road.

There was still that precipitously sharp drop to his right, and he moved quickly, trying to keep the same distance between his head and the man behind him. It would be short work to send him over the edge and worry later about the consequences.

They moved in tandem, walking steadily. And at length they came down the last curving slope, finally into the yard.

It was empty now, save for the dog, which, hackles up, came head-down toward Rutledge, growling. The trucks had gone.

He'd always had a way with animals, and he spoke to the dog, but it was taking its lead from the angry man with the weapon.

"Tessie?" He was shouting toward the main building. "Out here, if you please."

And the door finally opened. Tessie stood on the threshold.

"Who is he?" she demanded, her voice anxious. "Where did you find him?"

He told her, giving a location number. "Watching the yard with them glasses," he added for good measure. "Says he's a copper."

"Good afternoon," Rutledge spoke, then, keeping still while the dog circled him, "My name is Rutledge. I'm from London, Scotland Yard. My identification?" He turned his hand so that she could see it.

She said, staring hard at him, "You were here before. The foreman told me. Asking directions, you said then."

"Yes. I didn't know where to look before. I did today."

"What are you looking for?"

"I need to speak to Susan Milford."

"No one by that name here. I'm the only woman on this site."

"Then why is her Sunbeam here? In the quarry yard?" he asked in a reasonable tone of voice. "She was wearing a blue scarf around her throat."

Tessie looked just beyond him, at the man with the pry bar. "He's seen her, Eddie," she said.

"What shall I do with him?"

"Let me speak to her," Rutledge interjected. "The last thing you want is Scotland Yard coming up here and tearing this quarry apart looking for me. And if she's listening—" He raised his voice. "Susan? You'll have been told about me by Mr. Hastings. In Shrewsbury. You'll know it isn't safe to meddle with the police. All I need is an hour of your time. And then I'll leave."

"You'll leave if and when I say you do," Eddie said, moving a little, the pry bar still a weapon in his hand.

Someone appeared in the doorway behind Tessie, a shadowy shape in the dim interior. He thought he was being looked over.

The figure moved, and Tessie stepped aside, to let the woman in the blue scarf come to the threshold.

She wasn't traditionally pretty. But the force of her personality was there in her face, and he realized that she was quite attractive, like her half brother. There was strength in the line of her jaw, too, and her blue gaze was direct, and as clear of madness as anyone he'd met in the last two weeks.

"No' mad, but no' rational," Hamish was saying in his head.

But she *was* rational. Driven, tormented, but rational.

She was considering him now, looking at him speculatively, deciding what should be done about him. He could read it in her gaze. There was no anger in her face, no dislike of him or fear of what he'd come there to do. Just a weighing up of choices, the way a woman might decide which hat to wear or a man which cigar to buy.

As if he as a person was not the central issue. Something else was. And he had no idea what that might be.

And he knew with a sudden chill down his backbone

that she could order him killed, and both Tessie and Eddie would do as she asked.

Why? What had she told them that they would be willing to hang for her?

Searching for a way to reach her, he said, "I'm trying to find a missing child. I think you had her for a while, then lost her as well. I don't know where she is. I was hoping you might. She belongs with her mother. Will you help me find her?"

She heard every word, and then she nodded, and he thought with some relief that he had convinced her.

Too late he realized that it was a signal, and he couldn't duck the pry bar coming toward him. All he could do was lean away from the blow, hoping to take a little of the force from it before it hit him.

And then he felt the cold metal strike, a white light of pain, and then blackness.

He never knew that he hit the ground. There was only the blackness everywhere.

14

When he came to his senses, he wasn't sure where he was—or why. Only that one leg was cramping badly and his head ached as if an axe had been embedded in his skull. He could feel the weight of it, the blade pressing against the backs of his eyes.

It was several minutes before he could open them. When he did, the light was blinding. He shut them again. And as he did he became aware of the murmurs all around him, sounds he couldn't place. Soft whispers, as if there were people everywhere, trying not to disturb him.

There was a rhythm to their voices.

Frowning, he tried to make sense of it all. Were they singing? He couldn't hear words over the thundering in his head.

Making an effort that sent a shooting pain through his cramped leg, he tried to raise himself, then stopped almost in the same breath as he remembered the sheer drop to his right, down into the depths of the quarry, and how easy it would be to slide over the edge.

He opened his eyes again, squinting this time and able to raise a hand to shield them from the light, blinking against the force of it. His vision cleared a little.

He wasn't in the quarry. He was in the rear seat of his own motorcar.

Oh dear God in heaven, he breathed in sudden terror. *Hamish*—

The rear seat had been his realm since 1919, when he, Rutledge, had taken the motorcar out of the locked mews behind his parents' house—Frances's house, his parents had left it to his sister.

Frantic, ignoring the pain that seemed to be everywhere, he scrambled to find the door's handle and shove it wide, nearly tumbling out in moving silver—

Water. Shimmering, blinding water everywhere. Catching himself even as he was about to tumble in, holding himself rigidly on the edge of the rear seat by a sheer effort of will, he stared out at the moving water.

The tide was coming in. And his motorcar was axle

deep already, as the water whispered around him and eddied and stirred and tried to rid itself of this obstruction in its midst.

Where in God's name *was* he?

It didn't matter. He had to get out of there before the water was deep enough to reach the motor.

Gripping the back of the front seat, he somehow found the strength to swing himself into the front of the motorcar, his head brushing against the underneath of the top. Pausing just long enough to catch his breath, he looked up. The top was in place, but the slanting rays of the rising sun were lighting everything with a brilliance that made his eyes ache.

He got himself into the passenger's seat, moved across to his own.

He must get out and turn the crank. Now. *Now.*

Water filled his shoes and soaked the legs of his trousers. He held on to the frame, made it to the front of the vehicle, and shoved the crank into place. The motor, for a blessing, turned over, and he got back to his open door as fast as he could.

Looking around for points of reference, he realized he was on a long flat beach where the morning tide was coming in far too rapidly for his liking. And his tires had settled into the soft sand beneath them. But the powerful motor took hold, and the car rocked as it started forward.

He nursed it, adding power as he moved toward the stretch of dry land above the tide line, gray with the debris left behind by last night's tide.

Slowly, slowly he gained ground, and then his tires bit into harder packed sand, and he was out of the water, moving beyond its reach.

He stopped there to let his head ease a little. When he put up his hands to cradle it, he felt the encrusted blood on one side, and memory came flooding back.

Eddie, the damned fool, had hit him with the pry bar, and they had put him in his motorcar and driven him here. To the sea.

Here, *where*?

Porthmadog? Where the slate trains had always brought their wares to be shipped to England and even Germany, where slate had seen a huge market up until the war. But more to the point, this was a route that the quarrymen knew. It was a place they could reach even in the dark.

His other senses were starting to work, the cramped leg trying to reassert itself, tightening even as he made an effort to straighten it, his head throbbing with every movement.

What was that he smelled? Above the salt of the

sea, the dead fish odor of the tide line? It was some-how familiar . . .

Whisky. His clothes and his body had been dowsed with whisky. And anyone finding the motorcar and the half-coherent man inside would assume that he'd made it this far under his own power and was sleeping off his drunken spree, unaware that he'd stopped where the sea was about to come in.

It had been cleverly done.

He could hear someone's boots crunching in the sand, coming closer.

He looked up. It was the local Constable, trudging out to see what the reported motorcar was doing in the water of the little bay.

Rutledge braced himself.

"Good morning, Constable," he said. His throat was as dry as the sand beneath his tires now.

"Morning to you, sir." He was close enough now—Rutledge watched as the odor of stale whisky reached him on the sea breeze. "Had a happy night, did we now?"

"Not particularly," Rutledge said, and reached for his identification.

It wasn't there.

Swearing under his breath, he added, "I've come to Wales on police business. I was questioning a suspect when someone hit me, hard. And I awoke to find myself here."

"Indeed, sir. And you'll have some identification to be showing me now."

"I don't have it. It was taken by whoever put me here."

"Yes, sir, and was that your own whisky you've been consuming meanwhile?" He came closer, staring into the rear seat. "Ah, and there I see the bottle itself."

"It was poured on me, Constable. I didn't drink it."

But as the sun climbed and heated the interior of the motorcar, the odor intensified. "A waste of good spirits to pour them over a man and not into him." The Constable sighed, then said, "Perhaps you'd like to come along with me, now, sir. And we'll sort this out at the station."

What had they done with his identification?

He was trying to stave off the Constable while he searched for it. But it was nowhere, not on him, not in the motorcar's pockets, not under his feet on the floorboards.

The rear seat. He'd been pushed and shoved, to get him back there, his height creating problems—thank God they hadn't resorted to breaking his legs—!

Getting out was an effort, and reaching out to search behind the seat set his head to roaring like a goods train going up a steep incline. Persevering, he worked his fingers along the back of the seat, all but holding his breath. Behind him, the Constable had moved near enough to block any escape.

Twice he ran his fingers behind the seat, leaning in, closing his eyes against the sight of Hamish there, frowning at himself for his fear.

His fingers found a corner, and he tightened them, pulling gently. Something came, then caught on the back edge of the leather before suddenly pulling free and into his hand. He extracted himself from the seat, and turning, held his identification out to the Constable.

"It tells me who you are. But not how you came to be riding the incoming tide, or when you swallowed all that whisky." He looked at Rutledge's head. "Or how you got that bloody great lump on your head."

"Damn it, I need to see a doctor. The station can wait." The Constable's face was beginning to swim before him.

"I'll decide—"

His voice was cold and hard as he struggled to cope. "Do that. And afterward, the Yard will see to it that you're dismissed for obstructing an inquiry. Take your choice."

The Constable continued to argue with him but escorted him to a doctor's surgery just off a side street in the village. He'd been right, it was Porthmadog.

Dr. Llewellyn examined Rutledge's head and said, "That's nasty. What happened?"

"A pry bar in the hands of a large quarry worker. I was trying to persuade a murder suspect to see matters my way and talk to me. She declined. Her friend ended the disagreement. The next thing I knew, I was in the rear of my motorcar out on the strand as the tide turned."

The doctor sniffed, then stood back. "You reek of whisky, man."

"It's in my clothing. Not my stomach. Except for this damned headache, I'm as sober as you are."

In the end he was given a powder for his headache, and a patch for the cut there. He found a hotel—the Constable had to vouch for him before they would give him a room. His valise, in the boot of the motorcar, had not been touched. He bathed and shaved, combed his dark hair over the wound to make it less noticeable, then changed, while someone in the kitchen sponged his wrecked clothing. He felt at least presentable when he came down an hour later, planning to leave.

The woman behind the desk said, "Are you sure, sir? You don't look as if you feel quite well."

But he was angry now. He took with him the still damp clothing he'd been wearing, a packet of sandwiches, and a refill for his Thermos of tea.

When he reached the quarry two hours later and drove up to the pithead, there was a man now in the quarry office.

Rutledge had never seen him before.

He shook his head when he was asked to produce the woman by the name of Theresa and the workman called Eddie.

"There's no one here by those names. Are you certain they work here?"

"I am." He produced his identification. "If you lie to me, you will be charged as an accessory to their crimes, which may include murder."

The man's eyes widened, but nothing Rutledge could say would shake his insistence that he knew nothing about the two people the Inspector was seeking.

He even produced a list of employees for Rutledge to read.

It was proof of nothing except someone's ability to plan ahead.

He went house to house in the village at the quarry gates. But he met with the same shakes of the head, doors only half opened as he asked questions.

Susan Milford had vanished again. For all he knew, Theresa and Eddie were hiding in a bedroom or attic until the troublesome Londoner had gone.

In the end, Rutledge let it go.

As he drove away, swallowing another of the powders he'd been given for his headache, he was still very angry.

And the person he was angriest with was the solicitor, Hastings. Who sat like a spider in the center of this web.

It was a long way back to Shrewsbury. He knew he wasn't physically up to it, but his anger was still driving him, and he stopped when he had to, found a place to sleep for a few hours, then was back on the road again.

When he finally saw the approach to the Welsh Bridge very early in the morning, he thought for a frightening second that he was seeing double. For the bridge seemed to have wavered into two. Then it settled back into its familiar shape and he drove across it into the silent, dark city. He found the Prince Rupert, and asked the sleepy clerk if Sam Milford was in residence.

"No, sir. Not at the moment, sir."

He took a room.

He was asleep almost as soon as he reached the bed.

It was after ten o'clock when Rutledge forced himself to open his eyes. For a moment he struggled to remember where he was, then he got up, shaved, and changed. When he came down the stairs to Reception, he could smell a ham roasting, and it turned his stomach.

He went into the bar, but diners were in the middle of their breakfast, and he turned around without the cup of tea he'd wanted.

Leaving the hotel, he walked to clear his head, and by the time he was in front of Hastings and Hastings, he was once more in control. But not of the anger seething through him, and that worried him.

Hamish, who had been there on the long drive back, said, "It's no' your heid, man, it's the child. Remember that."

He crossed the street, went to the door, and knocked.

A clerk answered, but Rutledge brushed him aside. The man danced after him, protesting, but Rutledge was already across the room and opening the door to the passage.

Hastings was in his office. He got to his feet, his eyes hooded, as Rutledge opened the door and the clerk began to make apologies for the interruption.

"Never mind," Hastings said. "Shut the door behind you."

The clerk, stopped in midsentence, glanced quickly from Hastings to the set face of the intruder. Then he was gone, the door swinging shut with a soft *click*.

"Sit down, man, before you fall down." Hastings went to a cabinet behind his desk and took out a bottle with two glasses. "Whisky is good for the spleen," he said, and poured.

Passing one to Rutledge, he set his own down on the desk, then took his chair.

Rutledge didn't sit.

"I am here to take you into custody for obstructing an officer of the law in the pursuit of his duties."

"Very well. I'm an old man. I can hardly fight my way past you and escape into the street. So you might as well tell me what the charges are."

"Where is Susan Milford?"

"I have no way of knowing. I have discovered—as you appear to have done—that she's alive. Where she may be is another matter. Staying with friends, that's the message she left for me. She didn't tell me who they were or where they lived. She generally doesn't confide in me. And so I can't trouble her with questions."

"Why did she travel to Crowley, break into The Pit and The Pony pub, and steal a single photograph from the wall?"

"Did she? You saw her do this? You were a witness to this alleged theft?"

But he hadn't. He'd heard someone in the dark pub. And the next day Ruth Milford had discovered that a photograph was missing.

Rutledge smiled. It didn't reach his eyes. "Are you admitting that Miss Milford was in Crowley? That she did indeed take the photograph in question?"

"What was the photograph of? It might help, if I knew what this was about."

"It was of her brother. Taken on the night that he returned from enlisting in the Bantams. His neighbors had come to wish him Godspeed."

"To be perfectly honest with you, I don't know that Miss Milford doesn't have a copy of that same photograph. It would have been like Sam to have sent her one. If that's the case, why would she wish to steal her sister-in-law's photograph?"

"When the child disappeared last year, did Sam Milford suspect his sister had taken any part in that abduction? Did he demand that you tell him where she was?"

"No, of course he did not suspect her. Nor did Mrs. Ruth Milford. I believe I told you that it was a Mrs. Blake who brought up the half sister's name. She's related to Ruth Milford. A cousin, as I recall." He lifted his glass and drank a little, then set it down again. "It's good whisky, Rutledge. I haven't poisoned it."

But whisky didn't go well with the powders he'd been given.

"You led me to believe that Susan Milford had been suicidal. Why?"

"Because she has been in the past, and I have no assurances that she won't be in the future."

"Did she kill her brother? Or possibly have him killed?"

It was Hastings who was suddenly angry. "Susan Milford isn't a killer."

"She attacked the woman who had had the care of her father."

"She slapped her for saying something about the late Mr. Milford that wasn't true."

"She was the cause of my being attacked two"—he stopped, trying to remember—"three days ago."

"I don't believe you've met Susan, have you? How can you be so certain it was she?"

He gripped the back of the chair just in front of him. "Why do you protect her? At her brother's expense?"

"I don't. As her solicitor, it is my duty to protect her *interests.*"

"I thought she had taken her funds away from the trust. That tells me she also doesn't trust you."

Hastings smiled. "I don't believe there is any law that prohibits a client from asking whomever she pleases to represent her at any given time. As I was the manager of the trust funds in question, she had every right to consult someone else as she made the decision to manage them herself, going forward. It was all quite legally done. I assure you."

"What did she consult you about the other day, when she was here?"

"And you saw her enter my door? Susan Milford?" he parried. "But I will tell you this. I have been informed by my client that she is afraid for her own safety. She has no family. She does have a goodly amount of money in her own name, and as a woman she is vulnerable. The truth is, I don't know why she is in danger, or from whom. I am not even certain she knows. Therefore I can do nothing to protect her."

Rutledge looked at him. The wily old man in the chair behind the desk, sipping his whisky as if he were entertaining a favorite client, had just laid the ground-work for a plea of self-defense if Rutledge or anyone else tried to arrest Susan Milford for what had been done to him at the quarry.

Rutledge could picture her in a courtroom, telling the jury how he had spied on her with field glasses, claiming he was a policeman from London, and insisted on her accompanying him to England for questioning. Alone.

He had done no such thing. He had told Susan he wanted to ask her a few questions. But Theresa and Eddie could refute that, swearing that they feared for her safety and didn't know what else to do. *After all, Susan's own brother had recently been murdered, hadn't he?*

There was the briefest flicker of a smile in the so-licitor's eyes as he regarded Rutledge. One clever man saluting another. As if he'd guessed what Rutledge had just realized.

"It really is quite good whisky," Hastings said again after a moment.

"I haven't touched my glass," Rutledge countered. "Perhaps you'll finish it for me. Meanwhile, where is Susan Milford?"

"I have no idea. I will swear to that if you like. Your guess is as good as mine."

He was damned if he was going back to London with no one in custody, to sit in that cramped office of his and sort through reports he hadn't written.

Rutledge took advantage of the hotel telephone once more to speak to Sergeant Gibson. He'd little hope of finding him in on a Saturday, but his luck held.

He began with the truth.

"I've been out of reach. I've been here longer than expected, with nothing to show for it, except more questions. I shall have to start over, find out what I've missed. There is nothing to report on the child. And that worries me."

"Aye. Odds are, she's dead. But you asked about bones, when last we talked. I haven't received any reports that might be useful. It's the walkers who find them, most often. And it's not the season."

"She was not even three. In the open, they would be gone before they could be found."

"True enough. Anything more you need? Did you find the woman in Betws y Coed?"

"It served to muddy the waters, I'm afraid." He hesitated. "Find a way to break the news gently to the Chief Superintendent. I don't want to be recalled before this is finished."

There was an uncomfortable silence on the other end of the line.

"Gibson? Are you still there?"

"I am, sir. The thing is, Himself hasn't asked. Good day, sir."

And the connection ended.

Rutledge stood there, still holding the receiver, a frown on his face. That wasn't like Markham. It made him wary, just as it had made Gibson uncomfortable.

He was about to put up the receiver, and then in an unaccustomed moment of need, he changed his mind and put through a call to the house in London where his sister and her husband now lived. Frances had told him that they were having a new telephone installed.

She answered on the second ring, just as Rutledge was about to hang up, angry with himself for giving in.

"Hallo," he said. "I've been in the north for some time now. And I'm likely to be here another week. I thought it best to let you know."

"Ian, darling, I'm so glad you did. I stopped by the flat a few days ago. You weren't there, and Mrs. Cuthbert didn't know when to expect you. It's unusual to be away so long, isn't it? No problems, I hope?"

"Only a matter of distances. Keeps me out of touch more than I care for." He paused. "Any particular reason for stopping by?" And now he asked the question that had driven him to put through this call. "Important mail . . ." He stopped himself from adding "from the Yard?" There was no need to worry Frances as well.

"Nothing on the table by your chair. That's where Mrs. C. usually puts anything urgent, isn't it? No, I've just heard that a good friend of yours has got engaged. I thought you might have missed the announcement."

His mouth went dry, and he felt himself tensing, as if warding off a blow. "Has she indeed?"

"Not *she*, you silly man!" His sister's laughter came down the line, happy and lighthearted. "It was Patrick Nelson. Remember him at university? He is marrying one of the Browning sisters. It's a perfect match, don't you think?"

He found the words somehow. "I do. I'm happy for him. He's a good man."

But all he could think of was his relief at hearing it wasn't Kate.

Rutledge had meant what he'd said to Gibson, that he intended to start over, to find what he'd missed. And that meant returning to Llangollen.

On the way, he stopped in Oswestry to speak to Inspector Preston.

"Anything new in Mrs. Turnbull's death?" Preston asked as soon as Rutledge stepped into his office.

"There was a lead. It went nowhere. I'm looking for information today."

"Well, I've none to give you." The reply was short to the point of curtness.

"Then take me back a few years. Near the end of the war, there was a rape in Oswestry. A young woman had come here for a funeral. And someone attacked her. She was ashamed, she never reported that attack. But it's also likely that the man involved was sought in other assaults. Or he may even have been killed. If so, you'll have a record of that search."

Preston, suspicious, said, "What does this have to do with the Turnbull woman? Unless she *was* this woman?"

"I have no reason to think that Betty Turnbull was ever assaulted."

"Then why bring up this other issue?"

"Because that attack might have some bearing on the Milford murder. I think Sam Milford knew something. Discovered something. I have to rule out any connection." He gave the rough dates, as far as he could determine them.

"Well, I can tell you we had no assault cases that we didn't clear. Domestic matters, for the most part. Nothing outstanding, nothing unsolved. Unless it wasn't reported. And if it went unreported, it didn't cross our desk."

Rutledge made light of it. "Then it isn't important to my inquiry. That's all I needed to know."

He had been of two minds about Ruth Milford. And whether or not she had succeeded in killing her attacker. *I did what had to be done.* Her words had stayed with him. And Preston hadn't put them to rest.

He went on to Llangollen. The truth had begun to unfold in the shop of the tailor, Banner. That was where he'd discovered the unidentified corpse's name, had been led to Ruth Milford. And that was where she had been accompanied by a man who had waited for her outside Banner's shop as she ordered clothes for her husband's return from the war.

He, Rutledge, hadn't found that man, and apparently neither had Sam Milford. Still, that officer had either been on leave—or been recuperating from a wound. He either lived in Llangollen or was in a clinic nearby. The only other possibility was that Ruth and he had come there to conduct an affair because neither of them was known in the town.

But it was too late to begin when he pulled into the silent, empty streets. Too late, even, to find his dinner.

Rather than stay in the town, he drove back to a small inn he'd noticed on the outskirts, roused a sleepy owner, and took a room.

That was the last he remembered, for what was left of the night and most of the day that followed it.

The first order of business the next morning was to question Banner again, in the hope there was more he'd been able to recall.

Banner looked up as Rutledge stepped into the shop. "Good day, sir. I'll be with you in five more minutes."

And then he went back to the work he was doing.

When his client was satisfied with his sleeve length, Banner promised to have the coat pressed and ready for him by nine the next morning. He accompanied the man to the door, saw him out, then turned to Rutledge.

"Did you find the man you were looking for?" he asked.

"The man himself was a murder victim. I found his family. I'm now searching for his killer."

"I'm sorry to hear it. She didn't deserve to be unhappy."

"There was the officer who waited for her outside. He never came into the shop. But you deal with men's clothing every day. With their measurements. What else can you tell me about him?"

"As far as I know, I've told you everything. After all, that was some years ago."

"You told me he was in uniform. What insignia did you see?"

"I can't recall noticing. I was occupied with the woman, you see. Choosing cloth, considering measurements, picking out buttons."

"It's second nature to notice," he said again. "Just as I notice how people walk or stand. How they are dressed, whether they're nervous or anxious or angry. If they have something to hide. Do you have something to hide? Is that why you won't help me?"

Banner led the way to the tiny room where he kept his files. "I told you. I was reminded of my wife, talking to the young woman. I didn't want to know about the man in the street, waiting."

He hadn't wanted to think ill of the woman who reminded him of his wife.

Rutledge said, "Whether he was a friend accompanying her on an errand or her lover, I need to find him."

But whatever direction he tried, Rutledge couldn't shake Banner's belief that he couldn't recall any other information.

There was a hotel down the long hill from Banner's shop, The Broadstairs, and it offered a fine dining room.

That was busy today, and Rutledge had to wait in the lounge for the manager to spare him a few minutes.

When the man finally came in search of Rutledge, he looked harassed, as if this was the proverbial last straw. Straightening his coat, brushing back what was left of his thin white hair, apologizing for keeping the gentleman waiting, he led the way to his office. As soon as Rutledge crossed the threshold, the man shut the door, peering out as it closed, as if to be sure no one had seen them. "It's the busiest time of the day," he said, taking the chair behind his desk. "I do hope this won't take very long."

Rutledge told him why he was there and precisely what he wanted, using the date on Banner's bill as a starting point.

"The ledgers? From January to March 1917?" He was still holding Rutledge's identification, as if uncertain it was genuine. "I don't know what the law has to say about this sort of thing. Privacy of others, and all that."

"I must remind you, this is a murder inquiry."

"The class of person we host here—"

"—could be the very reason he chose this hotel. One would be less likely to find him here."

"Yes, yes, I see that." He seemed to realize he still held Rutledge's identification and passed it back to him. "Of course we wish to give the police every assistance."

There was a light tap at the door. "Come," the manager said.

A waiter poked his head around the door. "Table seven would like another of the wine bottles?"

"Let him have it. But not a third."

The waiter disappeared.

"The ledgers?"

Looking as if he'd been cornered by a stoat, the manager got up and unlocked a cabinet across from where Rutledge was sitting. Inside were shelves of ledgers, a date on each spine under the hotel's insignia. Finding the dates he was after, the manager pulled out two of the long, slim black-bound volumes and carried them back to the desk.

"This is one January 1917 through February of the same year. And this is March and April." Hesitating, he added, "I shouldn't leave you with these"—taking a deep breath, he finished—"I shall return as soon as possible."

And then he was gone. Rutledge moved behind the desk, opened the January ledger, and began to scan the names of guests.

It was slow, tedious work, deciphering the variations in handwriting, some names clearly written, others scrawled. He turned on the lamp sitting on the desk, but it helped very little. By the time he'd come to the end of January, he was beginning to think that Ruth Milford had chosen not to stay in such a public place after all, or that the officer had a house in the town.

He was halfway through February when a familiar name leaped out at him. Roddy MacNabb's grandmother had come in to Llangollen and spent a night at the hotel. He found her name again in the middle of March. What had brought her here?

Hamish, who had seemed to lurk over his shoulder as he went down the columns of names, said, "Escaping her daughter-in-law."

But he thought not. She wouldn't leave her grandson to the mercies of his stepmother unless she had a very good reason.

By the time he'd reached the end of March, he'd drawn up a list of fourteen names. Each was a married couple, and each gave an officer's rank for the man. He read them over again, and still was none the wiser. All they had in common was that they bracketed the date in question.

But on the day that Ruth Milford had ordered clothing for her husband, 10 March, 1917, there were only four couples. Lieutenant and Mrs. Davis, Captain and

Mrs. Thornton, Captain and Mrs. Griffith, Lieutenant and Mrs. Williams . . .

He went back again, skimming this time.

And Captain Alfred Thornton had stayed here three times. In mid-January, mid-February, and then in March. The first time, the room was in his name, and the other two times, he'd registered as Captain Thornton and wife.

Rutledge had finished by the time the manager returned.

"There was a Captain Thornton who stayed here several times that winter. Do you happen to recall him? Is he a regular who comes back from time to time?"

"The name isn't familiar. But there were convalescent homes in this part of Wales during the war. A number of officers came here to meet their wives, while they were recovering. Why? Do you think *he's* your killer?" His voice rose.

"That's a matter for the Yard to decide. There's a Mrs. MacNabb who stayed during that same period. Do you know her?"

He shook his head. "I don't. Well, if I saw her again—I don't mingle with the guests that often. It's not how I manage."

Rutledge believed him.

He repeated the exercise in two other hotels, The Llewellyn and The Denbigh. And found in the last of the two, The Denbigh, that Ruth Milford had stayed there in January. But there was no record of her returning later in the winter. Nor was there a Captain Thornton listed in the ledgers of either hotel. But he *had* stayed at The Broadstairs on that same date in January. Alone.

Sitting back in his chair at the manager's desk in The Denbigh, Rutledge considered the implications of what he'd learned.

Ruth had been to Llangollen *before* she had come to Banner's tailor shop. At least once, possibly twice before. And as far as Rutledge could determine, those were the only three visits she had made to the town. But she claimed she had never been there.

He referred to his notebook. The funeral she had attended in Oswestry was three weeks *after* her last visit to Llangollen—Captain Thornton's last visit as well, at least under that name, when he'd stayed with his wife at The Broadstairs.

Had Ruth Milford discovered that she was pregnant by the time she went to Oswestry?

Rutledge tried to piece it together. Apparently Ruth Milford had gone to Llangollen when she had claimed she was in Shrewsbury. Had she become pregnant then? For the journey to London had come *after* she had stopped going to Llangollen, as far as he could tell. Shrewsbury police had discovered that her husband couldn't possibly have been in London at that time, and so it was likely that Ruth had consulted a doctor in a town where she was sure no one knew her. Thus by the time she went to Oswestry, she must have been in a right panic over her situation. Somewhere in this time frame, she had told everyone that she had met with Sam in London. But of course that was too soon to announce a pregnancy from the visit as well. But she had had to tell Sam *something* before anyone mentioned the London weekend to him. Was it on her way to Oswestry that she came up with the story that she had been assaulted on the way home? She'd been fine when she was there, according to the grieving family. So the supposed attack had to have occurred afterward, as Fenton had suggested, when it was too dark to see the man's face.

If he was right, Rutledge told himself, there *was* no rape, because her daughter had been conceived in Llangollen, during her affair with Captain Thornton. By the time Ruth had gone to her friend's funeral, she had already known she was pregnant.

It made more sense that Thornton was Tildy's father. Not some unknown assailant. But a caring husband would have pitied her when she wrote to him about her harrowing experience, and accepted the child as his own—for his wife's sake. And Sam Milford, from all Rutledge had been told about him, was just that sort of man.

He went back over the facts, setting them out in order in his notebook. Thornton and Ruth Milford had stayed at separate hotels on the first occasion. The beginning of the affair? When she had been uncertain just what to expect—or what she had wanted from that meeting? When she still had time to back out, to go home with nothing on her conscience but loneliness?

Ruth Milford was nothing like Mrs. MacNabb's daughter-in-law. She would have gone into any romantic encounter with trepidation. Uncertainty. But the pull of that encounter had been stronger than she'd expected, and in the end, the affair had begun. Two more visits, this time staying at The Broadstairs as Mrs. Thornton.

And then it was over. But not finished . . .

It appeared that she had never told Thornton about the child. Had the whole affair ended badly? Was that why she had gone to the tailor to order civilian clothes for her husband's eventual homecoming? Guilt and uncertainty?

Thornton must have known she was married. But

how had they met in the first place? What had brought them together?

Rutledge remembered the old adage that still waters ran deep. Ruth had kept her secret from her cousin and everyone else. She had had to find an explanation for the pregnancy, and she had endured the shame of being raped rather than confess to her affair.

What had she told Sam Milford, even after he came home from France?

Not the truth, surely. He hadn't known the name of the father. Had never put a face to the man.

And yet he had died not very far from the town where his wife had been unfaithful. What had led him to the narrowboats and his death, instead of to The Broadstairs Hotel in Llangollen?

If it hadn't been for the shirt his wife had ordered from Banner, Milford would have remained an unidentified body, buried in a pauper's grave in a village with an unpronounceable name.

And Betty Turnbull might still be alive. Had she wittingly or unwittingly bridged the gap between Oswestry and the Aqueduct, telling Milford a lie that she had been paid to give him?

I've heard there's a small red-haired child living up by the Aqueduct. Don't know if she's the one you've been hunting . . .

Nothing would have prevented Milford from going there.

He closed his notebook, found the Denbigh hotel manager, and thanked him for the use of his office and access to the ledgers.

His next stop was the village where Sam Milford had been found in the River Dee. But on the way, he made a detour to call at three clinics where officers had been sent to recover from wounds.

They had been closed since shortly after the war's end, records turned over to the Army. If Captain Thornton had been a patient in one of them, no one remembered him.

15

The MacNabb farm was a little out of his way, but he went there before driving into the village.

Roddy was sitting against a tree in the yard, his face sullen, as Rutledge pulled in and stopped the motorcar.

"Hallo," he said, getting out.

Roddy ignored him, and Rutledge walked on to the house.

Mrs. MacNabb must have seen him—or was keeping a watchful eye on her grandson—for she came to the door and said, "I hope you aren't bearing more unhappy news."

"I've come to arrange the inquest, so that the dead man's family can bury him." As he reached the door, she opened it wider and invited him inside, sitting down across from him in the little parlor.

"You know his name, then. Who is he?"

He told her.

"And was it an accident, his fall?"

"I'm afraid it was murder."

"How awful for his family." Glancing toward the yard and her grandson, she added, "Please don't tell Roddy. He's only just able to sleep without nightmares."

"There will be talk about the inquest. He'll hear it from others. You should prepare him."

"Yes, perhaps you're right. Still. He's so young." She took a deep breath. "Have you found the person responsible?"

"Not yet. But I'm closer than I was on my earlier visit."

"Not one of us?"

"I don't believe so."

"That's a blessing, then."

She was on the point of rising when he said, "There is a question I must put to you. I was in Llangollen, looking at hotel registers. You stayed in The Broadstairs on two occasions. I'd like to ask what took you there."

Mrs. MacNabb rose, crossed quietly to the door, opened it quickly. There was no one in the passage. "Old habits die hard," she said, coming back, this time leaving the door standing wide. "She isn't here, she's gone back to Liverpool." He knew she was speaking of her daughter-in-law. "But I'm not persuaded that she will stay there. Very likely she will come home again, begging to be taken in. And I shall have to take her in, for my son's sake. Even though she is doing great harm to Roddy." She met his gaze. "I went to Llangollen to meet my solicitor. We talked, and I told him my wishes. I went again to sign the necessary paperwork. I have set up a trust for Roddy. This house is mine, much of our money is still safe and out of her reach. My son at least had the good sense to see to that. It is ironclad now. If anything happens to me, Roddy will be safe."

Something in the way she said it caught his attention. "Are you saying that she might harm you?"

"I could fall down the stairs—trip in the kitchen— stumble over one of the hens as I'm feeding them. And so I've taken measures to ensure my future and his. She has been told that as long as I am alive there will be a small income for her. It will cease with my death or if I am unable to assure my solicitor that I am still of sound mind and wish the arrangement to continue. This was set up during those two visits. A week ago I also agreed to continue payments even if she returned to Liverpool. And so she did, thank God. I am Roddy's guardian. She couldn't take him with her—I don't think it would occur to her to *want* him with her."

"You're very brave. Is there anything that the police can do?"

"No." She smiled sadly. "It's for the best, what I did."

"Why is your grandson upset today?"

The smile warmed. "He wants a dog. I'm not sure he's old enough to take proper care of one."

"A dog in the house might be all the protection you need, if she comes back and threatens you. And—Roddy needs a friend."

"I hadn't considered that. Thank you."

They were already at the door when Rutledge asked, "Do you go to Llangollen often?"

"I did on occasion in the past. But after my daughter-in-law came, it took all the joy out of any excursion. I simply didn't trust her."

"Another name I came across in the hotel ledgers was Thornton. Captain Alfred Thornton and his wife. Is it someone you know?"

"Are you telling me that he's a suspect?"

"No. Just—the name appeared on several different days. I would like to ask a few questions that might help me find the person I'm after."

"I don't know a *Captain* Thornton. But there's an Alfred Thornton out on the Chester road. He was our smith until the war, and after he came home, he opened a garage, lorry repairs his specialty. But he also maintains a motorcar service. One of the village lads took me to Llangollen in his father's carriage. Only fourteen, Tommy Daniels was then, lived on his father's farm a mile from us, and already motorcar mad. Later, when he went to work with the Sergeant, he persuaded him to set up a service for the villages around here. And now, I need only send Roddy into the village on his bicycle, and someone sends word to the Sergeant. It is a little more than I would like to pay but well worth it."

"Does this young man still work for Thornton?"

"Yes, he's one of the Sergeant's people. The one I still like best."

"Thank you," he said, "you've been very helpful."

He said goodbye to the boy as well, but got only a flash of sullen eyes for his trouble.

Stopping just beyond Roddy, he said, "You're the man of the house now. Look after your grandmother. She needs you."

Surprised, Roddy looked up.

"Don't let me hear that you've been ungrateful." And he walked on.

Rutledge went into the village and found Constable Holcomb, intending to go over the inquest with him and then the return of the body to Crowley.

"It's a wonder you found who he was. But you're no closer to who killed him?"

"I believe I know who killed Milford. One Joseph Burton, who has since been murdered as well. He was drowned in one of the Aqueduct basins."

"Here, I don't like the sound of that. Who killed *him*?"

"I don't know. Which is why I want to leave the inquest open."

"You're saying that this man Burton might have been killed because he'd been paid to kill Milford?"

"It's possible."

"Why was Milford killed? Do you know that?"

"Milford was too close to something that mattered to him. Let it go at that."

It was clear Holcomb would have preferred more, but Rutledge shook his head. "This has threads that go elsewhere. Milford and Burton aren't the only two dead. I'd rather not add to that number."

The inquest was arranged for a week's time. There would have to be another one in Trefor for Joseph Burton, and in Oswestry for Mrs. Turnbull. Sufficient to the day.

Preparing to leave, Rutledge said, "I stopped in to speak to Mrs. MacNabb. She tells me she sometimes employs the services of Thornton's garage when she needs to travel to Llangollen. What do you know about him?"

"Thornton? A good man. He learned his trade in the war and has made a decent living since he came home from France. Mrs. MacNabb always asks for Tommy, but I doubt she knows that the other young man who drives for Thornton—Wristen, I think his name is—had a brief affair with her daughter-in-law."

"Did he indeed? I understand the daughter-in-law has returned to Liverpool."

"And good riddance. There are wives who are sleeping easier since she left. Nothing I could quite prove, but *they* were certain enough of what was going on."

"Keep an eye on Mrs. MacNabb, will you?"

"That I will do."

Rutledge left soon afterward, driving out the Chester road until he came to the long, low building set back from the road that Holcomb had described. It was situated about halfway between Llangollen and Chester, convenient to both. There was a lorry in the muddy yard, two men looking under the bonnet.

He thought this had once been outbuildings belonging to the farm he could see in the distance. They had been refurbished and served now as a garage and what passed for a cottage connected to it.

He drove into the yard, got out, and walked over to

the lorry. The driver, glancing his way, nodded. But it was the man standing beside him that Rutledge was interested in.

He was of medium height, carried himself well, and had an attractive smile as he said, "Be with you shortly, sir."

Odds were that he'd been a junior officer. There was a cockiness behind the smile, as if he knew its charm. This was surely, Rutledge thought, the other young man who drove for Thornton, the one who had had an affair with Mrs. MacNabb's daughter-in-law. He was most likely in his late twenties.

"As a matter of fact, I've come to speak to Thornton. Is he in?"

"Yes, he's in the shed, looking for a part."

"Then I'll have a word." He walked toward the shed-cum-garage.

It was dimly lit but tidy. Across the rear wall, there was a long trestle table, and wooden boxes of varying sizes were set out on it in a row. A man was digging in one of the boxes, searching for something.

He had heard the footsteps, and said over his shoulder, "I've told you, it's important to keep like to like. How can I find what I need if it's in the wrong box?"

When Rutledge didn't answer, Thornton turned, realized it wasn't his helper who had come into the shed, and said, straightening up, "I'm sorry, sir. How may I help you?" He was of middle height, like the man working with the lorry driver, but older by eight or ten years. His sandy hair was threaded with gray, his face lined.

"Sergeant Thornton?"

Something in Rutledge's voice touched a chord of memory. Not for the man, but for the rank.

"I'm no longer in the Army, sir."

"Looks as if you've done well for yourself here."

"I'm trying."

"Apparently good help is difficult to come by." He nodded toward the yard.

Thornton sighed. "He's mad about motorcars and lorries, like Tommy, but Tommy is seventeen and willing to learn. Still, Wristen drives as if he'd been born at the wheel. A natural skill on the roads round about here. But he's like so many who came out of the war. There's an emptiness inside and he doesn't know how to fill it."

"What regiment?"

"Lately a Lieutenant in His Majesty's Forces, sir. Wiltshire."

"Good men."

"They were, sir. Some of the best." He glanced again toward the yard. "Nicely kept motor, yours. How can I help you, sir?"

"It's information I need, Sergeant." He took out his identification. "When were you demobbed?"

"Me, sir? Not until March of 1919."

"Were you in a convalescent home in early '17?"

"No, sir. Had a blighty ticket late in '16, and was sent back to the Front just after Boxing Day. Healed, they said, but I was far from it. Still. I survived."

There was no bitterness in the words.

"Have you ever taken your wife to a hotel called The Broadstairs in Llangollen? In particular, in January 1917?"

"On a Sergeant's pay? Not very likely! Begging your pardon, sir, but I'd like to know what this is about."

"I'm looking into a murder. And I came across a Captain Alfred Thornton who stayed in that hotel early in 1917."

"'Twasn't me, sir. And I'm willing to swear to it under oath. Not to say that there isn't another Alfred Thornton somewhere."

"I believe you. Did you ever encounter a Sergeant Milford? In the Bantams?"

"Milford? No, sir. I've met Bantams, of course, but that name doesn't pop up."

"He was killed not far from here. They found his body in the River Dee, just outside the village where your driver Tommy lives. He'd come here from Shrews-bury, looking for someone."

"I'd heard something about that. But there wasn't a name, as I remember."

"No. Not then. He never came here asking to be driven somewhere?" It wasn't likely. As Hamish was telling Rutledge. Trying to ignore the voice, he took the photograph of Milford from his pocket.

Thornton carried it over to the door for a better look, then shook his head. "No, sir. I've never seen him before. If he hired a motorcar, it wasn't one of mine."

He'd have made a good policeman, Rutledge thought. Steady, objective, not easily rattled.

Thornton was saying, "I don't much care for this business, sir. Using my name. It's my reputation at stake. If I could help you, I would."

"Mind if I speak to Wristen?"

"No, sir. He's all yours. And if he *did* use my name, I've no more use for *him*."

Rutledge went to speak to the younger man, well aware that Thornton was watching from the interior of the shed.

Brash as he was, when faced with Scotland Yard, Wristen shook his head. "I was never in northern England until the Sergeant asked me to drive for him.

Besides, in early 1917, I was not likely to be thinking about holidays. I may be many things Sergeant Thornton doesn't care for. I'm not a fool. I know that well enough. But I like working for him, you know. It keeps me straight." He looked away from Rutledge. "I should have died out there. In France. Twice a bullet had my name on it. How I lived, I don't really know. I feel sometimes that I'm on borrowed time. That I'm not really meant to be here, that someone got it wrong, and one of these days, they'll get it right, and I'll be gone."

"Have you told him that? Thornton?"

"God, no. He's Army, through and through, even though he's taken off his uniform. How do you make him realize that you want to do as much living as you can, while you can? He'd tell me how lucky I am to have survived the trenches with all my limbs intact. He'd got missing toes—trench foot—but he's learned to walk well enough without them. He wouldn't *understand*."

Rutledge believed him. But he showed Wristen the photograph of Sam Milford and asked if he'd ever seen the man.

Wristen hadn't. That appeared to be the truth.

Rutledge thanked him, nodded in the direction of the shed, and started back toward his motorcar. He'd turned the crank and was getting into the driver's seat when he heard a shout, and Thornton was walking rapidly toward him, his hand up in an effort to catch Rutledge before he could drive off.

The limp was pronounced as he hurried, more so as his left foot tired. By the time he'd reached the motorcar, he put out his hand to hold on to the frame.

"Sorry. Thought you might wish to know. There's a motorcar service in Chester. You might speak to them." He grimaced. "Our competition, now, but I worked for them for a year before I could afford to go out on my own. And I'd all but forgot—Henry asked me when he hired me if I was any relation to a client of theirs by the name of Thornton. Of course, I didn't know him."

Rutledge thanked him, and drove on into Chester. He found the motorcar service near the railway station, in a converted shop.

The owner, a man by the name of Henry, listened without much interest but was willing to show him their log of service.

And there, in January of 1917, was a listing that made sense.

A motorcar had picked up a Mrs. Milford at the Chester railway station and driven her to Llangollen. To The Denbigh Hotel. A third party had paid in cash for the journey and return. The name given was A. Thornton.

Mrs. Milford had made two other journeys to Llangollen and returned. Each time she had traveled alone, but on the second and third journeys her destination had been changed to The Broadstairs Hotel. The payment each time was in cash from A. Thornton.

It was all he could find. But Rutledge now had another link between Ruth Milford and Llangollen. And the train to Shrewsbury ran to Chester as well. It would have been easy enough to make the journey.

When he asked Henry who the driver had been, he was told that the man had died in the influenza epidemic of 1919.

Then Henry said, "As I remember, Mr. Thornton's solicitor made the arrangements. They often do, when a client comes in by train. See here? BBT. That would be Baldwin, Baldwin, and Tate. Most likely George Baldwin, a junior partner. He did a good deal of business with us."

But when Rutledge called on Baldwin, Baldwin, and Tate, he was told by the firm's clerk that George had retired in 1920 and moved to Carlisle to be closer to his daughter.

"Did he have a client by the name of Alfred Thornton? I'm trying to locate him."

The clerk's eyebrows flew up. "Thornton? Are you certain of that name? Yes? Then someone must be having a little fun at your expense. That's the name we use for various purposes. If someone is insistent on seeing one of the partners, we tell him the partner is in conference with Mr. Thornton. Or if there is something we need to do and don't wish to use the name of the firm, we use 'Mr. Thornton.'" He coughed slightly. "Er. A convenience, one might say."

"Then who might have used that name to hire a motorcar to travel to Llangollen in 1917?"

"I have no idea, sir. In that case it would have been a private matter."

"Was George Baldwin in the Army during the war?"

"I'm afraid not, sir. He was nearly sixty."

Rutledge pulled out of Chester twenty minutes later. It was some forty miles to Shrewsbury, but he had no doubt that he could make it.

He was not five miles from Shrewsbury when he glimpsed a Sunbeam motorcycle with a sidecar just ahead of him on the road, half-hidden between two lorries. He wouldn't have seen it at all, if the headlamps of the second lorry hadn't caught it.

He couldn't see the driver, only a shape with helmet and goggles.

Abandoning his own plans, he began to track the Sunbeam.

He lost it in the streets of the town, its very mobility against him as it sped in and out of what little traffic there was, and expected to find it in the yard at the Prince Rupert. But it wasn't there, and he began to search for it.

Hamish said, "It's nae use, it didna' stop here."

But Rutledge refused to give up. And then he spotted it, standing outside a pub that was already closed for the night. He stopped, got down, and went over to it for a closer look.

He knew almost at once that this wasn't the same Sunbeam he'd seen covered in army tents and brush just outside Little Bog. But he was beginning to open up the sidecar's covering when a man rushed out of the pub and shouted, "Here, what do you think you're doing, mate?"

He reached for his identification and held it up. "Scotland Yard. I'm looking for a Sunbeam that was connected to a crime. How long have you had this one?"

"Bought it secondhand when I was demobbed. What crime?"

Rutledge looked up. "Murder."

"Here, mate, I'm not involved in any *murder*—"

"It's Inspector. Not mate."

"Well, *Inspector*, I'm not mixed up in murder."

"Know anyone else who has one of these machines?"

"No. The only reason I have one is the price of a motorcar."

"Where did you come from?"

"Westmorland."

"Can you prove that?"

In the event, he could. Fumbling through a pack in the sidecar, he pulled out a sheet of paper. "See for yourself."

He had been in a clinic there for weeks. The doctors had taken out a shard of artillery shell from his knee, and he'd had to learn to walk again. "And bloody painful it was."

"Where are you traveling to?"

"Dorset. My family's there. A mate owns the pub here, I'm staying the night."

The accent fit. Rutledge let him go.

"A wild goose chase," Hamish told him as he got back into the motorcar. "Ye're obsessed with yon woman."

"It could have been her. He drove with abandon, just as she does."

"Oh, aye?"

Too tired to care, Rutledge tried to ignore the voice.

It was quite late when Rutledge finally reached Crowley. He left the motorcar in plain sight in the yard, and let himself into the inn, going up to the room he'd taken before.

Blocking the door with the back of the only chair in the room, to avoid any surprises, he went to bed.

For miles he'd seen nothing but foxes and stoats and hedgehogs on the road, not a single motorcar or lorry or farm cart.

The hours he'd had to be alert unrolled in his head as he lay wide awake on the bed, and for once even Hamish was quiet.

When he did drift into a troubled sleep, he was following two women, but when he got nearer, one face changed into another, Ruth Milford becoming Susan before changing back into herself, taunting him.

It was a measure, he thought when he woke from the dream with a start, of his failure to find any answers.

16

The aroma of baking bread brought him out of a restless sleep.

He rose, bathed and shaved, found a clean shirt, and then went down to breakfast.

Will gave him a long look, but served him with a reserved politeness.

But it was Ruth who came storming in and said coldly, "I hope you have something to tell us."

"Of a kind. The inquest into your husband's death has been set, and the body will be released for burial."

"Inquest? Then you know who killed Sam?"

He couldn't quite read her expression. Whether she was pleased—or alarmed. The post at the bar shadowed her face again.

"I have two suspects. I expect to narrow that to

one." He glanced toward the kitchen. "When does Will leave?"

"After washing up the breakfast things. It's easier to take our meals here, instead of cooking at home."

"Then perhaps we could talk elsewhere. I'd rather not be overheard."

She hesitated. "Anything you wish to ask me about Sam, I can tell you now. Here. There are no secrets."

"There are," he said. "And if you wish to discuss those here, we can begin straightaway."

She looked out the front windows, taking in the view, as if there were answers to be found there.

"Oh, very well. My house."

She turned on her heel and left. He had brought his coat down with him, and he went after her, careful not to close the space between them. By the time they had reached the Milford house and were sitting in the cold front room, she was visibly anxious.

Before he could begin, she broached the subject herself. "It's what happened in Oswestry, isn't? I can't tell you any more than I have. You aren't a woman, you don't understand what I've been through."

He realized that she had lived with her story for so long now that she more than half believed it herself. And that must have helped enormously with the guilt she carried with her.

"As a matter of fact," he said, his voice neutral, "I'd like to begin with the moment your train arrived in Chester, January of 1917. When you were put into a motorcar hired to take you to Llangollen, and The Denbigh Hotel there. Where was Captain Thornton waiting for you? Shrewsbury? Chester? Llangollen?"

Her gasp was audible, and then the color drained from her face. But she kept her gaze on his and said, "I'm not sure what you're talking about, Inspector."

He had carefully watched her eyes as he told her what he'd learned. He had seen her shocked reaction, the struggle to conceal it. She hadn't expected him to uncover a secret she had protected for years.

"It wasn't the first time you'd met him. You aren't that sort of woman. How did the affair begin?"

She retreated into tears. "What are you accusing me of? I don't understand any of this—" She rose, pointing to the door. "You will leave now, if you please."

He stayed where he was, in the chair across from the one she'd vacated. "This might have worked with Sam, even with your cousin. But I have seen the hotel registers. I've spoken with the tailor, Banner, and with the man whose firm provided the driver for your journey. I know you were meeting someone, and that you registered later as man and wife. Matilda isn't a child of an attack, she's a child of a liaison you had with an officer while your husband was in France, fighting for his country. You've lied to me from the start, and you lied to the police when Tildy was taken. Either you had something to do with her disappearance or you must know who did. And yet you kept that to yourself."

She stayed where she was, defiant. She had had *time* to learn how to lie.

"Did you tell your husband the man's name, or did you let him search for someone who didn't exist, except in your imagination? In the end, he must have found Thornton, and it cost Sam his life. The time for lying has passed. Tell me where I can find Alfred Thornton. And your daughter. If she's still alive."

"You're wrong. I don't know anyone by that name. I swear to you."

There was the despair in her voice now.

"Then you leave me no choice, Mrs. Milford. I am taking you into custody as an accessory to kidnapping and to the murders of three people."

It was harsh, and he'd intended it to be. That was the only way to break through the shell she had built around what she'd done, and make her face her own culpability.

Collapsing in her chair again, she was sobbing in earnest now, very real tears.

He handed her his handkerchief. She didn't appear to have one of her own. "Where is Thornton? If I clear him of any part in this inquiry, your secret is safe with me. It will not be brought out at the inquest. But you must realize that if this man is guilty of kidnapping or murder, you will have to testify. And I can't do anything about that."

"I can't. I won't."

His voice was very quiet in the small room. "Then collect your coat and whatever else you may need. We're leaving for Shrewsbury immediately."

"Oh, dear God, I wish I were dead," she wailed as he got to his feet.

Just then the door slammed back on its hinges and Nan Blake burst in. "Will said something is wrong, that that man was back, and needed to speak privately to you—is that true? Is it Tildy? *Ruth*—?"

He said, "I think you had better leave, Mrs. Blake. This isn't the time."

For several seconds she stared at Rutledge, trying to read his expression, then failing at that, she turned back to Ruth. Her voice was no more than a whisper now. "Oh, dear God, she's dead, isn't she?"

Ruth got unsteadily to her feet. "He's taking me to the police. You'll have to see to the inn. I can't—I don't know when I'll be back."

Nan went to her cousin, caught her by the shoulders. "*The police?*"

"It isn't the child," Rutledge said then. "It's another matter. Will you go upstairs and put some things into a valise? Mrs. Milford will be glad of it."

She turned on Rutledge. "I don't understand any of this. But before I let you take her away, you are going to explain what's happening. Do you hear me?"

Ruth said, "Nan. Let it go. I—it's nothing that you can fix. It's nothing any of us can change now. I'll have to do as he says."

But Nan Blake was adamant. "Look at you—you're in no condition to go anywhere." She wheeled to face Rutledge. "I'm taking her upstairs and putting her to bed. We'll see about this tomorrow. I'll have her solicitor here, if need be."

"Mrs. Blake—you're only making matters worse for your cousin. See to her things, and I'll bring around the motorcar. We leave in ten minutes. If you don't have a valise ready, we will go without it."

He'd commanded soldiers in battle. She heard that in his voice now. "You can't do this, it's wrong."

"My other coat, Nan. This one is my old one. And a scarf—gloves." Her cousin glared at her, still mulish. Ruth pleaded, "Please, Nan. I can't—this is more than I can endure right now. Let it go. Let me go."

Rutledge waited until Nan went up the stairs, but he could hear her talking to herself, demanding answers, worried.

"I'll walk to the motorcar," Ruth told him. "I'd rather."

"This isn't necessary, you know," he told her gently.

"I don't know any longer what's necessary. I've lost Tildy. I've lost Sam. A year from now when The Bog is closed for good, I'll lose the inn. There's nothing to live for, is there? You might as well hang me. Sam's death is on my hands, as surely as if I shoved him into that river myself."

He said nothing. He could hear Nan in the bedroom above, opening and closing drawers. She wasn't muttering any longer, and he thought she might be crying now.

And he was right. She came down the steps, the handle of the valise in both hands, a heavier coat under her arm.

Rutledge went to take them from her.

"I don't understand, Ruthie," she was saying to her cousin. "This makes no sense. What am I to tell Donald? Or Will? What are we going to do for credit, to keep the inn going? I wish you would tell me what to do?"

"I don't know," Ruth told her. "I can't see my own way clear any longer. I wish I could."

He helped her into the coat, nodded to Nan Blake, and opened the door.

They walked to the motorcar in silence, Ruth trudging beside him like a child going to the dentist.

He was fully prepared for her to change her mind before he had put her into the motorcar. To his surprise, she didn't. And he was forced to carry out his threat. But there was still time, he told himself.

Turning the crank, he got in and started down the incline. He could just see, as he prepared to turn toward the Shrewsbury road, the figure of Nan Blake still standing in the doorway of the Milford house.

The silence lengthened. Rutledge glanced at the woman huddled in her heavier coat. Her hands were bare, and trembling. He'd turned on the heater but it did little more than warm their feet.

Pulling to the side of the road, he fumbled blindly for the rug he kept in the rear seat. Finding it, he brought it across and handed it to her.

The last thing he wanted, if he was honest with himself, was to turn her over to Inspector Carson in Shrewsbury.

But women were sometimes harder to persuade than men. They held on to their loyalties longer and more intensely. Given what was about to happen to her, why was she so adamant about not giving him the man's name?

He mulled that as he drove. Had the love affair been that intense? What was the man's hold over her? Simple physical attraction was one thing. This seemed to go deeper.

And she had lost Tildy—to *him*? *Why hadn't she fought for her own child?*

He said, while they were still some miles from Shrewsbury, "Is your daughter still alive?"

At first she didn't answer. He thought she might not. And then she said, "How could I know?"

"Mrs. Milford—Ruth—I'd like to understand. Help me."

This time there was no answer.

He tried another tack.

"I can understand why you lied about the child, telling everyone else you'd gone to London for a weekend with your husband. But what did you tell *him*? He would have known London wasn't true." When she didn't answer, Rutledge asked, "Did you lie to him as well, did you tell him she was fathered in an assault?" She wouldn't meet his eyes. "Ruth?"

"What other choice was there? I couldn't rid myself of the child." There was infinite bitterness in the words. "I wouldn't have her branded a bastard. She was innocent of my guilt."

"You couldn't even tell your cousin what you'd done? You couldn't trust her with the truth?"

A shake of the head.

"But Sam must have accepted your lie. You've told me that he loved Tildy."

"How could he *not*? She was—she could enchant. There was something—she was never like me. I would look at her sometimes and wonder. That glorious hair—and she was spared freckles, except for the bridge of her little nose. Eyes such a clear green. It was as if God had given me something precious, and at the same time something that everyone knew couldn't have been mine. A joy and a curse. A constant reminder. And I loved her more than anything or anyone." The last words ended in a wail of despair.

He remembered something.

"The shoe. Why were you given a shoe?"

"To save the pub. It's supposed to be valuable. It's said to have belonged to Mary Queen of Scots when she was a child. But Sam wouldn't hear of it."

He turned his head to look at her, unable to believe what he'd just heard. "Do you mean that Sam knew the shoe—that it was the price of *Tildy*?"

"Oh, dear God, *no*! I refuse to—no, it was

unexpected—someone had promised to help. When it was possible. I'd stopped counting on it." Her mouth twisted in an ironic grimace. "Sam wanted to save it for Tildy's future. He thought we could find another way to keep the pub. But that was later. When the police arrived, and they saw it, they were convinced the shoe was some sort of omen. Or threat. Or, I don't know, some sort of horrid message. I finally just let them think what they pleased. I didn't care, as long as they searched for Tildy. Nothing mattered but that."

"Where did the shoe come from? Or—from whom?"

"I can't tell you."

He let it go. Yet—he found himself wondering— had Thornton, finally learning about Tildy, decided that the shoe would save the pub and a grateful Ruth would understand that and let the abduction go unsolved? Because that appeared to be exactly what she'd done, despite her shocked denial. Shocked because he'd guessed?

Changing his tactics, he asked, "Ruth, do you have any sense of what lies ahead for you in Shrewsbury?"

"I don't care."

Rutledge made one final attempt to break through her apathy. "If Tildy comes home, the man she believed to be her father won't be there. Nor will you, her mother."

"You should have considered that when you forced me to make a choice."

"I have a duty to the truth. To three people who were murdered. To a child who is out there somewhere, alive or dead. I'm very sorry that you are caught in the middle between my search and a man you must have loved very deeply to keep him safe in spite of the fact that he could very well have ordered Sam Milford's death."

"You could have trusted my judgment, my knowledge of that man. You could have believed me when I tell you that he has never harmed me or mine. You're wrong. You have been from the start."

"Or you could have trusted me to find out as quietly as possible if your faith in him is deserved."

She kept her eyes on the road ahead. "What kind of faith is that?"

As they drove into Shrewsbury, he knew he'd lost her.

When he reached the police station, she began to fold the rug into a neat square, handing it to him as he came around the bonnet to help her down and carry her valise.

She looked up at the facade of the station. "Will you tell Mr. Hastings where I am? I should like to speak to him."

"Do you know that Hastings is also the solicitor for your husband's sister? Susan Milford? I'm not sure where his loyalties lie. Or hers."

"It doesn't matter. I only need to put my affairs in order. So that Nan and Donald have the authority they need to sell the pub when the time comes."

"I'll speak to him."

The sergeant on the desk looked up as the man from London walked in with a woman whose eyes were red from crying.

"Inspector Carson, if you please?" Rutledge said, and waited.

Carson listened to what Rutledge had to say, then asked, "She has information that is pertinent to your inquiry, but won't give it to you. Is that what you're telling me?"

"Yes."

"What sort of information?"

"A name."

"Whose name? The kidnapper's? Or are you talking about the murder of her husband, Sam Milford?"

"Milford's death. Someone arranged to have him killed up at the Aqueduct. Then when it was done, killed the man who did his bidding. I won't know if this will clear up the kidnapping or not until I've found the person."

"When her daughter disappeared, Mrs. Milford was suspected to have had a hand in what happened. But

Fenton cleared her. In spite of her behavior on the day in question, there was nothing else that pointed to her. And then there was the shoe, which he believed was a taunt by the kidnapper. What did Fenton miss?"

"He didn't. It's what Sam Milford was searching for that cost him his life. But I don't know what he was after. He didn't tell his wife what he was doing, or anyone else that I am aware of. So far. But someone knew, someone kept an eye on him, and in the end killed him."

They had left Ruth Milford in Carson's office and were standing in the quiet corridor outside it, conferring in low voices.

"This is her husband and her daughter we're talking about. Why won't she help you? It doesn't make sense."

"She believes she's protecting someone who is not a party to any of this. But until I have interviewed the person in question, we don't know if her faith is misplaced or not."

"Man or woman?"

Rutledge shook his head. "I'm not at liberty to say."

"Damn it, if you want to shut her up in my cell, you can tell me that much."

"I can't. There's more at stake here than either you or I can be sure of. She wants to speak to her solicitor—Hastings—but he's played fast and loose with the truth about Milford's sister, who might well be involved in some way. And I'd rather not have him speak to Ruth for at least twenty-four hours."

"What's the sister got to do with this business?"

"Either nothing or everything. I have to eliminate her as a suspect, and she's somewhere in Wales right now, in hiding."

Carson took a deep breath. "When I took over here, that missing child was still very much on everyone's mind. As time went by, it seemed less and less likely that she'd ever be found. Do you think she's alive?"

"I don't know. There are days when I believe she could be."

"All right. I'll clap your prisoner in irons. And you owe me. I want to see justice done. Do you understand?"

"I do."

Carson opened the door and stepped into his office.

Ruth Milford, pale, her eyes still red from crying, was huddled in her chair. But when the two men came in, she rose.

"Good afternoon, Inspector," she said politely. "I am so sorry to trouble you, but I believe I am to be your guest for a while."

He said, "You won't find it very comfortable, Mrs. Milford. Cells aren't designed for women. There's little privacy, and you'll be watched day and night. Do you understand that?"

"I do. Yes."

"Do you want five minutes to reconsider your situation?"

"No. But thank you."

"Very well. This way."

Rutledge picked up the valise. But Carson shook his head. "Leave it. We must search it and decide what she can have and what she can't."

He led them to the rear of the station. Ruth Milford moved resolutely, and when he opened the cell door for her to enter, she walked straight inside. But it was several seconds before she could turn and face the two men.

If anything her face was paler, and her eyes seemed too large for her face.

Carson swung the door shut, shooting the bolt into place with a loud clang.

And then they walked away and left her there.

Preferring to leave his motorcar at the police station, Rutledge went on foot to the street where Dora Radley lived.

She wasn't in. He spent an unpleasant hour and a half in Hamish's company. It wasn't until shortly after three that she came down the street.

Seeing him almost as soon as he caught sight of her, she hesitated, then continued toward him. He stopped by the short walk to her door, and said, "We can have tea in a shop. Or we can talk in your parlor."

"I thought I'd seen the last of you."

"Sadly, no."

Once inside, he came to the point. "I know the work you do. You must have benefactors who contribute to the efforts you make on behalf of those women and children."

She said, "They are generous. I expect that's because they would rather give me their money than be called to work with the women I meet or take in a destitute child."

"I'd like a list of them, if you please."

Staring at him, she said, "I beg your pardon?"

"I'd like a list of their names."

"I will give you no such thing! I depend on these people, and I won't have you harassing them with visits from Scotland Yard. Do you know how quickly they would turn their backs on me, if that happened? I'd lose everything I've fought to do. No."

"I don't intend to harass them."

"Then why do you want such a thing?"

He worded his reply carefully. He couldn't tell her what he suspected, that she had wittingly or unwittingly provided information to someone that had been used to track Sam Milford. It could so easily be the same man whose whereabouts Ruth Milford refused to give him.

"Sometimes people know things that are helpful to the police, but aren't aware of the information they might have until they're asked. I may be wrong, but it's worth looking into, if I'm to find Tildy Milford."

"But there's no one among my benefactors who even knew the Milfords."

"Have you asked them?"

"Asked? No, of course not. I've had no reason to inquire." And then something changed in her face. A flush spread across it.

"Tell me," Rutledge said urgently. "If you won't help me, help Tildy and her mother."

"But he doesn't know them. I'm sure he doesn't. It's just that he does know a good many people who could be counted on to look out for the child if she was brought to an orphanage. They're often on the board of governors, you see, and so I asked him to help. Nothing more. And he made inquiries in Shropshire and Cheshire. Towns where I don't know anyone."

"And did he find any news of Tildy?"

"Sadly, no, but he *tried*. I was willing to ask his help, because I could see how much it mattered to Sam, and it's what I do, save children who can't save themselves.

And mothers who are at their wits' end, trying to provide for their families."

"Will you give me his name?" He waited for her to say it, confirmation. "And where I can find him?"

"No, not until I speak to him myself and ask his permission."

"It would be best if I spoke to him instead," he said persuasively. "In confidence. It's important, Mrs. Radley. Or I wouldn't ask." But her face was set. "Then perhaps we could find a compromise. If you will let me take you to him, so that you can introduce us, would that do?"

She was as stubborn in her own way, he realized, as Ruth Milford was.

He didn't want to threaten her. But he had no choice. "I've just brought Mrs. Milford to the Shrewsbury police and had her taken into custody for refusing to help the Yard with an inquiry. If you don't give me the information I need, I will have you taken into custody as well. Your benefactors will think twice about their generosity, if you spend several days in a cell like a common criminal."

She didn't believe him at first. But when he rose and began to charge her, she turned quite pale and said, "You can't do this."

"If necessary, I'll send for a Constable. My motor-car is still by the police station. We will have to walk there, the three of us. And your neighbors will see you in handcuffs being led away."

"You are a horrible man," she said, close to tears.

"I'm sorry. If I must do this to find a murderer and a lost child, I will do it."

She put up her hands to stop him. "I will give you what you want. Under protest. He's a solicitor."

For an instant he thought she was going to give him Hastings's name. Bringing him full circle. And not the name he wanted so desperately.

But when she spoke, in a low, stricken voice, he wasn't prepared.

17

"Alasdair Dale."

He said, "Lying to the police is not wise, Mrs. Radley."

"But I'm not lying. You wanted this information. I gave it to you. Now go. Please."

"How did you meet him?"

"He was a friend of my husband's. Didn't you know? Matthew was a solicitor before the war. They were in school together."

She had always been Andrew Clark's sister. Radley's widow. There had never been a reason to look into her late husband's past. He'd died in the war . . .

Reading something in his face, she said almost waspishly, "That's the trouble with the truth, isn't it? No one is comfortable with it. But I warn you. You can't bully Alasdair the way you've bullied me. He won't stand for it."

"When Sam Milford asked you about contacts in Oswestry, did you mention that to Dale? Did you tell him about Brewster, at the dairy farm? And Brewster's sister Betty?"

"I didn't know Brewster had a sister. But yes, I did ask Alasdair if he knew someone in Oswestry who might be in a better position to help Sam. I knew how important this was to Sam. But Alasdair didn't. He told me he'd never dealt with a solicitor there, or even had clients in the town. And so I had to give Sam Mr. Brewster's name after all."

The link was there. It was *possible*.

"And did you tell him that Sam Milford had been killed? That I had been sent from London to find out what had happened to him?"

"I was horrified, upset. And so I wrote to Alasdair. There was nothing wrong with that."

"What did you tell Dale about Sam's business in Oswestry? That he was searching for his missing daughter?"

"Well, no, not until he asked."

But none of this would matter, if Dale had no connection at all with Ruth Milford.

He walked back to the police station and went directly to Mrs. Milford's cell.

She was still wearing her coat, sitting wretchedly on the cot with its unpleasant blanket and the chamber pot against the wall.

He stepped inside, asked the Constable to give him ten minutes with the prisoner, and waited until he'd heard the man's footsteps receding down the passage.

"Have you come to gloat?" she asked, striving to keep up a brave front.

"No. To ask you if the father of Tildy Milford is Alasdair Dale. Not Thornton."

If he'd struck her, she wouldn't have been as shaken. That name, coming without warning, after all she'd been through to protect it, was too much. She didn't have any defenses left.

Still, she tried to lie to him, to deny the truth. Protesting strongly that she didn't know anyone of that name, on her feet at one point, begging him to listen.

"Dale was an officer in the Bantams," he told her. "For all I know, he was Sam's commanding officer. Is that how you met him? Through Sam?"

Giving up any more pretense, she sat down again on the cot and buried her face in her hands. "No—I-I knew him long before I met Sam. It had nothing to do with Sam, ever."

"If that's the truth, tell me."

He leaned his back against the frame of the door. Waiting.

Her voice now was little more than a thread. "I spent a summer in Ludlow, with my aunt. My mother had been ill, and Aunt Lily took me until she'd regained her strength. I was sixteen, and I fell in love. Alasdair was staying with friends, it was during summer hols at Oxford, and it was the happiest summer of my life. He was older, but we were going to marry as soon as I was eighteen. That's what we told each other. And then I was sent for, to come home. He'd promised to come and see me at Christmas. He wanted to speak to my father, he said. He never came, and in the new year, I learned he was to be married as soon as he came down. Only a few months away. But not to *me*. I thought my heart would break."

He said nothing. Letting her tell the story her way.

"Life has a way of going on. I survived, my heart survived. And later, I fell in love with Sam, and married him. I was very happy. When the war came, Sam wanted to enlist, but he was told that he wasn't wanted, that he was too short to be a soldier. It was a blow, a terrible blow." She looked at him. "You're tall, you've always been accepted wherever you go. You can't begin to know how men like Sam felt. They were healthy, they were strong, they wanted to fight, and they were turned away. And then Kitchener agreed to the Bantams. Sam left for Shrewsbury and then Chester as soon as he heard, eager to be in that first company. He was so fearful that there might not be enough men enlisting for a full battalion, but of course there were hundreds, and then thousands. Some of them walked for miles, just to sign their names. He said it was remarkable to see. And one man who barely even made the new height regulations offered to fight any six men there, to prove his worth. Sam came home a soldier, and all I could think of was, what if I *lose* him?"

She couldn't go on, weeping now. And then she wiped her eyes angrily and said, "He came home overnight, to show us his uniform, and an officer on his way to Ludlow dropped him at the bar. They had a few drinks, everyone there, and then the officer went on his way. I never saw him. I'd had a miscarriage. I hadn't even told Sam I was pregnant, I didn't want that to matter. To hold him back. Later, when my father put up one of the photographs he'd taken that night, so proud of Sam, and pointed it out to me, there was the officer—standing in the background. And I knew him at once. It was a shock. But he wasn't Sam's company—he just happened to volunteer to drive two or three of the men south, to give them a little more time with their families. By then the trains were overcrowded, one had to wait and wait."

She gave him an accusing glance. "That was the photograph you took from the pub. I'd managed to put it off in a corner, I didn't want it where I could see it every day."

"I didn't take it," he said. "I was nearly certain that it was Sam's sister who took it."

"*Susan?*" she repeated blankly. "Why would she want it? I don't understand."

"She was there—at Little Bog—when it was taken. I thought she must have come for it. I didn't know what it showed. Or why she should want it."

"No, you must be mistaken. She doesn't even know Alasdair. Besides, when my father sent a copy of that photograph on to Sam, he sent it to his sister. Proud of joining up. But she wrote to him and said she'd torn it up."

He let that go. "When did you see Dale again?"

"I'd gone to Shrewsbury. Mostly to speak to some of the firms that supplied the pub. It was December, and that evening I went to a friend's house, to a Christmas party. I hadn't seen her in ages, and when the invitation came, I was glad of it. My mother had recently died, I was missing Sam terribly, I hadn't had a letter in weeks. I was wretched. And in walked Alasdair. He was convalescing in a clinic outside Shrewsbury. He told me his wife had died in 1916, while he was in France. I was surprised, shocked, to see him. He was still on crutches, they thought they might have to do another surgery on his knee. And then in the new year, he told me he was being transferred to another clinic in Wales, while the knee healed. He asked me to come and raise his spirits. He even sent me a ticket for the train to Chester, where he had a motorcar waiting to drive me the rest of the way. I nearly tore it up. Instead, I went. And—and you must know the rest of it. Thornton was the name we used, so that no one would know. It seemed exciting at the time, and later—later it seemed tawdry. The last time I saw him, he'd just got his orders. The knee wasn't perfect, but he was eager to get back to his men. I was more than a little upset. That's why I went into the tailor shop, and I kept him waiting for me outside. I think I wanted to make him jealous."

"You never told him about Tildy?"

"Oh—no—no one knew. Not even Nan. Not even

the doctor in London." She looked up at him plaintively. "Will you let me go home now?"

"I'll take you myself. But I must ask. Are you certain he never learned you'd had a child?"

"I don't see how it's possible."

But Tildy didn't resemble either of her parents. She'd had that bright red hair and green eyes.

"Did Susan know you'd had a child, you and Sam?"

"I don't know—Sam tried to find her after the war. He'd lost track of her. He was afraid she might be dead—so many died in the influenza epidemic, and even the solicitor, Hastings, had no idea what had become of her—but he did his best to find her."

And that was where the solicitor Hastings entered this web of intrigue, like the spider in its center, controlling the various threads.

Hastings, who was Sam Milford's solicitor, who had drawn up his various wills. Who knew how to find Susan Milford. Who could have told her about Sam's pretty little daughter, and how unusual it was for parents of their coloring to have a red-haired, green-eyed child. How Sam doted on her. But the one piece of information Hastings had never had was the name of Tildy's father. Because Sam himself had never known it.

Hamish, who had been there in the back of his

mind for a very long time now, said, "Dale is fair, wi' blue eyes."

He found himself repeating the words aloud, to Ruth Milford.

"Alasdair's father had red hair just like that. I saw him, when I was sixteen, and I knew as soon as I saw Tildy, that she was going to look like him. I was horrified, and then I was glad I'd told Sam about the attack in Oswestry. You were right, I lied to him too. But it explained why Tildy didn't look very much like either Sam or me. No one in my family ever had such lovely bright hair. Or even green eyes." She bit her lip. "How could I confess to Sam that I'd had an affair? How could I hurt him like that? The lie was terrible enough."

He said, "I'll have a word with Inspector Carson. Then I'll take you home."

She looked him straight in the eye. "If there was any other way to reach Crowley tonight, I'd take it rather than go as far as the door with you. I'd *walk*, if I could." Then she asked, "Who told you? *Who else knew about Alasdair?*"

"No one else knew. Not in the sense you mean. Dale is associated with a charity here in Shrewsbury. One that Sam had also used to find if Tildy had been taken and then adopted somewhere else in Shropshire or Cheshire. I don't know if they ever crossed paths there. I don't know how Dale discovered that you'd had a child. Or even when. But Dale *was* told about your husband's search for Tildy. He must have guessed then, even if he hadn't known before."

He wasn't sure where her loyalty lay. Whether she would warn Dale that Rutledge knew his name.

Another thought occurred to him. "Did he give you the shoe? I need to know."

"All right. Yes. He did. He knew how worried I was about the pub, that last weekend in Llangollen. The German prisoners would be sent home at war's end. The Bog would be closed then. It didn't matter, they weren't allowed to come to the pub. Little Bog was already dismantled. We were struggling even then. He told me he'd like to help, but I didn't want anything from him then. I was too hurt, he was leaving and it was over. I felt—never mind how I felt. And then for no reason—all these years later—he sent that shoe. It had nothing to do with Tildy, I swear to you. And it wasn't as if he'd sent money. He knew I wouldn't accept money from him. But I told myself he could afford to part with the shoe now, and that meant that Tildy would be taken care of."

"Then Sam did know who sent the shoe?"

"He thought it was from a distant cousin of mine, whose heir had died in the war."

She had told so many lies . . .

"Don't look at me like that," she said, anger and pain and loss in her voice as she turned on him. "That Christmas, when I saw him again at the party in Shrewsbury, I needed to know if I still loved him. Alasdair. That's why, when he wrote to me in January, I agreed to meet him. But I didn't know until too late—in March, when he told me he had received his orders and was going back to France—that I wasn't in love with him after all. How much I loved Sam. And not very long after Alasdair was back in France, I discovered I was pregnant. That my sins were coming back to haunt me."

She kept repeating the story of their first encounter, as if trying to justify herself, find something that would excuse what she'd done, make it less her fault.

"Did Alasdair feel the same way about the past?"

"He swore that Christmas that he was still in love with me. But I knew better after Llangollen. That Romeo and Juliet romance in Ludlow hadn't lasted for either of us. We had grown into very different people without realizing it."

He was reminded suddenly of his engagement to

Jean. Blindly in love that summer of 1914, and with nothing in common but the past when he'd come back in 1919, a broken man.

He took a deep breath. "I'll speak to Carson," he said again, and left.

He didn't tell her that he himself knew Alasdair Dale.

"The name," Carson said. "You have it now, or you wouldn't be letting her go. Who was it? And is this person important to your inquiry?"

"He's a solicitor in Chester. I'm taking Mrs. Milford home, and then I'll drive up there and interview him. I'll know more when I've done that."

"Just remember that Shrewsbury is on your way. And the police station isn't difficult to find." He considered Rutledge, then said dryly, "Was it the cell that made her give up that name? We like to think ours are progressive, not medieval."

"It was a combination of pressures, most likely. But thank you. And—while I'm here. I'd like you to go on keeping an eye on Dora Radley. She's not directly involved, but she knows the man in question too. They are involved with the same charity, and there may be other connections I haven't uncovered. I'd like to know she's safe while I'm away."

"I'll see to it. I don't need one of your corpses showing up on my doorstep."

Ruth Milford remained stubbornly silent on the drive
back to Crowley.

It wasn't until they were within sight of the pub that
she said, "I'd appreciate it if you didn't stay here tonight. Or any other night. If there is anything in your
room, I'll have Will bring it down to you. Make your
excuses and go."

"My valise."

"Wait in the yard, then. Don't come in. I've got
to face Nan and Donald and Will. It's not going to be
pleasant, I don't know what to say to them."

"I kept my promise. Your secret is still safe."

She closed her eyes for a moment. "It was selfish,
wasn't it? I've regretted it every day since then. But I
don't regret Tildy. I've never regretted having her."

"Where is she, Mrs. Milford?"

"I don't know. I've never known. I have truly never
known."

She got out as soon as the wheels of the motorcar
stopped turning, hurrying into the pub without looking back.

He got down, set her valise by the door, but didn't
go in.

Five minutes later, Will appeared, tossed Rutledge's valise out into the yard, then slammed the door in his face.

Five minutes after that, he was on the road, driving back the way he'd come.

To Shrewsbury, and then to Chester.

Alasdair Dale had sent him to a tailor who had re-membered Banner, opening up the inquiry into the body found in the River Dee. Giving it a name. Had he expected the search for Banner to go nowhere? Or had he anticipated what Rutledge would do, speak to tailors until he found one who could tell him what he needed to know? Making certain he himself appeared to be helpful.

Had he known, even then, that the dead man was Sam Milford? And that the woman Dale had had an affair with in Llangollen had just lost her husband? That the child he'd fathered even existed?

He must have done. Dora Radley had confided in him.

Rutledge had a long drive ahead, most of it in the dark.

And Hamish was waiting.

Ten miles from Chester, Rutledge had to pull over to the side of the road.

He was tired, and in the dark the war had come back.

His men had been taken out of the line, exhausted, most of the original company dead or wounded, new men arriving and dying with frightful regularity. There was blood everywhere, bits of bodies stirred up in the mud and urine and dead rats—a hand appearing without an arm, a boot with a foot still in it, heads—sights men had learned to ignore, to keep their sanity and face the enemy. It had taken a heavy toll.

Rutledge endured the onslaught of memory, and in time, it began to fade. He couldn't have said how long it lasted, although his watch told him he'd sat there on the verge for over an hour.

Rubbing his face and eyes, he got out and turned the crank. Then realized as he got back behind the wheel that he was very low on petrol.

He just managed to reach a garage, but had to wake the owner, who had already retired. It was necessary to show his identification, but in the end, he got what he needed.

It was already dawn when he found a small hotel and took a room for a few hours' sleep before he could present himself at Alasdair Dale's chambers. He dared not risk resting any longer. News traveled fast, bad news faster. A different clerk, coming out to ask if Rutledge had an appointment, said, "Mr. Dale was called away on a matter of some urgency late last evening, sir. He left a message asking me to see to his diary and make necessary changes where possible. I wasn't aware that he was expecting someone this morning. If you'll give me your name, I shall be happy to arrange a more convenient time for you."

Had Dora Radley contacted him, told him that Rutledge was looking for him?

Rutledge produced a smile. "I'm an old friend. From the war. I won't be in Chester for very long. When do you expect Alasdair to return? He promised me dinner. Don't tell me he's already forgot?"

The clerk gave him a formal smile in return. It told him nothing. "I'm afraid I can't say until Mr. Dale lets me know his schedule. I'm so sorry, sir."

"There's another matter. I came in on the train, and I need transportation while I'm in town. It's possible that I'll need to travel to Liverpool. Does Alasdair use a driver? If he's away, the man might be willing to drive for me."

"I believe on occasion he's asked another firm of solicitors to find a driver for clients who are in town for a few days. They might be willing to help you as well. Shall I give you their direction, sir?"

Rutledge was tempted. But he wasn't ready to push his luck. "Never mind, Alasdair himself might be back before Liverpool. You didn't say where it was he went?"

"He himself didn't say, sir."

"Has he been in and out of late? I've written to him, and he didn't answer. Not like him to avoid me."

"He has a wide and busy practice, sir. Very much in demand."

It was useless. He thanked the man and left, before he was asked again for his name.

But where had Dale gone? Was he away on legitimate legal business? Or had Dora Radley contacted him as soon as Rutledge was out her door? A telegram? A telephone message?

Hamish said, "It's possible. Women trust him."

And that made Rutledge uneasy. It was a side of Alasdair that he'd never seen, in France. Dale had been a good soldier, a good officer. Even a good friend. But how a man dealt with other men was not always an indication of how he behaved toward women. As Betty Turnbull might have discovered, to her sorrow. But there was the fact that Dale had always been a very likeable man. People were often drawn to him.

He couldn't sit in Chester waiting for Dale to return. Nor could he afford to go haring off in the wrong direction in the hope of finding him.

He went into a small stationer's shop in one of the back streets, and found that they carried ledgers. He bought three, had them wrapped in plain paper, and then took them to a hotel just outside the city.

Asking for the manager, he explained that it was necessary to send ledgers to his solicitor, who was presently away from Chester.

"I don't have time to deal with this myself. I'd like someone to take the package to the address shown, and ask them to post the ledgers to Mr. Dale straightaway. There's a firm I wish to purchase, but I need Mr. Dale to have a look at these and tell me if I'm right about its future potential. I only have a matter of days to make my decision. I can't wait for him to return."

When the Bank of England note accompanied the request, the manager was happy to attend to the matter. "And what name shall I attach to this message, sir?"

"Gibson. I'm from the Firebricks Works at Ruabon. The Trefors gave me the name of their man. I am hoping he can help me."

He had no way of knowing who the Trefor House solicitor might be. But he wasn't entirely sure that Alasdair's clerks would know either. If they erred on the side of caution, his scheme would work.

When the transaction was completed, Rutledge thanked the manager and left. From a doorway down the street, he watched the man, package under his arm, find a cab to take him into Chester.

The post office was not that far from Dale's chambers.

Rutledge was there twenty minutes later, but it was another quarter of an hour before he saw the clerk striding toward the post office, the same package under his arm.

Shortly thereafter, he came out again, without it.

Rutledge waited until he was out of sight, then went inside.

It took some persuasion, but he got what he was after.

The package was addressed to Alasdair Dale, Esquire, in care of a hotel in Ludlow, Shropshire.

But *was* Dale in Ludlow? An innocent man with nothing to do with murder?

Or was it a clever bit of misdirection that would allow him to travel wherever it was that he intended to go, with no one the wiser, including his own clerks?

Where the hell was he now? And what was he planning to do?

Rutledge went to the Cathedral, where it was quiet and he could think, pacing in the cloisters with only his own footsteps to keep him company.

A cold wind had come up, but he ignored it, deep in thought.

He had no idea where Susan Milford might be. Or what her part in all that happened had been. He had to leave her out of the equation for the moment. Instead he had to weigh where the greater risk lay.

Dora? Or Ruth? Both of whom had connections to Alasdair Dale.

Dora knew now about the police interest in him, and she also moved in some of the same circles as he did, because her husband had been a solicitor. But Dora was not the sort to gossip. She might warn Dale of Rutledge's interest, but she wouldn't tell the world.

On the other hand, Ruth had gone through emotional turmoil for weeks now, since her husband's death. If she believed that Rutledge was wrong, that Dale was not guilty of that, she would go on protecting him. But if Rutledge had raised doubts in her mind, if he had given her even an inkling of her own guilt in all that had happened, she might take it into her head to do something rash. Could Dale trust her to protect him, or did he know her well enough to guess the damage she could do?

So far there wasn't enough evidence to convict Dale. Only to interview him.

Would he be foolish enough to try and silence either one of the women?

But if Ruth, distraught over her husband's death and the loss of her child, should take her own life, no one would be shocked.

And the blame, if any, would attach to him, Rutledge, for taking her to Shrewsbury and trying to shame her into confessing the name of her assailant in Oswestry.

Surely Dora Radley was safe. For the moment.

But Ruth wasn't.

And Dale had had a head start.

18

Rutledge left the cloisters and walked back to his motorcar, stopping only long enough to purchase sandwiches and refill his Thermos.

He was a very good driver. The roads were a different story, and once into Shropshire, the way they twisted and turned and sometimes doubled back on themselves made it nearly impossible to make good time. Nor was it safe, tired as he was.

Coming on an overturned lorry lying across a sharp curve in the road some miles outside Chester delayed him even more. He had to stop and sort out the tangle. But for a wonder the driver was alive, if badly shaken and suffering cuts on his face and shoulders.

Two other vehicles were on the scene, and he sent one to find the nearest doctor and Constable, while he positioned the other vehicle to keep its headlamps on the wreckage to prevent someone else from plowing into it, as they too had nearly done.

When the Constable arrived, Rutledge turned the accident over to him, and set out again.

Hamish said, "It could ha' been you, on yon curve. Slow down."

"There's no time."

"If ye're right, it canna' happen too quickly. No' if he wants the world to believe in suicide."

"He'll have thought it out. A mine shaft at Little Bog. A fall down the stairs. The rafters are high enough in the pub for her to use a rope. An overdose of laudanum to help her sleep. There are *ways*. He's killed before. Another death won't sit heavily on his conscience."

"Yon woman might. She's the mither of his daughter."

"If he cared about Tildy at all, it might make a difference."

"But if it was Dora who told him aboot the lass, he couldna' ha' taken her. She was already missing."

He nearly missed a turning, as Hamish shouted, "*'Ware!*"

As he fought the wheel in time, he realized that Hamish was right.

That brought him back to Susan.

And the child she claimed she'd had with her in Bed-dgwian. The child that had disappeared in the night.

What part had that played in all that had happened? If Dale didn't have Tildy—if Susan did—why would it matter if Sam Milford tracked him down as the child's father?

Why would Sam Milford have to die?

He drove on, steadily, as fast as he dared on the straighter stretches, slowing when he had to.

It was late as he crossed the bridges in Shrewsbury and sped past the stark outline of the Abbey, on his way to Crowley.

The night was overcast farther south, and with only his headlamps to guide him, he was grateful that the road was familiar. He concentrated on the uneven ruts and ragged verges, his teeth clenched.

It was Hamish who saw the glow first.

"There's light ahead," he said quietly. "It's no' a guid sign."

Rutledge slowed, wrenching his eyes from the road to look beyond the next turning.

There was an unusual brightness reflected in the dark clouds, a brightness that shouldn't be there. Fire. But he couldn't judge just how far ahead it was.

He sped up, used it as a beacon, and then watched it begin to dim rather than brighten as he grew nearer.

Fire, he thought. *It has to be a fire. But that can't be the pub. Surely not.*

Of all the ways he'd considered that Ruth Milford might commit suicide, burning down the pub around her hadn't occurred to him. But it was something that Alasdair Dale might think was fitting. She had wanted to save it, to stay as long as she could for her father's sake. Even when she knew it was only a matter of time before it would come to an end, whether she closed it or not. Her death and its destruction, freeing the Blakes to leave the village, was believable.

They would never receive their share of any sale, but the question must always have been, who would wish to invest in a dying pub, a dying village, and a dying lead mine?

The glow too was dying.

And then he was on it. Not the pub. Nor a lorry in trouble on the lonely road.

He stopped the motorcar well short, got out, and raced toward the dying flames, flickering over the wreckage of a Sunbeam motorcycle and sidecar.

Shielding his face from the heat, he tried to see if there was a body in the burning, twisted metal. There was a coat sleeve, partly ash now, hanging over the edge of the sidecar. But no charred bones showing.

Had the machine come to grief on the road? If so, where was the rider?

But as he looked at the tangle, he realized that the motorcycle had been struck by something, pushed off the road, and into the ditch in which it lay.

He ran to his motorcar and took out his torch, ran back, and began to circle what was left of the Sunbeam, searching for any signs that the rider had been able to crawl away.

The verge had been scorched and blackened by the fire at its height, but beyond that, the tall winter vegetation hadn't been touched.

Widening his circle slowly but surely, he wished for daylight to search for any marks in the dry jumble of grass and briars and scrub growth that ran just here along the road. The torch cast shadows that tricked him again and again into thinking he'd found signs, only to realize that these were winter-matted patches instead.

Swearing, he stopped and cast the light ahead of him.

He couldn't be certain it was Susan Milford's machine, he'd been wrong before, but here, so close to the turning for Little Bog, who else could it belong to? Still, he'd made that mistake once before.

Had someone come along and found the rider unconscious, and taken him or her to find a doctor? Leaving the wreckage to burn itself out?

Reluctant to give up his search, he moved on, then widened his circle again.

He had reached the road that ran toward Little Bog when he saw it.

Someone had fallen heavily, boots skidding across the ruts. It appeared to be fresh.

Kneeling, he brought the torch closer. There was a dark patch just there—

Pulling off his driving gloves, he touched the patch, and then holding the torch up, shone it on his fingers.

Blood? It was so mixed with the disturbed earth that even with the torch, he couldn't be sure.

He started forward, then changed his mind and went trotting back for his motorcar, driving to where the track to the mine turned in.

Once there, he left it running, walked on with his headlamps and his torch to pick out his way.

Twice more he found where it appeared that someone had fallen. What's more, there was half a boot print. A woman's. He was convinced now that somehow Susan Milford had survived the crash and was trying to get to a place she knew. But had she made it to the mine?

He was afraid to drive on, uncertain whether she lay

somewhere out of sight along the road, and in the dark he would pass her without seeing her.

Once she wandered off the road, and he lost her track. Casting about, he found where she had made her way back to it, and carried on. Her dogged persistence won his admiration as he followed her. He couldn't tell how badly she was hurt, whether she had been burned or was thrown clear. The blood worried him.

In the east a faint streak of brightness low on the horizon promised a gray and cloudy sunrise. But where he was, it was still dark.

Looking up, he could just make out the silhouettes of the Long Mynd in one direction and the Stiperstones to his left, black shapes against the horizon.

It was slow work. The next time he examined his surroundings, he realized that he was near the trees where she had hidden the Sunbeam under canvas and brush. He took the time to make his way there and search meticulously, but he saw no signs that she had got this far. There was no shelter here now.

He found one more place where she had tripped or had struggled with dizziness or felt faint. She had fallen heavily this time, and she had lain there for a space to gather the strength to go on, for now the traces of blood on his fingers were wet. He had seen wounded men on the battlefield do that—wait for the pain and the dizziness to subside before getting to their feet again—and under cover of fire from his own trenches had gone out himself to bring some of them in.

By the time he'd reached the outskirts of the Little Bog village ruins, he realized that in the dark, it would take him hours to search all of the cottages and mine buildings. In the dark it would be dangerous work. His motorcar was now some fifty yards behind him, and he debated what to do about it. In the end, he moved it into what was left of a shed, out of sight, but close by if he needed it in an emergency.

Then he began with the powder barn.

It was empty. No hearth now, no ring for a fire, the earthen floor showing only his own footsteps. Or so he thought.

In a damp patch just outside, where rainwater had puddled and then begun to dry, he found half an imprint of a man's boot. Old—or recent?

By now the day had broken and the pale light of a cloudy dawn showed it clearly. It wasn't his. But it was close to his size.

Had someone else followed her? He'd have had to be persistent, to come this far.

Was he still here? Or had he found what he was after, and then gone away?

Moving carefully now, Rutledge went methodically

through any ruined cottage that provided a bit of shelter. It began to rain, a light mist at first, then a more drenching rain. He didn't stop, his hat and the shoulders of his coat taking the brunt of it.

He searched the mine buildings, and then went into the wood just behind the stack.

And it was there he found her.

His first thought as he saw the toe of a laced boot, slim as the foot inside it, was that she had been buried where she lay.

He couldn't see her face. She was hidden under the trunk of a fallen tree, and the soft spongy soil around her had been scattered over the ground, masking her from view.

He stopped. There was no movement, nothing to indicate that she was alive.

Starting forward quietly, he knelt by the tree trunk, reached out and fumbled for an arm or hand to search for a pulse.

She erupted from under the tree, striking out at his face and shoulders. His hat went flying, and he was nearly knocked over.

Ignoring her flying fists, he got to his feet, reached out, and caught her shoulders, slowly pinning her arms even as she tried to kick out at his exposed shins.

"Stop—it's Rutledge. I've come to help you."

But she had already stopped flailing at him, her body going limp in his hands, her head lolling, her eyes closed. He hardly recognized her through the mask of blood that had dried across her face.

She had fainted. Whether from pain or shock or exhaustion, he couldn't tell.

He got her clear of the log, gathered her up in his arms, and started walking.

The driest place was still the powder barn. It was not particularly secure, but the rain was too heavy now to search for a better place or take her all the way back to the motorcar. He carried her inside and laid her against the back wall. Then he began to run his hands up and down her arms and legs. She whimpered when he touched her right ankle, and he could see that it was swelling. And again, when he touched her right arm. He thought it might well be broken.

There was a cut on her head, still bleeding a little, and her hair, which had come down, was singed at the tips, where the fire had caught it.

If there were internal injuries, he had no way of finding them. That she managed to reach the ruins in this condition was astonishing. The sheer will to survive must have driven her.

Rocking back on his heels, he looked down at her. The anger and resentment were gone from her face, but he knew it was the fact that she was unconscious that had erased them. They were still here, waiting for her to wake up. He had no illusions.

Was this Alasdair Dale's handiwork? And what about Ruth Milford? Was she still in danger? He needed to reach The Pit and The Pony, to warn her. But there was Susan, hurt and vulnerable. He couldn't leave her yet, not knowing if she was still being hunted.

Hamish spoke then. "He willna' touch the wife. No' today. It would be far too suspicious. He will wait. He's no' a fool."

There was truth to that. But Rutledge stood looking out at the rain, and argued with himself.

There was a sound behind him, and he turned quickly, thinking Susan was awake. He realized instead that she had curled herself into a knot, and was shivering. She was wearing only a thin jacket over a shirt and trousers. Her heavier coat lay in the ruins of the Sunbeam, half burned. She must have had to pull it off to free herself from the fiery wreckage.

He took off his own coat and spread it over her, but the shivering didn't stop. She was in shock.

Finally, he lifted her and pulled her into his lap, spreading the coat over both of them. But he kept his face toward the ruined opening. He had nothing with which to defend himself. He wondered if Dale was armed. Many officers had kept their sidearms, himself included, and even brought back German pistols as souvenirs.

After a time, the shivering stopped. He put her back against the wall, spread the coat over her again, then took a chance. The rain had let up only a little, but he ran for his motorcar, to fetch the rug he kept there. On the way back, he searched in places protected from the rain for bits of wood and dry grass, to start a small fire, making a bundle with the rug. It was a risk, the smoke would rise in the damp air, and give them away.

As Rutledge pulled the rug over Susan, Hamish said, "Take her to the pub."

But there was no doctor in Crowley, and no Constable. And he wanted to question her as soon as she was awake again. Then he would have a better picture of what had happened to her, and who was responsible.

Ignoring his wet coat and shirt, clinging heavily to his shoulders, he laid the wood out, put the grasses on top, and took out the lighter he'd carried since his first week in the trenches.

One of his men had made it out of a rifle casing and parts from another lighter. He'd used it to fire fuses in tunnels under enemy lines, and to light the candles in his officer's dugout to read maps in the black of night.

The grasses burned quickly, but the dry wood

caught as well, and the fire began to burn, taking some of the dampness away but not warming much of their surroundings. The smoke made him cough.

He looked at his watch. It was noon, but the day was dark, grim. As grim as he himself felt. The rain made a soft patter on what was left of the roof, and he had to fight his own drowsiness as what little heat there was began to reach him. It had been a long night, and he hadn't stopped with the dawn.

He had drifted into a light doze in spite of his efforts to stay awake when she spoke just behind him.

Coming alert with the ease of long practice, he turned and said, "Are you all right?"

"Yes. No."

"I need to know."

"My ankle hurts. And this arm. I've never felt such pain. It must be broken."

"Internal injuries?"

She started to shake her head, then stopped abruptly, putting up a hand. "Oh. No wonder it aches." She looked at the dried blood on her fingers, and then tried to sit up, crying out as she did. "My ribs—"

"What happened? I found the Sunbeam. It was still burning when I got there."

"How did you know where to find me?"

"I didn't. I had to track you here. What happened?"

"He must have known I was coming. I thought at first it was your doing. Suddenly my headlamp picked out something in the road. And I realized very quickly that here was a child's chair right in front of me. It looked—I thought she was sitting in it—and I was traveling at a great rate of speed. I was going to crash right into it. And so I didn't see the rope stretched across the road. I remember flying through the air and hitting the ground with such force I lost my grip on the handlebars and was thrown off. That's when I lost consciousness."

"The fire?"

"I don't know—petrol must have leaked onto the hot motor—or perhaps he burned it. I was barely conscious, and he kicked me in the ribs to see if I was alive. I managed not to cry out, and he left. I thought it was a trick, then I saw the flames, there must have been petrol everywhere, and my coat was burning, my hair—" She shivered again. "I don't know how I got the coat off, and tossed it back into the flames. And then I began to crawl."

"Was the chair still in the road? I didn't see it when I arrived on the scene."

"I don't know. All I could think of was getting away from the fire into the dark. I believed I'd be safe in the dark. I crawled, but it was too hard, and I somehow got to my feet and began to stagger off. When I came to—when I came to that road, I just—just followed it. But he must have come back to be sure I was dead, because he followed me, I could hear him calling. I found the fallen tree and got under it. I couldn't go on. I was having trouble breathing, my foot and my arm were on fire. I knew if I collapsed, he'd find me and kill me. The next thing I knew, you were touching me, trying to pull me out of the hole I'd made."

She lay back. "I'm so thirsty. And cold. I can't seem to get warm."

"Why were you on the road to Crowley?"

"I wasn't. I was going to Ludlow. I took this road because I knew—" She broke off. He thought she was going to say she knew it better because she had been there before. She had already avoided telling him that she recognized the Little Bog track.

"Why were you going to Ludlow? Do you have friends there?"

She didn't answer him.

Then she said, "I expect I should thank you. For this." She nodded toward the fire, then fingered his coat. "But then why should I be grateful?"

"You weren't as kind to me."

"No."

Folding up the rug he'd brought for her, he said,

"You need a doctor. Can you walk, leaning on my arm? I can't bring the motorcar to you."

"I don't need your help."

But she did, and still refused it. Getting to her feet was hard. Throwing his coat back at him, she used the wall and struggled painfully to her feet. She stood there for a moment, catching her breath. Her ankle had stiffened while she slept. Then holding her arm with one hand, she hobbled painfully toward the opening.

Rutledge let her go, following at a little distance as she made her way to the clearing where the mine buildings stood.

"Wait here." He left her then and went to bring the motorcar around.

When he got to where he'd left it, he saw that someone had been there before him. He'd left a stalk of dried wildflower where someone coming too close to the shed's opening would step on it.

He stared at it for a moment, thinking hard.

And then he spent a good quarter of an hour going over the motorcar. But as far as he could see, nothing had been tampered with. Under the bonnet. Under the chassis. The petrol tank in the rear.

He would know, once he began to drive it, he thought grimly.

Getting in, he carefully moved it out of the shed.

She was still there, waiting, as he came down the road. He'd half expected her to set out on her own, but of course there was nowhere to go. No Sunbeam, and she was barely able to walk.

Susan had difficulty climbing into the motorcar. With her ankle and the arm, she struggled, face gray with pain. But she got into the passenger's seat, and then leaned back, careful of her ribs.

He started down the road. They were still in the village ruins when he turned to her and said, "How did you come to know Alasdair Dale?"

19

He didn't think she was going to answer him. She sat there in her seat, upright, braced against the jerky movements as the tires bumped and dipped over the ruts in the road.

"Then tell me why you took Tildy from her parents?"

She never looked at him. Her gaze was on the road ahead, her profile cold with whatever it was she was thinking.

Without consulting her, he took her to Church Stretton, where he could find a doctor and ask a Constable to keep an eye on her.

He found a Dr. Matthews by the simple expedient of searching for a name plate on a surgery door.

An older man with sharp blue eyes, Matthews took

his patient back to the examining room, leaving Rutledge in the small outer room. There was no one else
waiting, and he paced the floor, too tired to sit and find
himself dropping into a light sleep.

It was nearly half an hour later when Dr. Matthews
came back to him.

"You say this woman was in a road accident?"

"Her Sunbeam went off the road. I found her not
very long afterward, but was unable to move her
straightaway."

"Hmmm. I believe that right arm to be broken, a
clean break. Painful, but it should heal with time.
There is heavy bruising in the ankle, and she must
stay off it for several weeks. I found a mark on her ribs
where she indicated she had been kicked by someone.
Painful bruising there but no indication that the ribs
are broken. The cut on her head explains some of the
vertigo she is experiencing. I don't particularly care for
that. She should have rest."

But it was Susan Milford that Matthews was referring to, and Rutledge wasn't certain she would listen to
his advice.

"Aye, but she doesna' have yon machine now. She
canna' do as she likes."

The Scot's voice was loud in the room, but Dr. Matthews appeared not to notice.

Rutledge said, "You must persuade her to take care of herself. I have no authority over her."

"The Good Samaritan who brought her here. Yes, I know. She told me, however, that she was afraid of you and didn't wish to be forced to leave here with you." He regarded Rutledge for a moment. "*Did* you cause her accident?"

He silently swore. "I did not." He reached into his pocket and took out his identification. "I'm looking into a death that occurred in Wales, but my search for the killer has brought me to Shropshire. She has no reason to be afraid of me, unless she had something to do with that death. I think it best if you keep her under observation for twenty-four hours. For her own sake. Can you do that?"

"Not against her will."

"Then give her something to make her sleep."

"Not with that head injury."

Rutledge said, "Are you certain she's not lying about the extent of her injuries?"

After a pause, Matthews said, "I can't be." Then in a different tone of voice he said, "*Is* she a murderer? Was she trying to escape from you when this happened?"

"I don't know," Rutledge said truthfully. "I won't know for twenty-four hours. If she presents a problem, call in the police and have them take her into custody."

"I don't want this responsibility," Matthews told him bluntly. "I have my family to consider—my other patients."

"And I can't trust her. She will have to stay here. In gaol or in your surgery."

He left without seeing Susan Milford. He thought that best.

But there were the questions she'd never answered.

The day had come down again, heavier rain now and lowering clouds. He set out for Crowley, stopping only briefly at the scene of the fire, using what little daylight there was to inspect the wreckage.

The place had been well chosen. There were trees on either side of the road just here, and he found rope burns on two of them, where the impact with the Sunbeam had cut deep into bark before the rope itself had broken. Someone had taken away whatever rope was left.

At least that part of Susan Milford's story was true. She was lucky, he thought, that the rope hadn't been set high enough to decapitate her. Instead the plan was for the accident itself to kill her, the Sunbeam tossed into the air and coming down with her still in the saddle. Instead, by some miracle, she had been thrown clear in time.

If there had been anything of use in the sidecar, it had burned, along with the valise, where only the handle and the hinges were left.

He walked a little way down the road, but if a chair had been placed there, there was no sign of it. Even if someone hadn't thought to sweep a foot across where it had been set, erasing any imprints, the rain had taken care of it.

"Or it wasna' there ata'," Hamish said.

But Rutledge believed her. It was the chair that had made her miss seeing the rope. The question was, why a child's chair? Had that been intentional—or simply chosen because a driver would do his or her best to avoid hitting it?

The other question was, how had Dale known she was following him? Had he seen her somewhere? On the Welsh Bridge, or by the Abbey? In a straight run of the road, where he could see her in the distance, keeping pace, never falling too far behind or gaining too quickly?

Or had the chair and the rope been intended for Rutledge? And caught Susan Milford by sheer coincidence? Had Dale stopped in Shrewsbury, and seen Rutledge's motorcar passing through? If he had taken another road south, missing the lorry wreck, he could have been well ahead, with time to lay his trap. But how had he come by a child's chair? Had he bought it in Shrewsbury or even Church Stretton?

Rutledge got back in the motorcar.

The worry now was Ruth Milford—

And where was Dale?

This was perfect country to hide in. Little Bog wasn't the only choice. There was the Long Mynd, the valley between two ridges, running not that far from here. Or the Stiperstones.

He drove on, and came to Crowley late in the day.

There were outbuildings behind the pub, including a stable where horses had been kept, and several sheds, all of them more or less in disrepair. How long had it been since travelers had put their horses or pack animals in the barn for the night, on their way to the mines or passing through on the Shrewsbury road?

Pushing and shoving, he got the barn door open, screaming of rusty hinges. It was damp inside, redolent of old, rotting hay. Looking up through the rafters, he could see the clouds hanging low. Debating whether to close the door again, he decided it was best to have ready access to his motorcar.

Then, knowing what his welcome would be, he took a deep breath and walked around to the yard door.

Somewhere in the distance he could hear crows calling, raucous voices echoing a little against the hill on which the pub sat.

The public room was empty, as it so often was these days. He stepped inside and closed the door behind him.

Nothing was out of place. No tables overturned, no signs of a struggle. He went to the window and looked down on the cottages. Only a few lights in the Milford house, as well as those neighboring it. A quiet evening.

He drew a breath in relief.

It would be the supper hour soon. If all was well, Will would be coming in to cook. He was too tired for confrontations now. Ruth had told him not to come back. And yet he had, to protect her.

Rutledge went up the stairs to the room he'd used before, sat down, and waited in the dark.

The aroma of food cooking in the kitchen reached him, floating upward. His feet were cold resting on the floor. But he sat there, patiently. It was apparent that no one had seen him arrive, or noticed the motorcar in the barn. He could hear voices but not quite make out what was being said. Still, the tenor was uneasy, as if those gathered there had very little to say to each other.

At length he heard the Blakes calling good night, and the yard door opening and closing. Will left soon after.

But Ruth was unaccounted for. He didn't think she'd left with the others.

Time passed, and he was on the point of going down when he heard a chair scraping across the floor just beyond the foot of the steps.

And someone moved to the stairs and began to come up them.

A woman's tread, he thought, lighter than a man's. In no hurry . . .

Was Ruth staying in the pub, not in her house?

But which room was she using? *His?* He hadn't turned on the lamp, but it hadn't appeared to be occupied. He moved silently, out of her sight if she came in.

She passed by his door. Her steps were slowing. And then he heard her go into the room next to his. It didn't take her long to get ready for bed. She moved around for a bit, then there was silence.

And then, in the dark, he heard her crying.

As if she'd kept up a front all day, and finally, here, alone, she could let herself feel something.

After a time, even the weeping stopped.

She was asleep.

Rutledge settled down to keep watch, sitting in the only chair.

It was still quite dark when he came awake with a jolt.

The stair treads, creaking slightly. Under someone's weight?

He brushed his hands over his face and eyes, trying to clear his head.

Coming up—or going down?

Going down. In the dark, someone had bumped into one of the chairs in the pub.

He moved as quietly as he could, out his door, down the passage to the next room. His torch was already in his hand, but he covered it with his fingers as he switched it on.

The covers had been thrown to one side, the sheets almost blindingly white in the torchlight.

And the room was empty.

He closed the door, walked back to the stairs. As he reached them he heard the yard door open and close.

Ruth had gone out into the night.

He kept the torch beam aimed to the floor, his fingers over the light to dim it further, picking his way through the tables and chairs, reaching the yard door and hesitating before opening it. She was nowhere to be seen.

Then he caught movement and knew she was standing just to one side of the pub, sheltered by the corner.

She stood there for a very long while, her arms wrapped around herself. Then she began to turn, back toward the yard door. He was going to be caught there, with nowhere to go—

But someone called her name softly, and she turned back quickly, hesitated, and then went toward the sound of the voice.

"I didn't know—I didn't think you would come."

Rutledge couldn't hear the response. Whoever it was, the speaker was out of his line of sight. But it was impossible to move nearer, for fear of giving his presence away.

"Did you kill Sam? I have to know. It's what *he* told me. Rutledge."

There was a reply but she said, "I didn't want to believe any of it. But Sam is dead, and *he* told me it was murder." Her voice rose a little. "I want to *know*—how did he die? Was it my fault? The lies I told?"

This time the voice was closer. "I never touched your husband. I give you my word—I'll swear on anything you like."

Listening, Rutledge was certain now that it was Alasdair's voice. And he could hear the ring of truth in it. But Alasdair hadn't killed Sam. He'd hired Joseph Burton to do it for him.

"I wish I had never met you again. Everything in

my life has gone wrong since then. Please. I want my daughter back. She's all I have left. There's no point in going on, if she's taken away from me too."

"I didn't take the child, Ruth. I will swear to that as well. I didn't know she existed until someone mentioned her to me. But I knew then she must be my child. Her age, her coloring—my father and grandmother had that red-gold hair. Elaine and I never had children, but I'd like to think they would have been as pretty as our daughter, if we had. Why did you never tell me?"

Rutledge, hearing him, thought, *Unless he'd* seen *the child, how had he been so certain of her coloring?* He was lying to Ruth. Why?

"You hadn't cared enough even to write, when you went back to France, I had to face all of it on my own. I wanted to hate you then. But when she went missing, and the shoe was right there, waiting for me. I thought it was to tell me not to worry, she was safe. You could give her so much more than a failing pub. I told myself it was for the best. She—Tildy was as sweet as she was pretty. She would have everything as your child. The best schools. The finest home and pretty clothes. It broke my heart to see Sam in such pain. But she was mine, not his. And you were her father. I'd always told myself that if you came for her, I'd let her go. But you hadn't. Until then. But now I want her back, Alasdair. You must give her to me. That's why I wrote to you last week."

"Ruth—I swear to you."

"Alasdair. If you won't give her back, I'll talk to that man. I'll tell Rutledge that it was you. And Mr. Hastings will see that she comes home. But I don't want it to be that way. I just want *Tildy*."

There was a hardness in her voice that brooked no refusal. And Dale, in the darkness just out of Rutledge's sight, heard it too.

"Ruth. I swear. I don't have her."

"But you do. You are the only person who has a reason for wanting her. She's your child. She's only Sam's legally. I'll even give you the shoe back." And she turned, walked purposefully back toward the yard door.

Rutledge had no time to think. He flattened himself against the inside wall, turning his face away from the door. She came inside, shut the door firmly behind her, leaving Dale somewhere near the edge of the yard.

"*Ruth*—" Dale called her name in anger and despair, but she walked straight across to the stairs and began to climb them, her footsteps dragging.

Rutledge heard Dale swear then, long and feelingly. After a bit, Rutledge had the sense that he was gone.

Ruth had made it clear to Dale that she would have

the child or else tell the police what she suspected, that he'd taken Tildy. And for whatever reasons he'd done it, there was no turning back the clock. Why? Because the child was dead? If he'd come to test Ruth's loyalty, he'd got his answer. And he didn't have the price of her silence. Or wouldn't pay it, for the very same reasons he'd abducted Tildy to begin with?

Rutledge straightened up, listening. In the silence, he thought he heard a motorcar moving away from the village. It had been left in the drive, he thought, where no one in the village would spot it. Ruth must have seen it, and gone down at once, before Dale had had a chance to reconnoiter—and find Rutledge's own motorcar in the shed.

Why had Dale ever allowed himself to have an affair with Ruth, so many years after he'd walked away? Had he been flattered? Lonely?

Or was there something between Sam Milford and Alasdair Dale? Something that went back to the war, and had nothing to do with the child they shared through Ruth?

Dora had told Dale about Tildy . . . but she was already missing by then. Dale already knew . . .

Rutledge stood there, his back still against the pub wall, trying to fit these new pieces of information together.

" *'Ware!*" Hamish said softly.

Rutledge kept very still. Was Ruth coming down again?

And then he heard someone walking away from the yard.

He slipped out the pub door, then moved to the corner of the pub, where Ruth had been standing only minutes before. But there was no one to account for the sounds.

He stayed where he was.

And in the distance, where the village cottages were spread out along the road, he could have sworn he saw a flicker of movement as a shape passed between two of them. He didn't see it again.

Someone had overheard the exchange between Dale and Ruth Milford.

Who had been listening? Will? In the very early morning hours, he often came up to the pub to start the bread rising. And he was devoted to Ruth. He'd helped keep the pub going when Sam was in the trenches, he'd stayed on when Sam came home. Quiet, patient, loyal Will. They had often seemed to forget he was there, in the kitchen, a part of the pub but not a part of the family. And he never seemed to mind.

Rutledge stayed by the corner of the pub for more than an hour, giving Ruth time to fall asleep again.

He'd been right about Dale coming to Crowley. Only it had been Susan who was nearly killed. And Ruth who had turned him away, even though Dale had tried to persuade her that he was innocent.

Rutledge was growing cold, outside in the early morning chill, but he was reluctant to walk back inside and run into Ruth somewhere in the dark pub. Or frighten her by coming up the stairs to his room. Finally, he went to sit in the motorcar in the darkness of the barn. He was too restless to sleep, anyway.

He could understand why Ruth had never told Dale about Tildy. She had let herself be drawn into that brief affair with him, trying to recapture a past when she had believed they were in love. He'd walked away the first time, breaking her heart by marrying someone else, someone from his own social world. Then, despite the three weekends they'd shared, Dale hadn't asked her to divorce Sam and marry him. He could have done—his wife was dead. Instead, he'd told her he was returning to the Front, and left her once more feeling betrayed. Only this time, she was to discover that she was pregnant, and he hadn't written to ask if all was well. It had made her bitter. And yet when she thought he'd taken Tildy, she had wanted the child to remind him of the mother. To haunt him. But it hadn't . . . apparently he'd never wanted Tildy for her own sake.

How had Dale found out about Tildy? Dora had told him enough for him to follow Sam and have him killed. But the child had been taken almost a year before that. Had Dale come to Crowley, seen her with Ruth, and realized who she was—then quickly driven on before anyone had seen him? Who would have noticed a passing motorcar on its way to The Bog? Or had he encountered Sam somewhere in France, and Sam had shared the good news? Rutledge found that harder to believe. Would he have talked about a child he hadn't seen and already knew was not his? *Someone mentioned her to me . . .* Who?

He got out and turned the crank.

Ruth was safe enough for the moment. And Susan Milford had nowhere to go, and no way to get there if she did. She could wait as well.

It was time he had another talk with Hastings, the solicitor.

It was just before dawn when he set out for Shrewsbury. Driving too fast on the muddy road, he tried not to recall how long it had been since Sam Milford had died—or how much time had passed since he'd spoken to Markham. Silence was unusual on the Chief Superintendent's part. A man who preferred to keep his finger on the pulse of every inquiry, he found it hard not to use the increasingly available telephone system to offer his opinion of whatever progress his officers had achieved. And so far there had been silence. Still. Better silence than to discover he was being recalled for not coming up with answers in a more timely fashion.

Hamish said, as Rutledge barely missed another deep rut, filled with rainwater and nearly invisible in the uncertain light, "There's no' a political gain here. There's no medal for finding the killer of the owner of a small pub aboot to close."

Still, Rutledge thought again, not convinced.

He rolled into Shrewsbury, the rain-wet streets glistening in the lamps, the roads quiet.

Rutledge went directly to the chambers of Hastings and Hastings.

There was no answer. When he looked at his watch, he knew why. Driving on to the police station, he asked for the direction of the solicitor's house. With some reluctance, the desk sergeant gave it to him.

It was a street of fine old houses, where old money resided in comfort. It suited the solicitor perfectly.

Rutledge began pounding on the door as soon as he reached it. The blows echoed on the quiet street, and somewhere a pair of dogs began barking inside one of the houses across the way. Another followed suit.

The door was jerked open. A butler was standing there, his nightclothes stuffed into his trousers, shirt over them, a coat over that. He had obviously dressed on his way down from his quarters.

"Leave at once or I shall summon the police," he said, his face grim.

"I am the police." He handed the man his identification. "Scotland Yard, here to see Mr. Hastings on urgent business. I'll wait inside."

The butler was peering at it. "Indeed, sir, but Mr. Hastings is asleep in his bed. I ask you to return to Mr. Hastings's chambers during regular hours."

"I'm sorry. This won't wait."

The staircase went up just inside the foyer. A voice came from the landing. "Oh, let him in, Franklin. He's not likely to go away. I'd like a cup of tea, if you please, with a whisky in it. Mr. Rutledge will take his plain, as he's on duty."

He started down the stairs, and Rutledge saw that he was wearing a robe over his nightdress.

So much the better. Hastings, he thought, wouldn't care for that at all. And would have to make the best of it.

Hastings led the way to a handsome book-lined study, gestured to one of the leather chairs, and sat down in the other. "You're younger than I am. Put a match to the fire. I feel the cold more often these days. Or shall I ask Franklin to give you a room, to freshen up?"

Ignoring the jibe, Rutledge did as he was asked, and by the time the fire was drawing well, Franklin had arrived with their tea.

Waiting until the man left, he said to Hastings, "This time I won't settle for less than the truth. I want you to know that now. Susan Milford was nearly killed last night."

He heard the quick intake of breath, then the quiet "Is she all right?"

Rutledge said, "I've seen to it. Someone put a rope across the road to Crowley. The Sunbeam was going at a high rate of speed. It crashed and began to burn. He tracked her, looking for her body. I found her instead, and he had to give up."

"Dear God."

"Sam Milford is dead. The child that he cared so much about is still missing. Ruth Milford has lied to me from the start, and so have you. Where is Tildy Milford?"

Hastings sighed. "I don't know. Not any longer."

"Did Milford *know* that you were a party to her abduction?"

"Oh, no, you're quite wrong. I was never that. Quite the opposite. I found her when the police failed."

Rutledge considered him. "And you did nothing to bring her home?"

"You see, I didn't know who had taken her. I still don't. And so I thought she would be safer if she was not found. Until we knew why." He stretched his legs, so that his feet were closer to the blaze. "Secrets are power in a way. I learned that long ago, and I have employed people to help me find out secrets I need to learn. But even they couldn't find the truth in this instance. Sadly."

"You said you found her. Where?"

"She was taken to Worcester. The police looked all over Shropshire and Cheshire. It was my people who decided to look farther afield. It was claimed by the person who brought her in to the orphanage that her mother had died, her father couldn't raise her on his own, and so he was forced to put her up for adoption. And because she was a pretty little thing, a family was found almost at once. *I* saw to that, arranged everything, and so she was placed where I could keep an eye on her. But Tildy is unusual. Her coloring made her noticeable. And Sam Milford was searching for her. Asking questions. By that time I'd discovered that she wasn't his child. And so I thought he would give up in time, that perhaps he was searching so hard because his wife was pushing him to find her. But Ruth wasn't, you see. It was Sam, not Ruth, who cared so deeply. Rather odd, don't you think? Still, it did explain why the mother wasn't as eager to have her back again. And so I left her where she was."

"How did you discover her history? Do you know the name of the child's father?"

"Not the name, of course. I was intrigued when Milford came in after the war and changed his will to include a child I didn't think he could have fathered. To my knowledge, he hadn't come home on leave at any time. I'd made a point to write to my clients who were serving their country. He'd replied several times and mentioned how much he missed his wife and the pub. I went to the clinic where the child was born. The name given there for the father was, as you'd expect, Sam Milford, but I placed some very discreet queries, and I found that he had not been in England when the child was conceived. It would have saved a good deal of time and trouble, if I'd merely asked Milford outright. It seems he knew about the child's father. Well, not *who* he was, of course. Apparently whatever

account he'd been given by his wife, he had been satisfied with it."

"Who did you ask about Milford's whereabouts in
1917?" But he already knew.

"A fellow solicitor. He'd served with the Bantams.
An officer. He was happy to help me."

"What was his name?"

"Alasdair Dale. A good man. We'd worked together a number of times on other matters. I knew
he could be discreet." He shook his head. "Do you
have any idea how many families lost their only heir
in the war? We've done what we could to trace blood-
lines. Not always successful of course. But we must
at least try."

"Did Dale ask why you were looking into Milford's
whereabouts?"

For once Rutledge had caught the solicitor off guard.
He shifted slightly in his chair, suddenly uneasy. "No,
of course not. He's discreet, as he should be." Hastings cleared his throat. "Alasdair's father was a solicitor. I'd known the family long before Alasdair was
born. I happened to mention when I asked him to look
into Milford's records that his young daughter had reminded me a little of Alasdair's grandmother. Beautiful
woman. The child had that same bright coloring."

Rutledge swore. Hastings had led Dale straight to

Tildy. And there was Trefor Hall, without an heir and leaving the sale of the property to the family solicitor. Was that Dale? Was that how he had come to know about the narrowboats and the Aqueduct? Was that how he had found Joseph Burton? It all made *sense*.

Hastings was still speaking. Justifying himself. "When the child went missing from where she'd been in safekeeping, I asked Dale to help me find her. I knew I could trust him. And I must say, he and I searched diligently. Sadly, we never succeeded."

Rutledge's voice was taut with his anger. "With all your scheming, all your secrets—did you have any idea that the man who was helping you search for that child was actually Tildy's father?"

Hastings's face drained of what little color it had, age spots standing out starkly on his cheekbones and forehead. "I can assure you. He is not. He would have told me, if I'd made such a terrible mistake. He would have *confessed* to me."

"If you had confessed to Sam Milford that you knew where Tildy was, you might have saved the man's life. He was followed to Oswestry, possibly by one of the minions you yourself have employed. And whoever hired them was worried enough about what Milford might learn in that obsessive search of his, to have him pushed off the Telford Aqueduct. Two other people have been killed as well. Susan Milford almost became the fourth victim."

"You are wrong. No, I refuse to believe you."

"Damn it, man, *I can prove it.* But why in the name of all the hounds of hell did you give that child to Susan to care for? She hated Sam."

"No, that's not true. She looked after Tildy beautifully. Tildy came to love her. Susan wanted to *keep* her. And I had to tell her that she couldn't."

"She wasn't a family heirloom, a clock or ring you could pass around. You were playing with the life of a *child*."

"Was I? With Sam Milford dead, who else would love her for her own sake?"

"Why does Susan Milford mean so much to you? You've protected her—and manipulated her—lied about her mental state—used her for your own ends."

"I knew her mother. Long ago. I made a promise. And I have kept it in my own fashion. She was happiest with Tildy. I saw a difference that gave me hope."

Rutledge stood up. "You tell me you've had help in all this. I need to speak to anyone who might have information I can use. I want to know who was following Sam Milford. Or me, for all I know. If you don't have the names by tomorrow, I'll have you dragged to the police station and put in a cell."

"Did it occur to you that the intended victim on the Crowley road was you?" The hooded eyes studied him. "*You* are in someone's way, you know."

"I'm in yours. And if I can find evidence that directly links you to murder, I will see that you are taken into custody and stand trial as an accessory."

"My conscience is clear. But I will give you a little free advice, Inspector. Who did that child threaten most?"

Rutledge shook his head. "No," he countered. "I've had enough."

And he walked out of the house.

20

He was, much to Rutledge's surprise, still sober. But Fenton's face seemed to sag as he opened the door and found Rutledge on his doorstep.

"Carson told me you brought in Ruth Milford. Then decided not to charge her."

"I needed information. She refused to give it."

"She must have done, finally. Or you wouldn't have let her go. Come in. We can't talk out here." He led the way to his study. "Drink?"

"I'm on duty."

"I'm not. I wish to hell I were. I can't seem to fill the hours of the day anymore. Once I could go eighteen hours without sleep, and then I only needed two hours and I was back at it again. Now I watch the hands of the clock move like treacle, and wonder how the hell I can make it through until dark. And in the dark I wait for sunrise. Not much of a life." He took a deep breath. "How can I help? You look as if you've gone eighteen hours back to back."

Rutledge had taken a room again, shaved, changed clothes, and tried to eat breakfast. He had been afraid to sleep, knowing how badly he needed it.

"Someone asked me a question just now. You might be better able to answer it than anyone else. Who did that child Tildy threaten most?"

"Threaten? She was two, going on three, for God's sake."

"Then why was she taken?"

"Because someone saw her and wanted her. It's the most likely answer. We went to The Bog and questioned everyone there. It's in the report, ask Carson. But I didn't hold out much hope—too close by, she'd have been recognized the minute she set foot out whatever door she was held behind."

"Who had a motorcar in Crowley?"

"Motorcar? There isn't one, to my knowledge. If anyone needs to take a train, the dogcart is available. It belongs to"—he closed his eyes, as if to see the report more clearly—"Will Easter, no, Esterly. He keeps a horse."

"How do they get their supplies at the pub?"

"They're brought in by van, from the vendors. That's been one of the problems. Crowley doesn't do that much business with anyone these days. There have been complaints about the distance, and a few firms have talked about delivery charges. Another headache for the pub, I should think. But that's why we never expected ransom demands. There didn't appear to be enough money to make the risk of taking the little girl worthwhile. She was taken for some other reason." He frowned. "Are you saying one of the van drivers came back for her?"

"Another possibility," Rutledge acknowledged, not wanting to tell Fenton what he knew. "The Blakes want to sell up. Would they have taken the child, thinking to drive Ruth into closing the pub?"

"I wondered about the cousin. If she was jealous of the child. But the signs weren't there. She was as devastated as the Milfords. No, there was something odd about the whole abduction. And yet there was nothing I could put my finger on, nothing I could work with. Nothing that made any sense. That's why I kept my eye on Ruth, because it had to be something about her. Not the child. The mother. And I never found out what that was."

On the drive back to Church Stretton to look in on Susan Milford, Rutledge fought the overwhelming drowsiness that was threatening to overtake him.

Hamish was there, his voice harsh as he said, "If yon lawyer is right, and ye're the target, no' the sister, then ye're running blind. Gie' o'er and sleep."

"I can't. I need to speak to her before she's had a chance to confer with Hastings. Then I'll rest."

"Aye, and if it's too late?"

"I'm safe until I am closer to Crowley. Leave it." He'd spoken aloud.

And he was right. He reached Church Stretton in its saddle ringed with hills, and went directly to the doctor's surgery.

Susan Milford was awake, but she refused to see him. Setting the doctor aside, Rutledge said, "This is no time for the vapors."

"Hardly vapors—she's threatened me with legal action if you come near her," Dr. Matthews began, then added, "Oh, very well, but I shall have to be there if only to referee."

She was dressed, though her clothes had seen rough usage, and there was a strong hint of burning Sunbeam about them. Sitting up on the examination bed where she had been brought last night, she eyed Rutledge balefully.

"I saved your life," he said. "In some societies, that would mean I would now be responsible for you as long as you lived. Thank God this isn't true in England.

Therefore, I can have you taken to Shrewsbury and put in a cell. It's where I put Ruth Milford, when she refused to cooperate. Apparently it wasn't a very pleasant experience."

She opened her mouth to retort, thought better of what she was about to say, and closed her mouth smartly.

"Why were you on the Crowley road two nights ago?"

"I wasn't. I was on my way to Ludlow. I told you."

"Why did you take a framed photograph from the pub?"

"I happened to want a photograph of my late brother. I'm sentimental that way."

"No, you wanted to see what Alasdair Dale looked like. Why?"

"I have never met this man. Why should I wish to have his photograph?"

"But he has Tildy, doesn't he? And he was on his way to Ludlow. He goes there often. You are still looking for her."

"I'm afraid I don't know what you're talking about." Her mouth had a mulish set.

"Who took her from her mother? Surely Hastings told you."

"I don't know anyone called Hastings."

Rutledge fought to keep his temper. "Indeed? I just spent the morning with your solicitor. He had quite a lot to tell me about you. Including the fact that you are quite mad, and I shouldn't trust anything you tell me—"

Her face flamed. "I am not mad." Her voice was tight.

"No? He showed me the letter you wrote shortly before you left Betws y Coed. When you threatened to kill yourself. I notice that you are still with us, very much alive."

"Here—!" the doctor interjected, but her words cut across his.

"He didn't. I don't believe you!"

"Ask him, when next you see him. Although knowing the man, you won't get a straight answer."

She faced him defiantly. "Go to hell."

He changed tactics. "Do you care anything about Tildy? Dale could very well be the man who had your brother killed. Does that count for nothing?"

"I don't think he did. I think it was Ruth herself. Or her cousin's husband. Donald Blake."

"Why would Ruth kill Sam Milford?"

"So she could marry Dale. A happy little family,

that." Her voice was bitter now. "A Chester solicitor. The best schools. Tildy would be too young to remember Sam. She would take to her new father, and come to love him. At least that's what Ruth must want."

But Dale hadn't wanted to marry her. She'd discovered that in Llangollen. And she had gone back to Sam Milford. She wasn't suitable, a pub owner's daughter, for the circles Dale moved in.

Still, her words were close enough to the truth.

He said, playing back her arguments, "What did Donald Blake have to gain, killing Sam?"

"I don't know. But it was Blake who took Tildy. It appears he was tired of waiting for Ruth to sell the pub. She was holding on to it for her daughter's sake, even though it was dying. He expected her to sell up, once Tildy was gone. Then he was going to play the hero after she'd done that, and bring Tildy back."

He stared at her. "Blake? Was this true? Or is that another of Edwin Hastings's little lies? He's a consummate liar, Miss Milford. I can't trust anything he tells me. Or you."

"He traced the child to Worcester. But I found out more. A man claiming to be her father had put her into an orphans' asylum, telling them he'd come for her again when he was able to take care of her. His description fit Donald Blake. But Hastings got her out of there, with a few well-placed donations. And I took her. Then she was taken from me." She closed her eyes at the memory.

"Then who killed Sam?" He was thinking out loud now, trying to work it out.

"I don't know. How could I know? Hastings thought Sam was looking for someone in Oswestry. Something to do with a funeral."

The assault was supposed to have occurred after the funeral of Ruth's friend. Had Milford been searching in Oswestry for anyone with red hair because of that? But what had lured him to the Aqueduct? A lie, passed on by Betty Turnbull? "Why did he have to die?"

"According to Hastings, it was because he wouldn't stop searching for Tildy. And that worried someone."

"Why did you want that photograph of Dale, if it was Blake who took the child?"

"Someone was starting a fire with a bit of newspaper. Never mind where this was. As they were crumpling it up, I saw a face I thought I recognized. A photograph of a couple who had just become engaged. A prominent solicitor and a very wealthy widow. But I'd seen him—I was sure of it—in the village where I was staying when Tildy vanished. I thought—I wondered if *he* had taken her. I know, it was—but I was desperate. I remembered that Sam had sent me a photograph when he'd enlisted. I found it, but I'd been angry, I'd torn it across. The man in the background wasn't clear. I thought there might be another at the pub, and I was right. And it was the same man. Hastings told me that this man didn't know Sam—but he must have done. When I heard that Sam was dead, I went to the Aqueduct. I intended to show that photograph to the narrowboat men. And one of them told me Dale had been there. I saw you as well, that night. I thought that you were after him too."

"Did you speak to Joseph Burton?"

"I don't know. I don't recognize the name."

Even so, he had enough now. He hadn't known to ask about Dale when he was at the Aqueduct. What's more, Susan had given him a possible motive. If Dale was about to be married, he might well have been horrified to learn that there was a love child who could be traced to him. What would his wealthy widow have made of that? Dale had no way of knowing that Sam was searching for the missing child or even for her real father because he wanted the little girl back, and had no intention of making his wife's affair public.

Nor did he know that Sam was unaware that Ruth had committed adultery. But in that late-night con-

frontation with Ruth, she had demanded that he
return Tildy—

A sense of urgency swept through Rutledge. "There
are some things I must see to—"

"Do you know where Tildy is? Is that it?" Susan demanded. "Is that where you are going?"

"Not yet."

"No. You won't leave me here! I'm going with you."

"It's too dangerous." And for all he knew, Dale had
already killed the little girl.

"No, I tell you, I have come this far. I must find
Tildy."

"You can't keep her, Miss Milford. She has a
mother."

"And what if she doesn't remember Ruth? But she
remembers me?"

"It doesn't matter. You aren't her family."

Something in her face changed. "That was cruel."

"Will someone please tell me what's going on?"
Matthews demanded, completely at sea.

She turned to him, pleading. "Tell him that I can
go, that I'm all right—you've seen to my arm, there's
nothing to be done about my foot except to bind it up,
and you've done that as well. My ribs too. I can travel
in that motorcar of his. *Tell him!*"

Matthews looked from one to the other. "You were going to call the police if I let this man near you—and now you wish to leave with him?" he began. "I am not convinced you are well enough to go anywhere—that blow on the head—I had to take three stitches—"

In the end, she got her way. She had begun to scream, bringing Dr. Matthews's nurse running, and then his wife.

Matthews, over the shrill cries, said, "Look, this has got to stop. Take her with you, for God's sake. They can hear her all the way to St. Lawrence churchyard. The Long Mynd for all I know. I've done what I could. She'll be all right. Just make her stop."

And she had, as soon as he agreed. Smiling at Mrs. Matthews, at the nurse, saying graciously, "I'm so sorry. But he's quite stubborn sometimes, you see."

Matthews helped her out to the motorcar, the nurse bringing up the rear with a pair of crutches, while Mrs. Matthews went to speak to the anxious couple in the waiting room alarmed by the disturbance.

As they pulled away from the surgery, Rutledge said, "That was unconscionable."

But she didn't answer him. He said, "There's a rug in the back. You haven't got a coat."

"I'll be all right."

He slowed, found it without looking, and handed it to her. "Don't give me any more trouble or I'll put you out at the nearest crossroads."

But it was a good three miles down the road before she wrapped the rug around her.

He wasn't sure just what he was going to do with her. He didn't want to drive all the way back to Shrewsbury, thirteen or fourteen miles behind them.

Putting her out of his mind, he began to concentrate on what lay ahead.

He reached the turning for Crowley, and said to the silent woman beside him, "You'll stay in the motorcar. Do you understand?"

"I want to see his face. Blake's. I want to know how he could take a child that young and give her to strangers."

"No."

"He doesn't know me. I can help you. Let me at least do that."

"No."

But when they pulled into the yard, Ruth Milford and Nan Blake were just coming out of the side door.

They stared at the motorcar, faces grim, as Rutledge prepared to get out.

Ruth, peering past him, said, "Is that—is that Sam's sister? What is she doing here?"

"I've come to talk to you. May I come in?"

"Go away, and take her with you."

"It's important," he said, keeping his voice neutral. "I think you need to hear what I have to say."

Ruth asked, "Is it about Tildy? Have you found her?"

"I know what happened the day she was taken from you."

She gave him a long look. "Is she alive?"

"I believe she is." But he didn't.

"Then come in. But *she* must stay out here."

"It's cold, and she has no coat. She was nearly killed two nights ago."

"I don't care."

Nan said, "Let her come in. I'll put the kettle on." And she went ahead, back into the pub.

Ruth made no attempt to help Susan Milford out of the motorcar. Rutledge got out the crutches, but Susan couldn't manage them with her arm. In the end, he had to help her limp into the pub. Ruth came behind them, shutting the door.

He settled Susan at one of the side tables, then moved closer to the bar.

"Where are Will and Mrs. Blake's husband?" he

asked Ruth as he pulled out chairs at one of the tables against the wall.

"Will has gone home. I don't know where Donald is."

"Never mind. It's you I've come to see."

She was still standing. "Tell me. If you know anything about Tildy, tell me."

He took a deep breath. "I know who took her. And what happened to her after that. Sit down. It won't be the best news I could bring."

After a moment she took the farthest chair from him, and sat down.

"Your daughter was taken by your cousin's husband. He took her to force you to sell up. She was placed in an orphans' home in Worcester. And from there she was adopted—"

"No. You're lying. I know who took her. I've always known."

"So you thought. But you are wrong."

"Nan?" she called. "Nan, come and hear this. Never mind the tea—"

Her cousin came to the bar, alerted by something in Ruth's voice.

Ruth said, "He's telling me that *Donald* took Tildy. To make me sell the pub. I told you he wasn't to be trusted."

Nan said, "Donald? No, why would he do such a thing? He loved Tildy as much as I did."

"I'm afraid it's true. And there is a solicitor in Shrewsbury who can show you whatever evidence you require," Rutledge replied.

"No, you're wrong—" Nan began, but Susan spoke then.

"It's true. Whether you want to believe it or not. Sam's solicitor found her, gave her to me. I had your daughter for weeks—months—"

They were all talking at once, arguing with Susan, blaming him, telling him to leave.

And in the confusion they didn't hear the side door open until Donald Blake stood there.

Rutledge was never sure afterward just how much he'd heard.

But from his expression, it was clear he'd heard enough. Slamming the door, he was gone, running across the yard and down the hill.

Rutledge went after him, leaving the door standing wide. Nan, crying her husband's name, came running at his heels. Rutledge, shouting over his shoulder, ordered her to stay there. She came on, without her coat, following the two men down the hill and toward the Blake cottage.

Donald got there first, went in, and slammed the door after him.

Rutledge got there seconds afterward, opened it again, and went inside.

Donald was in the front room, struggling with something that Rutledge couldn't see. And then he wheeled, and in his hand was a war souvenir, a German officer's dress sword, bare and pointed at Rutledge.

Nan came bursting through the door. "Donald— no—"

"Stay back, Nan. I'll deal with this," Donald said.

Rutledge said, "It will do you no good, using that. Don't add murder to what you've done."

Nan said, "Tell him, Donald—darling, tell him he's wrong. That you didn't have anything to do with Tildy's disappearance. Please—tell him!"

"I was going to bring her back—as soon as we'd signed the papers for the pub. I swear to you, Nan! But it was our only way out, don't you see? Ruth was going to keep that pub open until we had all been drained of every penny we had left, and then what? And Sam would have let her, he was besotted with her. And I had that cabinetry work in Gloucester that week, nobody thought anything about my going there. I got back a day early, and I saw the pram sitting outside the house—and suddenly I *knew*. She was asleep, I didn't *hurt* her. And I walked back to the railway station, got as far as Worcester, and it was done. It was our only hope, Nan. You must see that. I made certain she was safe, I made them promise not to let anyone adopt her."

Nan was crying, her hands over her ears, trying to shut out the sound of his voice. "I don't want to believe you. I can't believe you."

"Don't make it worse for her," Rutledge said quietly. "There's nowhere you can go."

"I won't go to prison. I did what I had to do, for the sake of all of us. I can tell you where she is. You can bring her home. But first you have to let us go. I've money put aside. Not much, but it will see us out of here."

Rutledge said, "But she's no longer at the orphans' asylum, Donald. She was adopted. They didn't wait for you to come back. She's gone."

"No, you're lying! I signed papers. She wasn't to be adopted. She was to come back with me as soon as possible."

"They lied to you. Or didn't believe you. They let her go. We don't know where she is, you see. And that's at your door. You can't bring her home. It's too late."

He stared at Rutledge, the point of the sword slowly circling between them.

"You're lying," he said again.

"The other woman in the pub—Sam Milford's sister—can confirm what I've just told you."

"She's mad—she's always been mad. Why should I believe her? Any more than I believe you." And he lunged.

21

Rutledge had been watching his eyes. When they widened slightly, he leaped to his right, crashing into the table by the window, knocking picture frames and ornaments to the floor.

Even so, he heard the cry as Nan fell back.

"Oh, God!" Donald shouted. "Nan, no!"

Rutledge was already getting to his feet, starting forward. Donald dropped the sword with a clatter, made it to the door, and was outside, running.

Nan, clutching her arm, was crying, "He didn't mean—" And then she slipped to the floor, fainting.

He went to her, took out a handkerchief, and wound it around the bleeding wound on her arm, tying off the corners. And then he went out, looking for Donald Blake.

He hadn't gone far. Rutledge found him on his knees in front of the Milford house, where once he'd found the unattended pram, his head in his hands, weeping.

Rutledge took him into custody, got him to his feet, and said, "You've done enough damage. Let's go."

"Nan? Did I kill her?"

"Nothing so dramatic. Her arm. She will be all right."

He got Blake as far as the motorcar, and left him by the dustbins.

Inside the pub he could hear voices. A shouting match between Ruth Milford and her sister-in-law.

He'd had enough. He walked in, and said, "Miss Milford, get into the motorcar, if you please. I've got a prisoner to take to Shrewsbury."

"With pleasure." She limped heavily to the door, grimacing with the pain.

Ruth said, "Where's Nan?"

"You'll find her in her cottage. Her husband cut her arm with his war souvenir. She'll need your help. It's been a shock."

"Why would he take Tildy? How could he do that to Sam and to me? I don't—I thought—never mind." She looked around for her coat. "I wanted it to be Alasdair. I *wanted* him to care for her."

"He's recently become engaged, Mrs. Milford. To a

very wealthy woman. The trouble is, I don't think he knows what to do with Tildy now. And that's worrying me. Do you know anything that will help me find her?"

"He wouldn't harm her. She's his *child*!"

"I don't think that matters to him now. He must have thought that Sam was searching for him to press a paternity suit. Once he got the child, he could deal with your husband. This marriage must matter more to him than you do." It was harsh, but she needed to hear the truth.

She closed her eyes for a moment. "I think in some corner of my mind, I wanted to hurt him the same way he'd hurt me. That's why I never told him about Tildy. When she was taken, I convinced myself that he'd give her all the advantages she would never have in Crowley. But deep down inside, what really mattered was the knowledge that every time he looks at her, he'll remember me."

"Wasn't it enough that Sam loved that child? That he'd provide for her?" he asked, curious. "He was a better man by far."

But she didn't answer him.

He turned and left.

On his way, he returned Susan to Dr. Matthews's surgery. The doctor wasn't pleased, nor was Susan, and Rutledge had to use all his authority to persuade both of them to accept the arrangement. There was no-where else he could safely leave her. He was too well aware that given the chance, she would go after Tildy herself, and take her where no one could find her.

And then at the door, as he was preparing to walk out, she limped after him and caught his arm.

"It's not just taking Blake to Shrewsbury, is it? If it were, I could go to my rooms at the hotel. You know where Tildy is, don't you? Let me go with you. She knows me, she'll feel safe with me."

"No."

Her grip tightened on his arm. "I want her. That woman doesn't deserve her. Promise me I can have her."

He didn't try to reason with her. He said harshly, "I must find her first."

But he'd been thinking that she might be somewhere near Ludlow. Where no one who didn't know about Dale's personal connection to the town would suspect to find her. He had no intention of telling anyone that he had come to that conclusion.

She let his arm go. "Don't shut me out of her life," she warned.

Rutledge delivered Donald Blake to Inspector Carson in Shrewsbury, charging him with kidnapping and at-tempted murder. It took longer than he'd counted on.

Inspector Fenton was leaning against a wing, waiting for him when he walked out of the police station.

"Carson sent me word," he said, "while you were attending to the paperwork. I never suspected Donald. Not seriously. He'd been away, and he could prove it. What's more, his employer neglected to tell us he'd left early. Just that the dates he was employed were correct."

"I should have. He didn't want me staying at the pub. He must have thought I knew more than I did."

"I said it had to do with Ruth. I just didn't know how. There's no way to charge her. But she ought to be charged. Have you found the child? What's to become of her? Ruth is an unfit mother. I've a cat that had more feeling for her kittens."

"I haven't found her. I'm going now to look for her."

"I hope you find her. I'll sleep better then." And he walked away.

Rutledge was turning the crank when one of the Constables came running out of the station, waving something.

"Inspector Rutledge? This was just handed to us. It was addressed to you, here."

It was a telegram. He took it, thanking the Constable, and closed the door before opening it.

The message was brief.

I've sent him a telegram. I told him I know what he's done. And why. In exchange for my silence, I will have Tildy again. It's finished. I've been such a fool.

It wasn't signed, but he knew who had sent it. Ruth Milford.

Rutledge swore.

If Dale had received his telegram, even if he wasn't already planning to silence her, Ruth had just invited her own death.

There wasn't time to speak to Carson. Rutledge put up the crank and was on his way south.

Even so, he was nearly too late.

When Rutledge reached the pub, only Nan was there.

She sprang up from her chair when he came in. "She went after Tildy," she said, her words tumbling over each other. "He didn't think I'd seen him. I'd gone upstairs to have a lie-down. And I heard voices. I was standing at the top of the stairs, when he told her where to find Tildy. And then he left. But I think he went after her. I didn't know what to do—Will has gone to Shrewsbury to pick up supplies. I'm all alone—"

"Where is Tildy?"

He expected her to tell him that she was in Little Bog. It was the ideal place to be rid of both the child and her mother. There were the pits, deep enough to keep their secrets for a very long time, even though they had been closed down. Boards could be removed, then replaced.

But she said, "Up on the Stiperstones. The Devil's Chair. Why would he leave her there? It's almost dark—Tildy will be frightened—she might fall—hurt herself. Ruth took the torch and went after her."

The Stiperstones were an outcropping of rock, a bare ridge jutting out of the landscape and rising in jagged tors to their highest point. It was unusual, a gray mass of stone where nothing grew. On the slopes leading up to it, saplings had become trees, obscuring the climb almost until the rock itself began. One of the highest tors, with its distinctive profile, was called the Devil's Chair, and the locals had for centuries believed he came to sit there and watch wild storms break around him.

Rutledge didn't believe the child would be there. But Ruth Milford had believed it.

He said to Nan, "Leave the pub. He may come back looking for you. Go to Will's aunt, and keep the doors locked."

"I ought to be here when they come down. They'll want food—tea."

"It can wait. Do as I say. I can't be in two places at once."

"Yes, all right. I'll go."

She caught up her coat and started for the door. "You'll find Tildy, won't you? To be sure she's all right?"

"I'll do my best."

As soon as he'd watched Nan walk to the Esterly house, he went back to the motorcar and drove to the stones, approaching from the west, their dark silhouette formidable against the eastern sky. He got as close to the tree line as he could. Then, leaving his hat on the seat, he started to climb.

It had been easy to pick out the formation locals called the Devil's Chair, stark above him. He couldn't see Ruth, and didn't want to take the time to use his field glasses. Even so, he was nearly sure there was *something* up in the Chair—a red scarf or coat. It seemed to flutter in the light wind.

Hamish, at his back, said, "It's your imagination."

But Rutledge knew it wasn't.

Once in the trees, he found it harder to keep to the track he'd picked out. Pushing his way through the dry undergrowth, avoiding fallen logs, climbing over minor outcroppings, he depended on his sense of direction to guide him. And as he climbed, he listened for any sound.

The wind was picking up, and he could feel the air cooling as night came down, taking with it any light he'd had until now.

He had nearly reached the ridge itself when he heard a gunshot, echoing, hard to pinpoint. He redoubled his efforts and finally came out into the open, the tors still rising high above his head.

The Devil's Chair, he realized, was to his right, and he began to climb across loose scree, hoping to reach the ridge just short of it.

It was not an easy climb in the dark, and he dared not use his torch. As he got higher, he could see the occasional flash of another torch, pointing this way and then that, frantically picking out pockets one minute and pinnacles the next.

Ruth hadn't found Tildy. She was still alive, still searching. He thought once that he heard her calling.

And then there was another gunshot. He couldn't see where it had come from. But the torch went spinning wildly into the air, before tumbling like some demented thing as it fell, lighting gray stone and the night sky by turns.

Silence fell, except for the wind and the sound of his breathing, the rasp of his boots against stone as he climbed. It was pitch-black now, and the jagged rock was cutting into his gloves as he sought for the next handhold, giving him purchase for the next move upward.

When at last he came out on the tor, he could see the Devil's Chair ahead of him, and keeping his silhouette low, he started forward.

It was rough going. Twice his foot slipped and he had to catch himself. It was a near-run thing the third time. He could sense the space where his foot found nothing but air instead of rock.

He was almost at the Devil's Chair when he stumbled, and reaching down, felt an arm. At the same time, there was a cry, quickly muffled as it was jerked away.

There was the sound of scuffling movement, scree falling, and another cry, cut short as the scuffling stopped suddenly.

He turned on his torch, covering the light with his fingers as he shone it down where the sound had stopped.

A distorted face, wide-eyed with fright, stared back at him. He barely recognized Ruth Milford.

He flicked off the torch almost at once, then said quickly, hardly above a whisper, "It's Rutledge. Where is he?"

"I don't know. *I can't find Tildy!*"

"Are you hurt?"

"Not badly. Cuts. Bruises." And then, almost on

a wail, "Her little scarf was caught on the Chair. I'm afraid she tried to climb down—that she's fallen—I keep listening for her crying."

"Who fired those shots?"

"I fired one. When I saw him climbing after me. And then he hit the rock just above my shoulder, and I dropped the torch. Please, find Tildy. I'll be all right."

He didn't tell her that the little girl was very likely not there. How could Dale have managed to get Tildy so far? It wasn't feasible. She would have been in the way. And Ruth's fall had to look like an accident.

"Stay here." He got himself past her without incident, and then moved on toward the Chair.

Even in the dark, it did look very much like a huge chair, and up here, it could easily hold the Devil and his helpers, Rutledge thought, as he swept his fingers over the stone.

His hand touched something, and as he felt for it, he realized that it was the scarf Ruth had found earlier. What he'd seen as a splash of color against the uneven gray of the tor.

But there was no child here. Alive or dead.

Somewhere behind him a voice called, "Ruth?"

Rutledge tensed, waiting for her to reply.

"I lied to you, Ruth. She isn't here. But I'll tell you where she is."

No answer.

"Did you realize that you damned near clipped my ear? I didn't know you were a good shot. I'd have been more careful."

There was the sound of a chuckle. As if he were laughing at himself. At his own carelessness.

At his ease. Certain that he had found her, and that he would be finished very soon.

"Let me help you, Ruth. Give me your hand, and together we'll both get down from this wretched tor. I'll help you back to the ridge. I could always see well in the dark, remember? You teased me about it."

He must have been groping in the dark, searching with his hands even as he talked.

"Tildy isn't here. I just needed to be sure you loved her enough. That you truly wanted her back. You're a widow now, sadly. It means we can finally be together—"

Rutledge heard a cry, bitten off as quickly as it had been uttered.

"There you are!" Triumph in the voice now. "Come on, give me your hand, it's cold up here, and that wind is rising. We need to go down. Ruth? I'm sorry I tricked you. Surely you understand why."

And then angrily, "Come on. We can't stay here all night. They'll be missing you at the pub soon."

He must have found her hand or arm, because

Rutledge could hear her cry out, and the scraping sounds of a scuffle, as if she was fighting him.

"Come on, Ruth, help me or we'll both fall."

She said something that Rutledge couldn't make out.

He couldn't risk it. Once Ruth was back on the spine of the ridge, she would be vulnerable. All Dale had to do was let go of her and push, and she would be off the rock with nothing to break her fall until she reached the bottom.

He flicked on his torch and shouted, "Over here, Alasdair!"

The man's reflexes were still good. He had let go of Ruth and was raising his service revolver even as Rutledge switched off the torch.

The shot reverberated as a shower of stone chippings flew to his left, peppering his face. He could feel them tear flesh, stinging all along his temple and cheek, as vicious as bird shot, barely missing his eye. Blood began to trickle in their wake.

Dale was closer than he'd thought.

Moving fast, Rutledge surged forward, the torch in his left hand, lashing out with it as Dale prepared to fire again. The blow caught him off balance, and Rutledge shoved hard.

Dale fell backward, grunting as he struggled not to keep sliding on the loose scree. Ignoring him, Rutledge reached down and caught Ruth Milford's outstretched arm, pulling hard. Somehow she got to her feet, and he swung her behind him. "Go down. Find the path," he said, and turned his attention back to Dale.

But the man had already begun scrambling back the way he'd come, stones scattering in his wake as Rutledge followed.

They made their unsteady way along the ridge, from tor to tor, and then Dale was sliding down, crying out as he lost his footing. The cry broke off as he caught himself with a grunt, and Rutledge could hear him just below, still picking his way down.

Rutledge started after him, heard him leap to the ground with another grunt, and start toward the trees.

He lost Dale in there, where it was black as pitch now, limbs slashing at him as he plowed his way through. The coating of leaves on the ground, slick from all the rain, was treacherous underfoot, and he found himself slipping and sliding, clinging to the rough bark of trunks as he kept going.

And then the trees were thinning, he was nearly in the open. Scanning for any sight of Dale, he stood catching his breath for a few seconds. But there was no sign of him. Rutledge was certain he'd come this way, at least until they'd reached the trees. But had he doubled back?

He started running, intending to skirt the long ridge until he could see Dale, but Ruth Milford came bursting out of the trees almost in front of him before he'd gone fifteen paces.

She was dazed, crying out as he came racing toward her, trying to turn back into the trees.

"It's Rutledge," he said sharply, catching at her arm, but she pulled away, ducking under the nearest limb, back into the trees.

He let her go, still searching for Dale.

In the distance he heard a motorcar start to move, reversing on the rough ground. Headlamps came on, blinding as they spun across him. And then the motorcar was speeding down the track, the light bouncing and lurching over the ruts.

He watched it go.

Then he turned and called Ruth's name, shouting until she answered him and he could guide her toward him.

As she came out of the trees, he said, "He's gone. In his motorcar."

She was shaking. "Why didn't he shoot me? He had the chance. *Why?*"

"He didn't want a bullet in you. Or me. Or I daresay he'd have made short work of us all the same. Come with me. The motorcar is this way. Let's get you back to the pub. Mrs. Blake is at the Esterly house. They are alone."

When he had got to the village, he stopped at the Esterly house to collect Nan, and then drove on to the pub. He went in first, found it safe, and then brought the two women inside. Only then did he go to the lamp by the main door and light it. Ruth, still shaken, was busy locking all the doors.

In the brightening lamplight, Nan Blake looked at Ruth, disheveled, her hair down her back, cuts and scratches all over her face and hands. "Did you find Tildy? Oh, please, say you did."

"She wasn't there. It was all a trick." Ruth sat down heavily in the nearest chair. Glancing toward Rutledge, she added, "You are bleeding."

He remembered the splinters of stone. They were beginning to sting.

"Mrs. Blake—can you make some tea? You and your cousin need it."

"Where are you going?" Nan Blake said quickly as he started toward the side door. "Do you know how late it is?"

But he had learned in the trenches how to go without sleep.

"I'm going after him. Lock up behind me. I don't think he'll circle back. Still—"

And he was out in the yard, turning the crank and getting behind the wheel.

Hamish said, "He willna' harm the child now. No' if she's still alive."

But Rutledge wasn't convinced.

He turned on his headlamps and drove out of the pub yard. And hoped to God that he was heading in the right direction.

Ludlow, with its castle high above the River Teme, was a busy town, and he avoided it, searching instead for the least likely village where it might be safe to keep a small but very noticeable child. Where a family or a woman would be glad of the income she brought with her.

But which? He had a map, he'd have to make a circle of possible villages and ask in each.

Dawn broke as Rutledge stopped for petrol, and took the opportunity to wash his face at the pump, even if he couldn't shave. He could do nothing about the small cuts, and his hands were scratched, his driving gloves torn in places.

The cold wind had kept up, and the clouds over his head were heavy. He wasn't surprised when he ran through a series of snow squalls, dusting the countryside with white and making visibility difficult at times. The wind seemed to sweep the interior of the motorcar with gusts that left his hands cold on the wheel. Pulling up his coat collar, he drove on.

By the time he found Stockford, hardly more than a hamlet on a tributary of the Teme, it was quite late in the day.

There was a stone bridge over the river where once there had been a ford for stock on an old drover road. A small church stood on higher ground, ancient yews surrounding the gate set into the churchyard wall. A general store was closed for the afternoon, and when he went to knock at the vicarage door, he saw the small sign in the window to his left.

RECTOR JAMES EASTON, WALFORD CHURCH, WALFORD. SERVICES IN STOCKFORD EVERY OTHER SUNDAY.

He left the motorcar in the vicarage's short drive and walked up the main street, past the shops and the general store, looking for someone he could speak to. But the weather kept them indoors.

Time was precious. He was about to turn back to the motorcar when he saw a face in a window, peering out at him.

He turned at once toward the door, and knocked lightly. Without urgency or threat.

The English didn't care for strangers knocking at their doors, and at first he thought the man he'd seen in the window was not going to answer.

The door opened just as he was about to turn away, and Rutledge realized why it had taken some time for the householder to get there. He was sitting in a wheeled chair.

"Can I help you?" he asked.

He was a Bantam. Rutledge was certain of it. Broad-shouldered, but no more than five feet tall, a scar running across his jawline. One leg was missing. Although a rug was spread over his limbs, the empty space on the left side was evident.

He changed what he'd planned to say, had used in his approach to the residents of four other villages. Instead, he began, "Captain Rutledge," and gave his regiment.

"The Scots." The man nodded. "Bonny fighters, they were."

"They were indeed."

"If you've come collecting for the funds, I'm afraid you're at the wrong door. I need more than I can give."

"In the Bantams, were you? I had a good friend there. Milford was his name."

The man shook his head. "Sorry, I don't know him. Not my battalion, I expect. But then I was invalided out in '17. He could have come up later."

"Actually, I'm looking for the Rector. Not here most days?"

"'Fraid not. Left us to our sins, mostly."

"I came in search of a grave. Our nanny. I can't remember the name of the village. The bridge looked familiar, but not the church."

"My Aunt Jo could probably help you, she's lived here all her life. What was the name?"

"Patricia Long. Nanny Long to us."

He shook his head. "Doesn't sound familiar."

Rutledge gestured toward the door. "Does she live with you? Your Aunt Jo? I'd like to speak to her."

"She lives in the last cottage before the bridge. Did you come from Ludlow? You passed it if you did."

"Thank you. I'll ask her."

He was about to turn away when the man in the wheeled chair said, "Tell her I'm waiting for my dinner. She usually brings it up."

"I'll be glad to pass that along." He thanked the man, and went back the way he'd come. He could see the cottage as soon as he passed the churchyard. It was small, tidy, with a garden in the back and a run for chickens.

He was nearly there when the words came back to him. *Tell her I'm waiting for my dinner.*

It was well past the dinner hour. Slowing, he kept his eye on the cottage. Had the words been a signal—or were they an indication that something was wrong?

Another squall of snow came through, dusting his hat and his shoulders, swirling around the chimney—

There was no smoke coming out of the cottage chimney. And it was quite cold, given the wind and the snow.

He began to run.

The door was locked. He pounded on it two or three times, then went round to the back. The kitchen door opened under his hand, and he stood there for several seconds, listening.

The silence was ominous. There were pots on the cooker, but when he put a hand on its frame, it was barely warm. An onion lay half chopped on a plate. It was already withering.

It explained why her nephew was sitting at his window wondering where his dinner might be . . .

Moving quietly now, he stepped from the kitchen into the narrow hall, where the stairs went up and the two front rooms opened into the entry as it widened by the outer door.

He could see her then. Lying sprawled at the foot

of the steps. Her white hair was dark with blood, and from the way her body was angled, he thought she must surely have broken her neck.

Going to her, dropping on one knee, he put his fingers at her throat.

To his surprise, there was a fluttering pulse. She was alive. But for how long? Stockford had no Rector, he hadn't seen a police station, and there was very likely no doctor.

He began to work with her, his Army training coming back to him as he ran his hand up and down her limbs. He touched her head, saw the swelling and the cut on her forehead. Impossible to tell if that was from the fall—or a blow that had sent her reeling down the steps. But when he tried to move her body, she whimpered.

"Dear God," he said under his breath.

What had happened to this woman, and why? If he'd found the person who was taking care of Tildy—*where was the child?*

He rose and took the stairs two at a time, looked in one bedroom, found a blanket on the floor and picked it up. Then he went into the other.

And there she was, in the ancient crib pushed against the far wall. Her knees drawn up under her, the side of her face pressed to the mattress. Her red-gold hair was matted, wet, and the sheet under her face was as well. The bastard had left her to cry herself to sleep, alone in the cold house with a dying woman by the stairs.

But she was alive.

He backed out of the room, so as not to wake the child, went down the stairs, stopping only long enough to spread the blanket gently over the quiet form. Then, unlocking the door, he ran.

The fire bell was outside the general store. He reached for the rope, and began to tug at the bell, long pulls that made it toll as if he were ringing changes.

Doors began to open up and down the street, and someone came out of the nearest house, shouting, "What are you about, man? Who are you—is there a fire?"

He knew he looked like hell. The dark shadow of his beard, the cuts on his face, his clothes rumpled. Hardly trustworthy. But he didn't stop until several men had joined the first man.

Letting the rope go, he said, "My name is Rutledge. Scotland Yard, London. There's a severely injured woman in the house above the bridge. I must go for a doctor. But she needs to be cared for now, until I can bring someone back." He reached for his identification and held it out for the nearest man to see, and then held it again for that man's neighbor. "Is there a midwife in Stockford? No? A woman who is good with caring for people? Find her. Bring blankets, pillows, get the cooker heated for hot water and tea. Keep that poor woman alive. But don't move her, do you hear me? Someone pushed her down those stairs. I want to know who. Take down anything she says. And for the love of God, *hurry*."

He started for his motorcar, when someone shouted, "How do we know it wasn't you who pushed Jo?"

He ignored the man, walking swiftly to the church-yard and his motorcar.

But he stopped at the cottage, leaving the motor running, and went up the stairs again. Scooping up her blankets, he wrapped them around the little girl and then lifted her into his arms. He wasn't about to lose sight of her.

He took her down to the motorcar as she began to whimper, and set her carefully in the footwell, close by the tiny heater, arranging her blankets around her to cushion her and keep her warm.

Looking behind him, he saw villagers running toward the house, some of them already carrying bundles of blankets. And someone had brought the nephew's wheeled chair out to the road, and was pushing it with all haste as the man shouted at him to hurry.

The bridge was nearly too narrow for the motor-car, but he had driven over it earlier, and now he made short work of crossing it a second time.

In the footwell, the child began to cry. And he began to talk to her.

Hamish said, "Ye canna' be certain she's Tildy. Ye're a policeman. There's no' any proof. No' yet."

Rutledge said, "Who else could she be?"

"Ye canna' tak her away. No' until yon woman can tell ye who she is."

But he *had* taken her. And he intended to keep her where he knew she was safe.

22

Rutledge had no idea where to find a doctor, swearing at himself as he realized he should have asked someone in Stockford. But in the third village down the road, he saw a Constable walking on the High Street, and hailed him.

"I need a doctor. It's urgent."

"That way, sir. Just beyond the church. I'll meet you there."

He found the surgery, ran to the door, and knocked.

The doctor himself answered. "I'm sorry, Letitia—" He stopped. "Sorry. You aren't Letitia, are you?" He looked at Rutledge's face. "And you appear to need my services." Peering at the cuts over the tops of his glasses, he said, "Come in. Are you hurt anywhere else?"

"Doctor—" He glanced at the bronze plate by the

door. "Doctor Masefield? It isn't for me that I've come."
He handed over his identification. "I have a badly injured woman in Stockford, a fall down the stairs. But it
appears that she was pushed. Head injury, no indication
of broken limbs, but internal pain—her ribs, possibly.
Bring what you may need. Meanwhile, do you have a
wife? A nurse? I've a very young child in the motorcar.
She appears to be all right. But it's urgent that I keep
her safe. Can you take her in, and let no one come anywhere near her until I have seen to her—um—nurse?"
He only knew the injured woman as Aunt Jo.

"Yes—my wife. She has some training. But this
child—"

A wail rose from the motorcar.

The Constable, just coming up the walk, turned
toward it.

"Wait," Rutledge called to him. "She's had a bad
fright. Doctor? Your wife?"

But he'd already stepped inside and was calling to her.

Rutledge opened the passenger's door, reached in,
and lifted the crying child into his arms, making sooth-
ing sounds as he turned back toward the surgery.

He heard the Constable say, "Well, I'll be damned."

Carrying Tildy close to his chest, his hand at her
head, he went back to the door, where a woman was
just coming into view.

"Let me take her," she said quietly, reaching out.

"Her name is Tildy. Matilda. She's been abducted from her parents. Don't let anyone near her, do you hear me?" He had to raise his voice over the child's bereft cries.

"She'll be fine. Come here, love, let's find you something to eat. You'd like that, wouldn't you? And we can visit—"

His bag in his hand, Dr. Masefield came running down the passage, cast one glance at his wife and the child in her arm, then shut the door, saying as he did, "Lock it, Mary, if you please." Turning to Rutledge, he added, "I'll take my own motorcar and catch you up. Constable?"

"I'll ride with the gentleman, sir, if you don't mind. But come back with you."

"Good, good. Carry on."

The Constable nodded to Rutledge, then got into the motorcar. "Now, then," he said, settling himself. "If you could just tell me what's happened, sir—"

They had almost reached the bridge as the Constable asked, "And you are fairly sure she was pushed. It wasn't a fall."

"You'll see for yourself. There—you can see the chimney just there across the river." Smoke was rising from it now, and he was glad of it. As he crested the bridge for the third time, he could see lights in the cottage windows and people moving about.

The two men went inside. Aunt Jo—he had no other name for her yet—lay where he'd left her, still covered in the blanket from the bedroom upstairs, although others had been added to keep her warm. She was awake, and in pain.

The doctor set his bag to one side and knelt beside her. "Well, now," he said, in his best bedside manner, "let's have a look at you. That's a nasty bump on the head. What happened?"

The Constable—Hardy was his name—had knelt just beside the doctor and was reaching for his notebook.

"My head aches terribly," the woman said. "And here—I think I bruised my ribs." Her voice was just a thread, but the doctor was taking her pulse, and he looked up at Rutledge. "Erratic, as you'd expect. Shock. Pain. But we'll be all right."

"What's your name, madam?" the Constable was asking.

"Josephine Priestley."

"Do you remember how you came to fall?" the doctor asked again.

"Yes. He was here—the child's uncle. And he bumped into me at the top of the stairs. At least I thought—but I'm sure I felt his hands against my back—I lost my balance then. I cried out, but he just stood there. After that I don't remember anything." Then she said restlessly, "There's been so much blood. They've used my best towels, but it won't stop."

"Head wounds sometimes bleed fiercely," Masefield said soothingly, already examining the cut. "I shouldn't worry."

"Constable. Her statement," Rutledge said. "The doctor and I will witness it."

"The child's uncle. And who would that be, madam? Do you know his name?" the Constable asked, as the doctor went on with his examination.

"Yes, of course I do. His name is Blake, Donald Blake. I've been looking after the little girl since her mother died."

But Donald Blake was in a cell in Shrewsbury.

Rutledge described Blake for the woman.

"That must be another uncle. This man is fair, lovely blue eyes. He was quite concerned about his niece. I thought he was very nice. Until now." She was agitated again. "I can still feel his hands—and he stood there. Letting me fall. Oh, dear God." She caught the doctor's hands. "Where is Julie? They told me a stranger had taken her—? What's become of Julie?"

Masefield answered her. "The child, yes? My wife is looking after her at the surgery. She'll be all right, Mrs. Priestley. It's you we want to worry about for the moment."

But the worried crease between her eyes didn't go away.

Rutledge asked quietly, "How long have you had the care of her?"

"Oh—for quite some time. She was no trouble."

A little later, Rutledge gave his own account of finding the woman and taking charge of the child. Constable Hardy took it down word for word.

"Do you know who this man Blake is, sir?" he asked, looking up, his pencil poised for the answer.

And Rutledge explained.

"A solicitor, sir? I don't know that I've ever had trouble with a solicitor before. Are you quite sure?"

"Inspector Carson in Shrewsbury can confirm Blake's whereabouts. And I have other witnesses who can identify the solicitor. Right now, I must go. I don't like leaving Mrs. Priestley here. See if you can get her into the doctor's motorcar. I'd feel better if she's at Masefield's surgery. And there's her nephew. The man in the wheeled chair. The villagers will have to see to him."

"What about the child?"

"I must take her back to her mother. She isn't dead. She's waiting. Then I must travel to Chester to make an arrest. Still, guard this witness closely. Send to Ludlow, ask for additional men for a twenty-four-hour guard on the surgery. She can identify Alasdair Dale, and the other victims who could do that are dead."

And he left, refusing to answer the questions fired at him by Mrs. Priestley's neighbors. Promising answers and an arrest soon.

But when he reached Masefield's surgery, and identified himself to Mrs. Masefield, who had blocked the surgery door with furniture, he could go no further.

Her face seemed to swim before him as he said, "The little girl?"

"She's very upset, but she drank a little warm milk and ate some biscuits." She looked at him. "You're in no condition to drive, are you? Help me push this chest back in place, and you can sleep in the examination room. The child is upstairs, in my bedroom. And I have hidden the key to my door."

"I have to go."

"You aren't taking that child with you. Scotland Yard or no, you aren't risking her life. I can't stop you. But I will not let you have her."

He slept. But only for three hours. And then, over

Mrs. Masefield's protests that the doctor would most certainly wish to examine her as soon as he came back from Stockford, he installed Tildy Milford in his motorcar once more, and set out to find his own proof of her identity.

Rutledge pulled up at the surgery in Church Stretton at breakfast the next morning.

He had driven through the night, not pausing at Crowley but stopping halfway to give the little girl more of the milk that Mrs. Masefield had sent with him. He even persuaded her to eat several biscuits. Not the best diet for her, he thought wryly as she stared at him, silent and suspicious, her green eyes large with mistrust in the reflected glow of the headlamps. But she took the food because she was hungry. He'd talked to her all the way, telling her stories that he only half remembered from his own childhood, asking questions that she could answer, but didn't, her green eyes filling her face, her lower lip always on the verge of trembling into tears. The sprinkle of freckles across her nose stood out against the fine, milky skin. Someone in her ancestry had bequeathed her these things. Now he was more worried about the future than the past.

When she was drowsy, he rested his head against

the seat and let the silence soothe her. But he was alert, watchful. He had been since leaving Stockford and choosing a roundabout way to Church Stretton, staying clear of the main roads, sharing the night with her and the animals he passed along the way, their eyes glowing in the headlamps as they slipped away.

She was still asleep now, her head against the leather seat. He got out of the motorcar and walked to the surgery door. Yesterday's squalls had given way to cold sunlight, but the wind had dropped, and it felt warmer.

He knocked at the door, and the woman he'd seen before answered. "Come in. We weren't expecting you today."

"How is the patient? Miss Milford?"

"Calmer today."

"Is the doctor available? I'd like to have him look at someone else."

She had tried not to look at the cuts on his face. "The doctor has his own patients—" she began, but he cut across her words.

"This is a police matter. Will you ask the doctor to see me privately in his office? And Miss Milford is not to know I'm here. Or why. Do you understand?"

She nodded. And while she went to find Dr. Matthews, he went out to the motorcar, bundled the child in her blankets, and carried her quickly inside, directly to the office where the nurse was holding the door wide for him.

"Good God," Matthews said. "Is that a child?"

"It is. Asleep from riding a very long distance in my motorcar. Will you examine her, please, and tell me what you find?"

Matthews looked at him questioningly, then took the bundle from him and spread out the blankets. The little girl sat up, sleepy and disoriented. Her face puckered to cry, but the doctor handed her the first thing that came to hand, a glass paperweight, and she began to examine it as he examined her.

After several minutes, he straightened, and keeping his voice low, he said, "She's fit. She doesn't say much, I can't speak to her frame of mind, but she's healthy, hasn't been mistreated, and seems to be a bright little thing." He gently took the paperweight out of her hands. "Doesn't she have any toys? Clothes? And she needs a fresh nappy. I'll see what my wife can do."

He left the room, and Rutledge took his place by the desk as Tildy searched for a new distraction. She saw a photograph and reached for it. He picked it up and held it for her to see.

"Dog," she said. And it was, a retriever, standing next to Matthews.

He picked up a pencil, then a pen, paper, whatever he could find on the desk, and she identified each object, reaching out for each in turn.

Matthews came back, a rag doll in his hand.

"Baby!" she exclaimed, and reached for it as well.

He changed her into clean clothes, then said, "What are you going to do with her?"

"Could you bring Miss Milford in here, please?" Ruth hadn't seen Tildy in months. It had only been weeks since Susan Milford had seen her, assuming that it was true that she'd had the child in her care.

"I don't think it's wise," Dr. Matthews began.

But Rutledge told him bluntly, "I don't have any choice. How else can I be sure who this child is? The woman who was caring for her didn't even know who had brought her there. Or where she came from. She's been told lies. And if this is the wrong child, I've got to start all over again."

"But there's her mother. Don't you even know who her mother is?"

"Her mother hasn't seen her for a very long time. She's likely to want to believe what she sees. Bring in Miss Milford. Or I'll go in search of her."

Matthews, lips drawn in a tight, grim line, left him there. And several minutes later he knocked twice at the door, then swung it open.

Susan's expression was grim and angry, and she was arguing with the doctor. But as she turned toward the room before her, her face changed, crumpling into tears. She stood there in the doorway, her gaze fixed on the child sitting on the desk, talking to the rag doll.

"You found her." She breathed, her voice husky, and then, "Gwennie? Gwennie, love."

The child looked at Rutledge, then turned toward the door. Her face lit up, and she tried to scramble to her feet, nearly pitching headfirst off the desk. He caught her, set her on the floor, and she ran toward Susan, clutching at her knees, laughing and holding on to her clothes.

Susan bent down to pick her up, winced, then sank on the floor instead and buried her face in the child's hair, talking to her.

Rutledge didn't stop them straightaway. Finally he asked quietly, "Why do you call her Gwennie?"

"It was my grandmother's name. Gwendolyn," she said. "Hastings told me she was called Matilda. It's an ugly name, I didn't care for it."

"Sam called her Tildy."

The child laughed and said, "Tildy."

It was a reminder. As he'd meant it to be.

Susan pulled her close. "You can't take her back. Not to Ruth. Please, *no*."

"I don't have an answer," he said. "But you have no legal right to her."

"I adopted her. From an orphans' asylum."

"But she was not an orphan. She had parents then."

"Legally she's Sam's daughter. I'm his sister. Why can't I be her guardian?"

"A solicitor will have to tell you what rights you have." It was a way out of the heartbreak he could see coming. "I have to take her to Crowley. It's my duty."

In the end, he had to take Susan with him. Dr. Matthews was adamant. "I can't have her upsetting my patients. Screaming the house down the minute you remove that child. I don't envy you what's to come. But I've done what I could for her injuries. Her own doctor can take her in charge now."

"I have three calls to make in Shrewsbury. If I promise to take her with me when I return, can I leave both of them here for a short period of time?"

"Yes. Yes, all right."

Rutledge didn't think Susan Milford noticed that he was gone.

He made his three calls. First to Carson, to be sure that Donald Blake was still in custody—he was. And then he went to Chester, to take Alasdair Dale into custody.

He found him in his chambers. He hadn't expected that.

If Dale was surprised to see him, he didn't show it. Instead, he rose from his desk and said, "The more I tried to erase the past, the bloodier it got. Did Ruth survive? Yes? I'm glad."

"You know why I'm here."

"Yes. I've put my affairs in order. In a way, I'm glad it's over, Ian. I'm tired."

"Was it worth it? The engagement cost you dearly."

"When I came back from France, nothing was the same. I couldn't settle to being a provincial solicitor again. Then I met Cecily. I thought I would do rather well in London. It was exciting, that prospect. But Hastings had mentioned a child when he asked me to look at the father's war record. I hadn't said anything then—but I suspected she was mine when I realized it was Ruth's husband and the date I was searching for was early 1917. What's more, Hastings had gone on about the little girl's hair. And he was right, you know. She's very like my grandmother, and my father has the same coloring. Still, she had a home, and I was certain Cecily's family wouldn't—they are sticklers for propriety, you see, I'd have lost her and everything that I wanted so badly. I asked Hastings what the father was after, and he thought Milford wanted to find the little girl's father, for a paternity suit. To help pay for that wretched pub. I'd already sent Ruth a family heirloom. I thought he wanted more."

Hastings's hand again, twisting the truth. Or perhaps, given his own lies, he couldn't recognize honesty in others.

"Sadly, Milford only wanted his daughter back. He was afraid her father had taken her."

"Was he?" Dale asked skeptically. He sighed. "By this time, the child had already been kidnapped. I'd helped Hastings locate her, I had a fair idea where Miss Milford had taken her. I thought that if the child disappeared forever, it would be for the best. There were people who might remember how friendly Ruth and I were in Ludlow. And Elaine had been dead for over a year before the child was born. I couldn't pass her off as ours. I had to do something, so I went searching for her, and took her. And I was right—she was the image of my father and my grandmother. *She* had been a great beauty in her day, there were people who still remembered that. All my relatives—there would have been no doubt. And so I took everything out of that house in Beddgwian—everything. It was a perfect plan. Even Hastings was caught off guard. But Milford was tenacious—he wouldn't give up. I told myself that I only needed to stop him, and all would be well. I'd killed in France. I knew how. But I couldn't bring myself—so I found someone who would, and paid him instead. And then *he* wanted more money, for his silence. Just as the Turnbull woman did. They were easier to kill, in a way. I didn't like either of them. Only it didn't stop there, did it? You were meddling, and there was Hastings. I was sure he would guess who was behind what was happening. People who could point a finger at me, and ruin everything." He shook his head. "I can't stomach any more killing. I'm not a murderer."

Rutledge looked at him. "Yet three people are dead because of you."

"Only three?" Dale said wryly. "Well, they can only hang me once." He moved the blotter on his desk this way and then that. "I broke off the engagement. I promised myself I would shoot myself before you came for me. The German pistol is in the drawer there. It would make matters easier for Cecily, at least. I found I couldn't do it. Rather sad, isn't it?"

He held out his wrists, walking around the desk toward Rutledge.

"I've made rather a mess of things, haven't I?"

"Did you have no feelings for your daughter?" Rutledge asked as he brought out the handcuffs. Dale had avoided using her name.

"I am not a monster, Ian. I didn't want to hurt her, just to make her disappear. She was all that stood between me and London. A few more months and I'd have been married, gone from here. All I needed was a little more time. I survived the war, somehow. I thought I could survive this as well. In the trenches, I was good at planning raids. It's not all that different, planning what I had to do here. The point, in both instances, is not getting caught. I was good at that too. If it had been anyone but you, I'd have been all right."

Rutledge led him out to where the Chester police were waiting. As soon as they had Dale in custody, he turned and walked away without a word. Sam Milford, he found himself thinking, had been worth ten of Alasdair Dale.

When he reached Shrewsbury, it was late, but he stopped at the Fenton house all the same. The man himself answered the door.

He watched tears fill the man's eyes as he broke the news. They spilled over and ran down Fenton's cheeks, but the man ignored them, unashamed.

"Well," he said. "It's true then. She's safe, the wee one." His voice was husky, and his gaze slid to the decanter of whisky on a side table. But he resolutely turned back to Rutledge. "Thank you. I can shut that door now. My wife will be glad of it."

He held out his hand, and Rutledge shook it.

The third call was to the solicitor Hastings. He was at home.

Rutledge spent more time there. He told the man what he thought of him, and what had happened. In that order.

"You've much to account for," he ended. "If I could arrest you for your lies and misdirection, I would. But you're a canny man, and you'd find a way out of it. The tragedy is that you haven't learned anything from the pain and the grief and the deaths."

Hastings met his gaze, but the man's eyes were impossible to read. "Have I not?"

"I have found Tildy Milford. I'm going to recommend that she be made a ward of the courts, so that her future can't be ruined by you or Susan or Ruth Milford."

"A wise man."

He couldn't stop himself from asking the question that was still gnawing at him. He had to be sure, he already knew what he would soon be called upon to do. "Given what you knew about Susan Milford's past, her instability, why did you trust her with a small child— and not any small child, her brother's daughter?"

"I knew I could trust Susan not to talk. Where else could I have put Tildy with any guarantee of safety for the child and her protector?"

And yet he had shared that secret with the one man who should never have been told about Tildy.

"I have five inquests to arrange and see through to a finding. In Oswestry, in that village by the Dee, at the Aqueduct, at Crowley, and in Stockford. If I see your hand in any of them, I will have you disbarred."

"You won't see my hand. I have no reason to interfere." He toyed with the letter opener beside the blotter. The one shaped like the Eiffel Tower in Paris. "I'm glad the child is safe. I was afraid he would kill her. Dale."

"He didn't. But he left her alone where no one knew her name, or where she'd come from, or what should be done with her. He abandoned her to whatever charity she could find. That was the ultimate cruelty."

"Well. He was to marry another heiress. She has connections to the family at Trefor House. You won't know where that is, of course." His gaze traveled across the shelves of boxes against the room's inner wall. "Dale's first wife had money. More than his own family had had. It was a sound match. But he's ambitious, and his fiancée could offer him money, social position in

London, possibly a career in politics. I'd heard he was considering closing his chambers and joining a new one in the City."

"He was willing to kill for that life, wasn't he? Sam Milford, Betty Turnbull, and Joseph Burton paid for that future. Susan and Ruth Milford and Mrs. Priestley nearly did. Three of his victims were your own clients. Rather a high price for one man's happiness."

"We must be thankful that he couldn't bring himself to kill the child as well."

Rutledge had to quell the urge to sweep everything from the man's desk to the floor. Instead he got up and walked out, too angry to stay.

When he had his anger under control once more, he went to the hotel and put in a call. It was to Melinda Crawford, in Kent. The family friend who had been such a large part of his life.

She came to the telephone at once. "Ian? Frances says you're in the North." He could hear the smile in her voice.

"Shrewsbury, in fact."

"Ah. Is there something I can help you with?"

He'd called on her before, in dire straits. But he couldn't tell her what troubled him now. "This close to Scotland—I was wondering if you'd had recent news from David." His godfather, the architect.

"As a matter of fact, I had a letter last week. They're well. David and little Ian. Fiona and Morag. They've invited me to come up, but I don't know if I can go just now."

She had her fingers in so many things. She was always busy. But she had always had time for him.

"You should go. You've always liked Scotland."

"And you should visit more often as well. David misses you, Ian. He still grieves for Ross." The son he'd lost in the war. Little Ian's father.

"I find it hard to get away . . ."

"It's time you took a little leave."

"Yes. When you write, send David my love, if you will."

"He'd rather hear it from you."

Rutledge took a deep breath. "I know." Then he said, trying not to make it sound like false cheer, "I'll give it some thought."

He rang off after that. Still uncertain.

But before he could deal with the problem of Tildy, he had to be sure he still had the authority to do so. And he put in another call to Gibson.

The Sergeant who answered the telephone at the

Yard reported, "Sergeant Gibson isn't here, sir. There's rather a push on. Could I take a message, sir?"

He couldn't speak to a man he only knew casually. "I'll telephone in the morning. Will he be in?"

"Yes, sir, I expect he will." There was a hint of amusement in his voice as he added, "I seldom see his desk unoccupied, sir."

Rutledge thanked him and put up the receiver, but stood there for a long moment afterward.

There had been nothing in the Sergeant's voice to indicate that Rutledge was out of favor, on the verge of being let go. Rumors were rife at the Yard. Still. The Chief Superintendent often kept his decisions to himself, preferring to witness their effect on the hapless officer standing in front of him.

In the end he went back to the hotel Sam had always used and asked for a room. Whatever he did tomorrow, it had to have official sanction.

Hamish remarked, as Rutledge climbed the stairs, "It's the coward's way out, ye ken."

But it wasn't. Another Inspector, coming late to the inquiry, might see matters very differently and do more harm than he realized.

And there were the inquests . . .

Lighting the lamp, he tossed his coat and hat on the bed and sat down at the small table that served as a desk. Taking out his notebook, for the next five hours he worked on his report, making sure that every detail was properly supported by fact. There must be no questions about the evidence, no uncertainty about Dale's guilt. Or the child's future.

As he worked, he had a passing thought about Dora Radley. Had she heard that Dale was planning to marry again? He thought not, she hadn't mentioned it. Still, he wondered if she'd had some hope in that direction. Sam Milford was married. Fond of him she might well have been, but Dora wouldn't have pursued any more than friendship. Still, she'd shared Milford's search with Dale. Because she truly wanted to help—or to curry favor with the attractive solicitor who had connections?

Sadly—or luckily—for her, she wasn't an heiress.

It was early when Rutledge tried to telephone the Yard once more. Sergeant Gibson was in, but at present was in the Chief Superintendent's office.

An hour later, when he called again, the Sergeant's gruff voice came over the line. "Scotland Yard. Sergeant Gibson speaking."

"Rutledge here," he said. "I've closed the inquiry and am preparing for the inquests. There will be several. A long story, but a successful one."

There was silence at the other end. Rutledge braced himself for what was coming.

"Himself just had an urgent telephone call. It was from the father of Mrs. Cecily Eastbourne."

Rutledge closed his eyes. "Yes?" He hadn't known her last name.

"Sir Henry wanted to thank Himself for the timely action of the Yard, in taking a Mr. Dale into custody in Chester. His daughter had been engaged to Dale, but fortunately it had been ended. He wanted to ask that the Yard keep all mention of Mrs. Eastbourne out of the picture. Himself agreed." Again a brief hesitation. "We don't know the facts in the case yet. Is that going to be possible, sir?"

Rutledge had already made that decision last night. There had been a little awkwardness in establishing motive, but he had managed to skirt the issue of the engagement. Instead, he had merely mentioned Dale's ambitions. Enough lives had been ruined.

"It has been done, Sergeant."

There was an audible sigh of relief. "I'll report to the Chief Inspector, sir. He will be most grateful."

Later in the morning, when he arrived at the surgery in Church Stretton, Susan and Tildy were sitting on the floor of one of the examining rooms, playing with a set of wooden blocks and the rag doll.

Susan looked up as he came in. But she didn't speak, going back to the game she and Tildy were enjoying.

Dr. Matthews, standing behind him, said quietly, "I am glad I'm not in your shoes. You do realize that that woman is either unstable, or has spent a lifetime using it to get what she wants."

"You don't care for her very much," Rutledge observed.

"I feel sympathy for the truly mad. They can't help themselves, and we can't always make them better. She manipulates."

But she had been taught by a master. Hastings.

"Is she safe to leave with that child? If I have to make that decision?"

"She loves her. You can see that."

"You haven't answered me."

"No. I haven't."

A little later, with Susan ensconced in the motorcar, Tildy in her lap, Rutledge left Church Stretton.

Once on the road, he said, "You will not make a scene. Promise me."

She played with golden ringlets, winding them around her finger as Tildy looked out the window, showing something to the doll. Mrs. Matthews had insisted that she keep it. Once Tildy had said, "Show Auntie Jo?"

"Later, perhaps," Rutledge replied. And didn't explain.

They reached Crowley and pulled up the hill toward the inn.

Susan's face was still, as if she had willed herself not to show any feeling at all.

As he drove into the pub yard, he saw Will looking out the glass of the side door. Then he was gone.

Rutledge got out. "Stay here. She doesn't know why I've come."

"I understand." She pulled Tildy closer, but Tildy was staring at her surroundings as if she had a faint recollection of them, and pulled away.

He walked across to the door and went inside.

The three of them—Ruth Milford and Nan Blake and Will Esterly—were standing in the middle of the pub, staring anxiously at him.

"I've brought Tildy home," he said, and Ruth's knees nearly buckled. Nan had to catch her arm and hold her up.

"She's been through an ordeal. I'll tell you more about that later. But she's healthy. I don't think she's suffered physically, but she has been shifted from pillar to post, and only time will tell. Wait—!" he said sharply as Ruth started toward the side door.

"There are two things you need to know," he continued. "The first is that I'm recommending that Tildy be made a ward of the court, to be certain she's all right in the years to come. You don't deserve her, Ruth. You'll have to earn the right to call yourself her mother. And I have brought Susan Milford, Sam's sister, with me. She had the care of Tildy when you were trying to persuade yourself that Tildy would have a better life with her true father. I have seen what that better life was, and I can tell you now that he gave her nothing. And you will treat Sam's sister with the respect she has earned. Do I make myself clear?"

"But she's mad—Sam told me she was mad."

"Sam was wrong."

He went back to the door and brought in Susan Milford and Tildy. The child was clutching Susan's hand, looking around her with wide eyes. Her gaze settled on Ruth, and she stared at her, frowning, before turning slightly and burying her face against Susan's leg.

Ruth stifled a cry. "She doesn't *know* me," she whispered in anguish.

"She hasn't seen you or heard your voice in a year. That was your choice, not hers."

Susan, watching the two women in front of her, said

nothing. But she put her hand down on Tildy's curls, gently smoothing them a little. Protective.

Ruth went down on her knees, holding out her arms. "Tildy? It's Mummy. Please, darling, come and give me a hug? I've missed you so terribly."

Tildy stayed where she was.

Collapsing in a heap, Ruth began to cry softly.

He said to Nan, "Close the pub. Leave Will to keep an eye on it. Then pack some clothing. I'm taking the three of you back with me to Shrewsbury. Miss Milford has rooms there. You and Mrs. Milford will share them with her and with Tildy. I have matters to see to. But what happens to Tildy will depend on what I observe in the next few days."

Nan said, "I shouldn't go—Donald—"

"You will. For Tildy's sake. Now get ready."

Susan was kneeling by Tildy, who was asking, "Why is the lady crying?"

"She hasn't seen you in a long time, darling. And you don't remember her. Go and tell her you are sorry you don't remember."

The child walked hesitantly across the space between them, and reached out to touch Ruth's hair. "I'm sorry."

Ruth looked up, smiled a little, then said, "I am sorry too."

She got up, touched Tildy's face with her fingers, and then ran upstairs. They could hear her choking sobs.

Nan followed her, after a glance from Rutledge. Tildy, surprised, went back to Susan's side.

Rutledge had started speaking to Will, when he heard Nan scream.

He went racing up the stairs, Will at his heels.

Nan was in the passage outside the room where Ruth had been sleeping.

She reached out and caught Rutledge's arm. "She's trying to kill herself—"

He ran into the room where Ruth was sawing at her wrist with a pair of scissors, blood all over the coverlet beneath her. He had to fight her for them, got them away from her finally, then pushed her back down on the bed.

"If you loved her, you'd want to live," he said harshly. "Instead, you're still thinking about yourself. What sort of mother are you? Now pack your valise, and go and sit in the motorcar." To Nan he added, "Bind up that cut. Will can stay here while you pack your own case."

It took him over two hours to put things in order.

Will, anxious and worried, said, "What will we do about the pub?"

"In good time. Just keep it closed for now. The family is in mourning."

He got Nan and then Ruth into the motorcar, wincing as they took over the space that had always been Hamish's.

And then he went back for Susan, who was sitting in a chair with a sleepy child in her lap.

She was looking around. "A pity the pub is closing. I'm sorry." She turned to Rutledge. "Sam was happy here." Then, "Did she really try to cut her wrists?"

He said, "I'm afraid so."

"I used to play at suicide. I never had the courage to go through with it. I see now I was as selfish as she was. What will happen to Gwen—Tildy?"

"I don't know."

He helped them out to the motorcar. Then he watched Will close and lock the side door. The man's face was sad as he turned and limped down the hill toward his aunt's house.

Rutledge turned the crank and got in.

No one said anything to him.

He pulled away from The Pit and The Pony, heading for Shrewsbury.

He had learned early on that murder always left living victims behind. Tildy was one of them. He wasn't sure the suite at the hotel would work. But for Tildy's sake he was going to give it a damned good try. And there were the inquests to get through.

Glancing across at the child asleep in Susan's lap, he thought of the small boy in Scotland, the one named for him. Ian had lost his father to war and his mother to murder. But his grandfather and the woman Hamish MacLeod had intended to marry at war's end had given the boy their love, to keep him safe.

If the three women in Tildy's life couldn't give her what she needed, he'd see that Tildy went to Scotland. She could share Ian's pony.

Or to Melinda Crawford.

He found himself smiling at the image of Tildy among Melinda's exotic treasures.

Hastings, by God, would find a legal way to see that it happened. To make amends . . .

If it came to that.

Acknowledgments

We wrote this book before Covid-19 became a household word—talked about every night on TV, seeping into everyone's nightmares all across the world.

A Fatal Lie went into production as the virus bloomed, and yet as production demands widened, there was always someone working who was available to do the job or see to the next step or make a decision about titles and font style and jacket art.

Emily and Julia were working at home, even as the virus exploded across the city—sometimes in difficult circumstances, but undeterred. Shelly and Laura got the copyedits done. There are so many others at HarperCollins who were doing what they always do to turn a manuscript into a book—design, jacket art, you name it. Ah, yes, that lovely jacket! And Lisa was there as well, as she always is.

We are grateful to each and every one of you! Yeah, Team Todd!

AND . . . a special thanks to Brian and Pauline, who introduced us to the Stiperstones, and to Sandy and Eddie, who owned the pub that was the inspiration for The Pit and The Pony.

Our thanks as well to Kathy and Nicky, great traveling companions, as we stayed in the Royal Goat Hotel, and later rattled over those mind-boggling roads in the quarry. It was also nice to be back in Betws-y-Coed again . . . we have such fond memories of that little town. We'd done much of this trip before with Pauline and Brian, but going back again for a fresh look led to this book. We never know where the story in our heads will suddenly find a home, it just happens. Travel does that. So here's to getting there and finding the perfect place for murder . . .

—*The authors*

About the Author

CHARLES TODD is the author of the Bess Crawford mysteries, the Inspector Ian Rutledge mysteries, and two stand-alone novels. A mother-and-son writing team, they live on the East Coast.